"Tell me, Sheriff, are stray bodies a common occurrence in Tombstone cemeteries?"

Caro knew she sounded too flippant, but he spoke before she had a chance to apologize.

"No, ma'am, they're not." She noticed his eyes spark with anger. "Which is why I'm here." He held his horse's reins in his left hand and touched his right thumb and forefinger to his hat brim, the characteristic mark of respect from a man to a woman in the Southwest. But his eyes didn't warm. "Sheriff Wyatt Earp Bodine, at your service."

Caro had never actually met anyone named after the legendary Old West lawman. But she was certain, somehow, that the name—like the skeleton—was for real. Not a gimmick for tourists.

"Caro Hartlan. I'm—"

"A Phoenix police consultant specializing in the high-tech end of forensics." Bodine kept his eyes on her. "Don't tell me you've decided to dig up business here?" he said with the barest smile.

Well, well. It appeared he had a sense of humor, after all. Still, she was determined to curb her characteristic joking remarks—at least until she knew him better. Much better...

Wrangler Dads
1. *Madeleine's Cowboy*
Kristine Rolofson
2. *Cowboy's Kin*
Victoria Pade
3. *Trouble at Lone Spur*
Roz Denny Fox
4. *Upon a Midnight Clear*
Lynn Erickson
5. *Cowboy at the Wedding*
Karen Rose Smith
6. *Dangerous*
Caroline Cross
Reunion Western-Style!
7. *Rodeo Rider*
Stella Bagwell
8. *Mustang Valley*
Jackie Merritt
9. *Holding on to Alex*
Margaret Way
10. *Home Fires Burning Bright*
Laurie Paige
11. *One More Rodeo*
Lynnette Kent
12. *The Reckoning*
Joleen Daniels
Conveniently Wed
13. *Seduction of the Reluctant Bride*
Barbara McCauley
14. *Temporary Husband*
Day Leclaire
15. *The Wilde Bunch*
Barbara Boswell
16. *Her Torrid Temporary Marriage*
Sara Orwig
17. *The Newlywed Game*
Bonnie K. Winn
18. *Gideon's Bride*
Amelia Autin
Holding Out for a Hero
19. *Midnight Prey*
Caroline Burnes
20. *Bulletproof Heart*
Sheryl Lynn
21. *Hiding Out at the Circle C*
Jill Shalvis
22. *Lucky Devil*
Patricia Rosemoor
23. *She Caught the Sheriff*
Anne Marie Duquette
24. *The Unlikely Bodyguard*
Amy J. Fetzer

Rawhide & Lace
25. *Cowboys Are for Loving*
Marie Ferrarella
26. *The Rancher and the Redhead*
Allison Leigh
27. *White Gold*
Curtiss Ann Matlock
28. *Texas Dawn*
Joan Elliott Pickart
29. *Rancher's Choice*
Kylie Brant
30. *Delightful Jones*
Patricia Knoll
Kids & Kin
31. *The Troublemaker Bride*
Leanne Banks
32. *Cowboys Do It Best*
Eileen Wilks
33. *The Rancher and the Baby*
Elizabeth August
34. *Boss Lady and the Hired Hand*
Barbara McMahon
35. *The Cowboy's Courtship*
Patricia Thayer
36. *The Farmer Takes a Wife*
Jodi O'Donnell
Men of the Land
37. *The Badlands Bride*
Rebecca Winters
38. *The Cowboy Wants a Wife!*
Susan Fox
39. *Woman at Willagong Creek*
Jessica Hart
40. *Wyoming Wife?*
Shawna Delacorte
41. *Cowboys, Babies and Shotgun Vows*
Shirley Rogers
42. *Home Is Where Hank Is*
Martha Shields
Secrets!
43. *The Rancher's Runaway Bride*
Judith Bowen
44. *Midnight Cowboy*
Adrianne Lee
45. *Remember Me, Cowboy*
Caroline Burnes
46. *The Other Laura*
Sheryl Lynn
47. *A Man without Love*
Beverly Bird
48. *The Return of the Cowboy*
Cheryl Biggs

MARRY ME,
Cowboy

SHE CAUGHT
THE SHERIFF

Anne Marie Duquette

HOLDING OUT FOR
A HERO

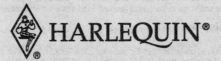

HARLEQUIN®

TORONTO • NEW YORK • LONDON
AMSTERDAM • PARIS • SYDNEY • HAMBURG
STOCKHOLM • ATHENS • TOKYO • MILAN • MADRID
PRAGUE • WARSAW • BUDAPEST • AUCKLAND

HARLEQUIN BOOKS
225 Duncan Mill Road, Don Mills,
Ontario, Canada M3B 3K9

ISBN 0-373-65332-8

SHE CAUGHT THE SHERIFF

This edition published by arrangement with Harlequin Books S.A.

® and TM are trademarks of the publisher. Trademarks indicated with ® are registered in the United States Patent and Trademark Office, the Canadian Trade Marks Office and in other countries.

www.eHarlequin.com

Printed in U.S.A.

ANNE MARIE DUQUETTE

has traveled extensively throughout the United States, first as an air force "brat," then as a member of the military herself. As a young girl, she started her writing career with lengthy letters to relatives and friends describing her impressions of countless new duty locations. A navy veteran, wife of a retired navy vet and mother of two, Anne Marie presently resides in California. However, she's equally familiar with Arizona, where she owned horses. The family spent one winter break sight-seeing in Tombstone, Arizona. While retracing the steps of lawman Wyatt Earp at the O.K. Corral and touring Boothill, this book was born.

Please address questions and book requests to:
Harlequin Reader Service
U.S.: 3010 Walden Ave., P.O. Box 1325, Buffalo, NY 14269
Canadian: P.O. Box 609, Fort Erie, Ont. L2A 5X3

A sad farewell to Romance Writers of America
members Marta Fulgham, Barbara Faith
and Emma Merritt.

Wherever you are now, ladies,
May the wind be always at your back,
The sun and stars before your eyes.

Rest in peace, good friends, and
Think of us as we will think of you.

Bon voyage from us all....

We at the San Diego chapter
Will miss you.

CHAPTER ONE

Wednesday morning

TOMBSTONE'S JUNE WIND blew blistering hot and desert-dry over Boothill Cemetery, but the wind was the last thing on Caro Hartlan's mind—or, she figured, on the minds of the tourists around her. Despite damp shirts and shiny foreheads, they all stared at the skeleton displayed at her feet.

Everyone was, to say the least, surprised. Including Caro. She'd just finished teaching a forensics workshop at Tucson's university and had decided to visit Tombstone in her spare time. She certainly hadn't counted on tripping over a specimen!

Nor had anyone else, she reminded herself. And most people weren't as accustomed to sights like this. The adults gaped at one another, gawked at the skeleton, then at Caro. The children flitted daringly back and forth between the bones and their parents' protective arms. They gawked at her, too.

"Don't look at me," Caro said with a slight shrug. "Just because I found it doesn't mean I know why it's here."

"Is it real?" one red-faced, sunburned tourist asked, even as he busily clicked photos of the grim sight.

"Can't be. It's just a re-creation," another tourist answered. "You know, like the mock shoot-out they do at the O.K. Corral every day."

The nervous crowd pressed closer to Caro to hear her response.

"Well…" Caro knelt down next to the remains. Her knees made little puffs of dust in the sun-bleached cemetery soil. "I'd say it's authentic. And definitely human."

Murmurs of disbelief, shock and excitement rippled through the crowd. The sunburned man with the camera wasn't quite so willing to accept her judgment. "And just how would you know?" he asked belligerently.

Caro stood up, brushed at her jeans, then brushed back the shoulder-length brunette hair from her face.

"It's my job to know. Forensics pays my rent. And I'd bet my last paycheck this skeleton is no joke."

The crowd gasped, and a few of the children squealed. So did a couple of adults.

"I don't get it," Mr. Sunburn said with an indignant snort, rudely elbowing a pleasant-faced woman—no doubt his wife—out of his way for a better shot.

"Neither do I," Caro replied easily. "As I understand it, the dearly departed are supposed to be *under* the ground."

A few of the crowd frowned at her answer. Caro's parents and younger policewoman sister, Desiree, back in Phoenix knew her glib tongue and black humor were coping mechanisms to help her deal with the terrible things she saw in her line of work. In truth, she was a compassionate woman with a big heart that bled for both the victims and their families when she worked a case. But of course these strangers couldn't know that.

She hunkered back down beside the skeleton. The ligaments and joints had long since disappeared, yet someone had carefully arranged the bones into their correct positions. *Someone highly skilled in anatomy.* There wasn't a bone missing or out of place, not even in the twenty-seven bones composing the hands.

That attention to detail bothered her. Someone had taken

great care to place this poor soul smack-dab in the middle of a popular tourist attraction. *But why?*

"Maybe one of you could walk back to the gift shop and get the manager to call for help?" Caro suggested.

Mrs. Sunburn left to do just that.

Caro continued to study the old bones with her trained eye. This was the desert, yet the bones weren't as well preserved as she would have expected. There were unmistakable signs of damp rot on them, so they certainly weren't from this cemetery. Caro was a Phoenix native, and she knew Arizona topography. Boothill sat atop a mile-high ledge of bedrock right in the middle of the Arizona desert. The cemetery sprawled among the cacti and aloe vera plants and rambled all the way down a steep, rocky hill— the final resting place of those buried with their boots on.

Clearly, this skeleton—male, judging by the narrowness of the hips—came from someplace else. She'd already established that the soil on these bones didn't match the soil in the cemetery. Not only that, the bones didn't bear the visible clothing traces generally seen with a corpse that had been in a casket. Clothing was often as durable as bone in the desert; however, this skeleton was as unencumbered as a plastic Halloween version, save for the damp rot.

And the trauma to the head... Caro got all the way down on her hands and knees and dipped low, her face only inches from the skull. She studied it carefully, examining the jagged fractures—almost certainly the evidence of assault. She closed her eyes for a brief moment. Caro Lynn Hartlan, Ph.D., might be thirty-five years old and an expert in forensics, but what she was about to announce never got easier.

"Stand back, people. I think we've got us a murder victim here."

That was the wrong thing to say. One thin young man

turned white and fainted, an even younger teen screamed like a banshee—and all hell broke loose.

Caro grabbed for the thin man before he hit the dirt. The screaming teen's mother whacked Caro over the head with a tourist brochure for frightening her son, and Mr. Sunburn gleefully started snapping more pictures. All this amidst more screams, exclamations and hysteria.

"Watch out!" Caro yelled as the fainting man narrowly missed falling face-first into the skeleton. Caro grunted and shoved just enough to save man, skeleton and herself from a three-way pileup.

"Couldn't you faint the other way?" She lowered the unconscious man to the ground and sank into a sitting position to rest his head on her lap. "You almost disturbed the crime scene."

"Is that all you're worried about?" the fainting man's girlfriend cried. "The crime scene?"

"Of course not!" Caro replied. "I caught him, didn't I?"

"Did somebody call the cops?" another person interrupted.

"Forget the cops. Just whistle for the sheriff!" came the anonymous suggestion. "There he is!"

"Who…?" Caro asked, confused. She didn't get to finish her sentence as one small visitor put fingers to his mouth and blew an ear-piercing whistle just inches from her head.

Caro winced, transferred her patient's head to his girlfriend's lap and stood.

"Here comes the sheriff!" someone yelled in her other ear. She winced a second time, both ears ringing. She decided to remove her backpack and retrieve the credentials that established her as a Phoenix-based, freelance bonded consultant and speaker on the subject of forensic science.

Caro wasn't sure how much a small-town sheriff was

likely to know about her specialty. A forensic scientist could be a medical examiner, the specialist who did an autopsy on the body at the morgue. Or, like Caro, a forensic doctor could be a criminologist, someone with more field training in criminology and law than hospital experience.

Whenever she was called in on a case, it was her job to examine the body at the crime scene, to provide information to the homicide detectives that would lead to an arrest and conviction.

Forensic scientists dealt with the relation and application of medical facts to legal problems, nothing more, nothing less. Their expertise could set a suspect free—or send him to death row... Caro was always conscious of the responsibility she carried, although in this case the murderer was probably as dead as his victim. But whoever had moved the bones was guilty of a crime, too.

An elderly gentleman wearing a gift-store smock caught Caro's attention as he joined the group by the skeleton and pointed. "There's the sheriff now!"

Caro followed the finger's direction. She gazed past the massive, head-high clumps of prickly pear and uneven wooden fence, which provided a protective barrier off to the side. Directly beyond that, the hilltop dropped a steep mile to the valley floor below. The desert mountains in the distance beneath a brilliant turquoise sky outlined a man....

A man coming straight up the incline of Boothill's dirt path on a horse!

Caro forgot all about removing her backpack, forgot all about her earlier plans. She'd traveled south to Tucson on business, but she'd made a side trip to Tombstone to follow up on her personal hobby—researching early forensic work in the Old West. Instead, she'd walked right into an old skeleton, had a man faint in her arms, been hit on the head by an irate mother and nearly deafened by a whistling spectator. Now she was watching some sheriff barrel up the hill on horseback. Up Tombstone's Boothill Cemetery, no less!

So much for her busman's holiday. Still, it was necessary to have a sense of humor in her kind of work, and an easy flexibility, and neither failed her now. Caro's lips curved in an ironic smile, then parted in awe at the sight of the approaching stallion.

Arabians were very common in Arizona; they were a breed that did well in the Southwest's desert heat. But this Arabian was a beauty, clearly an animal of show quality. He had a gleaming silver-white coat, a symmetrical body, a finely shaped head. Everything about him revealed generations of careful breeding.

Caro couldn't help smiling as horse and rider reached the top of the hill. The horse was magnificent. And the man—ah, the man. He was tall, perfectly balanced and leanly built. His expression seemed intelligent yet fully masculine—attractively masculine. Caro noticed curling, light brown hair beneath his Stetson. Jeans and boots like hers. Instead of a plaid western shirt like the one she wore, he had on a beige sheriff's shirt with insignia and badge, plus the shoulder harness and gun that went with it.

On the shirt's right front pocket was a bright yellow embroidered star, a replica of the Old West sheriff's star with circled points at the end and the whole thing set in a circle. A patch showing the Arizona flag adorned one shoulder.

On his hip was a pearl-handled Colt .45. Caro knew this was an official law-enforcement firearm, but it didn't look the part. This gun was a reminder of the wild Old West and the hard men who'd survived it.

The gun was just like the man, she decided. The stallion he rode, the pearl-handled revolver, the bullets slung around his waist—all were throwbacks to an earlier time.

The crowd parted as the Arabian drew closer. His rider slowed him to a prancing walk. Four silver legs were carefully guided around graves and cactus clusters with dressage accuracy, dressage grace. But it was the man who dominated the scene, just as he dominated the horse.

Caro watched rider and mount pull to a halt. She hadn't backed away as the others had. She stood her ground next to the skeleton, determined to preserve the crime scene. Even if it *hadn't* been part of a crime scene, she would have done the same. The man kindled her interest. And she wanted to meet him as an equal. She saw him take in the skeleton, the gawking crowds, the fainting man and his girlfriend, all in one quick glance—while she took in his ringless left hand.

I wonder if he's single. Then, *Not very professional, Caro.* But considering the striking sight he made, certainly understandable. And yet Caro hardly ever found herself responding to a man in such an...immediate way. Such an unabashedly sexual way. Like she was doing right now as she watched the sheriff dismount in a lithe, smooth motion.

Caro's admiration changed from approval of his physical attractiveness to something more as the sheriff immediately removed his canteen from his saddle horn and passed it to the fainting man's girlfriend, then asked, "Does he need an ambulance?"

Not bad, she thought approvingly. His first words were concern for the living, not fascination with the dead. Or a male response to her outright female ogling.

The girl murmured something to her boyfriend, who shook his head. He was already recovering. With the sheriff's help, the two were back on their feet in moments. It wasn't until the sheriff had checked over the boyfriend himself that he directed his attention to Caro.

"And you are?" The lawman's voice was deep and rich, yet quiet. But not so quiet that it didn't impress her with its strength.

"An out-of-town visitor who discovered this gentleman.'' Caro gestured toward the skeleton behind her, her gaze still on his. "Tell me," she asked, "are stray bodies in cemeteries a common occurrence in Tombstone?"

"No, ma'am, they are not."

Caro noticed his eyes spark with anger. This was a man who took pride in both his town and his job. He didn't like the skeleton, this situation or, she realized, her flippant question. She immediately regretted it, but he spoke before she had a chance to apologize.

"Which is why I'm here." He held the Arabian's reins in his left hand, and touched his right thumb and forefinger to his hat brim, the characteristic mark of respect from a man to a woman in the Southwest. The gesture was polite, but his eyes didn't warm.

Too bad her little attempt to lighten the mood had failed. She knew from experience that anyone who worked for the law needed a sense of humor, black or otherwise. Forensic scientists or sheriffs who didn't laugh now and then ended up sobbing, quitting or drowning job horrors in a bottle to save their sanity. But then, she doubted Tombstone had even a fraction of the crime Phoenix had. Her home had half a million people; Tombstone barely twelve hundred. Maybe the handsome sheriff didn't need to take refuge in laughter.

Introductions were made.

"Sheriff Wyatt Earp Bodine, at your service."

Mrs. Sunburn had returned with the manager, and her husband tittered and elbowed her when the sheriff announced his name. Bodine dropped his hand from his hat and ignored them. Caro knew her Arizona history, knew the Earps had played a big part in Tombstone's Old West days. She'd just never met anyone actually named after them before.

However, the way he'd introduced himself made her positive that the name—like the skeleton—was no gimmick for tourists. He was too serious to be joking.

"Caro Hartlan. I'm—"

"A Phoenix professor and police consultant specializing in the high-tech end of forensics, especially facial re-creations using computers and clay."

"So you've heard of me." Caro felt a flash of pleasure. She'd worked hard to establish herself, both as a consultant in the field and on the lecture tour. Her clay re-creations of skulls had identified a number of John and Jane Does, and put more than one criminal behind bars. Her Tucson university workshop had been sold out months in advance.

"I read about your seminar in the newspaper," Bodine said. He kept his eyes on her. "Don't tell me you're so bored you've decided to dig up business here," he said with the barest smile.

Well, well! It appeared he had a sense of humor, after all. Still, she was determined to curb her characteristic flippant remarks—at least until he knew her better.

Much better...

She had a tender heart, even if she had a tough hide, and she was willing to back down for a full smile from Wyatt Earp Bodine.

"I'm sorry about my earlier remark," she replied sincerely. "I think it's because I was in vacation mode, not work mode. And I'm used to police showing up in squad cars."

"Horses are a fine police tradition." His friendly expression faded a bit and challenged her to disagree. Caro did just the opposite.

She nodded. "I had the honor of riding a police horse in New York's Central Park a few years ago." She noted his surprise. "I was there for a summer internship, and I helped them capture a serial murderer who preyed on joggers."

"But why were you on horseback?"

"The killer was a pattern killer. He only chose certain paths in the park. None of us could figure out the pattern on foot or by map, but traveling from crime scene to crime scene on horseback broke the case. There were certain types of shrubbery at each location. The man was a Sunday gardener and preferred to kill next to his favorite botanical specimens. I identified certain pollens on the victims to help predict the next location. The police sent in a decoy jogger, and we nailed him."

"Nice work."

Some of the crowd had pressed closer to hear their conversation and added oohs and aahs of praise.

Caro smiled at the compliments. "Not to be blowing my own horn, however."

Yeah, right, Caro. Like you've ever been modest when it comes to your career. Still, she'd worked hard on that case and was proud of her work. She'd been able at least to provide a jail sentence to comfort the families of the victims.

"I was happy to see the culprit behind bars, but hated giving up that horse. A beautiful animal—like yours."

She boldly approached his Arabian and gave the velvety nose a gentle rub.

"As for drumming up business..." She threw the skeleton a pointed glance. "That I rarely do, but since I stumbled on this poor soul, I'm more than happy to extend my services. Professional courtesy and all that."

"Thank you for the offer." Disappointed, Caro noticed that the sheriff didn't commit himself either way. "For now, if you'll step aside, please," he said in professional voice, "I need a closer look."

Caro immediately did; he was the primary officer on the crime scene, and she had no permission to touch the body until he gave it.

Caro watched as Bodine tied up his horse, removed the walkie-talkie from his saddlebags and went to work. In a short time he'd called his assistant, an attractive redhead named Kimberly Ellis, to help him secure the area. He took statements from everyone present. Then he cleared the cemetery, except for Caro, his assistant and himself. He ordered the manager to close the cemetery until further notice, then—finally—directed his attention toward Caro.

The three of them were gathered around the dusty bones as the sun rose higher in the sky. By now it was almost midafternoon. Another deputy had dropped off some sandwiches and cold drinks earlier, to Caro's relief, and she was ready to begin work. If the sheriff permitted...

"Well, what can I do to help?" she asked.

"There's no reason for you to stay," Bodine said. "I'm sure I can set this right in a few days. It's obvious this is some juvenile prank."

Caro couldn't believe her ears. "It's not obvious to me at all!"

Bodine's eyes narrowed. "I know this isn't Phoenix, Doctor, but trust me, there's no need to interrupt your vacation. Your skill isn't needed to tell me that this skeleton is ancient. I'll run a query through the computer, get the original burial log and make arrangements to have him or her reinterred."

"*If* someone's missing a body. What if no one reports a grave desecration?" Caro demanded. Her attraction to Bodine instantly took a back seat to her work.

"This is a small town, ma'am. They will. And that'll be the end of it."

"You don't know that! Come on, Sheriff! You really don't want my help?" Caro said incredulously.

"That's what he said," Kimberly purred. The woman gave Caro a warm smile and gently laid her hand on Bodine's arm in a proprietary gesture. "Wyatt knows his stuff."

Caro gave Kimberly an assessing gaze. Physically the woman was a knockout. With her tousled auburn hair, lush curves shown off by tight jeans, and exotic gray eyes set in a carefully made up face, she seemed...aggressively feminine. Her appearance was a direct contrast to Caro's, whose build was taller, stronger, leaner, whose long, straight hair was pulled into a no-nonsense ponytail. And unlike Caro, Kimberly wore her emotions—and her heart— on her khaki work-shirt sleeve.

At least I know enough to keep my love life—what there is of it—private, Caro thought disdainfully. Clinging women gave all women a bad name as far as she was concerned, and made her answer Kimberly a bit more sharply than she'd intended. "I'm sure he does, Sheriff Ellis. But so do I."

"I'm not a sheriff," Kimberly corrected. "I'm the town's police dispatcher and office manager. And you can call me Kimberly. We're very informal here."

"I see—Kimberly. So tell me. Does this informal little town have a trained forensic expert? Or a medical examiner?"

"No, but Wyatt can get one from Tucson."

"I'd suggest you call one, then, if you don't want my services. Because this man was murdered."

"Murdered!" Kimberly tilted her head in a charming motion, her hand still tucked in Wyatt's arm. "*Please,* Miss Hartlan. I don't see any bullet holes in this poor thing."

Caro found Kimberly particularly patronizing, and Wyatt's acceptance of her on-the-job caresses irritating. "That's Ms. Hartlan or Dr. Hartlan, please. And this 'poor thing' is also a victim."

"So you apparently informed the crowd," Bodine said

with a raised eyebrow. "Want to explain exactly what you mean?"

"I don't have my tools with me, and of course I haven't touched the crime scene yet, but I can give you an off-the-cuff analysis."

"You have my permission to do so."

Caro glanced at him sharply. The sheriff had gone from friendly to coolly official as soon as she questioned his authority. Well, *he* shouldn't have questioned *her* knowledge! She didn't have one of the highest conviction rates on her cases for nothing.

"Wyatt, really, you shouldn't humor her..." Kim said in a soft voice, but Bodine abruptly straightened, shaking off her arm.

About time! Caro thought. Whether the relationship was a personal or professional one, she preferred a man's *full* attention.

"All right, Doctor. I'm listening."

Caro knelt down in the dust again. She picked up a stick to use as a pointer and began.

"Number one. This is definitely a male. The pelvis is steep and narrow compared to a female's. Number two. He's Caucasian. The nose ridge is narrow in relation to the height. In African and Asian skulls, the ridge is wider. The size of the eye sockets is also consistent with Caucasian heritage."

"This sure beats filing papers back at the office." Kimberly's eyes were suddenly bright with interest. She left Wyatt's side to get closer to the remains. Her departure didn't seem to bother Wyatt a bit, but it was certainly a relief to Caro. Maybe Kimberly wasn't the traditional clinging vine, after all.

And maybe I shouldn't be so hard on young lovers. Just because I don't have one of my own is no reason to drag out the sour grapes and—

"Go on," Bodine urged, interrupting Caro's thoughts. "We're waiting."

Caro pulled herself together. "Number three. This Caucasian male was a cowboy or suffered from rickets. Look at the bowed legs. The femur, the tibia and the fibula are all unnaturally curved. Since this is Tombstone, I'd go with the cowboy hypothesis, though rickets could also be possible, depending on the age of this man."

"How can you tell?" Kimberly asked.

"Well, for the age of the person at time of death, I'd need my microscope to do a calcification analysis."

"Incomplete calcification would mean a young adult, as full bone maturity hasn't occurred. Bone degeneration would tell us full maturity has been reached and for how long," Bodine explained to Kimberly.

Caro looked up at the sheriff, impressed. He might be country, but he wasn't out of touch with modern forensics. "That's true. But these bones are obviously not those of a child, so we can rule that out."

"Can't you tell how long the skeleton's been lying around?" Kimberly asked.

"No." Bodine answered again. He'd unbent enough to hunker down next to Caro. Kimberly quickly joined them.

"He's right. I can't. At least not yet," Caro conceded. "Skeletons rarely yield clues about how long they've existed in actual calendar time."

"What about carbon dating?"

"That process has too big a time margin for error to use on these bones," Wyatt told Kimberly, who was watching him with rapt attention.

"Right again, Sheriff. I see you know a bit about forensics yourself."

"A bit." He shrugged.

Caro suspected it was more than just a bit. "Only prehistoric artifacts are viable candidates for carbon dating,'' she said. "Even then it's not an exact science.''

"Then how can you tell?" Kimberly asked, obviously not pleased by the exchange between Caro and the sheriff.

"Oh, I still have a few tricks up my sleeve.''

"Tricks?" Kimberly echoed.

"Methods," Caro corrected. "I tend to have a somewhat flippant tongue at times. I'll try to be a little more precise.''

Caro bent low over the skeleton, carefully examining the bone surfaces. "Judging by clothing decomposition rates— this skeleton has no visible traces at all—and the insect and rodent marks on the bone, I'd say we're talking at least one generation older than us here. Possibly even two.''

Kimberly wasn't convinced. "You can tell that from just a few marks?''

"And other things, as well. I see no modern dental work on this man. No modern fillings, no old-style gold fillings, no bridgework—nothing but bad teeth and…" Caro gently touched a socket in the jaw. "Look at the clamp marks on the bone here. I'd hypothesize that this tooth was yanked out with a pair of old tongs—like those used by farriers to shoe horses.''

"That's Old West dentistry, all right," Bodine agreed. "But it still doesn't explain why this man didn't die a natural death.''

"Look at these breaks. The trauma to the skull and the legs couldn't have been self-inflicted." Caro gestured with her finger to several areas.

"But you said these bones are old," Kimberly protested. "They seem awfully fragile.''

"They could have broken during transit," Wyatt added.

"No. The two tibias and one femur both show serious splintering, which is how fresh bone breaks—like a twig off a living tree. Old, brittle bones break much cleaner, like dry wood. Same with the back of the skull. I noticed it earlier. These injuries most likely occurred at the time of death.''

Caro reached for the skull, hesitated, then checked with Bodine. "Do I have your permission to disturb the murder victim?"

"We don't know if there's even been a murder." There was a hint of impatience in Kimberly's voice. "And if this...man *was* murdered, the culprit's probably already been sentenced and tried."

"Kimberly," Bodine said, "please let me answer the questions."

Kimberly flushed, the red creeping up her untanned skin. But she refused to be silenced. "So far, I can only conclude trespassing and illegal disposal of a body. This is probably just some macabre, juvenile prank, right?"

"I doubt it," Caro replied. "Most juveniles aren't willing to work so hard for a prank. Digging up a grave is hard work. So is moving all these pieces of bone."

Wyatt rubbed his chin. "That's true. Kids would rather spray-paint walls."

"So far we have no proof this is a murder victim," Kimberly insisted again.

"Wrong. We do. This man did not die a natural death," Caro said firmly. She pointed toward the legs again. "These breaks are compression breaks. I've seen this same kind of thing in sky-diving and bungee-jumping deaths. Either this man fell a very great distance..."

"Or?" Bodine prompted.

"He was pushed. I only hope his killer—"

"If there was one," Kimberly interrupted.

"—was brought to justice. And as I'm sure you both know, there's no statute of limitations on murder."

There was silence in the cemetery. Caro was suddenly aware of the old tombstones surrounding her with their grim messages. The black letters were stark on painted white crosses and slabs.

Death by hanging… Murdered, poisoned, shot… Death by leprosy, death by smallpox, death by diphtheria… Shot, hanged, hanged by mistake… Death by Apaches, death by drowning, death by falling off a horse… Stabbed, shot, stillborn, suicide…

And that wasn't counting all the graves marked *Unknown.*

Caro wasn't superstitious but that didn't stop the fine hairs on the back of her neck from rising. Her scientific observations told her this death was no accident. Her gut instinct told her the victim's killer hadn't been caught. Why else would an old corpse—one never buried in this cemetery—show up here? It appeared that Tombstone's history of greed and violence had risen again.

This was no juvenile prank.

The desert wind blew through the cacti, hot and heavy, as Caro spoke. "You're a small town. I know you don't have a forensics expert or a medical examiner. I'm serious about helping out."

"For pay?" Wyatt asked.

"If your town can afford it. Free if you can't."

"The town can afford it."

"Wyatt, I think you should at least check the computer before hiring her on," Kimberly said sensibly.

"You need me now!" Caro directed her remarks to Bodine, not Kimberly. "A skeleton was deliberately left in the middle of Tombstone's biggest tourist attraction. Someone anonymously removed it, then reassembled it in perfect anatomical order for shock value." Caro had the satisfaction of seeing Wyatt start. She drove her point home. "Very few people can do that. Certainly not any juvenile prankster. What's more, the skeleton was left where they knew a trained forensic scientist would find it."

"Don't you think that's...well, a stretch?" Kimberly asked. "Surely it's no more than coincidence."

"I disagree. Maybe we could use some help, after all. Even the bones in the hands are in the right place," Wyatt mused.

So, Mr. Small-town Sheriff, you noticed that, too....

"Really, Wyatt," Kim protested. "A little anatomical knowledge doesn't mean murder. This is cattle country. Everyone who's ever butchered meat knows bones."

"And everyone reads the papers, too," Caro argued. "Sheriff, you yourself said you read the article in the Tucson paper about my workshop. It mentioned that I enjoyed researching early forensic work in the Old West. It also reported that I was heading here when my workshop was done."

Bodine gave Caro his full attention, the blue eyes piercing. "You think this—incident—has something to do with you, Dr. Hartlan? Something personal?"

"Doesn't it? I think someone took a great deal of time and risk to make sure I found this skeleton. I was even the first person on the scene."

"Coincidence, too," Kimberly added.

"No. The sign listed what time the grounds opened. But I was here a good hour early and got in." She saw Bodine's expression tense.

"Unless you jumped a five-foot fence and the six-foot-high cactus walls inside, you couldn't have. The only way to the cemetery is through the information-and-gift shop."

"It was unlocked, Sheriff," Caro said. "I couldn't find anyone, not even a guide, so I just walked in. The rest of the crowd showed up later—when I'd already found Mr. Bones here."

"If that's true," he mused, "then something isn't right."

"Of course it isn't! I'm positive pranksters had nothing to do with this!"

It was some time before Wyatt spoke again. "Are you serious about offering your services?"

"On one condition. You can hire me, but you can't fire me. Town budget or not, I don't quit until there's nothing left for me to find. Is that agreeable?"

"It is. But I want you to understand something. I'm in charge of this investigation. Forensic scientists assist the law, not the other way around. I'll bow to your expertise as long as you acknowledge my authority on this case."

"Sheriff, I wouldn't have it any other way."

Caro held out her hand and Bodine took it. They shook once, hard, then released hands, Southwestern style. "Consider yourself hired."

She nodded and went back to examining the body—and listening to the two officials consult with each other in tones that weren't low enough for her ears to miss.

"We rarely have to spend money to get the high-tech wizards out here," Kimberly grumbled.

"We rarely need them," Bodine replied quietly. "This is a peaceful little tourist town. The most trouble we usually have is with illegal parking and a few disorderly beer drinkers in the summer. Forensic skills aren't exactly our strong point. Maybe the doctor can teach us a thing or two, Kim."

Kimberly's reply wasn't gracious. "Well, I won't argue with that—and I'm not talking about forensics. *Dr.* Hartlan certainly proved us the fools here. We were both ready to write this off as a hoax."

"*I* was ready to write it off as a hoax. You don't have that authority. You're not a law-enforcement officer, Kimberly. I am. Remember that."

The formidable set to Kimberly's chin told Caro she wasn't happy about being criticized.

"Fine. I get it, sir. I'm just the dispatcher, sir," Kimberly added nastily.

Ouch! So much for young love, Caro thought.

Wyatt turned away from Kimberly. "I'm grateful for your offer, Dr. Hartlan. I'll look forward to working with you."

Caro had to give Bodine points. She would have been embarrassed as all get out if the situation had been reversed, yet he'd admitted his error, then corrected it by hiring her and putting Kimberly in her place. Too bad he couldn't smile just once—to ease the tension. He had a gorgeous smile. But she decided to keep that thought to herself.

"Do you need to send for anything?" Bodine asked her.

"No. Since I just finished my workshop at the university, everything I need is in my car—including my laptop and microscope."

"Where are you staying?" Kimberly wondered, still sounding sulky.

Caro paused. That was a problem. "I checked out of my Tucson hotel first thing this morning." Tucson was about seventy miles northwest of Tombstone, and it would take the better part of a day to complete a forensic investigation. "I'd planned on driving home this afternoon, but if you'll just point me toward the nearest motel…"

"There's only two, and they're always full in the summer."

"She can stay with me at the Bar E," Kimberly quickly chimed in. For the first time, she smiled warmly at Caro.

Before Caro could think of a polite way to say, *You couldn't pay me,* Bodine spoke.

"No. Dr. Hartlan will be staying at the Silver Dollar."

"Your ranch, Wyatt?"

Caro was struck by Kimberly's dismay—and by her own undeniable excitement. She would get a chance to know Wyatt Bodine, up close and personal. She wondered if Wyatt and his Girl Friday were an item, then decided they weren't. Kimberly was too obvious and Bodine too stand-offish for them to be lovers. It was also pretty clear that

Kimberly wasn't thrilled with Wyatt's suggestion. This looked like a one-sided affair of the heart to Caro. Which meant Wyatt Bodine might still be unattached. That fact made her more cheerful than she usually felt on a case.

These were the 1990s, and she was a 90s woman. She might not have Kimberly's voluptuous femininity, but in Phoenix she didn't lack for male companionship. Hmm. If Bodine's character was as appealing as his presence, maybe she'd buy him dinner when this case was over.

Heck, maybe I'll buy him breakfast, too.

Kimberly was still arguing with Wyatt's decision. "My house has much more room than yours."

"But you have an invalid at home. Your grandfather needs quiet." Bodine's face softened with concern. Caro was surprised at the difference it made. *They might not be lovers, but there's warm affection on both sides.*

"Kimberly's grandfather is very ill," he explained to Caro. "The doctors are extremely worried."

"And so am I. Wyatt, you're right, and I apologize. It's just that, well, I want to learn more from Dr. Hartlan myself. I'd rather be your partner—your deputy—than your dispatcher."

About-face there, Caro observed, watching the interplay between the two. First Kimberly didn't want to learn forensics, then she did. She waited for Wyatt's next move, interested to see how the man reacted under pressure. That was always a good thing to know.

"Our spreads are adjacent and you're only a few minutes away, Kimberly. You know my door is always open."

"But you have duties to attend to, Wyatt! Plus running your ranch. You don't need extra work entertaining guests."

Caro didn't care for the other woman's tone of voice. "I'm not here to be entertained, Ms. Ellis. I'm here to work. If you want to learn anything about forensics, I'd be happy to teach you—but it's a harsh subject. It doesn't belong around invalids. If you don't know that, let me be the first to tell you.''

And let me tell you I'd sleep in my car before I'd bunk down in the same house with you. It was a strong reaction, but instinctively she knew Kimberly wasn't a woman she preferred to be around.

There was a strained silence as both waited for Wyatt to speak. When he finally did, his question was odd, even surprising, and it caught her unawares.

''Why did you choose forensics as a career, Dr. Hartlan?''

''Huh?'' *What in the world does that have to do with my credentials?*

''Why forensics?'' he repeated. ''If I'm going to be taking a stranger into my home, I want to know something about her.''

''I don't snore, steal or swear. Well…I swear occasionally, but never in public. And rarely out loud.''

The sheriff's reaction didn't match her offhand remarks. His manner was watchful, waiting, serious, and he evidently expected her to be serious, as well. It was the manner of a patient and stubborn man, Caro realized.

She sighed. Obviously she was going to have to tell her story before she got any dinner or a place to sleep tonight. ''I made my choice years ago when I proved that my girlfriend's pet turtle had been poisoned by a jealous classmate.''

''Oh, please,'' Kimberly grumbled. ''Spare me.''

Wyatt ignored her. ''Go on, Doctor.''

''Well…'' Suddenly Caro was back in middle school. Her best friend, Emma, had proudly brought her turtle to class for a science project. Then that same turtle had suddenly turned up dead. Emma was heartbroken and blamed herself for not feeding the pet enough.

"I didn't believe her, of course," Caro explained. "Emma always took good care of her pets. She was just crazy about animals—she even walked around ants, for heaven's sake. So I was determined to prove her turtle hadn't died on its own. I remember how..."

She'd sniffed the chemical the class had used to euthanize locusts for dissection, the same squirming locusts her classmates had been afraid to touch. Caro hadn't minded the insects or the chemicals. She lived for science class. Plus, she'd rather have dead bugs to study than live ones. Bugs weren't puppies or kittens or horses. They were boring bugs—until you opened them up. *Then* they were interesting. She'd been one of the few class members to kill her own locust, instead of waiting for the teacher to do it.

So when Caro had smelled that same chemical odor around the aquarium, her keen senses and even keener mind had put together the pieces. She'd told Emma, then the science teacher, her suspicions. The teacher had taken care of the rest.

The guilty classmate had been sent to the school counselor, the turtle replaced by the boy's parents, and Caro had experienced her first triumph in seeing the truth exposed, all uncovered by her very own self. She was smarter than the killer, smarter than her teacher, smarter than everyone. And the disturbed boy was suspended to enter hospital therapy. That would be the last animal he killed, the last child he would ever torment.

Justice had been served.

It had been a heady rush of power for the young, intelligent child she'd been, a rush she'd never tired of feeling. Nor ever would, she suspected.

A slight smile crossed Caro's lips. "The other kids thought I was a freak, but I didn't care. Emma thanked me over and over for finding out the truth. She said..."

Thanks, Caro. I'm sad Shelly's dead, but it wasn't my fault. That makes me feel better...

Caro's eyes refocused, and she was back in the present, a bit embarrassed. But it *had* been her first case, and the sheriff *had* asked.

"Well, it doesn't matter what Emma said. It was a long time ago. Suffice to say that was when I decided forensics was for me."

Kim rolled her eyes with a "How touching" expression. Caro couldn't really blame her. It was a terribly sappy story. But Bodine didn't ridicule her; in fact, he'd sat quietly attentive throughout the whole thing.

"How old were you?" he asked.

"It was seventh grade. Twelve and a half, I guess."

Wyatt nodded. "I started becoming interested in law enforcement about then myself," he revealed.

"You'll have to tell me about it sometime. I'd really like to know," Caro replied, grateful for his understanding. She rarely revealed personal things to just anyone. In fact, she'd never told anyone outside of family about her experience with poor Shelly. For some reason, she knew she'd have been very disappointed if he'd rolled his eyes the way Kimberly had.

"There you go, my early career history in a nutshell," she said, trying to make light of the matter and cover her embarrassment. She glanced at her watch. Nearly five. "Now if I haven't put you both to sleep, I really do need to find a place for the night."

Wyatt's answer was instantaneous. "Kimberly, please drive your Jeep to my ranch so that Dr. Hartlan can follow you."

"But..."

"It's decided." His words were curt and full of authority as he turned from Kimberly back to Caro. "Doctor, I'm going to arrange for some backup to guard the crime scene until tomorrow. I'll see you both later.'' Bodine's words were a firm dismissal.

Caro watched as he untied his horse's reins and swung himself into the saddle. The Arabian came to life at the motion, hooves prancing eagerly in place. Then Bodine was off, riding out of the cemetery and down the hill to the desert floor.

But not before he touched his fingers to his hat brim and spoke one last time to Caro.

"Welcome to Tombstone, ma'am."

CHAPTER TWO

Wednesday evening

MORGAN BODINE jumped as the back door to the family ranch house slammed shut. He carefully put down the turquoise-laden silver piece and his rawhide hammer and listened.

The sound of stomping boots echoed in the stairway leading to the brothers' upstairs rooms. From his downstairs jeweler's workshop, Morgan followed the progress of the feet. He heard them progress to the bathroom upstairs, then a second door—Wyatt's door—slammed overhead.

"Wyatt? You all right?" Morgan yelled. This part of the ranch house, like much of Tombstone, was old but had been renovated. However, renovated wooden structures still meant thin walls and floors.

"I'm changing!" came the heated response.

Morgan tilted his head toward the ceiling. "That's not what I asked."

"That's all the answer you're getting!"

Morgan pursed his lips in a silent whistle as he heard the slam of a closet door. Friends and family alike agreed that Wyatt was the sensible one out of the three Bodine brothers. Virgil, now living in Boston, was the oldest, at thirty-eight; then came Wyatt, at thirty-six; Morgan, at twenty-five, was the quick-tempered youngest—and the first to admit it. Yet here Wyatt was stomping around like a Mexican bull with a wasp on his nose.

Morgan knew why. Tombstone was a very small town. Already he'd heard about the skeleton's discovery—and the hiring of that Phoenix forensic scientist. He'd also heard that it had been a murder and Wyatt had no leads or suspects.

"So, Wyatt," Morgan yelled upward again, "those two shutterbugs from the Tombstone paper get an eyeful?"

No answer.

"Wish I'd been there. Would've come over if I'd had the time."

Time. Even with their hired hands, that was one of the problems with working two jobs. Wyatt bred and raised Arabian horses on the family ranch, in addition to his job as sheriff. Morgan worked as a jeweler in his ranch workshop, and maintained a retail shop in town, as well. It was there, at Tombstone Turquoise, in fact, that he'd first heard the news.

"You could've called me if you'd needed me." Morgan stepped in as deputy occasionally, although it wasn't often that Wyatt needed help.

No comment. Morgan tried again.

"Kimberly making doe eyes at you again? Did you have to give her another reprimand?"

"So what else is new? You know Kimmie."

That didn't tell him much. Morgan decided to try one last time.

"You making doe eyes at that Phoenix gal, instead? You won't catch any grave robbers that way."

Crash!

Morgan knew he'd hit the bull's-eye long before he heard the sound of boots flying down the stairs. Seconds later a shirtless Wyatt burst into the room, his face a study in rage.

"Is *that* what this town's saying about me?"

Morgan picked up the silver-and-turquoise again, and

reached for his hammer. "Nope. That's just what I'm saying."

Wyatt was silent, which didn't surprise Morgan. Wyatt's color was up, which did, and Morgan knew his brother well. Wyatt wasn't one for outbursts of emotion. That was more *his* department. Jewelry making had a way of wearing Morgan's iffy patience thin, but Wyatt usually had plenty to spare. His next words confirmed Morgan's suspicion.

"You think some woman shows me up and I fall flat on my face?"

"Well, the way I hear it, the new lady showed you up—and Kimberly had a hissy fit that you invited her to stay here. So who are you more upset with? Kimberly or the Phoenix scientist?"

"Kimberly's harmless. I was angry at *myself* for not figuring things out before Caro Hartlan did! I hired her because she's good—really good. Catching the lawbreaker is what's important. My ego isn't."

Morgan met his brother's gaze. "So, what is all this about the skeleton being a victim in some old, unsolved murder?"

"It's not officially a murder yet," Wyatt said quickly. "And if it is, that's the last thing we need. We're a tourist town, Morg. If this is the bona fide thing..."

"If it's an old killing, our business might just boom. You know the morbid fascination most people have. Anyway, they'll probably think it's just a publicity stunt, not a crime."

"Either way, I can't be having the dearly departed popping up like weeds all over Tombstone. And this was no coyote digging up some old grave." Wyatt ran his fingers through his hair, something he rarely did. "I've got to get to the bottom of this."

"Good idea. Your reputation's at stake. Besides, isn't

this the last of your three-year term? You gotta be thinking about reelection.''

"My reputation is not a priority. If I find the culprit, my reputation will take care of itself.''

Morgan took pity on him. "I wouldn't worry, Wyatt. I'd say it's the person who dug up the skeleton—not this forensics woman—who made you look foolish.''

"He'll pay for his crime—and he'll pay for that, too.''

The anger in Wyatt's eyes gave Morgan pause. For a moment the man before him was a frightening stranger. Then the moment was gone, and it was only Wyatt again. Still, it took a few more passes of hammer on silver before Morgan trusted himself to speak.

"So, you hungry, bro?''

"Yeah.''

"Shame. You're late. I ate all the dinner. And Cook—'' he referred to the retired cowpoke who prepared their meals "—well, Cook threw a bit of a tantrum. You don't show up, you don't eat, he says.''

"Figures." Wyatt sighed. "It's been that kind of day.''

Morgan smiled. Yeah, Wyatt was back to normal. "Run upstairs and put on a shirt. We'll walk over to Carla's Cantina. It's Tex-Mex night. I'll order coffee and *sopapillas* and keep you company while you chow down.''

"Wish I could. But I've got to wait here for Caro.''

"*Caro?*''

"Dr. Hartlan—the forensics expert. I'll give her Virgil's old room to sleep in and we'll let her have the spare room beside it for her lab.''

"Yeah, but *Caro?* You two on a first-name basis already?''

"Not yet.''

"Then let Luciano earn his pay as foreman and wait for her. He can settle her in—unless you'd rather do it yourself?'' He spoke hesitatingly. ''It's not like you to appear too eager, Wyatt.''

''And it's not like you to play matchmaker, Morg.''

''Then hurry. I'll even buy the first beer.''

Wyatt grinned, his good humor restored. ''You're on.''

A minute later Morgan heard Wyatt moving around overhead, then coming down the stairs again. He wore a crisp Western shirt, the sleeves rolled up.

''So, is she really as pretty as they say?'' Morgan asked as he put away his tools.

''Who?''

Morgan wasn't fooled by his brother's casual air. ''The woman who's going to stay here.''

''She's smart as a whip. Doesn't miss much, that one.''

''I already heard that. But how's she in the looks department?''

Wyatt busied himself tucking his shirttail inside his jeans. Morgan knew a delaying tactic when he saw it.

''Well?''

''She's okay.''

''Last time you said a woman was *okay,* you almost married her. And Kimberly had a tantrum they heard across the border.''

Wyatt stopped abruptly. His eyes flashed a warning that Morgan had often seen directed at lawbreakers but hardly ever at him.

''Not that it's any of my business,'' he quickly added.

''You're right. It's not.'' Wyatt headed toward Luciano's quarters, leaving Morgan behind to secure the house.

That near-miss fiancée of Wyatt's had had more looks than brains, Morgan recalled; needless to say, things hadn't worked out. In the end, they'd parted amicably. Kimberly had ample supplies of beauty *and* brains, but there was no romantic spark there, at least on Wyatt's part. There was for Morgan, but unfortunately he struck out with Kimberly just as Kimberly struck out with Wyatt.

It was understandable. Because their land adjoined, the Ellises and Bodines had grown up together. Kimberly looked on Morgan as a brother, while Wyatt saw Kimberly as a sister, not a love interest. But this Phoenix woman could unbalance their precarious triangle.

Morgan let out his breath in another silent whistle. *Whoever Caro Hartlan is, she's trouble. Especially for Wyatt...*

THE SETTING SUN was far below the horizon, the streaks of orange and red completely gone. The furnace-blast wind was gone, too, replaced by a slight evening breeze that was cool and soothing, so soothing, in fact, that Wyatt leaned against the side of the brood mares' pasture fence to enjoy the star-studded darkness.

He'd seen the clear Arizona stars thousands of times. After all, he was Arizona born and raised. But he needed tonight's peaceful twilight as much as he needed the breather before Caro Hartlan arrived at the ranch.

Kim had called to say they'd be late; she had some unspecified business to take care of before she could lead Caro to the ranch. Meanwhile Caro had eaten dinner in Tombstone. By herself, he supposed—he felt a little guilty about that. Still, she should be on her way by now.

Wyatt hooked a boot heel on the railing and continued to gaze over his ranch. Like the town of Tombstone, he was a blend of contradictions. Wyatt E. Bodine was the son and grandson of a cattle rancher, yet he was highly intrigued by the law. He'd received his education mostly from the outdoors, books and the greatest teacher of all—experience.

He had a bachelor's degree in criminology and law enforcement, but he'd obtained it through the college's television and correspondence courses. The thought of sitting inside for four years had been abhorrent to him, but the thought of not getting into law had been worse. Maybe his destiny was in his name....

Wyatt had studied hard, breezing through any requirement tests demanded of him with perfect scores. That, and his sharp grasp of human nature, had earned him offers to work anywhere in the state of Arizona. But after a successful five-year stretch with the Tucson Drug Enforcement Agency, working the Arizona-Mexico border, Wyatt had chosen to pass up promotion, leave the DEA and come home.

This ranch, just outside Tombstone, was home. It was where he and his two brothers were born, and where his parents had lived out their long, full lives. They, like Wyatt and Morgan, loved the Old West heritage of their little town, so much so that their sons were named after three of the six Earp brothers—the three lawmen.

Morgan, Wyatt, and Virgil Bodine were brought up on horseback. They were blessed with the wide-open spaces of the Southwest. They also enjoyed the amenities of modern Tombstone. Wyatt had chosen to keep the town safe for its ranchers, miners and thriving colony of artists, while Morgan had found he was as skillful as a silversmith as he was as a rancher. If there was a sad note, it was only that Virgil had left Arizona for the bright lights back East right after Wyatt had run for election and won.

The Silver Dollar Ranch was the one place where Wyatt always felt a sense of belonging, a sense of home. But until today, until he met Caro Hartlan, he'd never realized how lonely a big ranch run by two bachelors could be. He hadn't noticed it during sunset, when his mind was absorbed by the sky's beauty as orange changed to brilliant red, then streaks of pink darted in and out of the dark purple horizon. He hadn't noticed it while he did evening chores on the ranch, either.

But now, with the work done, and the horses seen to and night upon him, now was the time he felt lonely. The lower the desert sun had fallen, the more Wyatt's world had seemed to shrink down to immediate sensation—until there was just the clean air of the desert in his lungs and the warm feel of the fence rails against his body. And a starry sky that belonged to lovers, not to him.

At least he had his burning passion for the law. The only person Wyatt was harder on than lawbreakers was himself. He'd sworn a sacred oath to protect his town, to uphold the law, and today he'd almost failed in that duty. *Would* have failed, if a certain woman with mocha-colored hair and dark eyes hadn't stood up to him.

Even his own brothers had never dared cross him the way she had. But Caro Hartlan had spoken her mind, proved him wrong—and entranced him in the process. He was grateful for her offer of help. And he'd been touched by her sharing that youthful memory. If only he hadn't looked like such a rube in front of her and Kimberly, so willing to take the situation at face value. Wyatt vowed to redeem himself in Caro's eyes.

He surprised himself so much that his boot heel slipped off the fence rung. Caro? He'd meant to say the townspeople. And his coworker, Kimberly. But somehow Kimberly faded into the background beside the tall, determined woman he'd just met. He remembered the obstinate jut to Caro's chin, the intelligence in her eyes, the facts she'd rattled off rapid-fire. She'd corrected him, brushed off Kimberly's rude protests and hadn't even broken a sweat.

And that wasn't counting the way her blouse and jeans had outlined a trim yet unmistakably feminine body. She didn't have carefully coiffed hair and makeup or creamy-skinned daintiness like Kimberly. But Dr. Hartlan had a strength he recognized and respected. Caro Hartlan, mind and body, was more exciting than a bag full of bobcats.

I wonder if she has the same claws, too—out of bed or in it. Might be interesting to find out.

Still at the fence, he noticed Kimberly's Jeep pass the long driveway approaching the house. Finally. A second vehicle—Dr. Hartlan's—turned into the driveway and drove slowly toward him. It would be the first time she'd seen Bodine land, the first time she'd see his horses. Wyatt wondered what she thought of his home.

WHAT A GREAT PLACE! Caro thought as she turned her car into Bodine land. There was a sense of history, an air of authenticity about the Bodines' Arabian-horse ranch. This was the real West with visible roots. She sighed in pleasure.

A traditional wooden gate stood high above the driveway and main entrance to the ranch. Ancient teddy bear cacti, many of the clusters easily six feet high, formed ragged rings around the base of the gatepost. In carefully hand-carved letters stood a weathered but still serviceable sign announcing the name of the ranch. Caro read the words aloud. "The Silver Dollar."

Underneath and to the right of the weathered sign hung a smaller, modern one with the ranch address, phone number and the words "Arabian horses for sale. Wyatt Earp Bodine, Proprietor."

Caro felt an ages-old longing for her own land, her own property. Somehow her rented condo in Phoenix seemed lacking as she took in pastures full of horses on the right, huge barns on the left and the main ranch complex dead ahead in the distance. Too bad it was dark and she was driving. She'd love to stroll up the long, cultured path unevenly bordered by high saguaro and occasional cottonwoods. Maybe tomorrow, in the brilliant light of the desert day.

This place had an easy, settled feeling that only family-owned, lovingly tended ranches possessed. Caro drank in the sights and sounds and smells of horses through her open car window, delighting in the clean desert air.

A few youngsters, frisky in the cool evening, ran alongside her car, racing her vehicle. Long legs flashed behind the fence railings, while manes and tails streamed in youthful exuberance.

Maybe postponing my vacation isn't such a terrible thing, after all, Caro told herself. *Maybe I'll get some riding in.* Like many Phoenix residents who didn't own horses, she'd still done a lot of riding, mostly as a child; in the desert horses were plentiful and hourly rates cheap. She had little time for riding now, but suddenly the longing for those open, carefree rides hit her hard.

That, and the longing to settle down with a man in a home of her own. A longing she only occasionally admitted. Then she noticed the sheriff leaning against a pasture fence.

He was still. Quiet. She knew he'd heard her car—knew he'd seen the two vehicles, hers and Kimberly's, drive up. But he didn't wave or make any other acknowledgment of her arrival. She watched him continue to stare out at the horses in the distance.

I wonder what he's thinking, she mused, driving past him toward the circular driveway.

I've got a lousy feeling about this case, Wyatt thought. Despite his long-sleeved shirt, he felt a strange chill as the moon appeared from behind the mountains. As a keen observer of the human condition and a brutally honest man, he suspected Dr. Caro Hartlan had discovered more than just some old bones.

And for the life of him, he didn't know whether that was good…or bad.

CHAPTER THREE

Thursday, early morning

SUNRISE WAS STILL a half hour off, but in the coolness of the predawn air at The Silver Dollar Ranch, Wyatt and Morgan were just finishing their morning chores at the stables. Wyatt was hurrying because he hadn't had much time to talk to Caro last night. He'd seen her pass him in the driveway, then his beeper had gone off. Five minutes later he'd headed out to take care of a rowdy drunk at one of the local campgrounds.

Morgan had shown Caro Hartlan to her room last night. Wyatt wasn't happy about that. He wanted to find out what made the lady tick. But last night the law had come first; this morning, feeding the horses did.

"I've given the ranch hands their assignments for the day," Wyatt informed Morgan. "And I'll be off the ranch, so if there're any problems with the horses—"

"I'll be in my workshop," Morgan interjected. "Luciano knows where to find me."

"So does half this town. You and your jewelry."

"Hey, if silversmithing is good enough for all those Native American men, it's good enough for me. Besides, the ladies love it."

Wyatt grinned as he walked the last of the brood mares out of the stable and toward the desert pastures. Morgan was right. Many women did love dating a man who owned and operated a trendy jewelry establishment. In addition to creating his own work, Morgan cultivated talented local artists, many of them Native American, to stock his store.

Which was a good thing, as Morgan's own work hadn't really caught on with either the locals or the tourists. Wyatt thought it nice enough; he proudly wore a turquoise-and-silver belt buckle of Morgan's creation. But then, jewelry wasn't his specialty, although it was fast becoming Morgan's.

Women did enjoy his big glass showcases. But it was Morgan's ready smile, easy laugh and ability to charm the rattle off a rattler that made him one of Tombstone's most popular bachelors.

Wyatt, on the other hand, was much more serious, less approachable, and unlike his brother, didn't indulge in light flirtations. He was an all-or-nothing kind of man, and not just with women, either. When he did something, he either gave it one hundred percent or he didn't do it at all. Period. And the law came first.

Which meant he'd have to solve this case fast if he wanted a chance to learn about this woman.

Who, he noticed with surprise, was up, dressed and unloading her car trunk. He'd expected her to be a city nine-to-fiver, not an up-with-the-chickens type like him.

Wyatt opened the gate to the pasture, unfastened the mare's lead and gave her a pat on the rump. It was all she needed to canter away toward the herd. She certainly was graceful, Wyatt thought fondly as he secured the pasture gate. And so was the woman.

He watched Caro for a few seconds unobserved. She moved lithely and with a lovely efficiency of motion. Such gracefulness was something you either had or you didn't. It couldn't be taught.

She didn't look as if she needed any help at all unloading her equipment. Of course, that wasn't going to stop him from going over and offering, and maybe getting to know her better. He told himself it was because he didn't like working with strangers, and last night's effort at conversation had been cut short.

Now's the time, he thought. His long strides took him swiftly to where she was parked on the circular gravel driveway in front of the ranch house.

"Good morning," he said. Automatically his hand reached for the brim of his hat—which, however, he wasn't wearing in the predawn darkness. He stopped himself, but not quickly enough, judging by the woman's amused expression.

"Let me guess. You're General Patton, and I'm the troops," she said with a saucy curve of her lips. "Sorry, but I'm not into saluting. If I was, I would've joined the military."

Wyatt hesitated, unsure of how to proceed. Caro reminded him of a green-broke horse. He couldn't tell exactly where he stood with her.

"Can I give you a hand, ma'am?" he asked politely, testing the waters.

Caro stopped what she was doing. "First of all, you can stop calling me ma'am," she said with a smile. "My name's Caro if you're feeling friendly. Dr. Hartlan if you're a wait-and-see kind of guy. As for your offer, thanks but I'm all set."

"You have three pieces, but only two hands. Let me help you."

"Thanks again, but no." She turned away from him and went back to her task. "I already took my clothes up to my room last night," she explained. "*These* pieces aren't luggage. They're a state-of-the-art microscope with interface and the computer that goes with it."

"They must've cost a small fortune."

"You'd better believe it. I'm still learning all the software."

"Well, if you want, I can take your kit there, instead."
He gestured toward a large toolbox arrangement with
wheels at the base and a carrying handle on top.

"I'd rather do that myself. It contains my field tools and
chemicals."

Caro removed the last of her pieces from the trunk and
slammed it closed. Wyatt's long-ingrained Western sense
of chivalry was definitely affronted now.

"I doubt you'll be able to get everything in the house in
one trip," he argued.

"I'll manage just fine."

"They look awfully heavy."

"They are, but I'm used to it. See?" Caro hefted the
computer under one arm, grabbed the microscope case with
that same hand, then lifted the toolbox with her opposite
hand.

Wyatt wasn't ready to give up, especially with the ranch
help watching her load up like a pack mule while he stood
there gawking. Men were solicitous of women in the Southwest. That was one convention that hadn't changed over
the years. "Don't be ridiculous, Doctor. Let me." He
started to relieve her of the toolbox, but she yanked it away
from him. Suddenly her eyes sparked fire.

"I don't appreciate being called ridiculous for any reason, let alone carrying my own possessions. I can look after
myself. And for your information, I don't like other people
messing with my tools."

"I was just trying to help. A logical person would've
accepted my offer. Even appreciated it," he said stiffly.

"Really? Let me ask you something. Do you let total
strangers ride your horses? Or clean your gun?"

Wyatt froze. She had him there, and they both knew it.
At least she didn't belabor the point.

"I see we understand one another," she said quietly.
"Let me put these away, grab what I need, then meet you

out here again. It shouldn't take me longer than ten minutes. I want to get to work removing the skeleton.'' She started toward the house, but not without a final polite smile. ''I hate unsolved murders—no matter how old they are. And my time is valuable.''

''That ten minutes would be five if you got off that high horse of yours,'' he said with a smile as polite as hers.

''Don't worry. I can make it in five all by myself. Just for you.'' Her eyes twinkled.

Wyatt was speechless. Was she teasing him? Flirting with him? What? After Kimberly's forthright attentions, Caro's subtlety was hard to read. It was irritating, infuriating—and downright exciting.

He gazed after her as she headed toward the screen doors at the main entrance. Ordinarily he would have hurried ahead of her to open the door, but the lady had made it quite clear she could take care of herself. *I won't open the door unless she asks me.*

She didn't. Caro reached the screen door, angled around to pop open the latch with one graceful swing of her hip, then quickly caught the door with the toe of her boot. Another swish of her hip and she was inside, equipment and all. Well, she was right about taking care of herself, Wyatt thought with grudging admiration.

Admiration for her spirit, *not* those shapely hips, he told himself firmly. Well, maybe those, too. He continued to study the house even after the door banged shut. It wasn't until his foreman, Luciano, passed him and spoke that Wyatt was startled out of his thrall.

''You know, boss, you could've given the *señorita* a hand.''

''I tried!'' Wyatt immediately said, uncharacteristically on the defensive with the man who'd served both his father and him. ''She wouldn't have any of it.''

Luciano's wise old eyes reproached him. He was more

family than employee, and Wyatt correctly suspected that Luciano was about to speak his mind.

"Maybe you should've asked more friendlylike. She's a guest. And she looks like a nice lady."

"I've met nicer," he couldn't help adding, his ego piqued.

"Then why are you staring at her window?"

Wyatt whirled around, annoyed to be caught searching for a glimpse of the woman. "I wasn't staring."

Luciano lifted one heavy shoulder in a shrug and deliberately reverted back to employee behavior. "If you say so, boss. But you know, things aren't always what they seem."

As Wyatt watched him walk away, he couldn't help thinking, *You're telling me.*

THE SUNRISE WAS a beautiful sight to behold, Caro decided as she sat next to Wyatt in one of his ranch trucks. She'd had a good night's sleep and a cup of strong coffee at The Silver Dollar Ranch and felt fresh and alert, alert enough to enjoy what she usually took for granted. Somehow the blazing sun seemed more primitive, more glorious, framed by desert mountains, instead of Phoenix high rises.

She rolled down her window, letting in the fleeting freshness of cool morning air, and inhaled deeply. It was moments like this she'd learned to savor, moments like this she locked away in her memory like gold in a safe. But these moments were more valuable to her than mere gold, for she could withdraw them when the terrible realities of her job threatened to drag her into depression.

They made the drive in silence, with Caro reflecting on the oddness of the situation. They were about to visit a nameless, guarded skeleton in a cemetery—Boothill, no less. She made no attempt to initiate conversation; neither did Wyatt. Not that she found the silence a hardship. It was companionable, relaxed, a fair trade for talk.

Caro took in another deep breath and sighed with pleasure. So far, she couldn't really complain. The skeleton was old, the crime scene untouched. No sobbing families were present, anxiously waiting for her to end their tortured suspense. Better yet, the victim was an adult, not a child. Child-murder cases were the hardest on Caro. Only someone in her line of work could really understand how sick, how depraved, how *monstrous,* some people could be.

It was one of the reasons Caro had never married, had pushed aside her secret desire for children. She'd seen too much evil, too much perversion as a forensic scientist. As far as she was concerned, no one, absolutely no one, was above suspicion. Dr. Caro Lynn Hartlan rarely trusted anyone save herself, her immediate family and the tools of her trade.

"Are you okay? Do you need to stop for anything?" Wyatt asked. "Coffee, maybe?"

The request held sincerity rather than just politeness, tempting Caro to break the peaceful silence.

"No, thank you, Sheriff. I don't need to stop. But," she added on impulse, "I would like to hear how you decided to go into law enforcement."

"It's a dull story," he said. Even the good-natured warning looked good on him.

He certainly is a handsome man, she thought to herself. Then she sternly told herself to back off. First, this was business. Second, the chiseled perfection of that face under the Stetson didn't necessarily guarantee good romance material. Still, conversation never hurt anyone.

"I'd really like to know," she urged.

Wyatt relented. "There's not much to tell. My older brother, Virgil, was small for his age as a child, and Morgan was always sickly. They tended to be targets for bullies. I grew up protecting them both, and other underdogs, as well."

"I see... Well, I wasn't protecting others as much as I was solving mysteries. I was one of those terribly nosy children who couldn't stand secrets."

"Let me guess. You opened the wrapping on your presents before Christmas."

Caro grinned. "Wrong. I peeked inside the closets to see what they were *before* they were wrapped."

"And just one turtle changed you from curious child to future forensic scientist?" He actually sounded interested, Caro noted.

"Well, there was the family thing. Dad's a cop, Mom's a judge, and my younger sister, Desiree, is just finishing at the police academy. Crime was always a part of the discussions at the family dinner table. And I was always interested."

"But not in becoming a law-enforcement officer or part of the judicial branch?"

"Nope."

"Why?"

"That's an easy one," Caro said airily. "Uniformed officers discover the crime, while judges and lawyers are there at the end. Forensic scientists, along with homicide detectives, always get the meat of the matter. I wanted the drumstick, not the leftover-turkey soup, so here I am. How about you? Were you another curious kid?"

"No. I was too busy making my own rules to worry about anyone else's. It was only those who broke my rules—like hassling my brothers—that I went after."

"That's still a long way from law enforcement."

"The justice system might be flawed, but the concept of fairness appealed to me. Maybe because children *aren't* fair. When I was a teen, I apprenticed in the summer with the sheriff's office doing pretty much what Kimberly does for me now. Eventually I signed up for law enforcement."

"You must have done well for the voters to elect you."

"Well enough to work with the Tucson DEA for five years before I was elected."

"You gave up the Drug Enforcement Agency?"

"Didn't like it."

"The city or the work?"

"Both. Border-town police chase a lot of drug smugglers. It's the bulk of their job, and that wasn't for me. I missed dealing with the public."

"So you returned here, campaigned for sheriff and won."

"Yes."

"Isn't that a big change from Tucson? The pace here must be so much slower."

"A lot slower. We get a few minor infractions—you know, the occasional shoplifter, illegal parking, tourist-traffic jams, expired commercial permits, a few loose cattle now and then. I like it that way. Any free time, my ranch keeps me busy, though I do antidrug work at the local schools, churches and Boy Scout troops."

"Really? So do I!"

"Ah, but do you show up on horseback? The kids love it—and around here, it's much easier to get places on a horse."

"Especially out-of-the-way cemeteries with unburied skeletons," Caro said glibly.

Caro saw the warmth leave Wyatt's face. The companionable atmosphere in the car started to slip away. *There I go again.* She tried to repair the damage.

"You'll have to excuse my smart mouth, Sheriff. My black sense of humor is an old habit. Try not to take my comments personally."

"I don't find death a joking matter."

"No, I agree. It never is." Caro's face grew sober. "But I'd rather joke around than cry in my beer. It's a release and a sort of defense when things get too grim. You worked for the DEA for five years. You should understand.''

Wyatt's lips drew together in a thin line. "I do understand. I guess it's just that I got out of the habit since I moved to Tombstone and got away from drugs, felonies and deaths.''

"But I haven't.'' Caro swung around in her seat. "Tell me, Sheriff. How many dead bodies have you discovered in your career? One? Two?''

"I've seen a couple in my day.''

"A couple. I'd like to see how you'd react to my little jokes after more than a hundred bodies. Because that's how many I've seen. Would you like to know how many were tortured to death? Mutilated? Would you like a breakdown of how many were babies? Children? Pregnant women? If you've seen the things I have, handled the broken pieces of people's once-healthy bodies…'' Caro stopped. She couldn't go on.

Wyatt placed a hand compassionately on her shoulder. "I didn't mean to upset you,'' he said. "I guess I've been spoiled working here in Tombstone. I do more community service than anything else.''

"I'm afraid my job is just the opposite—and always will be.'' She was quiet for a while.

"Maybe you shouldn't think about it so much,'' Wyatt suggested kindly. "Give yourself a break.'' He paused a moment. "How about letting me take you out for dinner some night soon?''

"I'll have to think about it. You see, I have three rules I never break when it comes to men.'' She peered out the window again, waiting to see if Sheriff Bodine was curious. *If he isn't, then he's a poor excuse for a lawman.* The best cops were the stubbornly curious ones—a trait she shared.

She waited. Wyatt didn't disappoint her. "And they are?''

"I don't date men who are taken."

"Sensible," he said.

"I don't date men I work with."

"Professional."

"And last, I never date men who look better in jeans than I do." She saw him flick her a glance and waited for him to take the bait.

"I never date men, period," he said, neatly avoiding her trap.

Caro laughed, and the gloom of earlier disappeared. "I'm impressed, Sheriff. That's the best answer I've ever heard in my little test. I usually get a 'Your loss' or 'You're in luck.' But you pass with flying colors."

"So tell me, Doctor, do you always test the men you work with?" Caro was pleased to note the trace of warmth in his voice.

"Men, women, dogs, cats, you name it." Caro settled more comfortably into her seat. "I want to know what I'm dealing with."

Wyatt searched for something to say, but settled for silence. What was it about this woman that caught him so totally unawares? He found himself out of his element with her, and he was a man who *always* had things under control. He didn't care for this strange, fish-out-of-water feeling, a feeling that remained all the way to the parking lot at Boothill. And, he reminded himself, with all that clever chitchat, she'd managed not to answer his dinner invitation.

Great. Now he had two mysteries on his hands—a displaced if lifeless body and a very-much-alive woman, a woman who'd already let herself out of the truck and was around back hauling out her equipment.

He waited patiently for her, and then they walked to the gift-shop entrance together—he empty-handed, Caro with a bag slung over one shoulder, a camera case over the other.

Wyatt knocked loudly on the locked door to the gift-shop/cemetery entrance. "It's Sheriff Bodine," he called.

A few seconds later "Catfish" Chilton, complete with the walruslike mustache that had inspired his nickname, let them in. Wyatt quickly performed the introductions; the elderly Catfish remembered Caro from the day before at the cemetery.

"Catfish was running his family's mine when my father was a boy," Wyatt explained to Caro.

"That was a long time ago, ma'am. I retired once, but retirement wasn't for me. So I putter around the cemetery and play docent to our visitors. Sorry your visit here was such a shock, ma'am. Here, let me take one of them bags for you."

Catfish's garrulous conversation was full of Old West charm. Wyatt watched Caro unthaw so much she even let Catfish take her camera bag. It appeared the lady could be gracious with the right man—which *he* obviously wasn't.

"Thank you, Mr. Chilton," she said.

"Call me Catfish, ma'am. Everyone does. If you'll follow me... I kept everything right as rain, just like the Sheriff ordered."

After first locking the front door, a spry, energetic Catfish led the procession through the store to the cemetery grounds.

"I'm gonna leave you to it," Catfish said. "I need to get the register trays for the cashiers, plus I need to man the phone. By the way, your little neighbor called, Sheriff."

"Kimberly?"

"Yep. She'll stop by later with that information you wanted, so I'll go wait for her. Oh, and ol' Milt—that's the undertaker, ma'am—he dropped off a transport box already. It's near the dearly departed and your grave guard."

He gestured ahead. Sure enough, the box waited next to a uniformed deputy.

"Milt said if you don't want to use your truck bed for delivery, give him a call." Catfish graciously handed Caro her camera bag. "It's been a pleasure, ma'am. Holler if you need anything."

"Thank you, Catfish. And thanks for the help."

Catfish tipped his hat, and after more fussing over Caro, finally took his leave.

"What a lovely man." Caro graced Catfish with one last sunny smile, Wyatt noted rather sourly. Then he sent the nighttime guard home for some well-deserved rest.

He and Caro were left alone amidst the tombstones, with only the desert sun and the skeleton for company.

Wyatt expected Caro to jump right into her work. Instead, he watched as she clasped her hands, closed her eyes and bowed her head. Wyatt blinked. She was praying!

She obviously didn't share his point of view that all of Boothill's permanent residents were long past the point of help. Still, Wyatt found himself unexpectedly moved by her concern for this poor soul.

After a moment she raised her head and opened her eyes to meet his gaze. "Melancholy name for a town—Tombstone."

"Blame Edward Schieffelin."

"Sorry, the name doesn't ring a bell."

"Schieffelin was a miner who prospected here for silver. But this was the center of Apache territory at the time. The soldiers warned him that the only thing he'd find would be a tombstone. When Schieffelin struck it rich, he decided to name his claim 'Tombstone.'"

"Because of the soldiers?"

Wyatt nodded. "He thought it was a good joke. You see, he found a mountain of silver that would eventually pay out eighty-five million dollars to Tombstone's inhabitants."

Caro straightened, her eyes lively again. "What a whimsical sense of humor. Mr. Schieffelin is a man after my own heart. Well. I'd best get started.''

And start she did. This time when he offered his assistance, she accepted. She only wanted him to take photographs, but it pleased him immensely. She handed him one of her two cameras and asked him to follow her lead, taking the same shots she did.

''Insurance purposes,'' she explained when he asked why. ''One camera might break down. And I always develop the film at two different labs. I don't like leaving anything to chance. Once we move the skeleton, we can't ever go back again.''

''Makes sense,'' Wyatt said, but she was already off and running.

Her plastic-gloved hands were everywhere, as were brush whisks, scraping knives and airtight sealed bags. Soil samples, bone samples, insect, pollen and debris samples were all taken and carefully logged.

''The more details I log, the easier it is to narrow down the original crime scene. Especially since we're actually solving *two* crimes—what happened to poor Mr. Bones and why he was removed from his resting place. Wherever that may have been. I need to know what's already present here so I can label what's been *brought* here,'' she elaborated.

That Wyatt already knew, but he'd never seen a crime scene worked with such minute attention to detail, not even when he worked for the city of Tucson. Dr. Hartlan was fast and thorough, yet not once did she treat the skeleton with anything other than respect. Any bone she lifted, she carefully, gently replaced. But she wasn't so cautious that she missed an inch, a speck, a detail of any sort.

By the time she was finished and the bones rested in the travel box, Wyatt doubted this woman missed much of anything. In fact…

''Lucky you're working for us,'' he said as Caro repacked her tools and he felt free to speak without disturbing her work. "The good guys, I mean. Because you're the type who could commit the perfect crime."

"I hope that's a compliment. Either way, it would never happen. I enjoy uncovering secrets, not keeping them."

Caro straightened, then brushed the dirt off her jeans.

"All through?" Wyatt asked.

"For now."

He checked his watch, which sat between the turquoise-and-silver band his brother had made him; it matched his belt buckle, as well.

"Kimberly should've arrived by now," he said. "With the three of us, it'd be no trouble to get the box onto the bed of my truck."

"I don't know if that's such a good idea."

Wyatt was puzzled. "It isn't heavy, just bulky. We should be able to lift it."

"I'm not talking about lifting. I don't know if I should move valuable evidence to your ranch."

Wyatt didn't like the expression on her face—or the tone in her voice. "Is there a problem?"

"Yes. I'd hate to compromise the investigation."

"Compromise?" That was a strange word to use. "Why would you say that?"

"Because, Sheriff, the evidence points to *you* as our body snatcher."

CHAPTER FOUR

Still Thursday morning

BODY SNATCHER? Grave desecrator? *Him?*

Wyatt felt the sun hot on his back, felt her words scorch deep into his soul. "Explain," he demanded harshly.

"Come see for yourself."

Wyatt approached the transport box, the lid propped up against the side. She knelt on the ground and gestured with one finger. Wyatt knelt, too, and peered inside.

"I don't see anything," he said.

"Look in the eye sockets."

He shook his head, still confused.

"Here. Use this." She passed him a penlight.

Wyatt lit up the skull. His insides went as cold as the graves beneath his feet. *It can't be my brand!*

But it was. There, reflected back silver in the light, were a silver *S* and a *D*. The *S* was inverted, the *D* was not. They stood back to back, just as they had for his father and grandfather and great-grandfather before him.

Silver Dollar. The brand marks of his ranch!

Caro gingerly fished inside the skull with a tapered finger and withdrew a set of keys, *SD* gleaming on the key tab. "I couldn't see this until I moved the skull." She traced the raised silver letters with her opposite forefinger.

"They're in the same position as the letters in your ranch sign," she said.

"They certainly are," Wyatt answered through clenched teeth.

"Well, then you can see my dilemma. I'd hate to set up shop on what could be our culprit's home turf."

Wyatt snapped off the penlight and handed it back to her. "I had nothing to do with this, Doctor. And if I *did* unearth this corpse, I'd have more sense than to leave my keys for you to find! These keys..."

"What?"

They're not mine! Mine are in my pocket. They're Morgan's! What's going on here? Instinctively he reached into the back pocket of his khaki pants.

He felt the cool, reassuring touch of metal.

Caro wasn't looking at him. She toyed with the penlight, then put it away in her shirt pocket to study the keys more closely. "Morgan did this, didn't he?"

Wyatt's mouth was desert dry. "Did what?" he asked hoarsely. *Dug up graves? Hid things from me? What?*

"Made this key chain for you. It's a perfect match for your belt buckle." She pointed to the turquoise-and-silver buckle at his waist, a birthday gift from Morgan in the same pattern. It, too, had the silver *SD* in the center. "You must have dropped them yesterday. Or last night," Caro said.

"I don't know how these got here," was his honest answer. *But I sure as hell intend to find out.*

Caro stared at him for a long, brooding moment.

"I believe you, Sheriff. But unless someone left them here intentionally—" she paused "—you lost your keys." Shrugging, she added, "Maybe when you were checking out the crime scene." She grinned, and her face lit with sudden amusement. "I hate to carry things in my pocket when I ride," she said. "I always end up losing them. But never in a skull."

Wyatt started to reply, then caught himself. He wasn't ready to admit that these were his brother's keys, that his brother might have had something to do with this. He owed it to Morgan to speak with him first. Surely he'd have a rational explanation. Sighing, Wyatt wished he'd noticed the hidden keys before Caro Hartlan had, though he knew he would have spotted them sooner or later.

In a situation like this, he relied more on intuition, on discerning motive, than on fact and analysis. The woman before him seemed just the opposite. In a strange sort of way, they made a good team. They might just solve this case—but first he'd have to find out what Morgan's keys were doing inside an unidentified skull.

"I'm well aware of that, ma'am." He held out his hand for the key chain. Caro, however, was still studying it.

"His jewelry is…different, isn't it?"

"Morgan's experimenting with styles. He wants to develop his own design. One of these days he'll hit on the right thing."

"I guess." It didn't sound like a compliment at all—more like a polite comment. Caro turned away and headed toward her toolbox, keys in hand.

"What…?"

"You live on a ranch and you drive an official vehicle. You won't need these keys. I'll dust them for prints, then tag 'em and bag 'em."

"But…you said you didn't think I was involved."

Caro's eyes suddenly narrowed. "That's true. And it does seem logical and probable that you simply lost your keys. However, I'm keeping them—just in case there's something else going on here. They *were* found at the crime scene. I don't know how you do things in Tombstone, but I go by the book. Evidence is evidence. No exceptions. Period. I don't care if you *are* the sheriff."

Caro Hartlan didn't flinch one bit. Wyatt admired her principles, but cursed them, as well.

"Of course you're right."

She studied him for a disconcerting moment, while Wyatt bemoaned his brother's foolishness. Then her seriousness was gone, and she was her easygoing self again.

"Glad you agree, Sheriff. Not that it would've made any difference to my decision." She placed the keys in a sealed plastic bag and carefully slipped them into a separate evidence pack. Next, she reached for the lid to the transport box, set it in place and fastened it down tight with her personal seal. "I've decided to go ahead with setting up my lab at your ranch, Sheriff. Hope that convinces you that I think we can work together. Now, I'm all finished here, so I'll see you later."

"Where are you going?"

"I'm catching a ride into town with Catfish after I load my tools in your truck."

"I can give you a ride."

"Don't you have to wait for the undertaker? Or are you bringing the victim back to the ranch yourself?"

"I can get someone else to do it. I wanted to go into town, anyway, to check in with Kimberly."

"Kimberly… Wasn't she supposed to be here this morning to learn more about forensics?"

"I'm sure she has a good reason for being absent. I asked her to run a computer check on any missing persons in this area. Maybe she's working on that. Or maybe the computers are down."

"I'm guessing this body is too old to be on the computers. Either way, I already have a ride into town—and some business to take care of."

"Like what?"

She frowned at his question.

"I'm just worried about you carrying the evidence bag around," he added. *And my brother's keys.*

"Oh, that." The frown disappeared from her face.

"Let me take it back to the ranch for you."

"Not yet. I'm going to separate the stuff in these bags later. I've halved most of the evidence, so I can mail out some samples for safekeeping."

"But what about the stuff you can't halve?" *Like turquoise-and-silver?*

"I'll store that at your ranch when I get there. Don't worry. I'll take good care of it. I'm just going to run a few errands and look after some personal business. Maybe I'll even pop into your brother's jewelry store and look around."

"He doesn't open until noon," Wyatt told her. "Better make it another time." *Like after I'm through talking to him.*

"Okay." They both turned at the sound of a horn honking. "Oh, there's my ride. See you later, Sheriff. Your brother, too. I have a few things I want to ask him."

He watched the slight sway of her shapely, jean-clad hips and thought, *Take a number, lady...and stand in line.*

"THANKS FOR THE RIDE, Catfish!" Caro slammed the truck door and waved goodbye to the grizzled old man.

"Anytime, missy." Catfish's truck backfired, kicked up some dust and chugged off around the corner.

Caro stood in place, absorbing the atmosphere. Despite yesterday's interruption, she was finally here in downtown Tombstone. She'd visited the historical site once before, when her parents had taken her and Desiree as children. Now she was here as an adult—and a professional.

So far she hadn't even had time to take a single hard-earned vacation breath or do her research on early forensics. She intended to make up for that, starting immediately. She'd already put in most of yesterday at Boothill, not to mention the hours this morning. She needed a break and couldn't think of a better way to get one than by pursuing her hobby.

She pivoted and set off at a brisk walk. She'd had Catfish drop her off at the Tombstone Chamber of Commerce and Visitors' Center on the corner of Fourth and Allen. Allen was Tombstone's main street and the location of the O. K. Corral. Most of Allen Street's buildings kept true to the original structures and locations of the 1880s. The whole town, complete with raised plank boardwalks and dirt side-streets made it seem almost as if she were stepping back in time.

But her thoughts remained in the present. *Strange, the sheriff's reaction to that set of keys. If it had been my lost set, I'd be thrilled to find them. But Bodine didn't seem thrilled at all. Maybe he was just embarrassed—or upset to have his possessions in an evidence bag. Still...*

Caro allowed herself to consider a thought she'd suppressed earlier. Was someone trying to make it look as if Wyatt was involved? Or worse yet, were her instincts about him wrong? *Was* he involved?

She shook her head. He couldn't be. She didn't *want* him to be!

"Son of a..." she muttered. *For the first time in ages I actually find a man I'd like to get to know better, and his keys turn up at the crime site.*

Her pleasure in the beauty of the morning faded, but Caro forced herself to put her current case—and the town's sheriff—to the back of her mind. She would focus on the present and herself; after all, she was supposed to be on vacation. And she *was* in Tombstone. It would be easy to tour any of the famous areas on foot. Tombstone's north-south streets started with First Street and ended with Seventh, while there were only four main east-west streets running through the historic district.

Safford and Fremont Streets were northernmost, then came Allen Street, where the Earps, Doc Holliday, Bat Masterson and the Clanton gang once walked. Below that lay Toughnut Street, named after one of Tombstone's original silver mines.

There was so much history—so much to see and do!

She hurried to the Visitors' Center, eager to become reacquainted with the town. She pulled at the door; it was locked. Caro glanced at her watch, then at the posted hours. It was still early—not even nine—and the Chamber of Commerce wasn't open yet.

That's what happens when you rise with the sun, she thought. *Well, no problem. I'll have breakfast and come back.*

Caro remembered seeing a sign for the Longhorn Restaurant. It opened early for breakfast and was only a block away on the corner of Fifth and Allen. She'd get some coffee and eggs, read a morning paper and take a breather.

That wish was not to be. It was summer, peak tourist season. Caro walked into a crowded room where she had to be seated at a table with another woman. Caro blinked. She'd seen the woman before. It was Mrs. Sunburn from yesterday at Boothill. Only this time she was crying.

Skeletons and sobbing didn't exactly make for easy introductions, but Caro didn't hesitate for an instant. She set down her newspaper and her camera pack, then gently touched the other woman's arm. "Are you all right?"

Mrs. Sunburn raised red-rimmed eyes. They were gray, set in an ordinary, weathered face beneath salt-and-pepper hair that had an attractive, professional salon set. Her makeup was blotchy and tearstained. Caro judged the woman to be in her midfifties.

"Is there something I can do for you?"

"Oh, no, I'm fine." Mrs. Sunburn raised a tissue to her eyes, obviously embarrassed. "Go ahead and order your breakfast. Don't mind me."

Caro removed her hand from the woman's arm. "I'm Caro Hartlan. From Phoenix."

"Marta Wenkert, from Paradise Valley."

Caro would have held out her hand to shake, but the woman was still clutching her tissue. Instead, Caro gave her a friendly smile. "Why don't we both order?" she suggested, flagging down the waitress. "I don't know about you, but I'm dying for a cup of coffee."

Marta managed a nod, but showed no willingness to talk once the waitress had served their drinks and taken their orders. Caro didn't try to force conversation. By the time their food arrived, Marta had regained her composure.

"Sorry about earlier," she apologized. "I usually don't fall apart like that."

Caro buttered her toast. "Would you like to talk about it?"

"It's nothing earth-shattering... I guess the experts call it empty-nest syndrome. My youngest daughter graduated in the spring with her engineering degree. She found a great job and just moved into her own apartment. And my oldest left two years ago. She flies helicopters for the Navy."

"You must be very proud of both."

"Oh, I am. But they grew up. You know how it is."

No, I don't. I don't have any kids—just cases.

"For years I took care of them. Now that they're gone, Frank—he's my husband—and I decided to travel a little. And then I'd planned to go home and look for a job."

"Sounds good to me."

"I thought so. But Frank—he's my husband—well, he doesn't want me to work. He wants me to stay home and take care of *him!* And now he's even complaining about this vacation. Said he'd rather be golfing in Tucson than walking around this dusty hick town. Said my idea to come here was the worst I'd ever had."

"That must be upsetting," Caro said tactfully.

"Tell me about it! I don't even play golf! Thirty years of marriage, and Frank's always had things his way. Well, the kids are gone and now it's my turn. I told him that. And you know what he did?''

Caro shook her head.

''He left me!''

''Left you?'' Caro gasped.

''Well, left the hotel for Tucson to go golfing,'' Marta qualified. ''Threw, actually *threw* money at me, then drove away in our car and stranded me! He told me I can catch a bus and join him when I've come to my senses.''

''It seems to me that perhaps your husband could use a little sense himself.''

''You can say that again. If Frank thinks I'm running after him, he's got another think coming. It'll be an icy day in Tombstone before I let him do that to me again...'' Marta's voice wobbled and trailed off. She viciously speared a forkful of egg, but didn't bother to eat it.

Caro's heart went out to her. ''Are you going to be okay?''

Marta closed her eyes, then opened them again. There was strength and determination in them now, not tears. ''You bet I am. I'm sorry, Ms. Hartlan. I don't mean to bore you with my problems.''

''Please, call me Caro, and it's all right.''

''No, it's not. I'm sure you have enough problems of your own—what with the skeleton and all.''

''You remember me?''

''Yes. And that skeleton.'' She gave a shaky laugh. ''Between old bones and Frank, this has turned out to be the vacation from hell. So, any leads on the case?'' Marta asked, deliberately changing the subject.

Caro took the hint.

''Nothing definite. Of course, it's still early in the investigation. I was just at Boothill, and...''

Caro filled Marta in on some of the forensic-collection details. Even though she kept her information very general,

Marta asked shrewd questions, especially about the photography.

"You're so lucky. You actually get paid to use your camera." Marta sighed and finished the last of her coffee. "It's been a hobby of mine since I was a kid. I love taking photographs—too many, according to Frank. Sometimes he takes away my camera bag to—and these are his words— save money on film. I'm glad I got it back before he left." She patted her camera bag. "That's why I came here. Tombstone's the home of Camillus Fly."

"The photographer? The one who took the photos at the surrender of Geronimo?"

"That's him. He took photos of almost everyone and everything in Tombstone—miners, saloon girls, lawmen, cowboys, hangings, shootings, buildings, even dogs. Fly had the largest studio between California and Texas, thanks to all those miners with money to burn. I can't wait to tour his old studio."

Caro smiled at Marta's enthusiasm, quite a contrast to her earlier despair. Obviously this was one subject Marta loved talking about—unlike, apparently, the absent Frank.

"Photography isn't a part of the job I particularly care for," Caro admitted. "It's simply documentation for me, and of course my subjects aren't very pretty. Usually I just get it over and done with so I can get down to the real business."

"But photography—even forensic photography—should be an art, not a job!"

"It takes a very strong stomach," Caro said. She started to signal the waitress for more coffee, but something in Marta's eyes—a hunger that had nothing to do with food— stopped her.

"Marta, this may sound spur-of-the-moment, but if you don't have any other plans, I could use an assistant."

Marta froze. "Me? Assist you?"

"Exactly."

"I'd love it!" The older woman's eyes sparked with excitement, only to be replaced with a look of wariness. "But why? This isn't charity or…or some kind of therapy, is it? Surely there's a deputy you could call on…"

Caro took a deep breath. Marta was a stranger, and Caro almost never trusted strangers. She rarely trusted, period. In this case, though, her gut instincts told her Marta could be trusted. And Wyatt—well, she *wanted* to trust him, but she didn't dare take the risk. Not right now.

I don't like finding Silver Dollar Ranch emblems near my crime scene.

"Whoever unearthed that skeleton might be trying to make it look like Tombstone's sheriff is involved," Caro announced. "Or maybe he really is. I don't think so, but I can't be a hundred percent sure. According to him, this is probably just vandalism. I think it may be murder. An old murder, but murder nonetheless."

There was no gasp, moan or other drastic reaction. Instead, Marta simply nodded her understanding. "Go on, please."

The woman has backbone, no doubt about it, Caro thought. She found herself telling Marta about the keys in the skull. "First, I believed he'd lost them, but I'm beginning to suspect they were planted there. Why, though? To implicate him unjustly—or to let me know he *is* involved?"

"What a mess," Marta said quietly. "I sure hope the sheriff's as upstanding as he seems to be."

"Me, too," Caro said. Shaking her head, she went on, "I don't like this case at all. Grave robbing, ancient corpses, planted evidence—maybe damning evidence. I've got to dust the keys for prints and hope I get lucky. If I do…" Caro tapped her forefinger against her lips. "Do you drive?"

"Oh, yes, but Frank took our car. And there's no place to rent one. There *is* a bus, though."

"Well, if you don't mind… I don't want the evidence kept in town if the sheriff or someone at his ranch is somehow involved in this. Neither do I want my film developed here in town. Plus, I'll need more photos taken if I manage to discover the original crime scene."

"You don't want to do those yourself?"

"I always take two sets with two different cameras. You'll do one, I'll do the other. That'll free up some of my time. And then I'll need help with the local research. Marta, you're a tourist. You've got the perfect cover to ask questions, especially if no one knows we're working together."

"They might be more honest with me," Marta said slowly.

"And you'd be more objective, as well. So, are you interested?"

Marta didn't answer right away. "You're not just putting me on? Trying to humor a weepy lady? Because I'm not usually like that. And I don't need humoring."

Caro sensed the pride in the other woman. "I honestly do need you, Marta. If I was working as a consultant for a big city with lots of employees, I'd have the luxury of requesting an assistant. But you're here and available, so if you *are* interested, I'd be really grateful. Being my assistant isn't going to be a glamorous position, but it'll certainly be a useful one."

Marta nodded. "If I take this on, where can I find you?"

"The motels are full, so I'm staying at the sheriff's place."

"What if he or someone from his ranch really *is* involved?" Marta asked anxiously.

"Until I have more proof than just a set of keys—keys that may have been lost or planted—I'll take my chances. Going by experience, I'd have to say Sheriff Bodine doesn't seem like a criminal to me, and believe me, I've met my share. Anyway, being out at the ranch means I'll be able to keep an eye on things. I'll check in with you every day."

"If I don't hear from you, what should I do?" Marta was deadly serious, and Caro answered in kind.

"I honestly don't think there's anything to worry about. But if you suspect trouble, call my family. My father's a policeman and my mother's a judge. Ask to speak with either one of them. Try my mom first. She's calmer." Caro scribbled down their home and work numbers on a paper napkin and passed it to Marta. "And speaking of family, it isn't too late to catch that bus, you know. I don't want to come between you and your husband."

Marta's chin lifted a fraction. "As far as I'm concerned, Frank and his golf clubs can take a flying leap into the nearest water hazard. I have money, a lovely room and I'm on vacation. I'm not leaving until I'm darn good and ready."

"All right, then."

The two women exchanged Tombstone addresses and phone numbers. Marta copied hers from the motel receipt, while Caro quickly looked up The Silver Dollar Ranch in the book at the public phone. Caro then reached into her pocket for the two rolls of film taken of the skeleton that morning. She also passed Marta the duplicate evidence bags to mail to her parents. The originals she kept, along with Wyatt's keys. Caro tried to talk Marta into accepting a retainer, but Marta would have none of it.

"I'm volunteering," she insisted.

Caro finally gave in, privately deciding they could settle up later. "Just one last thing," she warned as the waitress came back to present their checks. "This could get dangerous, Marta, especially if the sheriff or someone at his ranch turns out to be involved. I'm not saying we'll be dodging bullets—forensic experts are rarely a target for criminals—but it's been known to happen. Don't do this just because you're mad at your husband. You can bow out anytime.''

"This is what I want to do. What I *need* to do. I think I'll head out to Tucson today and take care of these." She gestured at the evidence bags and rolls of film.

"Great. I have to finish setting up my lab at the ranch. I'll call you tonight and let you know tomorrow's game plan. In the meantime, why don't you spend what's left of the morning doing some sight-seeing?''

"I did want to see Camillus Fly's gallery."

"There you go. I have some research of my own to do."

The two women rose. Caro started to reach for her check, but Marta grabbed it, instead. "I'll get that."

"Are you sure?"

"You've been kind to me, kinder than my own husband. Let me do this."

Caro knew she would offend the other woman if she argued. "All right," she said graciously. "But I buy the celebration dinner if—when—we solve this case."

"Agreed. And, Caro? Thank you for trusting me. You won't be sorry."

Marta gave Caro a cheery wave as they parted company.

Some people were so easy to read, Caro thought. If only that was true of Wyatt E. Bodine.

Caro stepped outside into the brilliant sunshine and squarely into the path of the man himself.

"A friend of yours?" Wyatt asked as Marta crossed to the opposite side of the street. "She looks familiar. Boothill, right?"

"Yes. We shared the same breakfast table."

"Are you ready to come back to the ranch with me?" Wyatt gestured at his truck.

"The ranch? Now?"

"Since you drove out with me this morning, you'll need a way back," he said. "The skeleton's already been delivered. I thought you'd want to get to work. I've arranged for one of the deputies to cover for me at the office."

"Your brother?"

"No, Morgan's working at his store today. His manager called in sick, and he has a new cashier they're still training."

"Who, then?" Caro asked curiously. "Kim?"

"She's a dispatcher only. I have a staff of three full-time deputies who work the evening and night shifts, and a couple of part-timers like Morgan to help out during vacations and such. So I'm free to get back to the ranch. If you want a ride, it has to be now."

"Well, then, I guess I'd better get started." Caro couldn't help looking down the street toward the sign advertising the O. K. Corral.

Wyatt obviously noticed. "Sorry to cut into your vacation. Maybe when we're done with the case I can show you around a bit."

Caro was tempted to jump at the offer, but business was business, so she was noncommittal instead. "Maybe. Thank you for coming to get me."

He touched his forefinger to his hat brim by way of acknowledgment, opened the door for her and shut it before climbing in himself. Then they were off.

The paved streets of Tombstone proper gave way to the dirt roads of the outskirts. The ground was dusty and dry, and the truck raised beige clouds as it traveled to the valley below. Tombstone was built on a mesa, with the Dragoon and Huachuca Mountains surrounding it. The traditional saguaros, the thin organ pipe and ocotillo cactus firmly established their claim to this patch of desert. Creosote scrub was abundant, interspersed with rare patches of green grass and blooming flowers grown by desert dwellers willing to pay dearly for water.

Caro noticed that most preferred to let nature take its course. Certainly there was a rugged beauty in the interwoven mesas and valleys and mountains, so why try to alter it?

The Silver Dollar was near the San Pedro River in the lowlands, a mere eight miles as the crow flies, but the indirect, winding route meant the drive was almost twice that.

"I can see why you ride a horse," Caro observed breathlessly after a particularly teeth-jarring drive through a dry desert wash. "I feel bruises forming already!"

"We can stop and let the dust settle for a few minutes."

Caro glanced at him gratefully. "Thanks, that sounds good."

A moment later Wyatt slowed and stopped at a fenced pasture. His land, he pointed out. The horses were still far in the distance. Wyatt climbed out of the truck, then went around and opened her door. Caro didn't make an issue of it. She understood that his courtesies toward women were an ingrained habit, not a statement on her abilities.

"I forget how rough this road is, I drive it so often," Wyatt said.

"Talk about one heck of a morning commute!" Caro quickly unfastened her seat belt and jumped down from the truck, trying not to react to his steadying hand on her waist. She took a deep breath when Wyatt released her.

He headed over to the fence and hooked a boot over a lower rail.

Caro followed him, but leaned back against the fence so they were more or less facing each other. "Sheriff, why would anyone in this town want me to find a skeleton? Let's talk about the real issue. Come up with anything?"

"Not yet."

"Too bad. We need a motive. In fact, we need two,

because we have two crimes here. But I'm betting the current one is somehow connected to the old murder. And we both know there're only three reasons for murder. Money, sex and power.''

"What about revenge?" he suggested.

"I think it falls under the last heading. It's the ultimate power trip.''

"Not in this part of the country. Revenge is revenge is revenge. Nothing more, nothing less. And revenge could figure in the second crime—if not the first.''

Caro considered that. The sun beat harshly down on her shoulders, adding its burden to the heaviness of Wyatt's words.

"All right, then, four reasons. Five if you count insanity.''

"That can always enter the equation. But I don't think it's part of this case.''

"I'm not so sure. You'd have to be pretty desperate to rob a grave, sneak around with a skeleton, then accurately reassemble it out in the open," Caro said with a frown. "I mean, think about it! That's hardly sane.''

"Sane enough if the victim meant something to you. This body was handled carefully, even reverently. Besides, you're forgetting something.''

"What?"

"Boothill to most people is a tourist attraction—a place to snap pictures and buy postcards. Take away the tourist angle, and remember that this is a bona fide cemetery. We don't even charge admission—we only ask donations. Maybe our culprit wasn't after shock value. Maybe he wanted the victim to rest in peace. That's certainly sane.''

"That's also speculation at this point. We won't know until we find the grave robber. I only know what criminals leave of themselves at the crime scene. I don't always have enough information to know how a criminal thinks.''

"It's not hard." Wyatt swiveled his way, his blue eyes as cold in his face as the sun was hot on her head. "There's a criminal—maybe even a killer—in all of us, Dr. Hartlan. Some of us ride herd on him better than others. But he's still there just the same."

For once Caro wasn't her usual nonchalant self. Her expression matched his. "I don't want to believe that. If what you're saying is true, our dark sides lie very near the surface."

"You have to think like a grave robber to catch a grave robber. Think like a drug pusher to catch a drug pusher. Think like a killer to catch a killer." His eyes shone with a strange burning light. "Frankly, I'm surprised. I just assumed that was how you'd achieved *your* success."

"Well, it isn't. Nor would I ever want success that way." Caro barely repressed a shiver and forced herself to ask the next question. "Is that how you achieved yours?"

"I have a perfect conviction record for every drug smuggler I arrested on the border. And for those very, very few who broke the law here in Tombstone."

"Impressive."

"It works."

"It's also dangerous. Perhaps too dangerous, Sheriff."

His eyes still glittered. "I can handle it."

"Can you? Last night I made a call to the head of the Tucson DEA. He couldn't tell me why you left Tucson. There was no family emergency, no health problem, no ruined reputation. You just left. Why? Because you couldn't handle the city? Or because you couldn't handle big-city crime?"

Caro watched the strange emotion in his eyes intensify. "You're checking up on me? And what are you saying, anyway? That shoplifting tourists and truant schoolchildren are all I'm good for?"

Caro drew a deep breath. "I don't know, Sheriff. You

took on drug cartels like a pro, then gave up big busts, promotions and glory for a walk-in-the-park job. There must be a reason. As your partner, your *temporary* partner, I think I have a right to know.''

He gently—so gently it sent shivers down her spine—took her wrist and drew her close. His lips only inches from hers, he said, "A right to know what? If I'm running scared? Lost my edge?''

Caro refused to back down. "Well? *Have* you?"

CHAPTER FIVE

Thursday, midday to midevening

WYATT COULDN'T BELIEVE the question she'd asked, couldn't believe she could be so bold—and so dead on the money.

"Evil is something we should all run from, Dr. Hartlan."

"If you believe it exists within us, where can any of us go? There's no escape. Ever."

"There has to be a safe haven. And for me, that haven is here—my ranch, my town." He willed her to believe it, even though he knew deep inside that this was a woman he could not intimidate. This was a woman who weighed all the evidence and made up her own mind.

Her face lifted to his, her expression as unyielding as the desert heat. She didn't argue with him, nor did she capitulate. But her refusal to accept his statement was there for him to see.

She actually had the audacity to smile. "As my grandmother used to say, if we believed everything we told ourselves, we'd either be extremely gullible...or very good liars. I tend to agree. What if she's right and you're wrong? What then?"

Furious anger rushed into his veins. He pulled her closer until no light passed between them, then pulled her closer still. He wouldn't let her get away with that challenge—but he couldn't hurt her, either. So he kissed her, instead.

Hard.

But instead of wilting under his attack, Caro absorbed it as easily as the Arizona desert absorbed the fury of a monsoon downpour, absorbed *him* until he stood empty, exhausted by his own onslaught. And she stood firm, strong, unyielding.

He admired her, even as he raged against the circumstances that had brought them together. Try as he might, he couldn't kiss her without the thought of Morgan's keys entering his mind. *Damn you, Morgan! You always did have the worst timing.*

Drained but not defeated, he released her. Caro stood apart from him, not moving. He waited to see what she'd say; for there was no way he was going to speak first.

"Was that your answer, Sheriff? Or was it supposed to hide the fact that you don't have one?" She tilted her head.

Her tone was breezy, even flirtatious, as if nothing had happened, but he noticed that her voice shook a bit. She bent over and retrieved his Stetson, which had fallen to the ground. Wyatt vowed to act as calm as she did as he placed it back on his head.

"I'm not normally at a loss for words," he said wryly.

"Which means I probably shouldn't expect another performance like you just delivered anytime soon?"

"A wise assumption, ma'am. Very wise."

He opened the truck door for her. What she said and did next took him completely by surprise.

"Then again..." she whispered, reaching around his neck with both arms. This time the onslaught was hers, not his. Her kiss was totally unexpected; so was the strength of her passion. Within seconds the energy she'd drained from him earlier was returned—doubled, tripled, quadrupled. Just when Wyatt thought he couldn't stand it any longer, she withdrew, leaving him breathless and desperate for more.

"What was that all about?" he asked the moment he could trust himself to speak.

"To prove a point." Caro coolly pushed back her tousled hair, the fall of heavy brown waves he'd run his fingers through. "I don't believe there's a killer in everyone, Sheriff. In some people, yes. Maybe even in you. That's not for me to say. But if there is…if you believe you could be one of them…"

"Yes?" Wyatt's fingertips itched to touch her hair again. He clenched his fists as he waited for her answer.

"I wanted to show you I'm not afraid, Bodine. Evil doesn't frighten me. It makes me sick. It makes me angry. It makes me want to rant and rave. It makes me cry until my eyes burn. But it's never, *ever* frightened me. That's why I can do what I do, day in and day out. That's why I'm so *good* at it. So if you're sitting on the wrong side of the fence with this case, be warned."

She stared him straight in the eye. "I'll track you down, whatever it takes. There won't be a place you can hide in this whole world."

"Or the next, I assume," Wyatt said, unable to resist the slight jab at her confidence—a confidence some might take for arrogance.

She laughed, a sudden refreshing sound that lightened the serious mood.

"I've never considered the possibility of becoming a ghostly Sherlock Holmes. Irene Adler, though, that's a thought. If anyone could do it, it'd be me. I'll take the matter under advisement, Sheriff."

The light in her eyes sparkled. It was still dancing as she climbed back into the truck and closed her own door.

Wyatt slowly walked around to his and wished he could defy evil the way she did. Wished he could shatter its siren call with a wisecrack. But he couldn't do that any more than he could ignore the twisted part of himself.… The evil part of his brain that thought like thieves and killers. The cunning, shrewd, remorseless genius that could instantly see through any scam, any conspiracy—and come up with a million better ways to execute it. That twisted intelligence of his was a loathsome fluke that fouled his sleep and fought with the goodness of his heart every waking moment. It was why he'd come home. To safety and certainty.

As a lawman, that secret, twisted part of him was his greatest strength—and his greatest weakness.

Not by one word or action had he ever hinted at it. Not one friend or family member in his life had ever even guessed at it—until now. Caro Hartlan was more dangerous than any criminal he'd ever encountered, because outlaws could only hurt his body. This woman—if she learned how right she was about him, how often he wrestled with his own personal demons—could destroy his soul.

How often had he played with making a discovered crime a perfect crime in his mind—long after the trial was over and the criminal jailed? How often had he forced himself to end such a dangerous mental game? It was an unhealthy fascination, and he knew it. The law was his choice, his destiny. But maintaining the law wasn't nearly as exciting, as seductive, as reliving the crime itself.

So far, Wyatt had been able to stay firmly, carefully, on the side of the law. Until now.

Caro's commitment to this case had already driven him to break his own code of scrupulous honesty. It disturbed him deeply. He didn't want to lie to Caro about Morgan, about the keys, but he owed his brother a chance to explain. They were family. Blood kin.

If only I could track down Morgan! So far he hadn't been in his usual haunts, including his studio—where he'd claimed he'd be.

Caro rolled down her window, startling him. "Are you coming, Sheriff?"

"I'm coming," he said. And they made the rest of the drive to his ranch in silence.

Once there, Caro went to the spare bedroom adjoining hers that Wyatt had decided she could use as a lab. "I'll finish setting up my equipment," she informed him. "Then I'm going to unpack the transport case and start working on the skeleton."

"Lunch is at noon sharp."

"I know. Luciano told me this morning." Already she was everywhere, unpacking things with that quick, easy grace of hers.

"Be warned, my cook is temperamental. No one gets room service. When Cook serves, you eat," he said. "That goes for everyone on this ranch."

"I snooze, I lose. Got it." She walked over to the door, grasped the knob and held it, waiting. Wyatt headed for the stairs.

"Aren't you going to stay?" Caro asked with surprise.

"I'll check in later. Right now, I need to track down my brother. If you miss lunch, dinner's at six sharp." *Morg, you'd better be there.*

"I won't forget." She closed the door behind him.

CARO TOOK A DEEP BREATH and let it out on a slow sigh. The coolness of the air-conditioned room was a welcome change from the already blistering temperature outside— and the heated emotions a certain sheriff had generated.

She didn't know which had shaken her more—the way he'd kissed her or the way she'd kissed him back. She usually had no problem holding her hormones in check. She was rarely so bold with men; her standards were too high. But unexpectedly raging hormones weren't the worst of it. Caro suspected there was more to her feelings for Wyatt Bodine than physical attraction.

Before finding those keys and seeing his strange reaction

to them, she'd definitely considered Wyatt someone she wanted to know better. She'd hoped that once this case was over, they could explore their attraction—and whatever else was between them. There were two kinds of single adults in the world as far as Caro was concerned: those you romped with and those you settled down with. Caro had thought Wyatt might be one of the latter. Now she wasn't so sure.

Generally she preferred that the men she dated had nothing to do with law enforcement. Seeing a man whose worst part of the day had been a blown business deal or a grumpy boss was relaxing, even interesting. She could put away the horrors of her job and concentrate on the ordinary.

Wyatt Bodine is no ordinary person, she thought. *But then, neither am I.*

With her customary discipline Caro got down to business. First she finished setting up her equipment at the large work table that had been moved into the room. Next she put on sterile gloves and spread a sterile white sheet on the bed. The transport box, delivered earlier, was on the floor waiting for her. She carefully unpacked the remains, laying them out bone by bone in human order. She'd been unable to really pack them well and they'd been jostled about during the drive.

Caro began by cleaning more debris from the bones, again packing it in clear plastic bags. Some of the specks she found were black and irregularly shaped. Her chemicals would give her a final verdict, but they looked like old silver-ore tracings to Caro. She took painstaking care with the debris, getting several samples of the silver—and various other materials—from the remains.

She neatly labeled the bags, then set them aside for slide preparation and study. Caro preferred to do her microscopic work later, preferably after she'd cleaned up. That way, any debris from the messier aspects of forensic work wouldn't contaminate the slides or the delicate equipment she used to analyze them.

Caro retrieved her tape measure and prepared to determine the victim's height. By measuring the long bones in the legs, she'd find it an easy enough task. An accurate mathematical formula had been developed by anatomy professor Mildred Trotter, a doctor who'd worked with the U.S. Army preparing Second World War soldiers for final burial. All Caro needed was the race, sex and one of the long bones from either an arm or a leg. In this case Caro could use a femur and a tibia from the same leg, a double combination that, according to Dr. Trotter, provided for the smallest margin of error. Caro made the measurements and wrote all her findings in a small spiral notebook. She'd do the calculations and transcribe her notes into the laptop later in the afternoon. Double sets of records, like double sets of photographs, ensured the safety of her investigation.

Caro continued her work, concentrating so intensely that the next time she checked her watch, she saw she'd worked straight through lunch. In fact, it was getting close to dinner. She straightened and rubbed her sore neck, a rueful expression on her face. She'd have less than half an hour to take a shower and change if she wanted some dinner, considering the strict ranch rules for chow times.

But first, dust those keys, hope for a print and a quick fax signal.

The keys jingled in her hand as Caro completed the procedure. She didn't know if she'd find anything. The hot desert sun could bake a fingerprint's oil in seconds, leaving nothing. But the results surprised her. A print appeared, as perfect as any she'd seen in textbooks, along with some adequate partials. Caro scanned the print with her scanner to load it into her computer, hooked the computer to the phone in her room and activated the fax and miniprinter.

There. I should get the results fairly soon.

She quickly stripped, showered and toweled off. As she was dressing, she heard the tiny beep that signaled an incoming fax. Caro grinned when she saw the name of a crime-lab friend on the log line, which explained the speedy reply. *Nothing like having friends in high places.*

She stared at the message.

"Prints identified from both partials and complete. Suspect one Morgan Bodine. Part-time deputy, Cochise County. Address, The Silver Dollar Ranch, Tombstone."

Morgan's keys? These are Morgan's keys?

What was going on? Why were Morgan's keys at the graveyard? And the biggest question of all...

Why didn't Wyatt tell me?

She read over the fax's beginning words again, then read the rest of it.

"Suspect's a registered law-enforcement deputy, Caro. This sounds like one heck of a juicy case."

"Now that's the understatement of the year," Caro agreed. She carefully folded the piece of paper, slipped it into a skirt pocket and faxed off a quick thank-you to her buddy in Phoenix.

Now what? she wondered as she finished dressing. She brushed her hair, then made her decision. She dropped the bagged keys into the pocket that held the fax. Time to rattle the family tree downstairs and see what shook loose.

After locking the window and outer door of her makeshift lab, Caro headed for the stairs. Her natural and professional caution stopped her. On impulse she retraced her steps. She retrieved her clay re-creation kit, spiral notebook, computer disk and the skull, and brought them into her bedroom.

Then she packed everything into her luggage bag—empty save for soiled laundry—locked the case and shoved it back under the bed. She felt very foolish at the action. Hardly an effective hiding place! Suddenly she remembered an old trick she'd learned from a case she'd once worked on. She hurried back for the length of rope Wyatt had used to tie down the skeleton and box for travel. The rope was still next door in the lab.

Caro pulled out the suitcase again and tied the rope onto the handle. And then, as the convicted criminal had done, Caro fastened the free end of the rope securely and out of sight behind the curtains. She opened the window, checking to make sure there was no one in the yard below. As quietly as possible, she hung the suitcase outside. She arranged some bath towels over it before closing the window and curtains.

To the casual observer it would look like some wet towels were being dried in the sun, since the rope and suitcase were beneath them. Of course, the outline of the suitcase was somewhat visible, even allowing for the jutting window ledge, but not unless you looked closely. However, until Caro could find a safer place for the evidence in town tomorrow, it would have to do.

Taking that extra time almost made her late for dinner. Everyone was already sitting down as Caro, clad in a denim skirt, short-sleeved blouse and comfortable sandals, hurried into the large dining room. Wyatt and Morgan both rose to their feet at her entrance. Kimberly, dazzling in an off-the-shoulder dress and evening makeup, did not. Nor did the elderly gentleman in the wheelchair next to her.

"Excuse me for being late," Caro said pleasantly. She turned toward the gentleman in the wheelchair. "Good evening. I don't believe we've met. Caro Hartlan."

"Hugh Ellis." The man held out his hand, which was as grotesquely thin as the rest of him. Caro took it, careful not to disturb the oxygen line that curved down from his nostrils. He looked to be in his nineties, she thought. Hugh's face had an unhealthy pallor and his grip was weak, but his hoarse voice still carried. "I'm Kimberly's grandfather."

"Pleased to meet you, Mr. Ellis."

"Call me Hugh. I may be a dying man, but I'm no high-falutin' dying man."

"Grandfather—Hugh, please don't say things like that." Kimberly's tone was anxious.

"It's the truth, isn't it?"

Morgan, still standing, reached out to put a calming hand on Kimberly's shoulder.

So, been looking for your keys lately, Morgan? Caro silently asked. But she maintained a pleasant enough air as Morgan spoke to her.

"Hugh tends to be rather blunt at Kimberly's expense. We're all very worried about him."

"Forget my health. Wyatt, go hold the lady's chair," Hugh ordered, but Wyatt was already coming around to do so. She was already familiar with his courtesies, and she found she enjoyed them. *Too bad the rest of the dinner isn't going to be as nice*, she thought as she sat down. The brothers followed. She noticed that Morgan's hand remained on Kimberly's shoulder. But Kimberly's attention stayed on Hugh—and Wyatt.

"Beating around the bush isn't for me," Hugh revealed. "Too much liquor and too many cigars wrecked my liver and my lungs. I lived the way I wanted, despite them damn doctors. I don't regret those years, nary a one, so don't feel sorry, Miz Caro. Or give me sermons."

Caro shook open her white linen napkin and spread it on her lap. "I'm a stranger. I'll leave the sermonizing to your nearest and dearest."

Kimberly looked at her sharply; Morgan stared at her in puzzlement. Wyatt's face registered very little as he watched them all. But Hugh surprised everyone with a wheezing cough that was his attempt at a laugh.

"Thank you for that, my dear. I get too many lectures as it is. Takes after my late wife in that respect." Hugh gestured weakly toward Kimberly, who flushed.

"I only fuss because I love you, Hugh. You're all I have left."

"I'm so sorry," Caro murmured.

Hugh turned away from his granddaughter to face Caro. "Save the condolences, ma'am. Kimberly's parents and brother are alive and well in California. My son gave up cattle ranching to work for some crazy computer company. Now he owns the company, my daughter-in-law is their software genius, and my grandson spends his time designing computer games for his parents. They've been after the two of us to join them for the last six years."

"Like I'd want to live in L.A. I'd have to borrow Hugh's oxygen bottle just to breathe." Kimberly wrinkled her nose for emphasis. "If the air didn't kill me, the freeway traffic would. Anyway," she said as she took a platter of fried chicken from Wyatt, "being a city girl isn't for me. Just as some women definitely don't belong in the country." She gave Caro a pointed look as she passed the food her way.

"Well, the city's been good to me. I do work I love and make a decent living," Caro replied, not rising to the bait.

"I don't need the city to make a living. I'm rich enough already," Kimberly announced.

"How…nice for you," Caro said politely, hoping Kimberly wasn't the type to go airing her personal finances in public. She wasn't, but it seemed Morgan didn't mind going into details.

"It's true, Caro," he replied. "The Ellis cattle ranch was deeply in debt, so much so that Kimberly's parents wanted to use the family's computer money to bail it out. But Kimberly wouldn't have it. She starting running the ranch when her parents left and Hugh became too ill."

"Kim turned things around so successfully she's been able to hire people to do all the jobs she used to do," Wyatt added.

Hugh snorted. Caro had the feeling the old man didn't approve of female ranchers. But any woman with the brains to pull a money-losing cattle ranch out of the red deserved full credit and every cent she earned.

"At the ripe old age of twenty-eight—"

Kimberly slapped Hugh's arm playfully. "Next time, say twenty-something."

"—my granddaughter became a lady of leisure."

"And then I decided to work for Wyatt. If I can turn a ranch around, I can certainly manage a small-town sheriff's office."

"She's been a big help. And she works for the city for free," Morgan said proudly. "Donates her paycheck to the local Scout troops."

Caro lifted her fork to her mouth. "Admirable." She had to give Kimberly points for being smart and for being so generous with her time and money. But chasing a man who didn't want her—even going so far as to work for him—didn't match up with those smarts. Kimberly would be better off chasing Morgan. Morgan obviously adored her, but Kimberly favored Wyatt, while Wyatt favored...

No one, as far as she could tell. Wyatt had a poker face when it came to his emotions. He wasn't as easy to read as Kimberly, who was still speaking.

"Playing the wealthy cattle baroness isn't for me," Kimberly was saying. "I enjoy working for the Tombstone Sheriff's Department. Who knows? Maybe I'll get my own law-enforcement degree, like Wyatt did."

"Just don't leave us for good. We couldn't do without you, Kim," Morgan insisted.

"Especially with a murder still unsolved."

Everyone at the dinner table froze at Hugh's words. Even

Caro with her glib tongue was taken by surprise. However, she was the first to recover and nod her head in agreement.

"Do I shock you?" Hugh said to her.

"You did say you were blunt," Caro replied. "And yes, I am a bit surprised. So far, I've been the only one here who's a hundred percent convinced the skeleton was a murder victim. You're the first person who's actually come out and agreed with me."

"Grandfather, please." Kimberly was obviously flustered, which was why, Caro supposed, she'd reverted to calling Hugh "Grandfather" instead of his name. "You're making a scene."

"Hugh, you're upsetting Kimberly. Can't we just have a quiet, pleasant dinner?" Morgan begged.

"I'd like to hear what Mr. Ellis has on his mind," Wyatt said.

"So would I," Caro seconded. "Everyone at this table seems more concerned with how the skeleton popped up—who moved it from where."

"You aren't interested in that?" Morgan demanded.

Caro's eyes narrowed at Morgan's angry stare. "I suggest you let Mr. Ellis speak, Mr. Bodine. You'll get your turn later." *Believe me, I'll see to that.*

"Well, missy, I see you believe in bluntness, too," Hugh wheezed. "I never did like being interrupted."

"Then why don't you tell us what you know, Hugh?" Wyatt suggested.

Hugh's expression was crafty. "Rumor is, Wyatt and Caro are keeping this case low profile. Unless high stakes are involved, people don't do that—or hold back evidence."

That's as good an opening as any. Caro reached into her pocket and withdrew the turquoise-and-silver key chain. "Like this?" The keys jangled in the clear plastic bag as she held it aloft.

"Hey, I've been looking all over for those."

"So they *are* yours." Caro glanced at Morgan, then swiveled toward Wyatt, her eyes holding both accusation and disappointment. Wyatt returned her gaze evenly.

"Where did you find them?" Morgan asked. He reached out for the bag, but Caro pulled it away.

"I found it inside our anonymous skull."

"Inside what?" Kimberly blinked.

"At the crime scene," Caro explained. "Either you're involved in this case—and I *am* going to call it a wrongful-death case—or someone wants it to look as though you are," she told Morgan.

She turned to Wyatt for assistance, but he sat steadfastly silent. As did the others at the table. "Don't all speak at once," she prodded.

"I have *my* keys," Kimberly sniffed.

"Well, I didn't put mine there! Wyatt must have borrowed them." Morgan turned to his brother.

"I didn't," Wyatt said quietly.

But you knew they were your brother's, and we'll talk about that later, Caro's expression promised him.

"You must have someone else's keys," Kimberly insisted. "One of the ranch hands or..."

Caro slid one hand into her pocket, pulled out the fax and passed it to Wyatt. "This says I don't."

Wyatt read the fax, then gave it to Morgan. Kimberly immediately peered over his shoulder. Morgan's next comment wasn't complimentary at all.

"Well, *Doctor,* aren't we the sneaky one?"

"Don't we all have something to hide?" Hugh asked cryptically.

"But why? What motive would Morgan—" Kimberly began.

"Not me!" Morgan exclaimed.

"—or anyone," Kimberly continued, "have to unearth an old skeleton?"

"Maybe the skeleton got in the way."

Now Wyatt seemed confused. "I don't understand."

"Don't you? There's more than just old bones being unearthed here," Caro answered. She stood up, taking her fork and the white linen napkin in her lap. She crossed to Hugh's wheelchair, knelt down and carefully scraped some soil from the treads of one rubber wheel onto her napkin.

"What is this—more party games?" Morgan asked.

"More like a laundry situation," Kimberly added. "I keep telling you, Wyatt, to use paper napkins. You're going to have to bleach that one by the time Caro's done with it."

Wyatt ignored Kimberly and tracked Caro's every move.

"What do you have?" he asked.

"I'll show you." She completed her scrapings and carried the napkin carefully to the table. Still standing, she ran her fingers over the dust, then rubbed her fingertips together. Using her spoon, she put a little of the dirt in the palm of her hand and added a few drops of water. If she wasn't mistaken—and she didn't think she was...

"Is there a mine on your ranch, Mr. Ellis?" Caro asked.

"Now it's Mr. Ellis again. That sounds ominous," Hugh said.

And *that* sounded like an evasion. Caro's professional manner kicked in. "Please answer the question, sir."

Kimberly replied for him. "There's no mine on Ellis land."

"Sheriff?"

"There's a mine on ours. Why do you ask?"

Everyone leaned forward to hear Caro's answer.

"Because it looks like there's precious metal in this soil."

Everyone leaned back again except Wyatt, who poked his finger through the dirt on Caro's napkin.

"Really, Caro, this whole town is full of silver tailings." Kimberly picked up her knife and buttered a roll. "And Tombstone's full of old miners."

"I realize that. But the town—more specifically, the graveyard—doesn't have this kind of soil."

"So?" Morgan demanded.

"So...the skeleton did. And so does Mr. Ellis's wheelchair."

Kimberly's roll dropped onto her plate with a soft thud.

"Are you saying Hugh's a grave robber?" Wyatt asked brusquely.

"No. I'm saying that the dirt on the skeleton came from Mr. Ellis's ranch—or from the Silver Dollar."

"You'll need proof of that. The soil around here is probably the same from one ranch to the next. Everyone has pretty much the same stuff."

"And everyone knows that Bodine land has an old silver mine on it. So do lots of the other ranches!" Morgan shouted.

"I have to agree." Kimberly's face was as pale as Morgan's was red. "Come on, Wyatt, that skeleton didn't come from your mine. It's been boarded up for years!"

Morgan, Kimberly and Hugh stared at Caro again.

"I want to hear the rest of what Dr. Hartlan has to say about this...wrongful death," Wyatt said.

"Correction. I've just officially upgraded it to murder, which is what I've suspected all along." Caro reached for more soil and more water, mixing both in her already muddy palm as she spoke. "Number one, I have a motive for the victim's death. Number two, he was probably thrown down a mine shaft after he'd been killed. The compression fractures on the long bones will bear me out. And I'd guess it's probably an old mine and an old murder, or the remains would've been discovered much earlier. Number three—''

Morgan lost his patience. ''Enough with the numbers, already!''

''Please, Morgan,'' Wyatt ordered. ''Go on, Caro.''

''Number three, I found precious-metal tracings on the skeleton, in addition to damp rot. And The Silver Dollar Ranch has an old mine on its land—''

''That silver was tapped out decades ago,'' Morgan interrupted. ''There isn't any more.''

''I want to ride out to The Silver Dollar Mine tomorrow and see for myself. Sheriff, will you take me?''

''That's a dangerous place.'' Wyatt didn't sound enthusiastic at all. ''Silver traces on the bones doesn't mean your skeleton came from our property. Or that there's anything in the mine.''

''I think the chances are very good there is. You see, Sheriff—'' Caro drew a deep breath ''—I suspect your mine isn't tapped out at all. I think it's yielding again, and quite richly at that. I also suspect the skeleton must have died for those riches, and he's somehow turned up again because of them.''

The room was filled with Morgan's hoots of derision, Kimberly's polite expressions of disbelief and Hugh's wheezing, which could mean any number of things. Even Wyatt's skepticism had overridden his usual poker-face look.

''Caro, your theory is faulty. There's no silver on this ranch, nor any motive for old murders or present-day crime.''

''I didn't say anything about silver. I said precious metal. I know what I've seen on the skeleton. And I know what I've just found in Hugh's wheels.''

She rose and held out her fist in the middle of the table.

It was Wyatt who took hold of her wrist, Wyatt who peeled back her fingers to the soil clasped in her hand.

A deadly silence fell on the room. Resting there in her palm—from a wheelchair that had crossed Bodine ranch land—were shiny flecks of metal.

"It's..." Kimberly's voice cracked and broke.

Wyatt's eyes met Caro's. No one bothered to finish the other woman's sentence. They could all see for themselves the glistening, noncorroded sheen, a warm, shiny luster that could mean only one thing.

Gold.

CHAPTER SIX

Friday morning

"GOLD! OF ALL THE preposterous claims!"

Outside his brother's official Jeep, Morgan Bodine strapped on the gun that his occasional stints as sheriff's deputy demanded. "It's even crazier than that woman thinking we're grave robbers!"

Wyatt unsnapped the collar of his shirt to catch the rare coolness of the morning breeze. "She's just doing her job, Morg. Can't fault the lady for that."

"The hell I can't!"

"She's doing the same job I do," Wyatt replied. "And you. You're one of my deputies, so I need to be able to contact you. Where were you yesterday?"

"Out with Kimberly."

"She was working."

"Not all day she wasn't. I took her to lunch."

"And you went over to the Bar E after dinner. Where you stayed till midnight—I heard you stumble in." Wyatt sighed. "I'll bet Kim tried to show you the door long before that."

Morgan's face flushed an angry, embarrassed red, and Wyatt knew he'd hit the mark. "Chasing her around like a schoolboy is beneath you, Morg, and you know it," he said sadly. "I'm warning you—"

"Save it, *Sheriff*. And while we're on the subject of

warnings, let me tell you that high-tech Sherlock Holmes you're chasing doesn't know a clue from a cactus!''

"Maybe not cactus, but I'm a whiz at fingerprint retrieval." Both men turned as Caro approached.

Morgan pointedly ignored her arrival, though Wyatt did touch the brim of his hat. "I'm off, Wyatt. I have better things to do than sit and listen to insults on my own ranch."

Wyatt dangled the keys to the sheriff's vehicle, regretting that this morning wasn't going to give him his chance to talk to Morgan privately. Morgan snatched the keys out of his brother's hand.

"Tell Kimberly I'll check in with her after Caro and I come back from the mine," Wyatt said.

"I hope you aren't wasting your time."

Wyatt's eyes narrowed. "Don't underestimate the lady, Morgan. I checked with the Phoenix police. Detectives fight for her services. The percentage of crimes solved on the cases she works is far above average. She's smart, and we're lucky we have her."

Caro was surprised—and pleased. "Thanks for the vote of confidence, Sheriff. I do work hard."

Morgan was fumbling with the gun belt, yet Morgan had grown up with guns. Was it Caro's imagination, or did he seem uneasy? Wyatt apparently thought the same thing.

"Morg?"

"Hmm?" Morgan wouldn't look Wyatt in the eye, Caro noticed.

"Anything you're not telling me?"

"Like what?" Morgan finally got the buckle to thread and fasten.

"Like about this case. Like how your keys turned up in that skull."

"I told you yesterday! I don't know! Now, are you going to believe me or are you going to call me a liar?"

"Morg, I—"

"Don't play big brother with me, Wyatt. I don't need it."

With those words Morgan climbed into the Jeep, viciously cranked the engine to life and sped off in a cloud of dust.

"My apologies," Wyatt said quietly to Caro. "It isn't like him to be so rude."

"I've ruffled a few feathers, I'm sure."

"Which was your intention?"

"Naturally."

"Well, you succeeded. Morgan's in rare form." *And Kimberly, as well,* he remembered. She'd called him early this morning to voice her complaints about Caro Hartlan. "My grandfather can barely breathe, Wyatt, let alone dig for skeletons and imaginary gold strikes!" she'd said. "I checked his favorite places—you know he can't go far—and I didn't see any metal anywhere. Except his aluminum wheelchair! Hugh's in bed from the shock, and I'm worried sick about him."

Wyatt had tried to soothe his childhood friend. He'd even used the affectionate diminutive of her name. "I'm sorry about that, Kimmie, but—"

"Sorry, my grandfather's mule! I don't know where that gold came from, and frankly I don't care! You do something about Dr. Know-It-All and do it soon, or you can find yourself a new dispatcher!"

Kimberly had hung up on him, her voice trembling with emotion. First Kim, then Morgan had joined in the outcry against Caro Hartlan. Wyatt himself wasn't thrilled with the events of last night, either, but he was forced to admit one thing. Caro Hartlan had made more progress in two days than he could have made in a week.

And although he hadn't told anyone yet, he'd come to the same conclusion as Caro had. His crime-fighting instincts never lied.

Someone on the Bodine or Ellis ranch knows more than he—or she—is telling. It looks like there's been one murder over treasure in the past. There isn't going to be another if I can help it.

"Come on, let's get out to the mine."

With Caro right behind him, Wyatt made for the barn, his steps slow, his expression thoughtful. A few seconds later he was throwing a saddle on one of the two horses he kept for personal use, mouth set in a grim line. Caro saddled the other. Wyatt felt that she knew he wasn't involved, but that wasn't particularly reassuring. It meant he might have to arrest one of three people, people he'd known all his life. A man he'd loved like a father. A woman he loved like a sister. A brother. And whoever might have helped with those crimes.

As he helped Caro finish saddling the Arabian mare, Wyatt muttered a curse. The horse pricked her delicate ears, while Caro tactfully avoided comment. Wyatt gave the mare a soothing rub on the neck, and she swung her velvety gray muzzle his way to lightly brush his forehead.

It would take more than an equine caress to brighten his mood, Wyatt thought dismally as he led the mare and his stallion outside. If he had to arrest someone he loved, so be it. His own code of justice demanded no less—no quarter given, no quarter asked.

This woman was responsible for what would almost certainly be a painful disturbance in all their lives. No, he reminded himself, she wasn't responsible for whatever had happened; she was merely bringing it to light. Still, how could he even consider any kind of relationship with her? And he had to face it, he was interested in Caro Hartlan. More than just interested. Intrigued and aroused by her mind, her body, her sharp wit.

Caro walked beside him, taking in the beauty of his silver Arabian—and the frown on Wyatt's face.

Obviously not a happy camper. Well, she wasn't too happy herself. Maybe his expression wasn't pleasant, but the rest of him was as attractive and fit as ever. Like her, he was dressed in boots, lightweight jeans and a long-sleeved yoked shirt as protection against the sun. Only tourists and sun worshipers dressed scantily in the fury of the desert's June heat. Unlike Bodine, Caro didn't have a gun strapped to her waist, and she'd settled for her Boston Red Sox baseball cap, instead of a Stetson.

Outside the barn, Wyatt mounted, the bullet belt and holster bouncing a bit at the motion. Caro found herself staring. She knew that most policemen carried their guns twenty-four hours a day. In some states it was even the law. There was no such thing as off duty unless you'd quit or died.

"I know you're an experienced rider, but I'm warning you, it's a long way to the mine," Wyatt said.

Caro smiled. "I'm an Arizona native, remember? And I'll take good care of your mare—whom you haven't introduced me to, by the way."

"Delicate Cactus Blossom. And mine's called Arabian Pride."

Caro stroked the mare's nose. "Delicate Cactus Blossom, huh, sweetheart? How about I just call you Blossom? You're a pretty one, aren't you? So, Blossom, ready to go stir up some bushes?"

"Pardon?"

"You have to stir up bushes and turn over rocks to find out where the snakes are hiding." She let her meaning sink in before swinging gracefully into the saddle. "Let's go, Sheriff. The snakes are waiting."

The trek out to the old Bodine mine began in silence. The old trail was faint but visible, and not a difficult ride. Wyatt was in no mood to talk—and obviously, neither was

Caro—despite the soothing coolness of the morning. A coolness that was fighting a losing battle against the sun.

The airborne predators were already circling, waiting for the ground animals to take advantage of the precious morning dew. Coyotes and other nocturnal predators waited to do the same before retiring from the hunt.

A hawk glided overhead. At its most primitive level, life was nothing more than survival of the fittest, Caro mused, not for the first time. She stole a glance at the man who rode beside her. Was he friend or foe? Hunter or hunted? Or perhaps both, like prey that would turn and destroy its predator—the deadliest kind of prey.

Caro hoped Bodine was an ally, believed it as strongly as she was able to believe anything. But even if he wasn't, she silently vowed she'd survive. She knew that the best offense was a good defense, that knowledge was, and always would be, power. It was time to start building on the knowledge she already possessed.

"Sheriff...why didn't you tell me those keys weren't yours?"

His head swiveled her way, his eyes hidden under the Stetson's brim. "Because I wanted to talk to Morgan first, give him a chance to explain. Before I could do that, you dropped your bombshell."

"That's hardly police procedure. The forensics expert and the primary officer for the crime are supposed to share all their information."

"I agree. So why didn't you tell me you'd fingerprinted the keys?"

Caro reined her horse close to his. "Fingerprinting is standard procedure, and anyway, I did tell you I planned to do it."

"Fine, but you could've told me when you received the results." He paused. "That's some little computer you have, ma'am."

"Silicon Valley's finest, and I wouldn't have had to use it if you'd been honest from the start."

"I was going to tell you those were Morgan's keys, damn it. You didn't give me enough time."

"Time to do what? Take them from me at the crime scene before I bagged them?"

Wyatt's reaction was swift and angry. "What are you trying to say—Doctor?"

"I'm saying, Sheriff, that your methods are somewhat…freelance. You want to kiss me on the job, okay, I can live with that. I can even enjoy it," she said bluntly. "But when it comes to letting someone take evidence or lie—"

"I never lied!"

"You deceived me by not telling me the truth. I believe that's called a lie of omission. Doesn't count favorably in my book."

"I've already given you my reason for keeping quiet about the keys."

"I see. Family comes first?"

"Justice comes first. But family matters to me, and so does fairness. As for kissing you…"

"Yes?"

"Rest assured, I won't make that mistake again."

Caro burned inside from anger and something else—a discouragement that surprised her with its intensity. They rode on, the stillness of morning broken only by the muffled thudding of horses' hooves and the creaking of leather. After a few minutes of this, she decided it was time for a change of subject.

"Tell me about The Silver Dollar Mine, Sheriff."

"What do you want to know?"

"Everything that could help us with this case."

"There's not much to tell. Bodines mined silver in the

early days, but the mine was tapped out long before the boom days ended.''

"What did your ancestors do for a living, then?" Caro asked. "When the silver ran out?"

"What everyone else did who didn't have a yielding claim. Fed those who worked the mines. My ancestors were all cattle ranchers, starting with Lem Bodine, who was the first Bodine to settle in Arizona."

"So you're the only Silver Dollar horse rancher?"

"That's correct."

Caro adjusted the grip on her reins. "Was Lem Bodine involved in the Earp-Cowboy wars?"

"No, he came into the picture a few years after the turn of the century. But Tombstone silver did play a big part in his life." He slanted her a curious look. "How much do you really know about all that—aside from the movies and high school history books?"

"Enough, I guess. I know that during Tombstone's silver-boom days, the Cowboys were almost a hundred strong. They were crooked cattlemen, drifters and fugitives who organized their own crime ring, with the protection of a corrupt political system."

"Then you know the Earps eventually broke the Cowboy rule," Wyatt said. "Including Tombstone's corrupt political system—the judges, the lawyers, the courts. The Earps set out to destroy that monopoly and saw justice served."

"Yes, but not without bloodshed," Caro recalled. "Most people only remember that the Earps and Doc Holliday survived the shoot-out at the O. K. Corral. They don't remember the rest of it."

Caro and Wyatt both fell silent and Caro reviewed what she knew about the fate of the proud lawmen, sons of a St. Louis judge. The corrupt courts issued warrant for the arrests of Wyatt, Virgil and Morgan Earp, as well as Doc

Holliday. Dead or alive. The hunters had become the hunted, who refused to surrender. The four men stood fast against the Cowboys—and suffered the consequences.

Morgan Earp paid dearly for his job as deputy. He was murdered by the Cowboys in December of 1881, a mere two months after the infamous shoot-out. The following March, Virgil Earp almost suffered the same fate; he survived a murder attempt, but was permanently crippled, thanks to a shattered arm and shoulder from a shotgun blast.

Wyatt and Doc were forced to leave their Arizona homes, and both men ended up in Colorado. Holliday gambled in various mining towns and died in a Colorado sanatorium of T.B. six years later. .

Wyatt was hounded by men—decent and evil—for the rest of his life. He and Sadie Marcus followed the mining camps, where Wyatt succeeded more often as a gambler, deputy or marshall than he did as a prospector. He eventually roamed as far west as California and as far north as Alaska in search of a fortune, which he found, and in the attempt to avoid notoriety, which was impossible. Eventually he settled in California to breed and race horses.

"It's sad to think of it," Caro said after a while. "The Earps, along with Doc Holiday, were responsible for breaking the rule of organized crime in Cochise County. Yet the town didn't appreciate the high price those men paid for that justice."

Wyatt pushed his Stetson back on his head. "You're wrong, Caro. The miners appreciated it, and so did some of the cattle ranchers. Not all of them were rustlers. My great-grandfather, who came to Arizona a few years later, raised cattle and sold them for honest prices. The Cowboys were long gone then, but the mines were successful from 1879 to the mid-thirties. So Tombstone was still a thriving town, with a market for beef."

"You're saying that thanks to the Earps, Tombstone offered cattlemen a decent living?"

"Pretty much. Lem's ranch in Texas had been overgrazed and wasn't doing well. When he got to Arizona, he originally tried mining. He laid claim to The Silver Dollar Mine to finance new Texas land. He didn't make enough for that, but when the mine tapped out, he was able to buy the surrounding land, outside Tombstone proper."

"I imagine it was cheap enough," Caro said.

"It was if you're talking money, not backbreaking labor. So Lem took his wife, his son and his herd of cattle to settle The Silver Dollar Ranch, which he named after the mine."

"They must have been determined people."

"They sure were. Without the Cowboys in power, Lem Bodine did quite well selling beef for the first few years."

"I imagine he did—but just for a few years?"

"The ranch prospered, but Lem died before his time. He might have avoided the Cowboys' reign of terror, but family history has it that Lem was caught in a cattle stampede. Nobody knew exactly what happened. And the remains were, well..."

Caro swiveled in her saddle. "What?"

"By the time a couple hundred head of cattle run over you, there's not much left to bury."

"Oh." Caro was silent. What a horrible way to die.

Wyatt sent his sharp gaze her way. "Just 'oh'? No witty comeback?"

Caro felt a dart of pain at his negative impression of her, and for once her answer was serious.

"Sorry to disappoint you, Sheriff. I may joke about my job. I certainly joke about death. But I never, ever laugh at pain and suffering."

After a few moments, during which neither spoke, she was surprised when he said, "That remark I made. I was wrong, way out of line. And I was wrong about something else. I should've told you the keys belonged to Morgan." He stopped his horse and held out his hand by way of apology.

The gesture looked and felt so sincere to Caro that she moved close to him, their thighs almost touching, to take his hand.

Gently their palms met. Then his grip tightened and he pulled, safely bringing her closer to his leaning body. His lips brushed her cheek. "I was wrong about you, too."

Before her uncharacteristically slow mind could come up with an appropriate response, his lips were on hers. This time there was a blatant male hunger she both recognized and responded to with a hunger of her own.

Their horses shifted impatiently. Caro didn't notice. The mine waited for them. She didn't remember. She knew their behavior was totally unprofessional—and she didn't care. Nothing mattered except what she was feeling now, what he was feeling: the elemental pleasure of male and female. Nothing mattered except their excitement, their desire.

That desire was so strong, so tempting, Caro knew she had to break its thrall now or end up making love on the desert floor. Frantically, she touched her heels to the mare's flanks. The Arabian, always ready to run and impatient at standing motionless for so long, responded instantly to Caro's touch. With natural grace enhanced by centuries of careful breeding, Cactus Blossom shifted effortlessly into the beautiful canter generations of Arabian owners had treasured.

The towering saguaros and creosote bushes were a dark green blur, while the thinner ocotillo and mesquite trees streaked Caro's peripheral vision with lighter green. Caro felt the mare's sureness, her steadiness, her familiarity with the trail in the smoothness of the ride and the excited pricking of the animal's ears.

She also heard Wyatt coming up behind her. On sudden impulse, she gave the mare free rein. Cactus Blossom burst into a gallop so eagerly that Caro laughed and crouched low, rider and mount caught up in the primitive enjoyment of flight.

Wyatt's stallion, too, moved into a gallop. The mare laid her ears flat against her finely chiseled head and responded with an extra burst of speed. Powerful muscles bunched and exploded in raw power.

Caro gasped with sheer exhilaration as the wind tore at her breath and hair, tore at the mare's silver mane and tail. She felt a strange identification with her horse as male pursued female in an ancient race. The female, unwilling to be caught by any male who wasn't fitter, stronger, more determined than she, stretched out even further.

Her hooves landed softly in the shallow sand, then dug hard against the rocky ground for power and traction. The stallion did the same, but his rider was much heavier than the mare's, and the mare wasn't in season. This time, the man and stallion slowed first. The females remained free.

It was the mare who first recognized that the race was over. Triumphant, she and Caro slowed down, allowing their pursuers to catch up. Caro patted the mare's neck and felt a moment's sadness, despite the magic of the desert morning, the beauty of the horse, the vigor of the race. Precious times like these were so rare in her life, and they seemed to end so quickly.

"Congratulations on your win. You're some horsewoman, Caro. I didn't stand a chance."

"I think the mare herself had a lot to do with it," she said graciously. "Not to mention her owner."

"I'm forgiven, then?" he asked. There was a simplicity in his words that erased some of the tension that always seemed to be present between them.

Caro found herself responding in the same tone. "For the cheap shot, yes."

"And the kiss?"

Caro allowed herself to unbend. "If I hadn't wanted you to kiss me, I would've shoved you off your horse."

"I believe you would've."

Then he grinned. Caro was immediately suspicious of that cocky, purely male grin.

"What?"

"It would've still been worth it."

All of a sudden she found herself feeling a little shy. "Thanks. And I'm very sorry about your great-grandfather," she added. "I wish his life hadn't come to such an awful end."

"Me, too. No one deserves to die like that."

For a moment, just a brief, flashing moment, Caro saw his deep concern and caring for others. There was more to this man than hot kisses and a handsome face. *But can I have faith in him where his brother's concerned? Even if he says he was wrong about the keys...* She continued to ponder that question as the ride progressed to the end of the trail and the mine.

If Caro hadn't been watching, if Wyatt wasn't there guiding the way, she would have missed the entrance to the mine. The sun had bleached the wooden planks covering the entrance to the same buff color as the land. The planks were further camouflaged by desert scrub.

Not until Wyatt reined his horse to a halt and announced, "Here it is," did Caro's eyes register the faint outlines of an entrance.

"If it was a snake, it would've jumped up and bit me," she said ruefully.

"Don't even say that. Snakes love cool areas like this mine, and so do the rodents they feed on. Watch your step," Wyatt warned. He reached for his canteen, but made no move to dismount.

"I will if you will," Caro replied. She swung one leg over the rump of the mare. Another fluid motion and she was on the ground, reins in one hand. She lifted her canteen from the saddle horn with the other, looped its strap around her shoulder, then removed a small belt-pack from a saddlebag and clipped it on, all under Wyatt's watchful eyes.

Caro gestured toward a treed rocky outcropping. "The horses will have shade there. Let's picket them and go explore the mine."

She loosened Cactus Blossom's saddle girth just a little for the horse's comfort, a habit her old riding instructor had taught her, then glanced at Wyatt. To her surprise, he hadn't yet dismounted.

"I don't think this is a good idea," he said. "Maybe we should just look around out here. Even if it's safe in there—which it isn't—we're going to have to pry off the boards in this heat."

"I'm not so sure," Caro said slowly. She left her horse tied to a sturdy branch, walked back to the mine and thrust aside a mass of old brush. "Look!" It parted easily at her touch, revealing a cleared area that led straight into a gaping hole.

Wyatt dismounted, his lips pressed together in the thin line Caro had seen before. It was an expression that revealed anger. Controlled anger. But this wasn't the time to analyze the sheriff's emotions. She had work to do. By the time he'd tethered the stallion and joined her, Caro had uncovered the entrance leading straight into the dark interior of the mine.

"I thought you told me this mine was boarded up," she said.

"It was. But I haven't been here in months—haven't taken a good look in years." Wyatt kicked at the dried, splintered planks of wood beneath their feet. "I'll have to get some fresh lumber and send some men out."

"I'd save my money if I were you." Caro carefully used a stick to probe at the shaded areas for scorpions and snakes, then squatted to retrieve something in the dust.

"What are you talking about?"

"The elements can decay wood, but only a crowbar does this." She held up a bent nail. "And look at these." She kicked over two, three, four planks of wood. All of them had bent nails.

Wyatt's face was set in a grim expression. She wondered if he was disturbed because he hadn't noticed the nails—or because *she* had?

"You're very good at this." He paused. "It worries me."

Caro boldly met his gaze. "Why?"

"Because your life might be in danger."

She didn't hesitate a beat. Collecting a few more of the nails scattered on the ground, she sealed them in the evidence bags she always carried in her jeans.

"It wouldn't be the first time I've been at risk. But I have a system, you know. I check in with someone several times a day. I let that person know where I'm going, who I'm with and what people I suspect."

It was the truth. She had phoned Marta with her itinerary early in the morning and arranged to meet her later on.

"So if anyone's planning on shoving me down a mine shaft, they won't get away with it." She finished with the bags. "Let's go."

He frowned. "After everything I've said about how dangerous this place is, you still want to go in?"

"Only if you know your way around," Caro qualified.

His expression became inscrutable. "And if I refuse?"

"I'll just go in without you."

He crossed his arms. "You don't have a very good poker face, ma'am. I think you're bluffing."

"Try me." Caro reached into her belt-pack, withdrew a small flashlight, manual compass and a computerized map recorder-plus-navigator. She flipped a switch, activating the tiny monitor. A glowing grid appeared on the screen with a loud beep.

Wyatt stared at the electronic instrument. "Another of your expensive toys?"

"Yep, mine and Silicon Valley's."

"You seem to keep those people in business." He gave the instrument in her hand a curious glance. "What is it?"

"A navigational aid. A computerized compass, actually. Nothing much."

"That's *all?* What's wrong with the good, old-fashioned kind?"

"Hey, this has built-in lights. Can't see the old-fashioned ones in a dark cave."

"Far be it from me to impede progress," was Wyatt's dry response.

You don't know the half of it, Caro thought. Her unit was more than just a compass. In fact, the instrument held a compact radar that could automatically record a fair backup map if she wasn't able to take the more accurate manual readings herself. But Caro, ever cautious, didn't feel the urge to tell Wyatt that.

"Just out of curiosity, how much would something like this high-tech compass cost?"

She told him. Wyatt was astounded.

"I can't believe anyone would pay that much when you can get a perfectly good compass for a few dollars!"

"Oh, you'd be surprised, Sheriff," Caro said smugly. "I bought stock in this company when they were first getting started."

Wyatt's eyebrows rose in amazement. "You played the stocks?"

"*Play,* present tense. I love high-tech gadgets. I'm even happy to share my stock proceeds with my parents and sister."

"Generous of you."

"Not really. They're family. There's no *my money* or *your money.*"

"Like the way we share ranch ownership?"

"Exactly. What, you think you're the only ones who know anything about family loyalty?" She held out the mapping aid. "Here. Want to try it?"

"No, thanks."

"Don't say I didn't offer." Caro shrugged, then expertly took her bearings with both the manual compass and the computerized navigator and entered the figures in her notebook. She lifted her chin, then headed for the entrance to the mine. "Last chance. Coming?"

"Only if I lead."

Caro gestured for him to go first with a satisfied sweep of her free hand. "Well, this time, anyway. After you, Sheriff."

They stepped inside.

CHAPTER SEVEN

Still Friday morning

THE AIR WAS STIFLING, the mine dark and dusty. Wyatt paused to let his eyes adjust to the dimness, and Caro did the same.

"Lovely place. I'm surprised it isn't in the tour books," she drawled as Wyatt brushed at the cobwebs that had fallen onto his shoulder. The resident spider dropped to the ground and scurried away. She took off her baseball cap and stuffed it in her waistband.

"I wouldn't do that if I were you," he said.

"I'm not afraid of a few bugs." She lifted the thick mass of hair from her neck, welcoming the air on her damp skin.

Wyatt gave her a concerned glance. "I suggest you tie your hair up, because you've got more than spiders to worry about."

"Like what?"

"Take a deep breath."

Caro inhaled. Immediately she wrinkled her nose at the fetid, moldy odor.

"Phew! What is that smell?" Caro couldn't place it. The stench wasn't that of death or decay—unfortunately her job had taught her to recognize those—but it was almost as bad.

"Guano."

"Guano?" she echoed.

"As in bat dung. And bats. The deeper we go, the more

there'll be. Which means even less chance of finding this mystery gold. And don't forget the snakes, scorpions and spiders. Sure you don't want to reconsider this plan of yours?''

"Sorry, Sheriff, but I don't mind creepy crawlies. Besides, I like bats.''

She received a sharp glance at her answer.

"I do,'' she insisted. "They keep the insect population down, and the fruit eaters aid pollination. Plus, their radar is a marvel of engineering. Even the government hasn't been able to build anything that operates at the speed and efficiency of bat radar. They're fascinating creatures.''

Caro reached for her hat and clapped it back on her head. "Although I do prefer to keep my hair free of guano.''

Wyatt's face registered grudging admiration. "Well, I'll say one thing for you. You're not squeamish.''

"It's not nature's creatures I worry about.''

Wyatt didn't respond other than with a crisp, "Follow me.''

Caro followed. The mine entrance was fairly level for the first thirty yards, then it gradually narrowed. The walls were sheer rock, but rock that had been attacked and weakened by the depredations of men and of time itself.

"I thought mines were supposed to be shored up with wood or something.'' Caro's voice had dropped to a soft whisper.

"There isn't much wood around. And with a whole mountain of rock on top of us, I doubt a few boards are going to make much difference.''

"Oh.''

He stopped. "You're not scared, are you? Claustrophobic?''

"Nope.''

"Because if you are, you'd better back out right now.

My brothers and I used to play in here as kids. Believe me, this is no easy stroll.''

"I'll be fine. Let's keep going."

By now the sunlight at the entrance was so far behind them it could no longer penetrate the darkness. Wyatt and Caro snapped on their flashlights at the same time. Any rodents that hadn't scrambled away at the sound of their footsteps did so then.

The temperature started to drop as they walked deeper into the mine. "Watch your footing," he warned. "It gets rough for the next fifty yards or so, but things will smooth out in the main chamber. Stick close and take it slow."

"I will."

Wyatt was a good guide. They stopped occasionally, and he waited without complaint as Caro took measurements and punched coordinates into her navigator. So far there was only one direction to travel, but Caro knew that could change. Many underground mines, especially older ones, fingered out into different tunnels as they followed the haphazard trails of silver ore.

The walls narrowed, growing so tight that Caro's shoulders almost grazed the rock on either side. She saw Wyatt take off his hat and turn his broad shoulders sideways. After a few more paces she had to do the same.

Just as she didn't think the passage could get any narrower without blocking their way, it gaped wide. Wyatt's beam of light diffused in the darkness. It was Caro's stronger torch that actually illuminated the rock on the far side of the wall.

"Only a few more steps." Wyatt led her a bit farther, then stopped. She did, too, casting her light around the huge chamber. The smell of guano was overwhelming.

"This place is enormous!" she gasped.

"Amazing what greed and dynamite can do to nature," Wyatt replied. "Good thing the bats don't mind."

He covered her hand with his and guided the flashlight toward the back of the cavern's ceiling.

Caro registered the warmth of his hand on hers. Then, what she saw illuminated by their flashlights caused her chin to drop in amazement. Hundreds, maybe thousands of bats hung upside down, their bodies packed tightly for warmth, their sharp claws curled around the ceiling's rough, jagged formations.

"They tend to cluster near the back. If you want to keep clean, it's best to stay here."

"I'm not going anywhere." Wyatt's guiding hand fell away from hers. Both of them lowered their flashlights, but not before Wyatt saw Caro frown.

"What? Smell getting to you?"

"No, I've smelled worse. But I was thinking... The skeleton we recovered had damp rot. I'm wondering if that's from guano."

"You didn't test for it?"

"No. It's not a test I routinely make, or even thought of making. I guess I should have," she said ruefully. "Still..."

"What?"

"You know, there must be other chambers around. Chambers with deep shafts," she added, mentally picturing the shattered, compressed leg bones.

"There are," Wyatt said. "But most flooded out a century ago. The few that aren't are filled with bats and dead ends like this one. I doubt our skeleton came from there."

"Are you certain of that, Sheriff?"

There was an uncomfortable pause, then Wyatt reached for her arms. He drew her toward him, just enough so she could see his face in the weak beam of his flashlight.

"I do have a first name, Caro. It's Wyatt. And I'm not in the habit of lying. Can't you trust me?"

Trust me... Caro wished she could see his eyes. But it

was too dark, and shining the light directly at his eyes would only blind him, a dangerous thing to do in a cave.

"I don't think you had anything to do with the skeleton," she said slowly. "But if Morgan's involved...then I'd have to ask where your loyalty would lie. With him? Or with me?"

"My loyalty would be to the truth—to the law. I follow the rules."

"I believe that, Sheriff." She couldn't bring herself to call him Wyatt, not just yet. "But I'm worried that your rules might not be exactly...textbook."

To her surprise, he laughed, his deep baritone echoing off the cave walls. "This from a woman who springs major evidence finds at dinner parties, scrapes gold off old men's wheelchairs and lets people think she's a dumb city slicker when she's anything but!"

He reached for a stray strand of hair that had escaped her Red Sox cap and tucked it in. "Your own set of rules is just as unconventional as mine. Lord knows what else you've done that I don't know about."

Caro thought about the suitcase she'd hung under her window—and the arrangement she'd made with Marta. Suddenly she was glad the darkness of the cave hid her guilty flush.

"However, if you wish to remain your cautious self," Wyatt went on, "do check at the city surveyor's office if you require confirmation. We can always come back if the skeleton tests positive for guano."

He studied her hair. "There," he said. "I think that's it." He released her arm.

"You aren't mad at me?" She was disappointed that he hadn't tried to steal a kiss in the dark, and annoyed for letting his touch distract her.

"How could I? We think alike. We're two of a kind, you and I."

"There *are* some differences," Caro said tartly.

The smile in his roving eyes was purely male. "And *vive la différence*. But remember one thing, Caro. Even the great Sherlock Holmes trusted someone."

"Sorry, but I can't see you in the role of the bumbling Dr. Watson, and I'm sure as shooting not giving up my magnifying glass."

He continued to smile. There was something in his gaze that both confused and thrilled her.

"You think I'm joking?"

He threw up his hands in mock defense. "No way, Ms. Holmes."

"Are you making fun of me?"

"Never in a million years."

Caro had no idea what to say. The possibilities, the fantasies she was dying to visualize, even verbalize, were too farfetched for her logical mind.

Finally Wyatt said, "Let's head back to the horses."

"Good idea," she said shakily. "You go on. I'll be right behind you. I need a few minutes alone..." *To get hold of myself.*

"Staying behind isn't a wise idea," Wyatt warned. "Even I won't do that, and I grew up around these caves."

"I won't be long."

"Why? What's so important that you can't— Oh." He broke off abruptly.

The good sheriff thought she had to answer the call of nature, Caro realized. She didn't, but she did want to be alone. And since she also wanted to take a few more readings and program those into her computerized map system, she went along with the pretense.

"Sorry to hold you up."

"I'll wait for you around the bend. Take your time."

"Thanks, Sheriff." Seconds later, the sound of his footsteps faded completely.

"This cavern might be too shallow for severe compression breaks," she murmured to herself. "But I wonder... does it *really* dead-end here?"

Maybe her little gadget could verify the truth of Wyatt's statement. Caro turned on the navigator's miniature radar. The *ping* stirred a few of the very mammals who'd inspired her instrument's creation, and they squeaked in response.

"Keep it down, guys," she said. "Your chattering's glitzing my machine."

A few minutes later her amusement was gone as the readings came winging back. "That can't be right!"

She took a second reading for confirmation. Then a third. Both told her the same thing as the first.

The cave doesn't dead-end as the sheriff claims!

According to her view screen, there was a second opening off to the side and way in the back. It wasn't large, it wasn't very accessible, but her computer showed that it could easily accommodate a man or a woman.

A chill went down her spine, a chill that had nothing to do with the cool dampness of the cavern. *Either Wyatt doesn't know about this—or he's deliberately deceived me.*

Caro clamped her mouth shut, feeling sick to her stomach. She stared at her view screen one last time, saved the map, turned it off and rehooked it to her belt with shaking fingers. She wanted to believe the best of Wyatt, yet every time she tried, she ran up against more questions. It was, to say the least, very puzzling.

And very unsettling...

"Is everything okay?"

Caro started at the sound of Wyatt's voice. He'd returned. "Not really, but I'll tell you about it when we get outside. Lead the way. I'm right behind you."

The desert sun was harsh and scalding after the coolness of the cave. She repositioned her Red Sox cap to get the maximum shade from the brim; Wyatt shifted his hat, too, and pulled out his sunglasses from a shirt pocket. He walked toward their horses, Caro right behind him. She watched as he checked on his mount and rubbed the stallion's nose before lifting his canteen.

Were his gently caressing hands—the same hands that had held her while he kissed her—those of a man of justice? Or did they belong to a lawman walking the edge—determined to protect his brother?

"You want to tell me what you found in there?" he asked. "I'm assuming it wasn't gold, or you would've shown me."

"No gold, but we may find something interesting yet. Here. Look at this." Caro punched up the last coordinates she'd taken, which showed the narrow passageway behind the bats, then handed Wyatt the instrument.

He studied it. "Well, I'll be… I didn't know about this!"

"Didn't you?"

Wyatt looked up sharply. "What's *that* supposed to mean?"

"For someone who grew up playing in these caves, you don't seem to know much about them."

He snorted. "What—you think I'm protecting Montezuma's treasure in there?"

"How about a gravesite?"

He started to answer, then caught himself. "Does this little gadget have printout capability?" he asked.

"It does."

"Then give me a copy."

"I can't. I have to tie it into my laptop at your ranch first."

Wyatt clearly wasn't pleased with her response. "It doesn't matter. I'm going to hike back for a quick look and see for myself what's there."

"Now?"

"Yes. Care to join me?"

"I can't. I don't have my equipment with me. I was looking for gold, not crime scenes, remember? If the remains came from that area, I want to be prepared."

"I'm ready right now," he said impatiently. "You can wait here."

"But—"

"I won't be long."

"Sheriff! Wait…"

He was gone with a speed she hadn't thought possible for such a big man.

"Great. Just great."

Caro decided to move the horses, since the shade had greatly diminished as the sun had risen higher. She approached her mare first, intending to tighten the saddle straps she'd loosened when she'd dismounted. She busied herself with the cinch, but found the nylon strap catching on something.

"What in the world…" She hadn't had a problem with the saddle before. She tugged slightly, then harder, without success.

"Everything okay?"

Caro whirled around. Morgan. Where had *he* come from? "You startled me!"

"Sorry, I didn't mean to. I drove out here to find Wyatt." He gestured toward the Jeep parked in the distance. "On business. Problem with that saddle?"

"I'm just trying to tighten the cinch. I loosened it earlier," she explained.

The mare snorted with irritation as Caro tugged again, trying to free the end of the cinch. She tightened her grasp on the reins. "What in the world is *wrong* with this thing?"

Morgan approached. "Maybe some of the blanket fringe has caught somewhere," he said helpfully.

"Here, hold the reins for me, would you please?" Caro asked. "I'm going to lift the saddle blanket."

"I'll do that," he said quickly. "You take the reins."

"I'm a big girl, Mr. Bodine. I'll—"

Caro froze, mouth open, her next words forgotten. Beneath the saddle blanket was a chilling sight. Her cinch strap had been cut. The knife mark was obviously recent, for the nylon edges were not at all unraveled.

"What is it?" Morgan leaned over and looked at the slash marks. Then his gaze swung from it to her face. "This isn't what you think," he said in a calm voice.

Deadly calm, Caro thought. Like the deadly desolation that surrounded them. She tried to speak, but all that came out was a parched, raspy sound. Her hand rose to her throat as she fought back panic. Morgan reached out his own hand in reassurance as Caro backed away one jerky step, then another, and another.

That cinch wasn't cut when I first mounted. I know! I checked! I always double-check. I saddled this horse myself.

"Don't be a fool!" he said harshly. "I didn't do this!"

Caro battled for control and forced herself to relax. "Of course you didn't," she managed to say. She even managed to inject some self-deprecatory chagrin. "Why don't you take off the saddle and see if we can fix it for the ride back?"

Morgan appeared to relax, too. "You're a sensible woman, Dr. Hartlan. For a moment there, it looked like you actually thought…" He didn't finish his sentence. Instead, he patted the mare's neck. "Come on, girl. Let's get this off you."

He's in uniform. Dare I try to get his gun? Or should I make a run for it? Wyatt, where are you?

Caro tensed again and bided her time. A few seconds for Morgan to rip free the last joined piece of the damaged cinch strap. A few more for him to reach upward for the saddle. Then his hands were full.

Now! her mind screamed. *Now!* Caro raced toward Wyatt's stallion. Her mad dash spooked the Arabian, made him skitter and start away, but Caro's reflexes were quicker. Already she had the reins in her hands, a foot in the stirrup, and then she was swinging herself into the saddle.

The stirrups were too long. Her seat was so loose she grabbed onto the saddle horn as she kicked the stallion to gait. The stallion balked and bucked just once, a warning to the strange rider. Caro slid about on the saddle—and stayed on. She wouldn't win any dressage contests, but she didn't care. *The man's carrying a gun!* If he had no qualms about cutting her saddle cinch, who knew what else he might be capable of?

"Dr. Hartlan! Caro!"

She exerted greater control over the stallion, her eyes never leaving Morgan's gun belt. Then she was kicking the horse again, hard, imposing her will on his, yelling, "Yah!" and racing away.

The heated air rushed through her hair as she urged the horse to greater speed. She hunched low in the saddle, listening, protecting herself, bracing for the sound, the feel of a bullet slamming into her back. She didn't dare turn around, not at full gallop and without stirrups. All she could do was listen to the pounding of her horse's hooves, her own ragged breathing...

And pray she wouldn't die with her boots on.

"Come back! Please! Turn around!"

She ignored Morgan's plea. His voice only made her urge the stallion to even greater speed. At first Caro instinctively headed back the way she'd come. But as she put more and more distance between herself and danger, she realized that returning to the ranch might not be a wise move, either. Not without Wyatt there.

Where should I go?

Caro braved a quick glance behind her. Morgan had not

taken pursuit in the Jeep; even that vehicle couldn't follow the rough terrain she'd deliberately chosen. And he hadn't mounted the mare. She now had a clear advantage. Luckily for her, Wyatt's stallion was one of the larger Arabians. The mare, on the other hand, was the smallish size one usually associated with the breed. Morgan was a big man. He wouldn't be able to travel fast riding bareback on the compact mare. Certainly not as fast as she could.

Caro decided to take another chance. She pulled the stallion up short, just for a moment.

First, adjust the stirrups to my length. Second, head into town, instead of back to the ranch. With Boothill sitting on a mile-high hill rising from the valley floor, navigation was easy. And Caro had seen horses, riders and hitching posts on Allen Street. She could leave the horse there.

But then what?

She remembered the walkie-talkie at Morgan's belt. He might have people looking for her, and Wyatt's silver stallion with the hand-tooled leather saddle and hanging silver fetishes would be spotted—and identified—in an instant. Even now, the fetishes were tinkling as she finished with her stirrups, their soft chimes carrying on the desert air.

Well, one good thing about a tourist town, Caro thought, was its crowds. Easy to conceal herself among all those people until she could find help, until she could reach Wyatt, or safer yet, Marta. It was early enough that her secret partner might still be in her hotel room. Thank goodness, Caro, like most regular riders, had taken to carrying her wallet in one boot. She could always grab a bus or a cab to the airport if she was ready to call it quits.

Which I'm not—not by a long shot.

She checked carefully behind her. No one. Mentally setting a course, she spurred Arabian Pride into a quick canter toward downtown Tombstone.

Locals and tourist alike stared as Caro reached the outskirts of town. The stallion's coat was lathered with sweat. Caro wasn't much better, her shirt as soaked as her mount's saddle blanket, her cap lost along the way. She felt light-headed from adrenaline letdown, thirst, the wild ride…and fear.

Caro approached the hitching post across from the public rest rooms at the end of Allen Street. A man she didn't recognize called out, "Hey, isn't that the sheriff's horse?"

"Sure is." Caro immediately dismounted. "Please walk him for me. I rode him hard." She thrust the reins into the man's surprised hands and hurried toward the boardwalk.

"But…where's the sheriff?"

"I don't know. We got separated," she said, not slowing her pace. She felt the curious eyes of other residents on her back, and she walked even faster, searching frantically for a phone. This town had public hitching posts, for heaven's sake, so where was Ma Bell when she needed her? And why had she left her cellular phone in the car?

Someone called her name. She flinched.

"Caro, hold up!"

She glanced over her shoulder and saw Morgan Bodine heading her way, with Kimberly right beside him.

Forget the cellular phone! She should've brought a few bodyguards!

Time for a new plan of action. Caro saw a group of about twenty tourists entering the Bird Cage Theater. She slipped to their midst, let herself be carried along through the brick-arched door, and prayed she'd lose her pursuers for good.

"All right, people, your admission price has been taken care of," said the tour guide, identified by his stick-on badge as Jackie from Jackie's A-OK Southwest Travel and Tours. "So bypass the cashier, and let's stick together."

Like a thorn on a cactus, Caro agreed.

The group moved into the front saloon area. They all

listened as Jackie, a Santa Claus-shaped man whose narrow, porcine eyes weren't the least bit jolly, spoke.

"The Bird Cage Theater was the Old West's most famous—or rather, infamous—honky-tonk in the 1880s. It never closed its doors once in nine years during Tombstone's silver-boom days. The entertainment ranged from gambling, faro, music, poker, theater, cancan dancers, shootings and, of course, prostitution."

Caro played the part of interested tourist and edged farther and farther from the door as Jackie continued his spiel.

"Ladies and gentlemen," he droned on, "this is the only completely original building in Tombstone that has survived with original furnishings. Nothing has been recreated or restored."

"Nothing?" someone called out. "It's all real?"

"That's right. The grand piano, the velvet hangings, the 140 bullet holes in the wall, the chandelier, the French-imported mirror—everything's the real McCoy."

The crowd murmured at the number of bullet holes and busily searched the walls for evidence. Caro, on the other hand, was watching Morgan's strides carry him closer to the Bird Cage. It wasn't *old* bullet holes she was worried about! She ducked behind a very tall man, making certain he was between her and Morgan.

Mr. Tall didn't seem to notice Caro's squirmings. "I don't understand, Jackie," he said solemnly. "How could everything survive so long?"

"Because of the owners—and the dry desert air. Tombstone's silver days ended when the mines finally flooded. The whole theater was sealed and boarded up in hopes that the mines could be pumped dry."

"Were they?" the man asked.

"They tried, but the technology just wasn't there. So the Bird Cage never reopened. For over fifty years it sat forgotten—until the government finally recognized its importance." Jackie's voice rose dramatically. "The theater was officially reopened in 1934 as a historic landmark of the American West. That's one reason for the theater's fame."

Caro watched Morgan approach the propped-open doors and peer in. She made herself shrink even more into the crowd as Jackie went on.

"...and before we go around the bar and downstairs to the theater area, I must insist that everyone keep their hands off the artifacts. To preserve this landmark's authenticity, nothing is roped off. No camera flashes are allowed, either, though fast film is permissible. Anyone touching or flashing—the artifacts, I mean..." He paused in a practiced way.

Everyone laughed except Caro. A quick peek showed that Morgan was getting closer and closer.

"...will be asked to leave."

Caro heard the group settle down a bit before Jackie continued.

"The second reason the Bird Cage is famous is that Wyatt Earp, Tombstone's legendary lawman, met Sadie, his last wife, here. Josephine Sarah Marcus was an actress, and reportedly quite beautiful."

"His last wife?" someone echoed. "Just out of curiosity, how many did Wyatt Earp have?"

"He reportedly married three times. He and Sadie were together for almost fifty years. Only Wyatt's death separated them."

"What about the second?" the same man asked.

"He had a woman he called his wife. Named Mattie Blaylock. She might have been common-law—history's a bit hazy on that."

"What happened to her?"

Caro's black sense of humor emerged, and she wondered if Mr. Twenty Questions was a divorce lawyer or a philanderer.

"Mattie? She committed suicide."

"Well, what about the first wife?"

Definitely a philanderer, Caro decided.

"Because of a typhoid epidemic, Earp's first wife died very young."

Caro prayed *she* wouldn't be numbered among those who died young. For a moment it seemed as if her prayers had been answered. She was overjoyed to see Morgan bypass the open doors and continue down the street. She exhaled a heavy sigh of relief as Wyatt's brother faded from view. Mr. Tall eyed her curiously.

"Just…drinking in the atmosphere," she said with a forced smile.

"Shh!" someone else said.

Caro shushed.

"Sadly, despite three marriages, Wyatt Earp had no children."

Murmurs of disappointment from the group.

"Now, you'll need to follow me to see the third and final reason for the Bird Cage's fame," Jackie announced. "For this, we'll be going around the bar to the left and down into the theater area. Please be careful on the stairs. And remember, people, no flashing!"

Caro grimaced as Jackie gave them all a broad wink. Obviously he was going for big laughs and bigger tips. But she was in no mood to be jollied along.

The group descended the narrow stairs single file. It was cooler in the theater than in the bar, but the coolness didn't seem at all refreshing to Caro. Despite the old red velvet curtains, the theater stage, the orchestra pit with its piano, there was no sense of cheer, no lingering atmosphere of good times. She didn't consider herself particularly sensitive to atmosphere, but there was an eerie, depressing feeling to the place she didn't like.

In fact, if she'd had her way, she'd be outside in the

sunshine. But safety and caution dictated otherwise. She forced herself to pretend a tourist's enjoyment and appeared to hang on Jackie's every word.

"Reason number three for the Bird Cage's popularity is... Are you ready?"

Nods. Caro gritted her teeth in frustration. Their guide's big buildup was about as subtle as a mule kick in the head.

"Okay, then. How many of you have heard the song 'She's Only a Bird in a Gilded Cage'?"

Numerous murmurs of assent filled the room.

"That song was written about this place. Look far, far up."

Everyone did, Caro included.

"See those compartments that look like theater boxes? Those were called the bird cages. Fourteen of them are suspended from the ceiling. From there, the men and their ladies of the evening could watch the show—or conduct their own."

Jackie's porcine eyes turned piggier. "The men merely stepped behind the seats and red drapes to the hidden beds."

Through rips in the curtains, Caro could see the rusting frames and dirty, stained mattresses.

"The men could have a little fun with their ladies. There was even a dumbwaiter that sent drinks upstairs for those men thirsty after their..."

A pause.

"Exertions."

Many of the people in the group chuckled. Caro wasn't one of them. She could only think of the women and their sad jobs; women forced to survive, determined to feed their children after the death of their men. Caro knew from her reading that many of the women were once reputable and still maintained pride in themselves and their sons and daughters. Strange as it sounded, these very women had helped contribute to the town's morale and physical health. Caro recalled that Tombstone's early churches were built through donations from these women. And during epidemics, common with the unhygienic conditions of mining towns, they worked as nurses, instead of prostitutes, very often for no pay.

Caro looked at the theater boxes above her. Jackie— showing good sense, considering the black looks she and the other women directed at him—quickly launched into a more sympathetic speech.

"I should add that women had very little choice in those days. There were few jobs—cooking, sewing or washing laundry paid very little. There was no welfare, no public assistance of any sort. Widows often had to choose between suicide and scandal. For every working girl in the Old West, there were just as many who killed themselves. Most of the suicides buried in Boothill are women."

"Death or prostitution? What a terrible choice!" Caro couldn't help exclaiming. Then she became quiet again, sorry to have drawn attention to herself. After all, she wasn't a member of the tour, and she certainly hadn't paid admission.

"But understandable," Jackie insisted. "Women weren't allowed to work the mines. But they were allowed to charge the men any amount of money they wanted for their favors."

Caro pivoted slowly, taking in the faro tables, the wine cellar, the dressing rooms and the poker room below the stage. Bullet-holed walls surrounded her; beneath her were wooden floors stained with ancient blood. Above were the fancy curtains and balconies of the "bird cages," the filthy beds behind them ready to accommodate any liaison. For the right price.

She studied a sign that listed all the common names applied to prostitutes at the time—calico queens, fallen angels and ladies of the night; scarlet, painted and shady ladies; soiled doves and, finally, Tombstone's own particular choice for its women. *Hell's belles.* If nothing else, Caro mused, she and the "belles" had one thing in common— they were determined to survive.

She decided it was time to concentrate on getting safely away from Morgan and his sidekick, Kimberly. The crowd, meanwhile, was growing restless, and Jackie switched their attention to a new topic.

"Come with me, people. Over here, we have Tombstone's most valuable antique—the Black Moriah."

"The what?" someone asked as the crowd moved forward.

"The Black Moriah, Tombstone's official hearse."

"A hearse," Caro mumbled to herself. "Just what I wanted to see."

"Trimmed in twenty-four-carat gold and sterling silver, this glass-and-black horse-drawn hearse enabled curious crowds to view the somber face of death." Jackie's voice dropped mournfully. "It was in the Black Moriah that residents made their last journey to Boothill."

Caro felt a shiver go down her spine. The shadow-box effect of the beveled crystal, the use of gold to adorn the final transport of Tombstone's unfortunates—it all struck her hard. In this sad, decadent place, she had a sensation of being surrounded by death, overwhelmed by it.

For the very first time in her career, Caro wondered if she'd taken on more than she could handle. But before she could answer that question, Mr. Tall suddenly swore. Someone, it appeared, had pushed him out of the way.

Jackie frowned. "Is there a problem?"

Caro's chin jerked up. She deliberately backed into the deep shadows cast by the massive Black Moriah.

The newcomer was Deputy Morgan Bodine.

CHAPTER EIGHT

JACKIE'S LITTLE PIG EYES fluttered as Morgan grabbed Caro's arm and pulled her out of the shadows. The crowd was frozen in that strange, unnatural moment of stillness before the storm breaks.

It broke hard as Caro yanked herself free. A younger man shrieked in surprise as Caro smashed her boot heel down on Morgan's toes. Morgan grunted, a sound that was cut short as the heel of her hand pistoned into his sternum, then curled into a fist for a hit dead square on his abdomen.

Morgan staggered but stood his ground. He grabbed for her attacking arm, but Caro was prepared for that, too. She made a grab of her own—for the freestanding metal sign that demanded in both Spanish and English, "Please do not touch the artifacts."

She aimed for his stomach and shoved. Morgan staggered again, but this time he lost his grasp on her wrist. Caro backed away, her advantage lasting only a few seconds. The deputy was up and advancing, tourists screaming or snapping pictures, and Caro searched desperately for a more effective tactic. She wasn't giving up without a fight.

She grabbed the metal stand like a baseball bat, took the at-plate stance and stood ready to swing at the Black Moriah.

"Touch me again, Bodine, and you can kiss your precious town relic goodbye."

"I don't think you'll do that," Morgan said over gasps

from the crowd. He even advanced a single step, holding his stomach with one hand.

"Don't think I won't," Caro warned, shaking her makeshift bat. "One good swing will shatter this to pieces. And I don't plan on stopping there. The gold on the frame goes next."

"Let's talk about this." Morgan took a second step toward her.

Caro refused to back down. "Guess who had the highest batting average in the girl's high school softball league for three years in a row?"

Morgan dared to take a third step.

Caro tensed, muscles ready. Her eyes were narrowed, her voice harsh. "I'll spread your tourist attraction all over this floor—if I don't aim for your lying mouth first." She meant it.

Morgan stared. The crowd stared. And Jackie stared at Caro with dawning recognition.

"You aren't with this tour! You didn't pay your admission!" Jackie slammed his hands on his pudgy hips and faced Morgan. "Arrest her!"

"Do, and you'll be picking up glass for the rest of the day." She shook the sign again in warning.

Morgan stopped his advance. "What do you want from me?"

"I want you to leave this building, you corrupt excuse for a lawman!"

"I won't leave. But I will back off."

He made good his words. All eyes focused on him, then shifted back to Caro. Only she had no idea what to do next—and Morgan knew it.

"It appears we have a standoff."

"Better than your trying to kill me."

There was a hushed murmur from the crowd. Mr. Tall giggled nervously. Jackie directed a verbal tirade toward

Caro. All the while, Morgan was talking to her, talking nonstop, but she didn't hear a word.

Because Wyatt had entered the room. She'd never felt so relieved, so grateful, in her life. She was so happy she could have kissed the man. *Heck, I just might kiss him anyway!*

Wyatt positioned himself between Caro and Morgan. "Give me the sign, Caro."

She did, for the posse was here. Despite her earlier misgivings about the sheriff, she felt safe next to him. She felt even safer as Wyatt immediately pulled her to his side and held her close. His calm, deep voice was the voice of reason.

"Care to tell me what's going on here?" he asked.

Caro was only too willing to oblige. "Your brother showed up. He cut my saddle cinch and—"

"I didn't cut your cinch!" Morgan yelled. Wyatt held up his free hand, and Morgan was silent.

"Go on," he urged Caro.

"I took your stallion and ran, but he followed—I don't know if he took your mare or his Jeep..."

"I have the Jeep," Wyatt replied, his arm still around her waist.

"I tried to hide in here with the tour group—"

"You owe money, young lady!" Jackie interrupted. He, too, was silenced with one hard look from Wyatt.

"When your...deputy showed up, I did what I had to do to keep him at bay."

"By threatening a valuable historical treasure!" Jackie squealed. "This could cost me my job!"

"She's jumping to conclusions!" Morgan shouted.

"Did you find anything in the mine? Like gold? Or more corpses?" Caro asked. "Maybe that's why he tried to kill me."

"For the last time, I didn't cut your damn cinch! You

have no proof of anything! And I don't know a thing about any gold or corpses!''

"I think we should move this outside." Wyatt spoke tersely.

"I want my money back!" one tourist demanded.

"Me, too!" another seconded. "I came here for a vacation—not to see riffraff and crooked cops!"

Caro felt Wyatt flinch. His arm tightened around her waist, and there was pain in his eyes at the blow to his badge, his character, his town.

Jackie started wringing his hands. "Please, people, Tombstone is a safe town. Let's just finish the tour."

Damn, I can't leave the poor man like this, Caro thought with sudden compassion for the tour guide—and more than a little guilt.

Despite her fear, she reached for Morgan's hand and pulled him against her other side so that Morgan, she and Wyatt were lined up in a row.

"Ladies and gentlemen," she said in a loud, theatrical voice, "may I present my two fellow thespians? These are—" Caro racked her brains for a couple of stage names. "—Tom and Dick Dollar. Please give them a warm round of applause for their performances today."

The audience gasped, then smiled and applauded. Wyatt immediately got into the act by removing his Stetson, waving it toward Caro with a big flourish and acknowledging her "performance."

"Harriet Silver, ladies and gentlemen," Wyatt said, as she did a little curtsy. Caro took over from there.

"And now, a round of applause for the fourth member of our little acting ensemble, your tour guide. Jackie hired us to make your visit to the Old West the most exciting it could be." Caro gestured toward Jackie, who, she decided, was the best actor of the bunch. He smiled and accepted the tourists' praise with nary a hint of confusion. *The man's a trouper. I'll say that for him.*

"Before our tour continues," Jackie began. "Now's your chance for photos of our little ensemble," he said without missing a beat. "Remember, folks…"

Caro silently groaned.

"No flashing!"

Caro noticed Wyatt signaling Morgan to leave with a jerk of his chin. Caro guessed it was because Morgan was in official uniform, while Wyatt was not. Some of the tourists started to protest, but Wyatt silenced them.

"Our deputy has another gig, ladies and gentlemen. But my leading lady and I can stay. Come on, Harriet," he said to Caro, "let's give them a good photo op."

First he pulled his Stetson low so his own face was in shadow. Then he grabbed Caro, swooped her across his arm and outstretched thigh and proceeded to kiss her senseless. His kisses were a delightful blend of dramatic license and genuine passion that hit Caro like a kick to the head—and heart.

Damn, I could get used to this! she thought, kissing him back—and putting on a show had nothing to do with it. High-speed film recorded their images as Wyatt lifted her upright again.

"Tom, Dick and Harriet Silver Dollar?" he murmured with amusement as he nibbled her ear.

"Hey, it was the best I could do on short notice!" She giggled, but her laugh had an edge to it.

Wyatt frowned and smoothed back her hair. "You okay?" he asked.

Caro nodded a yes, then shook her head for a more truthful answer. "My legs feel like rubber…" *And I just may be sick all over your shoulder.*

"I saw your cinch. Aftershock?" Wyatt whispered as he kissed her neck, camera shutters still clicking while tourists backed up to include as much of the Black Moriah in their photos as possible.

"Of course not! It's just been a while since I've ridden a horse. I'm out of shape, that's all." *Caro, you liar.* "Can we go now?" she whispered, nervousness warring with the pleasure at his caresses. "I need some fresh air."

"You got it, lady." Then to the crowd, "Last chance for pictures, folks!"

"Pretend I'm Sadie Marcus, and Wyatt Earp is taking me home," Caro improvised.

"In that case…" Wyatt stole one last kiss, then swept her up in his arms à la Rhett Butler and bounded up the wooden staircase of the Bird Cage Theater. They left to the sound of thunderous applause.

"Tell all your friends about Jackie's A-OK Southwest Travel and Tours." Jackie could be heard working the crowd. "We have the greatest tours in Arizona, and tips are welcome!"

Once outside, Caro felt the sun hot and heavy on her back, Wyatt's arm strong and steady around her waist.

"You want to sit down somewhere? Maybe get something to drink?"

"I'd like some water—anything. But first, let's get out of here." She threw one last glance at the Bird Cage Theater as Wyatt led her away from the tour bus toward a nearby family restaurant. A few minutes later, Caro was drinking a tall, cool glass of hand-squeeze lemonade, washing away the last taste of fear. She finished the drink in one long pull. Wyatt switched his untouched glass with hers.

"Thanks," she said gratefully.

"No—thank *you*," he replied. "You really saved my butt and Morgan's back there, plus a good chunk of our tourist trade."

Caro took a big swallow of Wyatt's drink. "I'm glad it worked out. But Morgan…" She paused, not knowing what

to say to the brother of the man who'd tried to hurt her—
maybe even kill her.

"Tell me about Morgan. From the beginning, please,"
Wyatt coaxed.

She did.

The way she always loosened her saddle when she dismounted. The way it was slashed when she went to retight-
en it. How Morgan had suddenly turned up and insisted on
fixing her tack. Why she'd refused. Her wild, primitive escape through the desert. Hiding from Morgan in the Bird
Cage Theater. Her fear of him as he caught up to her. The
way she threatened to bash in the Black Moriah if Morgan
took one step closer...

And the way Wyatt had shown up, just in time.

Caro finally relaxed. She was safe—safe with Wyatt.
Safe from Morgan. And safe from doubt.

WYATT LISTENED to her words in shock. He was shaken—
deeply so.

Caro could have been severely injured or even killed!
But by his own brother? It was unthinkable!

Wyatt reached for her hand, holding it tight within his.
Today had revealed some frightening things. His brother
was definitely a suspect. And he himself had left Caro
alone, subjecting her to danger; his failure to protect her
had made him feel like an alien in his own town. The tourists in the theater had been ready to turn on him—and Morgan; their hostility had been almost palpable.

Until Caro had brilliantly pretended to be an actress. She
was a quick thinker, something *he* usually was. But he'd
finally, however slowly, reached one inescapable conclusion: there was evil in Tombstone—evil Caro blamed Morgan for. He believed, had to believe, she was wrong about
that. Nevertheless, Caro, an outsider, had smelled the scent

of crime, perhaps corruption, when he, the sheriff, hadn't even recognized it. Had *refused* to recognize it.

The worst part—the absolutely worst part of all—was the way she feared his family. She honestly thought Morgan was guilty of attempted murder, and she suspected Wyatt might try to protect his brother, in the process breaking his sworn oath to uphold the law.

The sick taste in his mouth was something he hadn't felt for a long time. Not, in fact, since he'd left the Tucson DEA. He knew that whatever was wrong went far beyond a cut cinch and a misplaced skeleton. He'd have to find the real culprit to save Caro. He was afraid for her now, afraid her life was at stake. But it also meant he'd have to let loose that shrewd, remorseless part of himself. The part he hated.

That part of him could sniff out another's crimes like a coyote could a carcass. It had never let him down. Ever. But he still hated it, hated even more letting it surface.

I'm not ready for that. Not while Caro's sitting in front of me.

He didn't want her to see him become a cunning and ruthless hunter, a man who could identify with the worst in others. He wanted her to think the best of him. For now, Wyatt concentrated on easing her tension.

"How're you doing? Maybe I should've ordered us a couple of stiff Scotches, instead."

That got a spirited response. "Do I look like a swooning woman? I don't need liquor in a crisis, thank you. Now, a pair of handcuffs for your brother—that's another matter!"

"I'll take care of Morgan myself," Wyatt said tersely.

"You believe me, then?"

"I believe your cinch was cut. I don't know if I believe Morgan did it."

Caro abruptly pushed away the half-filled glass. "So that's how it's going to be." She rose to her feet.

Wyatt immediately jumped to his. "Caro, wait! You're reading this the wrong way!"

Her eyes narrowed, hard and accusing. "I don't think so, Sheriff."

She hurried toward the door, Wyatt right beside her.

"Where do you think you're going?"

"Anyplace other than The Silver Dollar Ranch! If you don't have Morgan detained for questioning by the end of the day, I'll be picking up my things—and calling for reinforcements from Tucson! Now get out of my way!"

"You shouldn't be out alone," he protested.

She ignored him. Wyatt went to stop her, but a local tour tram was passing just then and Caro quickly sprinted to catch it, leaving him behind. Wyatt felt a strange, stabbing sensation in his gut, but there was no time to analyze it.

He reached for his radio and contacted his office. Then he ordered one of his other part-time deputies to track down the tram.

"Keep an eye out for my brother," he ordered. "Keep an even closer eye on Caro Hartlan."

"Will do, boss. Over and out."

Wyatt approached the O. K. Corral, ahead on his right, intending to cut through the open area to Fremont Street, then head toward City Hall and the Sheriff's Department.

He strode casually through the admission gate, then across the dirt-floored area of the O. K. Corral, which held the stalls and antique carriage-and-wagon collection. He continued on into the open corral.

Before him stood the three-dimensional life-size models of the legendary heroes and villains involved in the shootout. He took a few more steps and paused in their midst. The Cowboys, brothers Billy and Frank McLaury, along with Billy Clanton, stood in bizarre vigil over the spots where they'd died.

Wyatt, Virgil and Morgan Earp were also there, Virgil

who was later crippled, Morgan who was later murdered in retribution for the three Cowboys' deaths.

And among them, another figure—the gaunt, tubercular, doomed man who was himself a cold-blooded killer, ex-dentist Doc Holliday. He became Wyatt's loyal friend, yet he never lost his reputation as a man to be neither admired nor trusted. Even Wyatt Earp vowed he was the most deadly man with a six-gun he'd ever met, and Earp was one mean shot himself.

Wyatt passed a trembling hand across his forehead. He wondered what the town would say if they realized Wyatt Bodine was more like Doc Holliday than Wyatt Earp?

The only difference was that Holliday readily gave in to his darker side when Earp wasn't around. Bodine suppressed his at all costs. He'd left the Tucson DEA because he was tired of thinking like a criminal. Tombstone had been his haven.

Until now.

Wyatt Bodine hated what he was going to do, but knew there was no alternative. He also knew he could control the heady criminal intelligence that was Wyatt Bodine, the man, at his worst, and Wyatt Bodine, the lawman, at his best.

Bodine took one last look at the figures, his gaze coming to rest not on Doc Holliday but on his namesake. The painted figure of Wyatt Berry Stapp Earp, named after Captain Wyatt Berry Stapp of the 1847 cavalry, stared silently back at Wyatt Earp Bodine.

"So tell me, Sheriff Earp. How did you do it? You never took a bribe, although plenty were offered—by men of power and women of beauty. Even the criminals trying to kill you admired you. You escaped every single bullet ever fired at you."

Wyatt studied the figure before him. Earp's statue was a realistic six feet tall, an impressive height at a time when the hardships of the West produced much smaller people. The artist had caught the lean, wiry muscles of legend, the handsome features, the straight nose, blue eyes and generous mouth partially hidden by the sweep of a light brown handlebar mustache.

"History says you died peacefully when you were eighty-one. *Peacefully!*" The word sounded like a curse. "How did you keep their filth from touching you—tempting you? Tell me!"

The painted eyes of the motionless Wyatt revealed nothing, nor did the living Wyatt expect them to. Bodine straightened his back and lifted his chin. He would have to fight criminals, his own dark nature—maybe even his favorite brother.

And he'd have to do it alone.

WYATT ENTERED the sheriff's office, closing the heavy old door with quiet deliberateness. Coming from him, that was as good as a slam. He saw Kimberly look up from her desk, eyes wide, lips wisely closed.

"It's all right, I won't bite," he reassured her.

He hung his Stetson on the hat rack and made for the phone at his desk. He lowered himself into his chair with the slow, easy grace that characterized all his actions. But he didn't rest his boots on the desk the way he usually did when he reached for the receiver, a relaxed attitude that indicated all was well. Kimberly, who'd started to rise from her own desk, noticed the omission and sat down again without speaking.

Wyatt put down the receiver and lifted one eyebrow. "You heard about Dr. Hartlan and Morgan?"

"Some, not all. This is a small town, Wyatt. Oh, if you're worried about your horses, I already had some of my men pick them up. They'll be trucked back to the ranch once they're walked."

"What about the Jeep?"

"Morgan took it."

"You've seen him?"

"No, but someone else did. He was headed back to the ranch." Kimberly set aside her paperwork. "He's probably there by now. So be honest, did *Dr.* Hartlan really think Morgan tried to kill her?"

"Yes."

Kim made a scoffing sound. "I hope you told her otherwise!"

"Doesn't matter. She thinks Morg's guilty and that I'm covering up for him. I can see how it could seem that way."

"Oh, please. Ms. City Slicker probably cut the cinch on some brambles."

"She knows horses, Kimberly. Our big-city forensics expert rides like an Apache."

Kimberly shrugged. "So she can ride. Big deal. So can almost everyone in this state. But her say-so doesn't make Morgan a suspect! We can't even be sure there's been a crime. For all I know, she might've cut the cinch as a ploy to get your attention."

"What?"

"Women in love have been known to do desperate things," Kimberly said softly.

"Caro Hartlan has brains, beauty and bucks, Kimberly. Even if it was her style, which it isn't, she doesn't need to play the helpless female to get a man."

"I have brains, beauty and bucks, too, Wyatt, and it didn't work for me. For us."

"We've already covered this ground, Kimberly," Wyatt said wearily. "Suffice it to say I don't believe Caro cut that cinch any more than I believe Morgan did."

"*Someone* did!"

"A trip back into the mine might help me find that some-one."

"How, Wyatt? You and I have known every inch of that mine since we were kids. We both know there's not much left to explore. The deeper shafts were flooded out long before we were born! We've already seen anything that's left to see."

"No—Caro Hartlan discovered a new tunnel today. The ground water must've settled since we were kids—because I'm sure not doing any pumping."

Kimberly shuddered. It was so uncharacteristic of her that Wyatt immediately noticed.

"What?" he asked.

"New tunnels, old tunnels, what's the difference? Wyatt, the air's so foul! The footing's so slick! If there *are* more passages, you'll need oxygen to explore, proper boots, spe-lunking gear, the whole works. I hate to think of you going in there. You could get hurt!"

"I'm well aware of that."

"You're really going to wade through all that guano?"

"Whatever it takes."

Kimberly whistled in awe. "Well, count me in. Not to explore," she added quickly. "I hate bats. But I can drive a Jeep out with gear and help guard the entrance against unexpected visitors."

"I'd appreciate it, Kimberly. We need to ensure that the horses and tack are safe." As he spoke, he calculated the possibilities: if Kim *was* in some way involved in whatever was going on, he'd be able to keep a watchful eye on her, maybe even catch her out. If she was innocent, he could use her help.

"Are you sure Caro's cinch was really cut, Wyatt?" she was asking. "Maybe it split from normal wear."

"I'm sure it was cut, Kimberly."

"I wonder who *did* do it."

"That makes two of us. Any suspects?"

Kimberly rose, her curls tumbling gracefully about her shoulders. She crossed the room to his desk and perched on the corner. "Besides Morgan, my grandfather and me?"

He flinched inside at her words, but revealed nothing. "Kim, dear..."

"Kim, dear, has your jealous side tempted you to kill off the competition?" Kimberly mocked. "Kim, dear, has your senile, invalid grandfather finally gone off his rocker? Kim, dear, you know I love you like a sister?"

"Caro Hartlan has nothing to do with the way I feel about you."

Kimberly's expression turned ugly. "Why don't you admit it, Wyatt? You find her exciting. I can see it in your eyes when she's around. I can see it now when you say her name."

Wyatt flung himself out of his chair. "She's an outsider, Kimberly. She'll be leaving soon."

"Which makes her all the more appealing, doesn't it?"

Wyatt's patience had already been sorely tested today. "You know how I feel about personal conversations when we're working," he said irritably. "I have a case to solve. Back to business, please."

"Sorry, Sheriff. I forgot."

Kimberly's tone was sarcastic, but she swung her legs around and seated herself sedately. Her feelings were hurt, and he knew it. But Kimberly had her pride. She wouldn't belabor the point.

That in itself made Wyatt relent. He followed her to her desk, and this time he was the one who hovered above her.

"I'm sorry, too. If only you and Morgan..." Wyatt ran a hand through his hair. "You know how Morgan feels about you, Kim. Couldn't you and he...?"

"Forget it!" she snapped. "Having a deputy for a husband is one thing. Having a criminal is another!"

Wyatt's concern for Kimberly was shoved aside at his brother's name. "What are you saying?" he asked.

Kimberly bit her lip. "Nothing."

"Tell me." His voice was as quiet as his movements had been when he'd closed the door earlier. And, like earlier, the quiet spoke volumes to the woman who'd known him since childhood.

"Look, I don't know anything about any secret mines. Or skeletons. And I don't know where that gold on Hugh's wheelchair came from. Neither does he. But if there were any rich veins around, I'd bet my last buffalo nickel Morgan would be scrambling for it."

Wyatt stared at his longtime friend. *Morgan in financial trouble?* He must have spoken the words aloud, because Kimberly answered, her expression as somber as his.

"I've heard things, Wyatt—things that worry me."

"Why the hell didn't you say something?"

"Because he's your brother! Because I don't have any proof!"

"Doesn't matter. I want details."

She hesitated. "It's just grapevine talk."

"Which can be very accurate."

"Which is why you should speak to Morg yourself."

"I'll do that." Wyatt grabbed his hat and a set of car keys from the wall. "Because you're wrong about Morgan. He's an honest man."

The words sounded hollow, even to him....

CHAPTER NINE

Friday afternoon

"YOU POOR THING!" Marta exclaimed. She and Caro were standing by the door of her room in the Triple B motel—the *B*'s standing for Boothill's Bunk and BBQ. "I had no idea forensics could be so dangerous! Although you did warn me...."

"Well, nothing like this has ever happened before."

Marta handed Caro a glass filled with tap water. "Here. Sit down and drink this."

"Are you sure? I smell like horse, guano, sweat."

"I'll open the sliding window. Now sit before you drop."

Caro did as she was told, although she did choose the dinette's patio-style plastic-covered chair, instead of the freshly changed bed. She gratefully slugged down the water.

"More?" Marta offered.

"Please." Caro handed her partner the empty glass.

"Let me run out for some ice and soda. I'll be right back. Will you be okay?"

"I'll be fine."

The older woman patted Caro's shoulder, then left. While she was gone, Caro took time to compose herself in the bathroom. First she carefully washed and rinsed her face and hands. Next she reached for the comb in the back pocket of her jeans and ran it through her hair.

She returned to the dinette table to empty her pockets and sort through evidence. Then she made a phone call—to the sheriff's office. By the time Marta got back Caro was almost herself again. In front of her lay the tiny navigational computer.

"You're looking perkier!" Marta grabbed two glasses, unwrapped them, then joined her.

"I feel much better."

Marta smiled. She pulled the tabs and poured out the sodas. "I've ordered us some lunch from room service, too. So relax, okay?"

"Thanks, Marta, you're very kind."

After a companionable silence during which Caro collected her thoughts, she began her story, starting with the horseback ride to the mine and ending with her tram ride to the Triple B. Marta was a quiet, sympathetic audience. When Caro finished, Marta simply took her hand and squeezed it.

"Praise the Lord you're all right."

"Amen," Caro seconded. "But this doesn't end here. I have a feeling things are going to get worse before they get better. So before our partnership goes any further, I have to ask—do you want out?"

"Out?"

"Yes. This may not be an easy case to solve, Marta. It could take forever. If I even solve it. So if you want to go back home and patch things up with your husband, don't let me stand in your way."

Marta shook her head. "I already tried, and a strange woman answered my phone. I've heard her voice before…" Marta compressed her lips. "Let's say I doubt I have much to go home to—unless it's a divorce lawyer."

It was Caro's turn to squeeze Marta's hand, but Marta would only take so much sympathy.

"Hey, I'm a grown woman. Until I decide what I want to do, this case is a good distraction."

"But if you get hurt...if someone comes after you because of me..."

"I'll just pretend the attacker's my husband and his mistress and go straight for the jugular. I'm staying and that's that. Now, tell me what we do next."

Caro had to hand it to her new partner; Marta was much calmer than she'd thought any woman could be under the circumstances. Marta had such strength, such determination, Caro knew she could confide in her.

"Let's start with this." Caro slid the navigational computer across the table. "If I can get the map printed out at the front desk's computer, I want the printout mailed to my parents today so they can have the Phoenix police seal and store it in the evidence locker."

"Shall I enclose a note of explanation?"

"A short one, perhaps. You don't have to go into detail. I've done this before, and my parents know the routine. But before you mail the packet, enclose your name and personal information as witness that this evidence hasn't been tampered with."

Marta reached for her purse to jot down notes. "Got it. Anything else?"

"See what you can dig up on the Bodines and the Ellises. So far, all the evidence has turned up in their presence or on their land. I have no reason to believe this case concerns anyone other than them. And my money's on Morgan."

"This is a small town," Marta said. "How far back do you want me to search?"

"Parents and grandparents, for sure. Great-grand-parents, if you can. One good thing about Tombstone, it's full of old photographs and old newspapers, and lots of records." She paused. "There were two newspapers the miners could buy—the *Epitaph*, which was pro-Earp, and the *Nugget*, which was pro-Cowboy. And of course Camillus Fly's photographs—an expensive thing back then— were just the thing for the newly rich to purchase and send back home.''

"I know all about those," Marta said.

Caro nodded. "Tombstone had a court seat, as well. There should be something about the Bodine and Ellis ancestors at the Old Court House here in town. I think I'll cover the court's museum records and leave you to the newspapers and photographs.''

"Got it. How will I get this information to you?"

"I'll call you tomorrow from the Silver Dollar."

Marta's pen actually fell to the floor. "Surely you aren't serious about going back to the ranch!''

"All my equipment and clothes are there. Not to mention one poor, nameless skeleton.''

"Oh, so you're going to pack up first and then move— where, here?''

"Nope, I'm staying put. I want to hear Morgan's explanation, and I'm not going to be able to do that hiding my head in the sand.''

"You'd be safer here! I don't mind sharing the room.''

Marta's concern warmed Caro's heart, but she was determined. "Marta, if someone really wants to hurt me, I won't be safe anywhere.

Marta retrieved her pen and tapped it against the table. "There's only one thing left for me to do, then, and that's come with you.''

"No. You're my ace—I need a partner.''

Marta's lips set in a tight line. "I don't care for card analogies. And I don't care for your plan.''

"Neither do I, Marta." Caro rose and walked to the door. "But it's all I've got.''

THE LATE AFTERNOON seemed strangely subdued as Catfish drove her back to the Silver Dollar. Wyatt had sent him for her after she'd called, and she met him when she left the hotel.

"The sheriff said you'd probably rather drive with me, instead of him. Said you were somewhat skittish."

"I wasn't then, and I'm not now," she said firmly.

Catfish heaved a sigh of relief. "Thank goodness. I'm too danged old to put up with any hysterical woman."

The words were gruff, although his eyes were kind.

"You're in luck. I'm not in the mood for shrieking," she said with a smile.

But her smile faded the closer they drew to the Silver Dollar. She felt a sudden wish to be back in Phoenix, safe and sound in her own home, or perhaps at her parents'. Anyplace but this ranch.

As if reading her thoughts, Catfish said, "The sheriff— he's one good man, you know. The best."

Caro couldn't think of an appropriate response, so she said nothing. Catfish turned onto the ranch's drive and took her all the way to the main house. "End of the line, missy."

Caro started to open her own door, but Catfish moved surprisingly fast for a man "too danged old." He came around to her side, opened the door and helped her out with old-fashioned courtesy. Then he pressed a slip of paper into her hand.

"You ever need anything, Doc, you gimme a call."

Caro thanked him and put the paper in her jeans pocket. However, Catfish wasn't ready to leave it there.

"Before I started mining, I used to be one doozy of a cattleman. I could find the best piece of prime stock out of a herd o' thousands. I know good blood, missy. Them Bodines got it. Know you don't believe me, so until you do, keep my number handy. Agreed?"

"Agreed."

"Then shake on it." Catfish spat in his right hand and held it out.

Without batting an eye, Caro immediately followed suit. She shook hands, managing to suppress a slight grimace.

"You're not bad stock yourself," Catfish said as he withdrew his palm and wiped it on his jeans. Once more Caro imitated his actions.

"I never did like fussy, fancy women. Give me the sensible ones any day. Even Kimberly won't shake an old man's hand proper."

"I'm not Kimberly."

"That's a fact. She keeps telling me what a city girl you are. But you don't act like a city girl. Appearances surely can be deceiving."

You're telling me! "Thanks again, sir."

Catfish doffed his beatup hat with a grand flourish. Then he was back in the truck and driving away. Caro waved, missing his straightforward kindness already.

As she looked around in the still, hot afternoon, a tall figure stood watching, one boot resting on the bottom rail of the brood-mare corral.

Caro lifted her head, took in a deep breath and walked toward Wyatt Bodine. The sun glared off the metal corral pipes, standard construction in the desert where wood was expensive, quickly splintered and destroyed by the sun.

The Arabian mares scattered at her approach, despite their swollen bellies. Streaming tails and manes painted the air with swirls of silver and black. Caro couldn't help but admire the horses' beauty. And yet she couldn't allow herself to be distracted from the task ahead of her—determining exactly what crime had been committed—and by whom. So many pieces of the puzzle were still missing. Potentially deadly pieces.

She shivered, despite the heat. But she didn't back down from approaching Wyatt. It wasn't until she joined him at the rail, her pose identical, her eyes on his mares, that he spoke.

"So here you are, walking into the spider's parlor. You're either the most courageous woman I've ever met— or the most foolish."

The corners of Caro's mouth tilted upward. "I've been called both. And I won't argue with either."

"Why?"

"Because it's my job. Because I knew the risks when I signed on. If you're one of them, so be it."

"I'm not, you know."

"Then I have nothing to worry about, do I?"

Wyatt nodded. They watched the mares settle again. Some of them ambled back to the fence, cautious around Caro, yet emboldened by their owner's presence. One mare trotted up to Wyatt. But when he stuck out his hand to caress the black velvet muzzle, she tossed her head and sidled over to Caro.

Stroking the arched neck, Caro tangled her fingers in the silky black-and-silver mane. The mare stood regally, accepting the caress. Caro continued to stroke her until the mare tossed her head with a snort, whirled on her back legs and cantered back toward the herd.

Caro was suddenly aware of Wyatt studying her and boldly returned his gaze.

"Is there anything you *aren't* afraid to take on?" he asked.

"Not when I think I'm right."

"I'm not certain of this, Caro, but—" Wyatt sighed deeply "—I think my brother *is* somehow involved in whatever's going on."

Caro dropped her foot from the bottom rail of the pipe corral. She gripped the top rail with excitement. "Did you find him?"

"Not yet. But he may be in financial trouble."

"Financial trouble? With all this?"

She gestured toward the Arabians before her. Each animal was worth thousands of dollars, as were the unborn foals. There was a great demand for Arabians in the arid Southwest, as well as elsewhere in the world, a demand certainly great enough to keep the Silver Dollar in business.

"I find that hard to believe," Caro stated flatly.

"About three months ago, Morgan took out a loan against his share of this ranch."

"Weren't you worried?"

"No. My brothers and I each own a specific third of the Silver Dollar, and we all have complete power when it comes to financial matters concerning that third. We only have one restriction. If we want to sell, we have to offer the land to blood kin first."

"Surely Morgan doesn't want to sell."

"No, but he does want to expand his jewelry business. His original operation was in kind of a small place on the outskirts of town. He wanted to target sales to the tourists and move to the center of town.

"That must have cost him," Caro said.

"You'd better believe it. The bank did what Morgan requested, and that was to mortgage his share of the ranch."

"Oh, no! The horses, too?"

"No, the horses are mine and mine alone. I gave up cattle for horses and sold my share of the herd to the Ellises. Virgil sold them his cattle when he left home, and Morgan did the same a few years earlier to open his jewelry shop at the first location. But I need land to raise my Arabians."

"Don't you have enough now?"

"Only because I pay rent to both Virgil and Morgan to lease their share of the ranch. If we lose Morgan's share, it'd be a tight squeeze to have enough exercise and grazing area for the horses I already own. I have no ready cash to start up elsewhere."

"Surely you could get a loan if worse came to worst."

"No. Equine stock is considered a high-risk collateral for a loan. One sweeping illness, the death of the few prime breeding stallions and it's easy to wipe out a lifetime's worth of work. The banks know that."

"Have you talked to Morgan about this?"

"Not lately. Like I said, it was his share of the land, and he said he knew what he was doing. What worries me is what else I just found out."

Some of the heavier mares lay down, secure in their familiar surroundings. A few others dozed on their feet, while most continued to pick at what remained of the evening alfalfa bales. But Caro's mind wasn't on equine appetites. She hung on Wyatt's next words.

"Even if Morgan lost his share of the land, I could manage. But Virgil gave Morgan power of attorney to manage his share, as well. He mortgaged that, too."

"Oh, no!"

"Oh, yes. I checked with the bank myself."

"But why would Morgan do such a thing? Or Virgil, for that matter? I would've expected Virgil to give *you* power of attorney."

"Morgan was doing me a favor. I have two full-time jobs—Morg mostly works on his jewelry. Occasionally helps me out by acting as a deputy when I need him." He shrugged. "We thought it was a viable solution."

Caro shook her head in disbelief. "Doesn't what Morgan did seem like...well, a betrayal of trust?"

"No, Morgan wouldn't do that. Virgil said he could do whatever he wanted to increase the family fortune, so to speak. Morg probably figured he could make himself and Virg some money in the jewelry game. I thought his business was doing well."

"Perhaps not," Caro suggested. "Morgan would have to put out a lot of cash to get established. There's the rent on the downtown building. Equipment. Staff. Silver isn't that high, but it adds up. Turquoise costs, as well—and if he decided to go into goldsmithing and move up to faceted stones like diamonds, that could cost a bundle.''

"I see we're back to the gold again." Wyatt's lips thinned, and his eyes grew dark. "One thing's for sure—if there's a hidden stash of gold on this ranch, Morgan doesn't have access to it, or he would never have mortgaged the Silver Dollar. Damn, I wish I knew why he did it without telling me!"

"We'll find out." Caro suspected this might be the connection she'd been seeking, yet what she felt most intensely was concern for Wyatt. This was his brother.

"I have to find him first."

"Morgan's missing?"

"I don't know if 'missing' is exactly the right word. But he isn't at his jewelry store in town. He isn't on the ranch. No one's seen him over at Hugh's. I thought it might be Morg when I heard Catfish's truck."

Caro felt a small twinge of disappointment. So Wyatt hadn't been waiting for her. Not that it mattered, she told herself. "Where's Morgan's car?"

"He uses the Jeep, and it's still parked at my office. I checked with Kimberly earlier. The two sheriff's cars are there, too, so he didn't take one of those."

"Did Morgan have any business in Tucson?"

"No, he would've told me if he did. We usually have feed and supplies to pick up, so we always let the foreman know when we're going to the city. But Luciano hasn't heard from Morgan. I hope—''

Wyatt abruptly broke off, but Caro knew what he'd been about to say.

I hope he's all right.

"I do, too."

Wyatt slowly turned to face her. "Thank you, Caro. I think you mean that."

She bit her lip and swallowed hard. "I mean it, Wyatt."

Wyatt nodded, then went on, the dread discernible in his voice, "I'm worried. It's not like Morgan to disappear."

There was risk in the desert. Caro had grown up knowing that. Whenever she was going to be gone for any length of time in the scorching wilderness, she always let someone know her schedule. And whether on foot, horseback or driving, she carried her knife, rifle and canteen—all of which her mother had bought her.

Caro thought back to her youth. Her mother had taken her out to the desert, setting up tin cans for target practice. Caro had started out with a BB gun and graduated to a rifle. Her mother had done the same with her younger sister.

"You have to learn to protect yourself, honey," her mother had said. "This is the desert. You have to know how to survive, how to keep yourself safe and some-times…how to kill."

Caro hadn't like hearing that. Neither had her younger sister. Caro had cried at the noise of the bullets until her mother had shown her the scars on one leg, where she'd been savaged by a javelina; the wild desert boar with the massive tusks.

"The desert is your home, Caro," she'd told her daughter that day. "If you and your home are friends, instead of enemies, you'll survive, just as I did when I killed that javelina. So cry all you want, sweetheart, but reload the rifle while you're crying, and let's start again."

Yes, shooting and riding and hiking and learning the ways of the desert were part of growing up for Caro. She and her sister knew the harsh realities of the Southwest. Children grew up fast in the desert, or they didn't grow up at all. It was as simple as that.

For Morgan, a local, to be missing was serious indeed.

Wyatt took off his Stetson and whacked it against his thigh in frustration. "Morgan's nowhere to be found, two-thirds of the Silver Dollar's mortgaged, I have unidentified bones popping up, a forensics expert who thinks I'm trying to protect a conspirator who tried to kill her—and who happens to be my brother—and a tapped-out mine that might not be tapped out, after all. What next?''

"A quick shower and dinner, then we go look for your brother,'' Caro said decisively. "Or I can just put on a fresh shirt and snack in the car.''

Surprise registered on his face. "You'll help me look for him?''

"You take your car, I'll take mine, and we'll cover twice the territory.''

Wyatt paused, and the light in his eyes faded.

"What?''

"I've been waiting to tell you,'' he said. "After this morning I had your car checked. Your saddle cinch wasn't the only thing tampered with.''

"Let me guess. Someone cut the brake lines.'' The look on his face confirmed her suspicions. "How clichéd! Really, you'd think whoever this was—'' she was careful not to say his brother's name "—would have a little more originality,'' she said sardonically.

"Sometimes the old tried-and-true methods work best. I had your car towed to town, Caro. It wasn't safe to drive. You'll have to go with me.''

"I'm game.''

"I hope there's no real emergency here. Morgan may just be delayed someplace. But I'd feel better if I checked.''

Caro didn't know if he planned to protect his brother or not, but she didn't doubt the fear in his voice. Whatever had happened to Morgan, Wyatt wasn't in on it. She certainly wasn't ready to trust him completely—she didn't dare—but some of her suspicions had subsided.

"Then let me wash my face and put on some clean clothes,'' she said, heading for the house. "If you could grab us some fruit and maybe a couple of sandwiches, we can get started.''

I want to find Morgan just as much as you do, she silently thought. I just hope he hasn't skipped town. Maybe she'd give Marta a quick call and ask her to come along. Three sets of eyes were better than one. *And it won't hurt to have a chaperon—or a witness.*

Caro hoped she'd be in; she couldn't really leave a message at the desk. And if she wasn't in, maybe she could at least write a quick note to drop off later if they didn't find Morgan.

Paper and pencil. I'll get them from my lab, she decided. Then she stepped into her lab—and screamed.

CHAPTER TEN

Still Friday—early evening

CARO'S SCREAM was one of pure, unadulterated rage...

The table she'd set her equipment on was lying sideways on the floor, along with bits and pieces of what had been her microscope, all her camera equipment and laptop computer. Her field tools had been broken and scattered all over the floor. Forensic chemicals had been poured over her cameras and film. The foul-smelling reagents were now eating into what was left of her toolbox, as well as the throw rug and hardwood floor.

And worst of all—*the skeleton was gone!* Where the transport case had been was now empty, that space the only clean area in a sea of devastation.

Caro stood there, debating whether to scream again from rage or flat out curse, when Wyatt rushed into the room. "Are you all right?" he asked.

"You tell me, Mr. Ranch Owner! I leave the house for one day and come back to...to..." Caro gestured wildly toward the wreckage at her feet.

"But are you okay?" he demanded.

"No, I'm not okay! My evidence is destroyed or missing... Well, at least we know where Morgan is!" Her voice was harsh, accusing, as her suspicions about Wyatt rushed back full force.

"What are you talking about?"

"Morgan isn't missing at all! He's probably taking a late

run out to your mine to hide the skeleton in one of those secret caverns. Did you know about this plan or was it all his idea?''

"I don't even know where Morgan is, let alone why—I mean, if—he'd do something like this!" The unflappable Wyatt Bodine looked as shaken as Caro felt.

"Well, if he didn't, then who did? Where were *you* when I was trying to hide from Morgan at the Bird Cage Theater?"

"I certainly wasn't here! Think—if I was going to ruin your evidence, I'd do better than pouring acid all over my own floor."

"You know something, Sheriff, I'm awfully tired of these half answers of yours. I feel like getting my suitcase and…"

Suddenly Caro remembered where she'd put her suitcase—and what she'd hidden in it.

Oh, please, no! My evidence!

Caro dashed out of the lab, ignoring Wyatt's anxious, "What is it?"

Caro didn't bother answering him. She yanked open the door to her bedroom, Wyatt right behind her. This time, she did swear at the sight, instead of screaming.

"Damn it! Look at my room!"

It was a shambles. Her clothing had been yanked out, along with the dresser drawers themselves, and thrown all over the floor. The bed linen had been stripped down to bare mattress, the mattress slashed open on the floor. Caro's eyes flicked to the window, but before she could check on her suitcase, Wyatt joined her.

His jaw worked, and the skin over his cheekbones stretched taut. "If Morgan's involved in this, I'll throw him in jail myself."

Caro stared at him. Wyatt was either the world's best actor or he really was as shocked as he seemed. Until she figured out which, Wyatt mustn't know about the suit-case—*if* it was still there. It was time for a distraction, a way to get him away from the window and out of her room. She immediately dropped to her knees and started picking up her clothes.

Wyatt joined her on the floor and started to assist. Caro rudely, purposely, snatched a teddy out of his reach.

"My lingerie's had enough trauma for one day, Sheriff. Go get your cheap thrills somewhere else!"

What happened next was a blur. In seconds Wyatt had grabbed her arms and yanked her up, the lingerie in her hands fluttering to her feet. His fingers held her fast, her face inches from his.

"Listen to me, lady. You're not the only one who's had a rotten day! My house has been vandalized, my investigation compromised, and worst of all, my brother's missing."

Caro shoved free with a violence of her own. They faced off like two bulls in a rodeo pen, her charade of a distraction now turning into a full, heated brawl. "I'll trade you my slashed cinch and cut brakes!"

"Caro, this is getting us nowhere! What do you want from me?"

"How about a more professional way to conduct an investigation?"

"I'm working on it! Can't you get it through your head that I'm not the enemy here?"

"Oh, pul-leeze! Do I look like I just fell off the hay wagon?"

"You may not look like it, but you're starting to sound like it. Think, Caro, think! This is my home, my ranch. And I'm the sheriff here. If I was trying to cover up a crime, don't you think I'd be more subtle? Give me some credit!"

Caro hesitated. Bodine was an intelligent man. And Morgan *was* missing.

"Better yet, lady, give me your trust." This was said in a quiet voice.

"Trust? Tell me this, Sheriff. If Morgan's guilty of grave robbing, cinch slashing, car tampering and destroying evidence for Lord knows *what* reason, just how hard are you going to work to put him behind bars?"

"As hard as it takes!"

Caro's breath came out in a scoffing gust of air. "You expect me to believe that?"

"You don't have a choice. Because the way I see it, you need reinforcements, and you need them now."

"I need something, all right. But I'm not sure it's you!"

"That's too bad, because I'm all you've got."

Oh, I have a few aces up my...suitcase, Sheriff. At least, I hope I do. Caro drew a deep, shaky breath. She'd decide whether to trust the brother of a possible criminal later. First things first. She had to get Wyatt out of the room to check.

"Well, Caro?" He was waiting for her answer. "Are we a team or not?"

What to do? Time and time again, her judgment had triumphed over that of others with more experience, more expertise. Caro never trusted anyone. It was her greatest strength; it always had been. Besides, her instincts had already been borne out once—when it came to Morgan's keys. Why should this case be any different?

"I suppose I could use a little help from you," she answered slowly, making sure she didn't commit herself to the "team." "Just as you could use my help to find Morgan."

He gave a satisfied nod. "Wise move, ma'am." Then he turned and stared at the mess on the floor. "I'll send a couple men to clean up. Then you and I can compare notes.''

''Give me fifteen minutes,'' Caro replied. ''I prefer to pick up some of my things myself.'' She glanced pointedly at the intimate apparel scattered around.

''Fifteen minutes. We'll grab a quick bite and decide whether to ring the alarm for Morgan or not.''

''Fine. Shut the door behind you, please.''

As soon as he'd left the room, Caro locked the door and raced to the window. She flung open the glass pane, grabbed at the rope and yanked up the suitcase and towels. With trembling hands she threw the towels on the floor. Her heart pounded as she rested the suitcase atop the slashed mattress.

''Please, please, please...'' she prayed as she worked the locks. ''Be there, be there!''

The locks popped back and Caro flipped open the lid. Her breath caught in her throat. The off-white of the skull filled her gaze. The skull was untouched. Film, notes, computer disk—all were still safe. The instruments she could replace. The evidence she could not. Evidence that might incriminate Morgan far more than a stray set of car keys did. She had to find out if Morgan was involved—and how deeply—and she had to do it alone. Without Wyatt.

Caro breathed again. She grabbed a fresh but wrinkled change of clothes from the floor, tossed it in, fastened the suitcase, patted her boot to make certain her wallet was still there and hurried to the window. It took only a few seconds to lower the suitcase to the ground with the rope. So far, so good. She was next. It was time to leave, with or without her damaged car. With or without Morgan. As the official forensic investigator on this team, she knew her first duty was to protect the evidence, and protect it she would. Which meant getting everything to Marta, the only person she could afford to trust. The only person she *knew* couldn't possibly be involved. She had to put her confused feelings for the sheriff completely out of her mind. At least for now.

Caro was betting that the Silver Dollar hands, like those on most working ranches, left the ignition keys in their vehicles during the day. Wyatt even did the same with his sheriff's Jeep when he parked on his own land.

This time-saving tradition would make her task possible. As some of those trucks and cars were parked behind the house near her room, her escape would be that much easier.

Caro made sure the rope was still securely fastened at her end and thrust one leg out the window. "I hope you don't mind, Sheriff, but you'll be eating alone while I borrow one of your cars," she said aloud. "I've decided to drop in on Marta for a while."

A few minutes later Caro and her suitcase were safely inside a ranch vehicle speeding away from the Silver Dollar toward Tombstone.

"MRS. WENKERT ISN'T IN? Are you sure?" Caro asked the desk clerk at the Triple B."

"Yes, ma'am. But she did leave a message and a key for you." The clerk passed Caro both items, then politely looked away as she read the note.

Dear Boss—In case you decided to come by, am off researching for you. Talked to the manager at Boot-hill Cemetery. I thought someone like him would have a good slant on the old Tombstone generation. He has an odd name, Catfish, and we're having a working dinner. Make yourself at home. Will give you a ring later. Hope the case is coming along smoothly. Best, Marta.

"Oh, hell," Caro mumbled, disappointed.

"Is there a problem?" asked the clerk. "Do you wish to leave a reply?"

Caro folded the note and shoved it in her jeans pockets. "Thanks, but I'm all set for now."

The clerk looked at her suitcase. "If you're going to Mrs. Wenkert's room, I'll have someone carry that for you and let you in."

Caro automatically gripped the handle even tighter. "I'll take care of it myself. But thank you." She gave the clerk a parting smile, pivoted and headed toward Marta's room. One thing about small towns—they certainly knew how to treat their visitors.

Or so she thought...until she stepped into Marta's room and felt a hand—Sheriff Wyatt Bodine's hand—grasp her wrist. One of his booted feet slammed the door shut, while his free hand reached for her suitcase. Caro and the suitcase eluded him, but she found herself still caught in his other hand.

"You!"

"Yes, ma'am. Too bad you don't know all the shortcuts. Or that half this town called to tell me someone was stealing my truck and hiding it behind the motel."

"Let go of me!"

"I can't do that. We need to talk, and I'm tired of your disappearing acts. Grabbing a greased javelina's easier."

"Well, why don't you grab the door handle and show yourself out?" Caro replied, protectively cradling the suitcase.

"Why? Afraid I'm the local lingerie thief? What's in the suitcase, Caro?"

"Nothing!"

"Good. Then you won't mind if I borrow it—just like you borrowed my truck?"

"Let go of me!"

"Not until you hand over the suitcase."

"Over my dead body!"

"With pleasure!" Wyatt approached, his free hand extended.

"Touch my suitcase, and I'll…I'll…" *Damn! He's right between me and the door!*

"What? Scream? Sob? Swear?"

"No, this!" Caro slammed the suitcase square into his stomach as he made a second grab for it. Wyatt grunted, and his hand on her wrist loosened. She ran for the door, still holding the suitcase, but Wyatt recovered with amazing speed. In another second he'd tackled Caro, her suitcase and his Stetson flying through the air. The suitcase squashed the Stetson to the floor with a loud thud just as the two of them landed on Marta's bed. Caro found herself crushed beneath the rock-hard muscles of the Stetson's owner.

"I'm getting very tired of you, lady," Wyatt ground out, his voice still breathless from her blow.

"And I'm sick of your unprofessional behavior! I'm warning you—this is your last chance to let me go!"

"Over *my* dead body!"

"Fine. Have it your way!" Caro flung out with all her might and deliberately rolled them both off the bed. Her weight, now on top, slammed into his as he hit the floor. She scrambled to her feet and grabbed the suitcase, ready to run.

But his strong hands grabbed her left ankle and sent her flying back to the floor where he still lay. As Caro hit the carpet the suitcase snapped open, the skull flying up in one direction, the computer disks, clay kit and her notebooks scattering in others.

The skull fell and hit Wyatt dead on the nose, and he roared in pain. "Son of a desert-whelped cur!"

Caro grabbed for the skull and her computer disks. Wyatt grabbed for his bleeding nose and Caro. He missed and she began to crawl toward the skull. Wyatt clutched her shoulder and yanked her back, causing her to drop the skull. Both of them toppled to the floor again, Wyatt on top, Caro on bottom. The skull stopped its topsy-turvy roll and settled, right side up, mere inches away, garishly leering at them.

And then the door opened.

Caro saw Marta and Catfish step into the room and freeze in shock. Catfish stared at Wyatt, Marta stared at Caro, and Wyatt—as far as she could tell from her position under his body—was staring at the skull.

Catfish cleared his throat in embarrassment. "Them youngsters sure don't neck proper anymore, do they, Miz Marta?"

Marta pushed Catfish's escorting arm aside. "Necking, my Aunt Fanny! This looks like assault to me!"

"Breaking and entering! Assault and battery!" Caro glared at her captor.

Wyatt glared right back. "*I'm* filing assault and battery! And grand theft. She stole a ranch vehicle."

"Borrowed it!" Caro furiously corrected. "And only after the brake lines in mine were cut and someone stole the skeleton!"

Everyone started talking at once.

"Your brake lines were cut? When…"

"Unless he just *told* me that to strand me without a car!"

"Someone stole the skeleton? But the skull is here…"

"Not that she'd tell me about it!"

"What's going on?"

Caro yelled to make herself heard above everyone. "GET OFF ME, YOU BIG OX!"

Silence. Then Wyatt was off her, Marta was helping her up, and Catfish was closing the open door against the curious eyes of other guests. Caro contented herself with shoving the hair out of her face and reaching for the skull again.

Marta hurried over to fuss and comfort. Caro went to pick up the scattered evidence, while Catfish dragged Wyatt over to a chair, thrust a large cotton handkerchief at his nose and tossed him his squashed Stetson. Wyatt threw it to the floor.

"Someone want to tell us what's going on?" Catfish said.

"We can start with you telling me what the hell you're doing here!" Wyatt glared at Marta.

"She's a friend of mine, and I'd watch your mouth in the presence of ladies," Catfish warned.

Wyatt wasn't repentant in the least. "There's only one lady here, and it isn't *her!*" The look Wyatt threw Caro was one of pure fury. "If she isn't turning my job into bedlam, she's trying to break my ribs or bust my chops."

"Only because every time you turn up, evidence about this case disappears!" Caro rose to her feet to drop an armful of evidence, skull included, on the little dinette table. "You call yourself a lawman! The real Wyatt Earp must be turning in his grave."

Wyatt flew from the chair as if launched by a cannon. Catfish grabbed his shoulder, stopping the younger man's forward momentum with surprising strength.

"Back off, Wyatt," Catfish ordered. Wyatt did, calming himself with great effort.

"I told him that, too, but he didn't bother to listen to me!" Caro said furiously. "Of all the lawmen I've worked with, you are the most stubborn, vague—"

"Enough, everyone!" Caro and the two men jumped at the whiplash crack of Marta's voice. "Sheriff, sit down. You too, mister. And, Caro, a few deep breaths wouldn't hurt."

"But—"

"Take them!" Marta commanded. "And then sit down on the bed."

Caro's eyes didn't leave Wyatt for a moment as she obeyed. The deep breaths helped.

"Better?" Marta asked crisply.

"A little."

"Good. Now, what's going on here? Tell me everything, starting with…" Marta pointed to the skull.

Catfish nodded his agreement. "That's as good a place as any, don't you think, Wyatt?"

Wyatt refused to answer, but Caro had a mouthful of complaints about the professionalism of Wyatt's investigative procedures. In her fury to protect the evidence and perform her own professional responsibilities, she dismissed all other emotions. The more-than-physical appeal Wyatt had always held for her—*still* held—was just a distraction, she decided angrily. It sure wasn't an issue during their no-holds-barred fight, and it wouldn't be now. By the time she was through, she had everyone's undivided attention—and sympathy. Except Wyatt's.

"Looks like you scared this poor little gal to death," Catfish announced.

"She isn't a girl, she's a *woman*," Marta said fiercely, getting into the act.

"You tell them, Marta! I don't scare easily," Caro snapped.

"By the looks of things when we walked in, Doc, I won't argue. You was holding your own. More than holding your own," Catfish said, admiration in his voice. "While you—" Catfish shook his head at Wyatt, disappointment expressed for the whole male species "—Lord knows what you had on your brain."

"I wasn't making any moves on Caro Hartlan. Nor was I waiting here to destroy the skull." Wyatt picked up his battered Stetson, attempting to punch the hat back into shape. "I didn't even know she had this stuff hidden away."

"Not stuff—*evidence!*" Caro howled, hovering over the assortment on the table, even pulling it closer when Wyatt started to approach.

"I'm not going to hurt your precious evidence. You have my word."

"Right. Like that amounts to a hill of beans after the way you manhandled her," Marta sniffed. "You should call the state police and have him arrested!"

Catfish tried to defend Wyatt, but Wyatt, now in control of himself, held up a restraining hand. "Who exactly are you, ma'am? *Besides* one of the witnesses that day on Boothill?"

Marta looked to Caro for guidance. Caro made the introductions. "This is Mrs. Marta Wenkert, my investigative assistant."

Catfish stared. "You told me you were just a tourist interested in local history! A librarian who read a lot of Tombstone books." Catfish's voice rose as Marta smiled proudly.

"Good cover, huh, boss?"

"She's in your employ?" Wyatt asked.

"That's right. Considering the caliber of help I've received on this case, surely you aren't surprised," Caro said dryly.

"Well, *I'm* surprised, dang surprised!" Catfish glared at Marta, standing next to him. "You could've said something, woman!"

"I was undercover," she explained.

"I don't care about you playing Mata Hari! But you could've told me you was hitched! I didn't know you was *married!*"

Marta gaped at him. "What does that have to do with anything?"

"I wouldn't be showing you around town if I'd known you was married *or* on an official investy-gation!" Catfish replied. "I've a good mind to bill your boss for my time, *Mrs.* Wenkert!"

"You do that, you old fool. And while we're on the subject of money, my boss will be charging *your* friend for her microscope, computer, tools, car repairs...and...and whatever else she can think of!"

Wyatt ignored the growing storm between Catfish and Caro's assistant. He moved closer to the table where Caro herself sat guarding the evidence.

"You said the bones showed damp rot."

Caro nodded.

Wyatt held out his hand. "May I?"

"Not on your life. Or this poor soul's."

"Then I must ask *you* to smell the remains."

"Smell?" Marta echoed. Even Catfish lifted a questioning eyebrow.

"Yes, smell. Remember what we were discussing out at the mine?"

Caro did as he requested. She inhaled deeply, her eyes narrowing. There was something about that faint odor. She'd only smelled it once in her life, but the smell was unmistakable. She recognized the faint, pungent fetidness even before Wyatt spoke.

"Recognize it?"

"Bat guano?"

Wyatt held out his hand again for the skull. This time Caro passed it to him. He rotated it so that the biggest area of damp rot was before his nose. He sniffed just once, his lips together in a thin line, and nodded in affirmation.

"Number one, the skeleton probably came from my mine. Number two, if I was in on this, I wouldn't have told you a thing about guano rot. And last, if Morgan doesn't show up tonight, we begin an official search tomorrow. I want everyone ready and waiting at first light at The Silver Dollar Mine.''

"We're going to look for your brother there?'' Marta asked, filling the ominous silence.

"Yes.''

Catfish played with his long white whiskers. "You don't think…''

Caro's eyes lifted to Wyatt's. She confirmed her own suspicions. "He's hiding out in the mine?''

Wyatt's words rasped like a file shaping a tombstone. "Hiding—or worse.''

CHAPTER ELEVEN

Saturday morning, early

LONG BEFORE the desert sun rose over the mountain peaks, the search party was under way. The night had been frigid, with a chill that went beyond mere coolness. Most of the searchers—there were nine in all—were traveling out to The Silver Dollar Mine by vehicle. Only Wyatt and Caro elected to go on horseback.

Despite the body heat of the Arabian and the warmth of her flannel-lined denim jacket, Caro shivered. The man riding beside her—hiking boots in place of his cowboy boots—broke the silence for the first time since the two of them had set out an hour earlier.

"Cold?" Wyatt asked. "I have coffee if you want."

Yes, she was cold all right. But the cold was more inside than out. Her very heart felt icy.

"Thanks. I'll pass."

A few seconds later, Caro shivered again.

Wyatt noticed. "Let me give you that coffee," he insisted.

"You don't understand. It won't help. It's not that kind of cold."

"Then explain it to me."

Bodine's gaze was piercing as he reined his stallion to a halt. Caro followed his action with the gentlest pressure on the bit. The desert wind blew strong, threatening to rip her hair from the confines of her borrowed hat. The cold slapped her face, stabbed through her jacket, chilled her bones.

"Funny thing about evil, Sheriff. I can feel its power like a poison burning the bloodstream." Reins still in hand, Caro rubbed at her arms. "It's like biting into a piece of bread that's just started to turn bad. You may not see the mold, but one bite, one taste, and you know. You *know*."

The wind kicked up, gusting and howling. Tails and manes blowing almost parallel to the ground, the two Arabians closed their eyes, their lids and delicate lashes protecting them from the stinging sand. Wyatt remained motionless.

"You have a bad feeling about Morgan, too, don't you?" he said. It was a statement more than a question.

"Yes. Maybe he isn't involved at all," Caro replied. "Maybe someone wants it to *look* like he's involved."

"I'd already come to that conclusion, Caro. I didn't think you ever would, especially after what happened yesterday. What changed your mind?"

"A couple of things." Caro paused and gathered her thoughts. "For me, helping to solve crimes isn't just gathering evidence, Sheriff. There's a lot more—gut feelings, too."

"True. I'm a believer in a cop's intuition. But intuition never sent anyone to jail."

"I think you know better, Sheriff. Any fool can throw materials into plastic bags at a crime scene. Not everyone knows how to take that evidence and use it to track down a criminal, target the way he acts. You do. And I may seem obsessed with the evidence itself, with facts, but I also have a sharply honed intuition. I rely on it. And so far, my intuition says you're in the clear."

"About time you figured that out. What convinced you?"

"I always *wanted* to believe it. But what finally convinced me was the way you acted yesterday in Marta's room. You proved that you don't know any more about what's going on than I do. Starting with the fact that you tackled me for the suitcase.''

"I said I was sorry about that."

"I'm sorry I had to fight back so hard. But I had to make absolutely sure the evidence wasn't compromised by you—covering up for Morgan. And you can't say I didn't have grounds to worry. You've done it once already."

"I was wrong," Wyatt admitted. "But I'd do anything for Morg. Well, almost anything," he amended. "I won't protect him from the law."

He touched his heels to his horse, and they both started forward again. Wyatt massaged his ribs with one hand. "I'm glad you don't feel as battered as I do. Where did you learn to fight like that?"

"My mother. A girl can never be too careful, she always said. Anyone's capable of killing under the right circumstances. Not that I agree with her, but I still had to listen."

The wind howled again. Wyatt's Stetson blew off his head. He ignored it, even when the chin strap caught and jerked the weight of the hat against his throat. Caro watched him, the predawn darkness hiding his face.

"No argument, Sheriff?"

"Your mother is right. We're all killers deep down."

"Your logic is faulty. Don't think I'm capable of murder just because you say you are." Caro shifted in the saddle. "I know how good cops work—and bad ones. You have to think like the criminal you're chasing, feel what he feels. And unlike him *you* have to control it." She paused. "You don't like that part of yourself, do you?"

Wyatt's tight smile was without mirth. "Understandable, isn't it?"

"Of course it is. I do understand. But most of my friends don't. They can't see why I chose a job like this."

"Why did you?"

"Because I have a gift. Like you do. Because I can see beyond the blood and gore and the sadness and tragedy to the actions, the motives of the person who caused it."

"And you call that a gift?"

Her expression was rueful. "Well, it certainly isn't something I would've chosen for myself. I'd rather be a concert pianist making beautiful music. Or an artist painting in a Paris studio. But I have no talent for either."

There was a hint of sadness that Wyatt would never have expected. But then it was gone.

"Sheriff, I faced who and what I am years ago. I accepted it, and I use my abilities for good. Like you. You don't enjoy the more grisly aspects of your profession any more than I do. But you take pride in seeing justice served—I know you do. I know because of your record with the DEA. And because of the conflict you've felt over Morgan."

Wyatt couldn't believe what he was hearing. Her words touched him deeply, left him with a glow of warmth, but he was afraid to fan that glow into anything else.

"Caro," he finally said, "I have to tell you something. If anything's happened to Morgan—if I find out he's hurt or..." He couldn't say the word. *Dead.* "I'll kill whoever is responsible. I'll be serving my own kind of justice. And there won't be a thing you can do to stop me."

"Perhaps not, but I'll try my best. And my best is good, Sheriff. *Damn* good."

He didn't know how to answer that. Didn't *want* to answer that. He willed her to back off.

They stared at each other as the wind increased. Caro's hat almost blew off her head before she caught it. In the distance, a herd of horses moved restlessly, their actions evidence of the coming storm.

She urged her mare to a canter, leaving Wyatt behind in the shifting sands and bloodred light of the rising sun.

Wyatt watched her long, graceful form as her mare traveled ahead in an easy canter. Something deep inside him— even deeper than the darkness he tried to hide—moved and flexed. It was a strange feeling, a mysterious, primitive yearning, a compelling drive Wyatt had never experienced this strongly, this completely, before.

Caro Harlan had brains, beauty and courage. She was his equal, maybe more than his equal. Wyatt found himself wanting to know more about her. *Everything.* From her most closely guarded secrets to the way she made love....

But we have to survive this case, survive this first. Whatever happened to Morgan isn't going to happen to Caro— or to me.

THE SEARCH PARTY—or some of it—was waiting outside the entrance to The Silver Dollar Mine. As she dismounted, Caro recognized Marta in Catfish's old truck. She waved as Wyatt took her reins to picket the horses, a job he preferred to do himself. Marta and Catfish both came out to greet her, Catfish touching his hat brim in the automatic gesture of respect.

"Where is everyone?" Caro asked when they were within earshot. "I don't see Wyatt's truck."

Earlier Wyatt had said he'd have a trio of men come out in a ranch vehicle. That group hadn't arrived yet, and the vehicle was supposed to carry all the rescue and first-aid gear.

"The road out here takes much longer than the trail, ma'am. But Luciano's truck should be here any minute."

Sure enough, a vehicle's headlights were visible in the early sunrise. Then a second set appeared behind the first. Catfish frowned. "That lead truck's not one of Wyatt's. Did you invite someone else?"

"No." Caro shook her head.

Catfish glanced at Marta.

"Me, neither," she confirmed. "Everyone I know in Tombstone is here."

Wyatt approached, the horses now picketed. "It's probably someone from the Bar E. Hugh told me his horse trainer's daughter is into caving and climbing. I asked her to help us out. One of Hugh's men is driving her over."

But Wyatt was wrong. It wasn't Hugh's foreman driving the Bar E truck; it was Hugh himself. Wyatt hurried over to meet the newcomers. The second truck parked; Luciano and two other men hopped out. Wyatt's attention wasn't on them, though. He stood by Hugh's now-open door, barely noticing the dark-haired young woman in the passenger seat.

"I can't believe Kimberly let you do this!" Wyatt's forehead furrowed with dissapproval as he saw the oxygen lines and Hugh's pallor. "Does she know you're here?"

"My granddaughter may run your office. She doesn't run my life," Hugh wheezed. "Now make yourself useful and get my wheelchair. And get me some coffee while you're at it. I'm parched."

Wyatt gestured toward the bed of the truck with a curt motion of his jaw. His men immediately set to work removing the chair from the rear, but it was Wyatt himself who lifted Hugh from the truck and put him in it.

Caro approached to see if she could help. Wyatt shook his head, so she turned to the trainer's daughter, who looked to be in her midtwenties, and said, "Hello. I'm Caro Hartlan."

The younger woman nodded politely, but didn't extend her hand. "Jasentha Cliffwalker. Pleased to meet you, Dr. Hartlan."

Caro dropped her own hand. Handshaking was not a Native American custom, and the climber's black hair, bronze coloring and facial features, as well as her name, spoke more of Apache ancestry than Spanish. The serious brown eyes held intelligence—and steel. Caro recognized a kindred spirit. Despite Jasentha's obvious youth, Caro had no doubt the woman was as capable deep within the caves of the earth and on its highest peaks as she herself was in the midst of a crime scene.

"Please, call me Caro."

The woman nodded her acknowledgement, but not necessarily her assent. Her bearing and manner had a certain dignified reserve, and Caro suspected Jasentha wasn't about to lower that reserve until Caro had earned the privilege.

"Thank you," she said. "If you'll excuse me, I need to unpack my gear."

Caro was left standing alone. That didn't bother her, but the frustration of not being able to assist did. She was competent outdoors, thanks to her mother and grandparents, who'd been ranchers, but search and rescue of the living, as opposed to search and recovery of the dead, was beyond her expertise. Obviously Wyatt thought so, too. He rejoined them, Hugh safely in his chair.

"Caro, I want you to stay here with Marta, Hugh and my two hands," he said. "Jasentha, Luciano, Catfish and I will head into the cave. If we find anything or need more help, I'll send Catfish and Luciano back out. They'll keep you posted."

Caro refused to be dismissed. "Wherever you want your men posted is your business. Where I and my assistant go is mine. Marta, are you comfortable staying here without me?"

"I'm going if you're going," was Marta's loyal reply.

"Neither one of you is in charge of this expedition," Jasentha said. Everyone looked up at her words, but it was Wyatt who challenged her.

"I'm the sheriff here, Jasentha."

"I'm the expert on caves. If you expect to stay safe or to use my services, you will all follow my orders." She spoke softly, confidently, firmly. Caro recognized the professional tone as the same one she herself used.

Wyatt seemed willing to bow to the young woman's authority—not happy about it, but willing. "I'll trust your judgment concerning the terrain. But when it comes to making any other decisions about Morgan on this case, be prepared to step aside."

Jasentha nodded once. "You, Catfish and the forensics doctor may accompany me. The rest will wait."

"Luciano knows how I work, and he's a good man to have around. Caro—Dr. Hartlan is an unknown quantity," Wyatt protested.

"Caro Hartlan and Mrs. Wenkert are the only outsiders here. We need them to protect the integrity of this search."

Wyatt's face turned almost as pale as Hugh's. "What are you saying, Jasentha? That *my* integrity is not to be trusted?"

"No. What I am saying is, you know the rules. So I insist that Dr. Hartlan accompany us. Marta will remain behind with Hugh. As will Luciano."

Wyatt shook his head. "You know that cavers always travel in pairs, Jaz. Caro doesn't know the mine. Catfish does."

"Ought to," Catfish agreed. "Used to work it."

"She'll slow us down if we need to send for help," Wyatt warned.

"Then you and your foreman will go for help. The woman may remain at my side." Jasentha finished unloading her gear. "Now follow me."

Wyatt frowned, but Jasentha ignored him. She merely slung the last of her ropes over her shoulder, put on her miner's helmet with its attached light and distributed helmets to the other three.

Jasentha led the way. One by one they squeezed into the

small opening at the entrance. Wyatt followed her, Caro close behind; Catfish brought up the rear.

As before, the sun's rays quickly faded into a gloomy coolness that soon changed into a black chill. Jasentha turned on her headlamp, and everyone else did the same. Caro was the first one to switch on her flashlight, for the others exhibited a surefootedness she didn't feel.

"Take your time," Jasentha suggested. "I don't want you hurt."

But Wyatt had already fallen back to walk at Caro's side. "I'll keep an eye on her."

"And I'll keep an eye on him." Caro gestured Wyatt ahead. "If I need anything, Sheriff, I'll yell."

"As you wish." Wyatt returned to his earlier position.

The four of them made steady progress to the large chamber Caro had visited with Wyatt. Already the bats were returning to their den through a small opening high in the ceiling. Caro hadn't observed it before; her equipment hadn't picked up that crack. In fact, she would never have noticed it even now if it wasn't for the incoming traffic. As the nocturnal mammals settled down for the day's rest, Caro unclipped her navigator from her belt, intending to make a manual adjustment.

"I'll do that if you want," Jasentha suggested.

Caro looked up in surprise. "You know how to use one of these?"

"Yes. I also know where this cave vents above ground. If you want your data to be accurate, I can help."

Caro immediately passed her instrument to their guide. As Jasentha busied herself with the adjustments, Caro checked carefully to make certain her hair was completely tucked under her miner's hat, safe from the falling guano. She wrinkled her nose at the smell, then remembered Wyatt's earlier words. "Sheriff, I thought you said we'd need oxygen to work around the bats."

"I thought we would."

"Wrong." It was Jasentha. She gestured upward as she spoke. "With large colonies of bats like this one, ammonia gases usually do necessitate oxygen tanks. But this area is well-vented. Your mining caves get plenty of air, Sheriff. There's a shaft that runs up to the natural cave system above. We'll be entering some fair-size chambers."

"But those could be filled with bats, too!" Catfish protested.

"They are," Jasentha confirmed. "But one thing you don't have to worry about is being able to breathe. The same shaft that provides the Silver Dollar chambers with air also vents the natural caves and up to ground level."

"Well, if you're sure it's safe," Catfish grumbled.

"I am," she assured them. "We don't need tanks any more than I need this." Jasentha held out the navigator for Caro to take.

"I didn't know about the vent above us, Jasentha," Wyatt said. "That's why I wanted you here."

Jasentha didn't comment but merely announced, "We go up."

"Up?" Caro couldn't help saying. "We're going to climb up through the air shaft?"

"Yes. The footing will be damp and difficult, but the climb isn't impossible if you're careful."

The expedition continued on. Jasentha led them to the far end of the large chamber, toward the sloping wall. The ground was slick with layers of new guano upon layers of old, the smell overpowering, but it didn't seem to bother their guide or Wyatt. Caro wasn't thrilled to have fresh urine and droppings splatter her helmet and jacket shoulders. Neither was Catfish. He swore eloquently every time he was hit. Caro couldn't help wincing a few times herself.

"For someone who can work with the goriest of corpses,

Caro, I didn't think a little organic material would upset you," Wyatt said smugly.

"At least I'm not holding out for an oxygen mask," she muttered to herself. But the tomblike atmosphere carried her words clearly.

Jasentha giggled, the sound at odds with the quiet dignity she'd so far displayed.

"Are you enjoying yourself, ladies?" Wyatt asked, annoyed.

"I can only speak for myself, but I do believe I am," Caro replied. That prompted another giggle from Jasentha. Even Catfish chuckled.

It was Jasentha who broke up the festive mood. "Flashlights on your belts, please, and gloves on your hands. The rocks are sharp, and we'll have to make do with the lamps on our helmets. Follow my footsteps. The climb gets steeper here. Go slow and pay close attention."

Steeper, it appeared, was putting it mildly! Caro thought fifteen minutes later as they labored up the rock wall. They were almost level with the bats on the ceiling, and yet still they continued to climb. The angle was steep, the footing slippery, and worse yet, Caro had no idea where they were headed. Even Wyatt had lost his bearings.

"Where the heck are we?" he asked when Jasentha stopped to allow them a breather. Caro was panting heavily, as was Catfish. Wyatt was only slightly winded, while Jasentha didn't seem tired in the least. Her voice was relaxed when she answered.

"I told you, your mine connects with a series of natural caves directly above. I'm taking you from here to there."

"How long's it gonna take? Damn!" Catfish scrubbed at the guano on the knees of his pants. When he noticed a splotch on one end of his fine, waxed white mustache, he became so frustrated he ran out of swear words. "This isn't a job for a retired man, Wyatt! Jasentha, couldn't you have taken us around this filth?''

''There *is* another way.''

''*Now* you tell us!''

''You could've said something earlier,'' Wyatt seconded.

''It would have made no difference. The three of you could not have made the climb.''

''I'm having a hard time with this one?'' Caro took off her filthy gloves before reaching for her canteen and unscrewing the cap for a swig of water.

''You may be slow, but at least you don't complain,'' Jasentha said pointedly.

''Oh, I have my moments,'' Caro admitted before taking another swallow. ''Especially when it's dark, I smell like guano, and—'' she paused ''—I don't know what's going on with Morgan.''

''I don't, either, but the sheriff *can* be trusted. If he believes Morgan is in here, we'll find him,'' Jasentha assured her.

''In this dark?''

''We'll see daylight soon. After we climb up and around this next bend, we'll come out on the floor of the caves. They umbrella over this mine for miles.''

Wyatt paused, the canteen halfway to his lips. ''I never heard about a set of caves connecting to the Silver Dollar before. I thought I knew every nook and cranny of this place. Obviously I was wrong.''

''That's because you aren't a bat,'' Catfish said, some of his good humor returning at the promise of daylight.

''Or a people who sent generations concealed from their enemies in these mountains,'' Caro added.

Jasentha swiveled her head to face Caro. Even in the dim illumination of the battery-powered headlamps, Caro could see her surprise. ''You know about the early Apaches?''

''Some.'' Caro drank one last swig of water and secured

her canteen, aware of Jasentha's close scrutiny but not disturbed by it.

Jasentha said something to Wyatt, not in English or Spanish, that Caro wasn't able to follow.

"Am I missing something?" she asked curiously as everyone rose to their feet. She followed suit.

"If I had wanted you to hear, Doctor, I wouldn't have spoken Apache," Jasentha replied, but her words were kind and her smile sincere.

"Oh." Feeling slightly chagrined, Caro pulled on her soiled gloves again. "Well, I'm ready when you are."

Jasentha checked on everyone, then adjusted her backpack and Wyatt's. Catfish and Caro wore none.

"About ten more minutes, and we'll be feeling the sun," their guide assured them.

Ten minutes to the dot, Caro saw that Jasentha was right. Warm sunlight streamed through the cold granite above them, illuminating handholds and toeholds that seemed old and well-worn.

"You've been here often, haven't you, Jasentha?" Wyatt asked quietly.

"A few times," was all she said.

"More than a few," Wyatt remarked, but he didn't pursue the matter. Like the others, he was intent on climbing toward the sun. Below them, their earlier route faded into darkness, along with the smell of bats. One by one they switched off their headlamps. Another fifteen minutes of steep climbing, then they were over the ledge. The strong, dusty heat of blowing desert air hit their nostrils, and the sunlight—what there was of it—warmed their shoulders.

Caro sighed, tilting her face toward the light in pure pleasure. "Hello, sky." She slipped off her helmet with one hand and gulped in the clean air.

Below them was the bat's entrance to the caves and the mine, above them the cloudy sky, and all around them were the spires and pillars of strange rock formations. The massive rocks prevented any kind of a view—or even a detailed rendering on Caro's navigational computer.

"Where are we?" Wyatt asked their guide.

"We're a good mile above the valley floor, and still on Silver Dollar land."

"I've never climbed this area before. I always thought this particular formation was inaccessible without climbing equipment," Wyatt marvelled.

"Caves can be great shortcuts," Jasentha said. "But right now we have to hurry. There's a storm brewing. Follow me."

Even as she spoke, the sun dipped behind the mushrooming thunderheads. "Please leave on your hat," Jasentha said to Caro. "There are falling rocks in this area. These mountains are very old—and many sections are heavily weathered."

Caro reluctantly put her hat back on, unable to suppress a shudder. Her soiled clothing, the prisonlike strangeness of the area, the rolling clouds above—it all threw an eerie pall over an already depressing situation. She knew how she'd be feeling if it was her sister who'd gone missing. Caro glanced at Wyatt. His face was tight and drawn, his worry and pain almost a palpable thing.

Impulsively she put her hand on his shoulder. "We'll find him, Wyatt. I know we'll find him."

"Maybe we already have," was his grim reply. "Look."

All eyes swung to Jasentha, then followed the direction her finger was pointing. Despite the gusting winds of the brewing storm and the rolling clouds, there were birds aflight, large birds, gliding in a circular pattern that spelled trouble—or worse.

"They're..." Caro couldn't finish, for she—and everyone else—recognized that black circle of death.

Vultures.

CHAPTER TWELVE

"MORGAN..."

Wyatt was the first to speak—if you could call his strangled gasp speaking. He was also the first to react. Without bothering to wait for Jasentha's lead, he immediately started off through the winding, twisting maze of rock, using the circling vultures as an overhead guide. Caro and Catfish hurried to keep up. He was moving so fast even Jasentha had to hustle to catch up with him.

"Sheriff, let me lead!" she called, but Wyatt was having none of it.

"My brother's out there!"

Wyatt forged boldly ahead as if he'd been born among these rocks, instead of seeing them for the first time. The only thing he concentrated on was the vultures above and their ominous shadows on the uneven rocky ground at his feet. He felt a restraining hand on his shoulder. If it was Jasentha's, he would have shaken it off.

But he knew it wasn't his guide's. The shock of recognition that ran through his body, the warming of his skin against hers, told Wyatt it was Caro.

"Please wait for Jasentha," she said quietly. "You can't help Morgan if you're hurt yourself."

Wyatt stared at her. For a moment he hesitated, drawn to this woman and her compassion—for him and, he sensed, his brother. But then thoughts of Morgan flooded his mind, and the moment was gone.

It had been enough time, however, for Jasentha to catch

up and regain the lead. But with or without her, anyone could easily have found the yawning pit. They came upon it abruptly just around a bizarre cluster of sheared, off-center rock formations.

The very blackness of the hole before him made his head spin, and Wyatt wasn't a man afraid of heights. He shone his flashlight down into its depths, but his beam couldn't reach bottom. Caro's beam joined his as she spoke. "Everyone! Flashlights and hats on! Center your lights with his! Now!"

She snapped out the order with the forcefulness of a drill sergeant. Even the reserved Jasentha was scrambling to obey her. It suddenly struck Wyatt that Caro Hartlan was a damn strong player to have on his team. He felt a sudden rush of gratefulness that he filed away for later. Right now they had work to do.

"Don't get too close to the edges. We don't want anyone else falling in," Caro warned. Her flashlight and hat beams merged with his. Then Jasentha's. Then Catfish's. The strength of the single beam was wide and powerful, except for one side where the light was wavering. Wyatt realized that the shaky beam was his. His fingers clamped down hard on the flashlight and steadied it.

When he did, his light caught on the bleached, off white shape of bone. "Morgan?" he gasped, his professional reactions gone, replaced by reeling emotions. Once more Caro's logic sounded clear and true.

"Morgan hasn't been missing long enough to show up as a skeleton," Caro said matter-of-factly. She lowered herself from her kneeling position to her belly and edged even closer to the pit. Jasentha reached for Caro's belt to give her an extra margin of protection, but Wyatt's hand was there first.

"Be careful, Caro," he said tersely.

"Hey, careful's my middle name. Everyone, follow my beam again. Same location."

Everyone did. Once more the beams merged, allowing them all to focus on the bones below. Beneath his hand Wyatt felt the tense muscles in Caro's back relax.

"What?" he demanded.

Caro sat up and the beams diffused once more. "Unless I'm sadly mistaken, our old friend from Boothill has been traveling again."

Wyatt couldn't share her relief. He looked up and saw the circling scavengers of the desert. The turkey vultures, with their black feathers and bloodred throat that gave them their name, were still above. Still waiting, still circling.

"Vultures don't bother with stripped bones," Caro said. "Merge the lights again."

"We'll start from the north end and circle down to east, south and west," Wyatt ordered. "Then everyone spiral in, same direction, tighter circle. Follow my lead."

There was no question as to who was in charge now. The other three did exactly as he asked. There wasn't a sound as the light traveled in tighter and tighter circles. The bottom of the pit wasn't wide, but its jagged ledges made coordination difficult and slow...

Until Jasentha gasped aloud. "Is that a boot?"

"You've got a good eye, Jaz. Track up on it," Wyatt commanded.

Again hats and hands coordinated the light's focus. Wyatt watched the beam travel up past the legs to a beige khaki shirt—*a beige that only a sheriff's officer wore.* And then, higher, up to the face.

Wyatt nearly dropped his flashlight into the pit. "Oh, my God!"

The other three leaned forward to confirm what his own eyes had already told him.

"It's Kimberly."

"Kimberly?" Catfish echoed. "Kimberly Ellis?"

Wyatt nodded.

"Is she..." Jasentha's voice trailed off. She suddenly sounded very young, her confidence shaken.

"I don't know." His own voice sounded strange. He'd found another person he loved, but not the brother who was missing. The sick fear in his heart grew as he reached for his backpack with its first-aid gear and walkie-talkie.

It was Catfish who voiced the words Wyatt himself didn't dare say aloud.

"But if that's Kimberly, where in tarnation is your brother?"

"We'll worry about Morgan later," Wyatt replied hoarsely. "Right now, we have to reach Kim."

Caro was already helping Jasentha take off her backpack. "Let's get her out of there, Sheriff." Caro glanced up at the ever-darkening sky. "Fast."

Wyatt tried to contact his office with his walkie-talkie, then realized he might not get an answer due to the pillars of rock interfering with reception and the gathering storm clouds disturbing the atmosphere. He tried again and again as Jasentha unpacked her climbing gear. By the time the ropes were anchored securely and the body harness unrolled and spread on the ground, Wyatt had given up.

He reached for the buckles that would loosen the harness; its girth had been fitted for Jasentha and wouldn't fit his larger body.

"What do you think you're doing?" Caro demanded.

"I'd like to know that myself," Catfish said.

Wyatt blinked at the concern in Caro's voice. "I'm going after Kimberly."

"Bad idea." Jasentha reached out to take the harness from his hands. "I'm the rock expert. You aren't."

"That's right," Caro agreed. "Plus, Jasentha doesn't weigh anywhere near as much as you, Wyatt. I think, for safety's sake, for *Kim's* sake, we need one strong man and one strong woman to pull her up.''

"Hey!" Catfish protested. "What am I? The old gray mare?"

"She's right," Jasentha said. "You are an elder. Your mind is wise and strong. Your body, as is the way of elders, is not."

"Kimberly might need medical help. I'm trained in first aid." Wyatt stared straight at Jasentha. "I know for a fact that you aren't."

Two spots of color appeared high on Jasentha's cheeks. Wyatt watched her lose her temper for the first time since he'd known her. "You told me you accepted my authority as leader!"

"Rocks, yes. Lives, no. Consider yourself demoted."

Caro intervened then. She curled her fingers around the harness with one hand, then reached for Wyatt's shoulder with the other. "I'll go down."

"You?"

"Yes. I've got more medical knowledge than anyone in this group."

"Medical knowledge of the dead?" Catfish interrupted.

"Doesn't matter. Dead or alive, the human body is still the human body."

"She's right," Wyatt said unexpectedly.

There was silence among the four. The wind picked up and blew harder as the sun darted behind the rising thunderheads. The vultures above had to flap hard to keep from being blown away from their prospective meal.

"Have you ever done work rope before, Caro?" Wyatt asked.

"Some. I'm no expert, mind you, but most murderers like to hide their victims' remains in deserted areas. There's rarely a paved path to the body's location. I have to get to the crime scene any way I can, and that's included ropes."

"So you aren't afraid of heights?"

"Nope."

"What about the dark? And snakes? What about—"

Caro held up a hand to silence him. "Please, Sheriff. Give me some credit. I know what I'm doing."

Wyatt heard the determination in her voice. "All right," he said curtly. "But for God's sake, be careful."

Caro nodded. "I'm ready to go. Jasentha can supervise the ropes, and the three of you can lower me down. I'll let you know if Kimberly can be moved."

"It's a good plan, Wyatt," Catfish said. "What do you think, Jaz?"

"It could work," Jasentha's reply was stiff.

"Then we're agreed," Caro said matter-of-factly. She gently pulled the harness from Wyatt's grasp and pivoted to face Jasentha. "Now, help me put this on."

Jasentha soon had Caro outfitted and ready to descend, complete with Wyatt's backpack containing the first-aid kit and a second rope and harness for Kim so that Caro wouldn't have to remove her own. Jasentha went over some last-minute details regarding the gear. Wyatt watched Caro lean over the edge of the pit, her eyes dark with concentration and the reflected gloom of the deep.

"Sure you want to go through with this?" Wyatt asked softly as he made certain the beam on her hat was working properly.

"Hey, at least I won't be bombed by bat guano," Caro said. She attached an extra flashlight—Wyatt's—to her belt. "Besides, I can ID a broken bone with my eyes closed and one hand tied behind my back. So lower away."

"Someday I'll find out what you *are* afraid of."

Caro shrugged. "It's no big secret. Get me out of this hole in one piece and maybe I'll tell you."

"It's a deal."

Wyatt reached for her shoulders. At first she thought it

was to help her maneuver her weighted-down body into a sitting position on the ledge. But suddenly he placed two hands on her face and pulled her close. His lips descended on hers for a kiss that was hard, fast and sweet.

His movement unbalancing her, she grabbed his chest for support. Wyatt used the excuse to pull her even closer. Then, as quickly as he'd begun the embrace, he ended it.

"What...what was that for?" Caro asked shakily.

Wyatt almost smiled. Caro Hartlan could be rattled, after all. "For luck. So you know you have something to come back to."

Caro blinked, but before she could say anything, Wyatt passed her the rope, pressing her fingers around it. "Hold tight," he warned. "Because here we go."

She made a thumbs-up gesture and gave them all a confident nod. "By the way," she called up as her head dropped below the lip of the pit, "my uncle's a lawyer. So don't drop me, or I'll sue the pants off the whole bunch of you. Starting with Wyatt."

Jasentha lifted one eyebrow and Catfish snickered, but Wyatt refused to join in their amusement. He recognized her attempt at black humor for what it was, understood the reasons for it, but wouldn't, *couldn't*, laugh. His eyes were intent on her miner's helmet as it dropped lower. And the lower she went, the more his heart choked his throat. Praying for her safety and Kim's, he continued to feed the rope.

Occasionally Jasentha called out to check on Caro, but her answer was always the same. "I'm fine. Keep going."

They lowered her carefully with an almost maddening slowness. The pulley system Jasentha had hooked up and around a nearby pillar was working perfectly. It took most of Caro's weight, so no one was straining. But no one was taking the situation for granted, either. The deepness of the pit and the darkening sky didn't help.

The wind whipped Jasentha's long hair about her face.

Unearthly moans issued from the pit. Wyatt's hands clamped so tightly on the rope that the progress of the feed was actually stopped before he realized it was the wind, not Caro or Kim moaning. Jasentha had to call his attention to it.

"Sheriff, loosen up! You're giving Dr. Hartlan a jerky ride here."

Wordlessly he did. The minutes passed, and the darkness and wind increased. The smell of approaching rain filled the air. And in Arizona, with its massive downpours and flash floods, a geographical depression was one of the worst places to be. Wyatt's nerves were stretched taut. He almost yelled out to Caro, but she beat him to it.

"I'm down!" she called out, her voice a hollow echo in the deepness of the pit. "Give me some slack, then hold up!"

They did, everyone up top waiting anxiously to hear about Kimberly.

"She's breathing!" Caro yelled. "And I'm right about the skeleton. It *is* our old friend! No sign of Morgan."

Wyatt exhaled deeply. Kimberly was alive! As for Morgan, he'd hang on to that old truism, "No news is good news," for now. *Just for now, until I know Caro and Kimberly are safe.*

A flash of lightning. The rumbling crack of thunder reverberated among the mile-high rock formations. The wind increased so much that even the huge, strong-winged vultures disappeared to seek shelter. The moans from the pit sounded like a woman crying.

It *was* a woman crying! Wyatt's adrenaline shot up so high it gave his mouth a metallic taste, but then he heard Caro's soothing voice comforting Kimberly.

"Caro! Kimmie! What's wrong?"

"Looks like Kimberly's awake," Jasentha said with satisfaction.

"And unhurt," Catfish added. "She's squalling like an angry cat, instead of a wounded bird."

His words were confirmed a few minutes later when Caro yelled to the group that Kimberly was ready to be pulled up. The smaller woman was dirty and hungry, but otherwise unharmed. Her mental state wasn't nearly as stable as her physical one. As soon as she was hauled to the top, Kimberly flung herself into Wyatt's arms and once more broke into hysterical tears.

Wyatt folded Kimberly in his arms and held her tight as she tried to talk and cry at the same time. "It was Morgan," she sobbed. "He lowered me down there because... because..." A new onslaught of tears.

Wyatt held her tighter, but he had no time to try to decipher her disjointed story. All he could think of was Caro still at the bottom of that pit. No matter that Kimberly was someone he'd grown up with, no matter that she seemed to be accusing Morgan. He couldn't bear the thought of Caro alone down there in the dark. He motioned Jasentha to join him at the pulley and passed the weeping Kim to Catfish.

"Take care of her, Catfish. Try to find out what's going on with Morgan. I need to get Dr. Hartlan up before the rain starts flooding the caves."

"Oh, so we're back to *Dr. Hartlan* now, not Caro?" Jasentha asked with a smirk.

"Your manners do your parents shame. Now shut the hell up and pull," Wyatt ordered.

"Like your manners are any better. Well, Sheriff, I'll pull, but you'd better pull, too. Catfish isn't helping, and your friend down there weighs a ton!"

A few minutes later Caro was pulled from the pit. Wyatt stared at the broken pieces of skeleton shoved into the spare sections of her backpack.

Jasentha shook her head at the sight, but said nothing.

Wyatt allowed himself the luxury of speech. "You and that damn skeleton!"

"Not all of it! Just a few shards to keep as evidence." Caro pushed back the metal helmet, where an indentation from the inner hat band was visible on her forehead. Wyatt reached out to smooth it away, but Caro thought he was after the shards.

"Hands off! This poor skeleton—what hasn't been smashed into a million pieces down in the pit—has already been roughed up enough."

Wyatt's hand dropped, but not his temper. "There were only two of us hauling you up, you fool! You could've been killed!"

"I said it was only a few pieces!" Caro yelled back.

"You..." *You scared me half to death! The rope could have broken! I could have lost you!*

The thunder accompanying another flash of lightning drowned out his next words. It didn't matter. He pulled her close and held her even tighter than he'd held Kimberly, so tight her harness pressed its outline into his chest, so tight he could feel her heart beating against his. He could have stood that way forever, but Jasentha once again took charge.

"We have to get back to the mine before the rain starts. Stow the gear now, or we'll be going home on a stretcher, instead of our feet."

That broke whatever spell Caro's presence in his arms had woven. They separated, Wyatt to put his miner's hat on Kimberly, Caro to be unharnessed by Jasentha. The gear was packed just as a light rain started, and they were hurrying as fast as they could to the cleft that was the connecting spot between the elevated surface and the natural caves. They left the caves for the mine only seconds before the downpour began. And had their feet back on the guano-filled lower level of The Silver Dollar Mine just as water started streaming down the incline.

Despite the filth under their feet and the foul smell as water mixed with dried guano, all of them, Jasentha included, sank down into the muck for a much-needed rest. Wyatt found himself with Kimberly in his lap, her shaking arms around his neck, her face buried in his shoulder. He stroked the hair that was below the miner's hat, wished the curling red locks were a straight brunette, and hated himself for wishing Caro was in his arms when his friend Kimberly was suffering. When his brother was missing. But Caro had somehow become just as important as family and old friends. Maybe more so…

After a while Kimberly raised her head. "Morgan…"

"What about Morgan, sweetheart?" Wyatt asked. The oft-used endearment now sounded strange on his lips. Suddenly he knew he would never be able to call Kimberly that again. Kimberly didn't notice his distraction. She was ready to talk and nothing would stop her.

"He's crazy, Wyatt. Crazy! He got into trouble with his jewelry store. No one wanted to buy his gold work and—"

"What gold work?" Wyatt asked sharply. "Morgan makes turquoise jewelry."

"He wanted to get into the wedding market. But I guess his gold bands and diamond engagement rings were too expensive for Tombstone."

"Diamonds? Hoo-ee, Wyatt, you didn't tell us Morg was into diamonds!" Catfish said.

"I didn't know."

"He *was* into diamonds," Kimberly repeated. "He had a jewelry consignment shipped to Phoenix, only no one there wanted them, either. He was in debt, so he mortgaged…he mortgaged…"

"The ranch. I know, Kimberly."

Kimberly laid her hand on his cheek. Wyatt permitted it

to remain. "Morgan decided to leave town rather than face you. I'm so sorry, Wyatt. I tried to stop him, but…" A fresh torrent of tears.

"Leave town!" Catfish burst out. Caro, Wyatt noticed, was silent. Like Jasentha, she was listening carefully.

Kim nodded, her hair bouncing from beneath the helmet. "He came to see me. Said he was taking all his jewelry to Los Angeles."

"Los Angeles!" Catfish burst out again. Wyatt threw the older man a quelling look.

"Keep going," he urged Kimberly gently.

She wiped her wet cheeks with the back of her hand and made a visible effort to calm herself.

"Morgan said there had to be a market for his jewelry in California. He was going to sell his rings, pay back the mortgage and have some money left over for…for us."

"But he left you in the pit!" Jasentha protested.

"Because I said I was going to tell you. He said he had something to show me first—something important. In the mine. So I followed him. We climbed up through the mine—to those caves. Oh, Wyatt, don't look like that. Morgan may be crazy, but he didn't hurt me!"

"So what do you call being thrown down a hole?" Catfish asked incredulously.

"He didn't *throw* me. He lowered me. Left me water, too. He said maybe some time alone to think things over would change my mind, make me want to go with him. He loved me. He'd show me the world. And he promised he'd be back for me later, when he'd squared things with you and Virgil about the mortgage."

"With me?"

"Yes. But he didn't say *when,* and I had no food, and I was so scared, and that awful, filthy skeleton was down there with me, and…and… He's insane, Wyatt! Insane!" Kimberly dissolved into another torrent of weeping.

Catfish and Jasentha both came to Wyatt's aid, patting her shoulder, holding her hands, fussing over her. Caro did not. She had risen, and stood some distance apart from everyone.

That's not like her. Wyatt knew of her empathy for people, her sense of fairness, her passion for life. *What's wrong?*

He carefully eased Kimberly over to Jasentha, then rose and joined Caro. She was looking up at the rivers of water racing down the inclined edges of the cave.

"What is it?" he asked.

"This storm." Caro dropped her voice to a soft, confidential level that only he could hear. "Awfully convenient, wouldn't you say?"

Wyatt was confused. "I don't understand."

"Can't climb back up in this weather to wait for Morgan now, can we?" she asked. "I doubt even Jasentha could do the climb in that downpour."

"Don't think I don't know it. What rotten luck!"

"Is it? Arizona weather this time of year is pretty predictable. Any native knows about the monsoons. I think there's something rotten in this cave, and it's not just the guano." Caro stared pointedly in Kimberly's direction.

"You think she's lying?"

"Don't you? Do you honestly believe your brother would kidnap someone—someone he loves—dump her down a shaft and just leave her there?"

"I... No. No way on this earth."

"Who's Kimberly protecting? Either Morgan or Hugh or..."

"Me?"

Caro shook her head. "No. No," she said again in a stronger voice. "Wyatt, I'm sorry I doubted you."

Relief at her confidence in him was short-lived. Caro

didn't know the *real* Wyatt. Or the real Morgan, either, for that matter.

"Morgan lied, that's a fact," Wyatt said. "But why do you suspect Kimberly?"

"I noticed something when I hooked her up to the harness. Something *you* would've noticed if you weren't so worried about Morgan." Caro gave him that sleek, satisfied smile he'd learned to recognize as pride in her work.

"What?"

"Look at her clothes."

Wyatt glanced over at Kimberly. "So?"

"According to Kimberly, she and Morgan traveled this way up to the surface."

"I still don't follow."

"Think back, Sheriff. Think about her appearance when you pulled her out of the shaft. Think about the way she smelled."

Wyatt frowned. Suddenly his breath caught as he relived Kimberly's throwing himself into his arms. He remembered her uniform smelling of cologne and dust and sweat.

But not of guano. There wasn't a smear, a stain, a single whiff of guano about her.

Caro's expression was grim as realization swept through him.

"Kimberly lied."

CHAPTER THIRTEEN

Saturday, early evening

THE EVENING RAIN was still falling as Caro stepped out of
Marta's motel-room shower. She could hear it beating on
the windows as she dressed, pulling on the spare clothing
she'd packed with the skull. Her soiled clothes were already
sealed and left outside for the laundry service. And she'd
cleaned her boots in the motel parking lot before coming
in out of the rain.

She was alone.

Marta had driven Kimberly, accompanied by Hugh, to
the local clinic to be checked out, and then driven the old
man and his granddaughter back to the ranch. Catfish, Luciano, the two ranch hands and Caro had caught a ride in
the other truck. Despite the violence of the storm, Wyatt
had ridden Arabian Pride back to the Silver Dollar; he'd
led Cactus Blossom.

Everyone had thought Caro's suggestion of unsaddling
the horses and turning them loose to find their own way
home blasphemous. "Leave his horses?" Catfish had
sounded as if she was asking him to drown kittens.

"The horses will go straight home," Caro insisted. "You
know that. If you ride, you could get struck by lightning!"

Wyatt had merely shrugged.

"City girl," one of the ranch hands had mumbled.

Then Wyatt had retrieved the mounts, unsaddled her
mare and thrown the tack in the back of the truck. Caro

had watched with disbelief as he mounted up, the tethered mare already close to the stallion's side, the rain already puddling in the brim of his Stetson.

"You can ride home with the hands, Caro. I'll see you later."

"If you don't get yourself killed first!"

Her words sounded heartless, but they were born of fear. Yet no one else seemed to be worried, not even the hands. Obviously this was a cowboy thing. If Caro knew that horses were herd animals, obviously these cowboys did, too. The horse's instinct to rejoin the herd was so strong that a loose, unattached animal would immediately seek out the shortest way home, an instinct that would prompt the mare to follow Wyatt's stallion. Caro wasn't concerned about her. But any rider could be a target for Arizona's monsoon lightning...

The drive back was silent, and the hands had worn dour expressions. She knew that their frowns weren't merely disapproval of her for "abandoning" her mount; they were in a bad mood because the search for Morgan had been called off. Lightning wasn't the only danger the searchers faced. The monsoon rains caused flooding above and *below* the ground. The caves, their deeper shafts already flooded since the end of Tombstone's boom days, became more dangerous than usual.

Dangerous to the searchers. Dangerous to Morgan. Caro was deeply worried about him *and* Wyatt, and the atmosphere in the truck was not reassuring. She was glad to be dropped off at the hotel. Luciano politely offered to take her back to the Silver Dollar, but Caro had, no less politely, refused.

"Perhaps you could have someone pick me up in a couple of hours?" she suggested. "I have some things to take care of first." She wanted time alone to collect her thoughts—and the suitcase full of evidence.

Caro finished dressing, ran a quick brush through her freshly shampooed hair and then turned on the heat in the room. The ride back had been cold.

She needed limber fingers for what she was about to do.

Caro was deep in her work when she heard the sound of a key turning in the lock. She looked up as Marta walked in. "Welcome back, stranger. I was wondering when I'd hear from you. Any word on Morgan?"

"Afraid not. The rain's keeping everyone grounded. Even Wyatt."

Caro nodded, then returned to her task. "So they kept you a long time?"

"Not really. Catfish and I stopped for a cup of coffee, then we decided we might as well order dinner since we hadn't eaten, then—"

"I meant, did the clinic and Kimberly's doctor keep you a long time?"

"Oh." Marta blushed. "Them." She left her wet purse and too-large raincoat—a raincoat Caro suspected had come from Catfish—in the bathroom.

"How *is* Kimberly?" Caro prompted.

"Calm. Unhurt. At home. And milking her experience for all it was worth."

Caro raised one eyebrow.

"Oh, all right, I'm sorry. She had a tough time of it, but she's fine now. She needs some backbone."

"Like yours," Caro said over her shoulder. "You've got more backbone than just about anyone I've ever worked with."

"Good thing, too," Marta said briskly. "Or my husband would've driven me crazy years ago. He sure isn't…" She paused.

"Catfish?"

Caro didn't bother to hide her smile. "Marta, I've seen the way you look at him."

"He's in his seventies. That's a good twenty years older than me!" Marta said indignantly. "Besides, I'm a married woman. Just because my husband cheated on me doesn't mean I intend to stoop to his level."

"*Looking* never hurt anyone, married or not," Caro replied.

"I'm a little too old to be staring at some sheriff packed into his jeans. Not like *some* women."

"I wasn't talking about the sheriff."

"Well, I wasn't talking about Catfish." Marta deliberately changed the subject. "So, what are you doing here?"

"I'm organizing the few remaining tools I have and repacking the evidence." Caro gestured toward the open suitcase. "I'm heading back to the Silver Dollar and what's left of my lab. My ride should be here in fifteen minutes. I think it's about time we found out exactly what our mystery man looks like."

Marta reached for her purse. "Count me in."

It was Catfish himself who came to pick up Marta and Caro. The rain was still falling, and the two women were glad to be back in the snug confines of The Silver Dollar's ranch house. A friendly fire was going, just warm enough to dispel the damp and welcome the three wet travelers.

Wyatt was waiting for them. A quick cup of coffee in front of the fire to dry off, then all four trooped up to Caro's makeshift lab.

"Thanks for the coffee," Caro murmured to Wyatt as they climbed the stairs. "Any word on Morgan yet?"

"Not a thing. Not one damn thing."

Caro gently placed her hand on his arm. He let it rest there until they reached the landing, his face still grim. She could think of nothing else to say.

Once in the room, Caro took a seat and got to work.

"I tried to fix or replace as many of your tools as possible," Wyatt said. "If you need anything else..." He looked so dispirited, with such an uncharacteristically defeated air about him, that Caro impulsively suggested, "Why don't you stay? Marta's going to help, and there's enough room for you and Catfish if we move the table.

Wyatt—and Catfish, as well—didn't need to be asked twice. A few minutes later, the four were comfortably situated and watching Caro begin her work with the clay.

"What are you doing?" Catfish asked. "Packing the skull in clay? I thought you used plaster to protect the evidence."

"I'm not protecting the skull. I'm re-creating the face of the man this belonged to."

Everyone stared, fascinated, as Caro measured the thickness of clay she'd used to re-create a facial muscle with her calipers. "This is a fairly new science. What happens is that—"

"—Forensic experts re-create the victim's face using precise, gender-adjusted formulas for muscles, cartilage and teeth," said Marta. "And it's all done in the same layers as the muscles are found, only in reverse, of course."

"You know about this?" Caro asked in amazement when Marta stopped for a breath.

"Oh, yes. I loved *Gorky Park*. Saw it twice."

"You and Catfish..." Wyatt murmured.

"What *about* us?" Marta bristled defensively.

"Catfish likes crime movies, too," Wyatt said.

Marta swiveled toward Catfish. "I always read the books first. For instance, much as I liked the movie, I preferred *Gorky Park* as a book."

Only half-listening, Caro studied the skull's face, frowned and added a pinch more clay around the eyes. "Like to help, Marta?" she offered.

Marta backed away. "Oh, no. I couldn't. I didn't go to college. I was just a mother and homemaker."

"A good, honest profession," Wyatt said.

"And one that probably taught you more about life than my classes ever did, so don't sell yourself short," Caro said.

"Baked many pies?" Catfish asked.

Caro grinned. *He's not here to watch my technique, that's for sure.*

"I've won ribbons for my pies," Marta said proudly. "They're all homemade, too. None of those box mixes."

"Then you're hired." Caro tossed Marta a chunk of modeling clay. "Go ahead and work that for me until it's soft. Pretend you're kneading bread dough."

"Do you know how to cook?" Wyatt asked Caro.

"Yep. But I don't do it often."

"Whyever not?" Marta's voice was curious.

"Same reason I don't watch crime movies. I just don't have time."

"What do you do for meals?" Wyatt asked. "Go out for dinner with your boyfriend?"

Caro almost blushed. *It appears Catfish isn't the only one not interested in my clay.*

Catfish winked at her. "I think the good sheriff's fishing, Doc."

"And I think you and I should have another cup of coffee," Marta said firmly, rising to her feet and pulling Catfish with her. "Just holler if you need anything, boss."

Marta tossed the lump of clay to Wyatt, then the older couple left. Caro continued with her work.

"To answer your question, Sheriff—no, I don't often go out for dinner. I mostly raid my parents' house for leftovers."

"That's not very appetizing—especially when you're eating alone. *Are* you eating alone?"

"Subtlety isn't your strong point, is it," Caro said, secretly pleased at his question.

"No, it's not. So—are you?"

She looked him squarely in the face. "Most of the time, yes. I'm afraid my job frightens some people off. *Especially* guys who don't work in law enforcement. You know what one of my dates told me? He said dating me was like dating an undertaker."

Wyatt's eyes glittered with anger. "Then he was a fool, and a mannerless fool to boot."

"Well, I had to forgive him. I'd come home that day smelling of formaldehyde." She shrugged. "Face it, I don't have a pretty job. But it's mine, and I'm not giving it up."

"I'd never ask you to give up anything."

Caro didn't know what to say to that. *Is he trying to tell me something? But we've only known each other three days.*

She held out her hand, and Wyatt passed her the lump of softened clay. "Were you able to ask Kimberly anything?" Caro asked.

"You mean like why she was lying? No. If she lied to us before, she'll lie to us again. I'd prefer not to tip our hand."

Caro found that she liked the way he said "us" and "our." It seemed final proof that they were a team now. She sliced off an excess portion of clay with her scraper, then carefully smoothed over the area with water from a bowl. "My guess is that she's protecting someone—either an Ellis or a Bodine. Someone's hiding a secret—one I suspect goes all the way back to Tombstone's Wild West days. And I'd bet my last pair of boots that this old skeleton holds the key."

"I can't argue with that."

"I'll have to see how Marta's doing with those background checks I asked for." Caro added a little more water to the lump, then tossed Wyatt a clean, wet hand cloth.

"I'll get her," he said. "Would you like some more coffee?"

"Please."

Shortly after Marta and Catfish rejoined her, Wyatt reappeared with a fresh pot of coffee and a hot plate. While he set that up, Caro asked Marta about the background checks.

"No skeletons in the closet yet. I mean—" Marta broke off and stared at the clay-and-bone mosaic. "I think I've been listening to your bad jokes too long."

"They do tend to rub off," Caro said with a quick smile. "But there *has* to be some dirt somewhere. Skip the financial checks for now. I'll have a friend of mine in Phoenix do them by computer."

"I can easily handle those," Wyatt said.

"Thanks. That'll free Marta—"

"And me!" Catfish chimed in, his eyes on Marta, not Caro.

"All right." Caro continued, "I'd like the two of you to go four generations back and get me whatever photos you can find of the Bodines and the Ellises."

"You think this—" Wyatt pointed at the skull "—belongs to one of our families?"

"It has to. It's the only thing that makes sense. If we can match a face to a photo, we might be able to make a dent in this case."

Marta's eyes glinted with comprehension. "There are all those Camillus Fly photographs. I saw hundreds of them—in Fly's Photography Gallery. Plus, I've looked through lots of the books publishing his work. And of course there's the display of his photographs at the Old Court house. There's even before and after pictures of criminals sentenced to die by hanging."

Caro shivered. "And people say *I* have a grisly job. So, how many photographs do you think we'd have to search through?" she asked.

"Fly was a prolific photographer even by today's standards."

"That's right," Wyatt put in. "He took over five thousand photographs just of Geronimo and the Apaches."

Caro was flabbergasted. "Using those old cameras?"

Marta nodded. "He and his wife developed thousands of photographs of Tombstone and the old mines around here."

"I've seen some of those, Marta, but I need shots of faces, not old mines. They won't help."

"They might," Wyatt contradicted. "Fly was a would-be miner who never had the luck with silver that he had with photographs. Even though he built his business into the largest photographic studio between San Francisco and El Paso, he never lost his fascination with miners."

"You think this poor old guy is connected with The Silver Dollar Mine?" Catfish asked.

"Yes. And I'd bet Fly had photos of The Silver Dollar Mine," Caro said.

"It's going to be a lot of work, looking through all those photographs," Wyatt warned, but Marta wasn't discouraged.

"At least we're here in Tombstone. What better place to buy collections and reproductions of his work? Or to look through the archives? I can start as soon as you say the word."

"You mean as soon as I finish the skull." Caro dipped her fingers in the water bowl again. "It's going to take me most of the night."

"Then I'd better get us something to eat," Marta said briskly. "Sheriff?"

"Help yourself to the kitchen. Catfish, you know the way."

The sandwiches and fruit arrived about twenty minutes later. Marta also took responsibility for the coffee, making a third pot and then a fourth. All the while, the skull beneath Caro's fingers slowly and steadily took on a life of its own.

She stopped only once to rub her stiff neck. Wyatt stepped in and kneaded her shoulders—which Marta and Catfish seemed to find inordinately interesting, to Caro's annoyance.

"Hey, he's doing it for therapeutic purposes only," she said.

"Sure, Doc." Catfish sniggered, but one dark glance from Wyatt shut him up.

"Of course she won't get a good re-creation if her arms are stiff," Marta said loyally, although her eyes were twinkling, as well.

"Be quiet, both of you, and let me get back to work," Caro scolded, but she let Wyatt finish, enjoying the sure touch of his hands. They were gentle and supple with a restrained strength and an instinctive feel.

He's probably just like that in bed, Caro thought, then felt her face grow hot. She forced her mind back to business—but not without a grateful, "Thanks, Wyatt." She took another swallow of coffee and resumed her clay sculpting.

The hours ticked on. Catfish was the first to bow out, electing to get his "forty winks" on the couch downstairs in front of the fire.

Wyatt left next on police business; cattle had gotten loose during the earlier storm and wandered into someone's backyard.

That left Caro and Marta.

"Hey, you're getting close to the end, aren't you?" Marta said around three in the morning, when no bone was left showing in the face. "That's really something. Is this the way our guy was supposed to look?"

"Well, pretty close, if I've done my job right." Caro rose from her chair, back aching. "I've made the eyes gray, since we have no idea what color Mr. Bones's eyes really were. I still have to do the hair. Wish I had a clue."

Marta stared at the head. "Why don't you just use black? It's a neutral color—like gray—and the photographs I'll be looking at will be black-and-white, anyway."

"Hey, that's a good idea," Caro said.

"Even blondes can show up looking as though they have dark hair in old black-and-whites," Marta pointed out.

"You're pretty knowledgeable about this. Lucky for me."

"Frank thinks it's stupid to be so interested in old pictures." She paused and said reflectively, "You know, I haven't missed the louse one bit."

"Mmm." Caro rummaged through her wig bag for a man's black wig with longish hair, as it was worn in the Old West. "If you don't mind me asking, have you made any progress with Frank?"

Marta sighed. "He says he doesn't want a divorce. He says the affair is over. He wants me to forgive him and come back home."

Something in the tone of Marta's voice made Caro ask, "You don't want to? Forgive him, that is?"

"I haven't decided if I want to go home to him. But that's my problem, not yours. I'm here as long as you need me." The other woman's face was sad but determined.

Caro reached for Marta's hand and gave it a sympathetic squeeze. "I'm sorry."

"Don't be. I haven't thought about Frank all day, until now." Marta released Caro's hand, and gestured her back to work. "You know, maybe I'm better off without him. This is the most freedom I've had in years."

"Trust me, being alone isn't all it's cracked up to be." Caro picked up one of the straight pins that would anchor the hair to the skull.

"Neither is being with Frank," Marta said bitterly. "He isn't the man I married—not anymore. He's changed, and not for the better.'' She rose and walked purposely toward the coffeepot. ''You want another cup?''

''No, I'm almost done, and then I'm calling it quits. Why don't you get some sleep? Lie down in my room—it's next door.''

''Sounds good to me.'' Marta yawned hugely. ''What about the skull? Are you going to just leave it here, or should I take it with me tomorrow and photograph it for you?''

''I think I'll leave it here. It should be safe enough with Morgan gone.'' She felt a new stab of fear as she said the words. Fear for Morgan—and for Wyatt. She forced herself to sound as efficient as possible. ''You could photograph it once the clay's set—not before. I don't want to risk ruining it.''

''Yes, the poor old thing had enough...trauma the last time, with you and the sheriff rolling around on the floor.''

''I explained about that!''

''Sure you did.''

Caro paused in the middle of making one last-minute adjustment. ''You know, that Catfish is a handsome man. Do you know if he's seeing anyone? Do you want me to ask him?''

''Oh, all right, I can take a hint. Good night, boss. I'll see you in the morning.''

''Good night, Marta.''

Caro was left alone. She fussed a bit more with the hair until she felt satisfied with her efforts. Then she tidied the lab, cleaning up clay, cleaning her tools and lining them up on the table, since she no longer had a toolbox to pack them in.

With one last yawn, she stretched, pushed her chair under the table and admired the head one last time. It was remarkably lifelike; so lifelike, in fact, that Caro spoke aloud.

"There. All done. I don't know who you really are, mister, but I hope I've done you justice."

"If you'd lived a couple hundred years ago, Doc, they would've burned you at the stake."

Caro whirled around. "Wyatt!" She smiled. "I'll take that as a compliment."

They both studied her re-creation. "If we're lucky, we'll be able to identify this man soon. There must be lots of people with roots in early Tombstone. *Someone* has to know who this poor soul is. It's our job to find out."

"There's no need. I can tell you who he is right now." Wyatt's jaw set in a granite line.

"That man is Lem Bodine."

Sunday morning, early

IT WAS STILL RAINING, still gloomy in the predawn glow. Most of the storm's fury had abated, but there was a thin drizzle and the remains of a wind that continued to make horse's tails and manes whip about.

But Wyatt wasn't outside tending them. For the first time in a long time, he let Luciano and the rest of the hands feed the stock without him. He needed a chance to think.

Wyatt gazed out the window. He wore old jeans, his feet and chest bare, a half-drunk cup of coffee in his hand. He watched the brood mares off in the distance, most of the herd crowded under the metal canopies that the horses preferred to their stifling barns in the summer. A few hardy mares grazed in the drizzle.

Kimberly was home with Hugh, since Jamie, the deputy who'd worked last night, had promised to stand in as temporary dispatcher. Caro was sleeping in. He remembered her shocked face.

"Lem Bodine? Your great-grandfather? The one who died in a cattle stampede?"

"Lem Bodine, who had fallen—or been pushed—to his death," Wyatt corrected.

"But...are you sure it's him?"

"Caro, I'd recognize that face anywhere." He shook his head in admiration. "My God, you are good."

Wyatt remembered how her face had flushed with pride at his words, but as usual, she'd remained her logical, practical self. "Maybe if I could see a photo, I'd know for myself," she said. "I need one for evidence, anyway. Do you have one?"

"No, but there are some of Fly's in the Old Court House. They're too fragile to be removed from the glass cases."

"I'll need at least a reproduction of it," Caro had said.

"You can take a photo of the photo," Wyatt suggested.

"Both my cameras were wrecked."

"You can borrow mine."

"Thanks. You know," Caro mused, "it would be better to have the case open—less reflection from the glass."

"You're bonded, aren't you?"

"Yes."

"Then I'll give you the keys to the building. Including one for the display case."

"Thanks—again," she'd said gratefully. "I'll do the Old Court House photos in the morning. Marta's going to photograph the skull. In the meantime, is there someplace safe I can put it?"

"Store it in my private safe. Let me buzz Luciano. He'll show you where it is and how to change the combination. Then only you will have access to it. Good enough?"

"Yes." She'd smiled. Luciano had arrived a moment later and the skull had been carefully transferred to the safe. Then she'd yawned again, accepted Wyatt's offer to sleep in Morgan's room since Marta was fast asleep in hers, and left. She wasn't there to hear him say to Luciano, "Keep close watch. I don't want anything happening to that skull or to Caro Hartlan.'' *Especially* Caro Hartlan.

Now the sky glowed with the last of the dawn. Wyatt hoped Caro was still sleeping. He wished *he* could sleep.

His mind was weary from his racing thoughts, and his heart was sick with worry over Morgan. He still had no idea where to look for him or why Kimberly had lied. Were the two in this together? The whole town knew how Morgan felt about Kimberly.

And who'd been dragging the skeleton around? Who'd displayed it on Boothill in the first place?

Wyatt had plenty of work to do, but he was having difficulty concentrating on it. Instead, he was remembering the feel of Caro's body against his, above his, below his, strong, supple, with both a woman's tenderness and a stubbornness that intrigued every male part of him. If Marta and Catfish hadn't walked in on them at the motel and then played chaperon tonight…

What? Would he have declared his surprising craving for her? Ever-constant exasperation with her? His admiration for her independence, determination, intelligence?

He desperately wanted to wake her up—ostensibly to discuss the case—but his watch told him it was probably too early for that. She'd been working late into the night.

Caro Hartlan. She didn't miss much and that meant she was a threat to someone. Maybe two or three someones. And now the way she'd re-created the face of Lem Bodine—it was enough to set his nerves on edge, make him fear for her safety.

Wyatt set his coffee on the windowsill and rubbed his aching forehead. It was time for some answers, answers only a local could get. Caro had shown him the way; it was time for Wyatt to take the lead again.

For starters, why *was* Kimberly lying? Why had the seriously ill Hugh driven to the mine? Was Morgan in on the plot, whatever the plot was? Was there really gold hidden somewhere on this land? And most important, would he be able to keep them all alive?

The sun burned through the mist with desert power, desert brightness, and suddenly the gloom of the morning was fighting a losing battle. Renewed vigor flowed through Wyatt's veins. It was a good day to search for answers, and he'd begin with Hugh Ellis.

The sun was just rising as Wyatt set off for The Bar E Ranch. He was travelling there, as usual, on horseback, although he wasn't riding his favorite stallion. Pride had been given a well-deserved rest. He rode a younger gelding, one whose physical configuration was too flawed for breeding, but whose temperament and smooth, easy gait was a relaxing change.

The air felt clean and brisk after the rain, another welcome change, but the ground was only slightly damp. The gelding tossed his head and pricked his ears with cheerful excitement. Wyatt loosened the reins in answer to the animal's mood, letting him canter at his own pace.

The Bar E ranch house was almost deserted, not surprising this early in the morning. The hands were out with the horses; the cook and household help hadn't yet arrived. It was Hugh himself who answered the door.

"Morning, Hugh. I thought you'd still be resting," Wyatt said.

"I'll have plenty of time for that when they plant me six feet deep. Now get inside before you let in half the stable flies."

Wyatt stepped into the hallway.

"Coffee?" Hugh asked.

"Thanks, but no. I'm here on business."

"Figured as much when you didn't hang up your hat."

The hat rack by the door was used by social callers. Those who kept hat in hand signaled to the host that the visit wouldn't be long, or politely waited to be told if it was a good time to stay.

Here I am, Hugh, hat in hand, looking for answers.

Hugh coughed and wheeled his chair over to a well-worn but inviting couch, and waved him into it. "Sit down a spell, anyway."

Wyatt did. "How's Kimberly?"

"Fine. That girl's like a cat. She always lands on her feet. Tough as nails."

"The Ellises always were."

"Not all of us, Wyatt. Not all of us." The older man looked terrible this morning, face pale, breathing ragged despite the oxygen line to his nose. But Wyatt knew his sympathy wouldn't be appreciated. He waited silently until Hugh had the breath to speak again.

"Any word on Morgan?" Hugh asked after a moment.

"Nothing."

"Not even from the forensics woman?"

"She has some ideas," Wyatt said, remembering the likeness of Lem Bodine he'd walked in on last night.

Hugh's gaze was piercing. "You like that little gal, don't you?"

"Dr. Hartlan's a first-rate forensic scientist," Wyatt said firmly. "Tombstone's lucky to get her."

"That's not what I meant, young man, and you know it." Hugh looked unhappy, but his words were matter-of-fact. "Maybe if you settled down with someone, Kim would find someone else."

"I wish she'd settle for Morgan. He's always loved her."

"And Kimberly's always loved you, Wyatt. There'll never be anyone else for her as long as you're unattached."

"I couldn't marry my sister—that's what Kimberly is to me."

"Two men and one woman in love, and nary a match among the three. A sad state of affairs for a dying man."

Hugh wheezed, then broke into such a fit of coughing that Wyatt rose from his seat, worried.

"Let me get Kim," he said. "I'll—"

"No," Hugh choked out. "She's sleeping. There's nothing anyone can do for me, anyway. You and I both know that."

Wyatt sat down again. Deep inside he recognized the taint of evil. Hugh was hiding something; something Wyatt suspected he wanted to share. But just as he was about to speak, Wyatt heard Kimberly's voice in the distance.

"Hugh, if that's Wyatt's horse tied outside, tell him I'll be right down!"

Hugh's face turned even paler, and Wyatt hadn't thought that was possible. He half rose in his seat, alarmed, as Hugh gasped, "I want you to ride through the west pasture!"

"Hugh, I—"

"Do it! Make the time! One of the hands spotted—"

Both men heard the sound of steps on the stairs. Wyatt rose to his feet. Hugh wheeled over to Wyatt's side.

"—Caro Hartlan's baseball cap. Go get it, Wyatt!"

Wyatt frowned. Was the old man's illness affecting his mind? "Hugh, I don't care about some hat. I have a brother to find, work to do!"

"Go now, before Kimberly gets here!" Wheelchair or not, Hugh all but pushed Wyatt out the door. "Remember, the Bar E's west pasture! Hurry!"

Confused, Wyatt left, more from fear of upsetting the man's delicate health than because he'd finished his questions. Something was wrong with Hugh's statement. It smacked of an out-and-out lie, and this from a man who'd been like a father to him. First Morgan, then Kimberly, now Hugh...

Is there no one I can trust?

Then he realized—Caro Hartlan was the only person who hadn't deceived him. She might have suspected him at first, she might even have withheld information from him, but he'd never once caught her in a lie. He was sure he never would. Wyatt recognized the golden vein of good in her that nothing could ever tarnish.

Caro Hartlan and I have some serious talking to do, Wyatt decided. *But first, I'm going to ride through the Bar E's west pasture.*

KIMBERLY ELLIS stood at the window, watching Wyatt swing up onto his horse and ride off at a good clip. Her face was sad, her eyes dark with emotion. "Good heavens, Grandfather, what have you done?"

"What I should've done years ago. I'm an old man, Kim. I want to die with a clean conscience."

"So you told Wyatt?"

"I told him nothing. Nothing!"

"You might as well have! You pointed him in the right direction!"

"Wyatt's a good man. He'll do the right thing."

Kimberly pivoted to face him. "This could be a disaster for all of us! You, me, Morgan, *all* of us! It could ruin my parents' reputation and…and their business, and they have nothing to do with this. We'll all be ruined! Have you ever thought of that?"

Hugh buried his face in his hands. For once Kimberly didn't rush to his side. Instead, she went back to watching Wyatt, the gelding taking him ever farther toward the horizon.

"No good can come of this, Hugh."

"Please, Kimmie," the old man begged. "I had to do it!"

Her eyes glittered with tears. "And now it's too late."

CHAPTER FOURTEEN

Still Sunday morning

WYATT CURSED the distance to the west pasture and blessed the gelding's high spirits and willingness to run.

What was out here? What had made Hugh so frantic?

Thank goodness he'd ridden out on horseback. In most of off-road Arizona, it was still the fastest way to cover any distance.

His horse snorted and increased the speed of his canter; Wyatt made no attempt to rein him in. Whatever was waiting for him in the west pasture, it was best to find out quickly. As long as it wasn't another body—like Morgan's. His heart raced in fear. Everything was so puzzling.

And then, suddenly, it wasn't.

Wyatt pulled his horse to an abrupt halt and dismounted. If it hadn't rained, if Hugh hadn't urged him toward the west pasture, he would never have noticed it.

The fierce desert sun often baked the land to a uniform hue. Time and heat could fade the most vivid of colors. But this soil was fresh and damp from the rain, and the sun was just beginning to peek over the east horizon. The dark patches stood out vividly against the light buff color of the desert floor, despite the cattle scattered over the area, grazing on the sparse grass. And because of the rain, Wyatt could smell the faint, uremic smell emanating from those patches—patches that glittered in the sun.

Guano! And gold!

The horse tugged impatiently at the reins as Wyatt hunkered down to run his fingers through the soil. Flecks of gold dust clung to his fingers, held fast in the mucky texture of the guano.

Wyatt grabbed a handful and stood, bringing his palm close to his eyes. Understanding ripped through him like a .45-caliber shell. Caro was right. Someone was mining gold from The Silver Dollar Mine! And hiding the tailings under hundreds of cattle feet. If the rain hadn't released the smell of guano, he would never have suspected a thing.

But who was doing the mining? Kimberly? Hugh? Morgan? All three of them? No, that couldn't be right. Morgan was too busy with his jewelry-making, with his store and the ranch and the occasional stint as deputy. Hugh? Perhaps—but then why had Hugh suddenly decided to drop such a broad hint? Why hadn't he told him the whole story? What was Hugh afraid of?

Suddenly Wyatt thought of the number of across-the-border laborers he'd seen in Tombstone recently. They were easily noticed—not locals, not tourists. Work was often scarce in Mexico, and Arizona ranchers employed many legal border-crossers. Although most spoke little or no English, as a rule they were hardworking, honest men determined to support their families. Wyatt himself employed them, both on a temporary basis and as permanent help—like Luciano.

But this wasn't the time of year ranchers needed extra help with calving or branding. If someone wanted a labor force—a labor force that spoke little enough English to believe they were doing honest work...

It was a definite possibility. The gold was being mined by someone. What if that someone made regular trips across the border—avoiding the highway checkpoints—and exchanged the gold for cash in Mexico? Maybe even for American dollars... Mining equipment could be found.

Mine pumps could be bought. A labor force could be amassed. Mexico was, after all, a mining country.

But who was the ringleader? Who was the master deceiver? And how would he find out?

Wyatt threw the damning clump of evidence down with such violence that his good-natured gelding skittered nervously. He swore and clamped down so hard on the reins that the leather cut into his palms. The more he learned about this case, the more confused he became.

The motive—greed for gold—was simple enough. But Morgan wouldn't hide the discovery if the gold was from the Silver Dollar. Morgan would haul it in and spend it like a shot. Could the metal come from Bar E land? But where was it, and who was mining it? A Bodine? An Ellis? Both? Neither? The only two people in the clear were Caro and her assistant, Marta.

Wyatt's brain kicked into overdrive. *I'm missing something. Something I've seen, something I've discarded earlier—but shouldn't have.*

He remounted. He couldn't retrieve the information yet, but he'd remember it soon. He knew he would. His mind habitually filed away everything—everything a criminal had done. It allowed him to anticipate that criminal's next actions. Something told him that Morgan, not Kimberly or Hugh, was the weak link here. Morgan was the key to this puzzle. *I have to find him!*

It was time to review this case, time to find that vital information he'd bypassed. *And I know just the woman to help me do it.*

CARO FINISHED PACKING and boxing the completed skull, which she'd retrieved earlier from the safe. Marta shook her head in dismay. She had awakened soon after sunrise, alert despite her few hours' sleep, and detailed the ever-willing Catfish to help her prepare a substantial breakfast, since Cook wouldn't arrive until later. Then she'd shot two rolls of film to record the face on the skull.

"I don't know about this, boss. I don't think I should leave you just yet."

"I need you in Tucson." Caro tossed the wrapping tape on her work table. "My car's ready. The garage called—they open early and we can pick it up now. We'll get Catfish to drive us there. I want you to take this skull and all your film to Tucson."

"But you won't have any backup here in Tombstone!"

Caro ignored Marta's protest. "Develop the film in Tucson, then courier the negatives and the skull to my parents. We can start searching through the record books when you come back with the prints. Let me get you my keys." She rose from her seat.

"Where will you be?" Marta asked curiously.

"At the Old Court House. I understand they have some mining archives. I want to track down the picture of Lem Bodine and do a little research on The Silver Dollar Mine. You can drop me off there on your way."

"Aren't you at least going to have some breakfast? You should eat. I had a good nap, but you've been up most of the night."

"Maybe later."

"Caro, I worry about you. Listen, Catfish is working at Boothill later today. If you need any help…"

"I shouldn't. Ah, here're my keys. Come on, Marta, find Catfish and let's get rolling."

The drive from the ranch to downtown Tombstone was an easy one, enlivened by the banter between the older people. After a few more protests and words of caution from Marta and Catfish, Caro exited the truck. She'd asked that Catfish drop her off at the edge of town—she wanted a brisk walk and some fresh air. He beeped in farewell and was gone, headed for the garage.

The morning still smelled of last night's rain; the sun hadn't completely burned through the damp. In a few hours the freshness would be replaced by the familiar desert heat. Until then, Tombstone looked the way it did in nineteenth-century photographs. The rain had erased tire marks on the dirt sidestreets. The earliness of the hour meant no tourists and almost no cars. The boardwalks were silent, the hitching posts empty.

Caro felt as if she'd stepped into yesterday as she walked from the eastern edge of town down Fremont Street. Places and names from the past surrounded her. She passed the Pioneer Home Museum, then turned south down Fifth Street. She walked past the Oriental Bar, once a faro house that Wyatt Earp had owned a share in, now a crafts-and-jewelry shop. *Will I ever shop for a wedding ring with a man I want to spend the rest of my life with?*

The Crystal Palace, old Tombstone's most popular meeting spot, just across the street from the Oriental. *Will I ever gather with friends for a friendly chat, a chat about kids and dogs, instead of corpses and murderers?*

Caro rounded the corner and left Fifth for Allen Street. On the corner was the Bird Cage Theater, home of the Black Moriah, old Tombstone's only hearse, *the very hearse I threatened to destroy because I found myself in over my head. Is my whole life to be nothing more than a study of death?*

Next was Big Nose Kate's Saloon, named after Doc Holliday's girlfriend, the tough-as-nails "soiled dove" who risked her own neck in a noose by breaking him out of a Dodge City jail after Doc killed a card cheat. *Will someone ever love me enough to risk his life for me? And I for him?*

Then came the O. K. Corral, scene of the final big confrontation between organized crime and the law, between good and evil. *The law won that time, but will justice triumph again?*

She passed the sheriff's office. *Whose side are you on, Wyatt Bodine? I need to know once and for all. The law's? Or your family's?*

The sun rose even higher in the sky, and as businesses started to open, tourists and locals alike lined up for breakfast and coffee. Caro kept walking.

She left Allen street for the corner of Toughnut and Third. There she approached her final destination, the Old Court House.

She stopped to admire the building, its warm red bricks edged with larger, attractively contrasting beige ones. She admired the balconies, pillared entryway and churchlike steeple sheltering a small cupola. In front was a graceful oak tree almost as old as the building itself.

You almost didn't notice the hangman's platform in the walled exercise yard. Three rope nooses rose above high brick walls, the hemp's pale color stark against the turquoise morning sky. The desert breeze made the nooses tremble and sway.

Caro shivered.

For a moment, just a moment, she had the same eerie feeling of sin and shame and death she'd felt at the Bird Cage Theater. This was no frivolous tourist display. This was the site of trials, some just, some rigged. It was the site of executions, both deserved and undeserved. Caro could almost smell the sweat of the condemned men, hear the excitement of a town that closed businesses to watch, and sense the raw animal fear of death approaching.

Then a hand descended on her shoulder, and Caro jumped.

"Sorry. Didn't mean to startle you." Kimberly smiled, her expression apologetic above the spotless, starched beige of her uniform shirt. "Pretty grim sight, isn't it?"

Caro reined in her fancies. "No more so than the electric chair. I hate it all."

"You don't approve of the death penalty?"

"No! Do you?"

"Of course."

"Killing's still killing," Caro said tersely.

"I'm surprised by your opinion, considering all the murders you've worked on. Killers deserved to be killed. What if it was your child or your spouse who was murdered?"

Caro turned back to the Old Court House, where the three nooses still swayed in the breeze. "If I could be certain that every single convicted man or woman was guilty of the crime and sane while doing it, maybe I'd share your point of view. But I've seen too many deranged criminals, too many witless juries and too many clever lawyers to believe in perfect justice."

"You don't believe that suspects who're innocent go free?"

"No. Too often it's the other way around."

Now Kimberly seemed startled. Her face went a deathly pale, Caro studied her carefully. "You look like a deerskin dragged through the rocks," she said frankly. "Aren't you supposed to be resting? Yesterday must have been quite an ordeal for you."

"I'm...I'm fine. I just needed a good night's sleep."

"But still—"

"Wyatt needs me," Kimberly said fiercely. "Morgan's still missing, and last night's dispatcher needs to be relieved. He's been working overtime this morning because I had a late start."

"Then why aren't you at the sheriff's office?" Caro asked. "Why come after me?"

"Actually, I wanted to talk to Wyatt. He wasn't at the office or the ranch. I came over here to look for him."

"I thought the Old Court House was a historic site, not a working office."

"That's right, but Wyatt said something about you wanting to look up some old records. And the Court House doesn't open for another hour.'' Kimberly gestured toward the sign in front. ''You're too early.''

Caro read the sign carefully; it listed the hours and gave a short history of the building. In 1881 Arizona established Cochise County and named Tombstone as its seat. But the silver rush ended in 1886 with the flooding of most of its mines. Tombstone lost much of its population after that and as a consequence lost its status as county seat. The Old Court House sat empty for years—from 1929 until it was renovated in 1955—and reopened as a historical site and museum.

''Wyatt gave me a key and the code for the alarm system.''

''Oh. I didn't know that.'' Kimberly continued to stand there as Caro read the signpost a second time.

I know about all the silver mines that flooded back then, when ground water seeped into the shafts. But I wonder…has the ground water in The Silver Dollar Mine settled? Or is it being drained using modern technology? It was an intriguing question, and one Wyatt hadn't brought up.

''Care for a personally guided tour?''

''I…'' The nooses swung again in the wind and Caro felt a sudden foreboding. She'd never been one to ignore her instincts, and she didn't plan to start now. ''I wouldn't want to take any more of your time, Kimberly.''

''I don't mind.''

''But I do, especially after your ordeal yesterday. I'll just go on my own.''

Kimberly still hesitated. ''There's a lot of valuable artifacts in there.''

''I'm a registered law-enforcement investigator,'' Caro firmly reminded her. ''Bonded as well, which is why the

Sheriff gave me a key. Besides, didn't you say you needed to get to work?"

"I don't know…"

For some reason, Kimberly's obvious reluctance only made Caro more determined to do her research alone.

"Go ahead, check with the sheriff." Caro glanced pointedly toward the walkie-talkie on Kimberly's belt. "I don't mind waiting."

There was a pause, then Kimberly gave in. "I imagine it'll be all right."

"I hope you feel better soon," Caro said politely. "Tell the sheriff I said hello."

Kimberly nodded. Caro thought her smile looked a bit forced.

"Say hello to your assistant for me, too," Kimberly said. "Where is Marta, anyway? She's not at the hotel."

Word sure travels fast in this town! "She's out for breakfast, I imagine," was Caro's casual answer. "Why?"

"Catfish wanted me to ask."

This was the second time Caro had heard the woman lie. She managed a smile. "Oh, I suppose they'll hook up sooner or later."

"Maybe I should give Catfish a call. I'd better use the phone inside the Old Court House."

There was an expression in Kimberly's eyes that rang more than just warning bells in Caro's head. She reached for her mobile phone and held it out. "Here, save yourself the walk and use mine."

Kimberly blinked. "I had some business to discuss with him, too."

"Why don't you go sit in your car? That should be private enough. After yesterday, you really should pamper yourself."

"You're very kind." Kimberly's voice was too sweet. "But I guess I'll use the phone back at the sheriff's office."

"If you're sure..."

"I'm sure."

Caro refastened the phone to her belt as Kimberly finally left. She watched the other woman walk away, watched her get into the car, watched her drive off. Then she waited a few minutes to make certain Kimberly—and the gooseflesh on her neck—wasn't coming back.

Caro stepped inside and, cautious as always, locked the doors behind her before proceeding. The interior of the courthouse was cave-cool—the thick old bricks retaining the chill of last night's storm. Her footsteps echoed on the hardwood floors, the wood dark and polished with a century-old patina.

Straight ahead was the docent's desk and a stand of books and brochures. To the right was the period cubbyhole desk and original sheriff's office, plus other displays. Caro wandered through it, nothing in the photographs and displays really catching her eye. She left the sheriff's quarters and headed toward the courtroom.

The carefully handcrafted judge's bench, jurors' chairs, witness stand and bookshelves were works of art, a striking contrast to the primitive hangman's noose outside.

Caro's black humor reasserted itself. "Sorry, Your Honor," she said aloud, speaking to an invisible judge, "but I don't feel like lingering. I've been in too many courtrooms as it is."

Her words bounced off the high ceilings and echoed in the room. Suddenly they didn't sound funny to her. She was mentally tired and emotionally exhausted from seeing courtrooms and morgues and murder sites. And from interviewing men and women whose every word she questioned again and again. Was it asking too much to find someone she could trust? Someone she could spend a lifetime loving?

The face of Wyatt Bodine flashed in her mind.

Caro gave herself a shake. She was mooning over Wyatt E. Bodine like…like Kimberly Ellis! Time to act like Caro Hartlan. "Come on, get to work. Don't waste all that tuition money the folks spent on you." She stifled a yawn and pulled out the pencil and little spiral notebook she kept in her jeans pocket. The sooner she finished, the sooner she could get back to the ranch and take a nap.

"I'm getting too old for these all-nighters," she muttered to herself. Then she unfolded the floor plan she'd grabbed off the docent's desk on the way in, got her bearings and set off for the main display room.

The first thing that hit her as she entered it were the hundreds of black-and-white photos. Like everything in Tombstone, they were a study in contrasts. Exhibited were rich and poor, cultured and uneducated, decadent and decent. Pictures of prim, churchgoing women in yards of hand-sewn material appeared next to scantily clad prostitutes. Dirty, ragged miners with swaybacked, dispirited mules contrasted with elegantly dressed dandies in shining carriages drawn by prancing horses—all purchased with lucky silver ore.

And then there were the photos of hanged men, their swaying boots and final open-coffin poses recorded for all time.

Caro found the whole exhibit fascinating. It held the same gruesome pull as the Bird Cage Theater did. Horrific, yet mesmerizing. She had to force herself to concentrate on business, not emotions, and jotted down a few observations.

She headed decisively for the O. K. Corral exhibit and immediately noticed that the photos and drawings of the infamous shootout were all recent. Funny—you'd have thought that Camillus Fly, that most prolific of photographers even by modern standards, would've taken pictures of the incident and its characters.

But there were none. In fact, there was even a cryptic

note explaining that no photos of the incident were to be found—and no photos of the crime scene *after* the incident, either. This, despite the fact that Fly's studio stood next door to the O. K. Corral. By fair means or foul, Caro thought, someone had hidden, probably destroyed those photographs.

There were, however, plenty of photos of the Earps from shortly before and immediately after the infamous shooting. Caro quickly read the display narrative.

Wyatt Berry Stapp Earp, born March 19, 1848, was an athletic man, she learned, a boxer, frontiersman, buffalo hunter, railroad builder, freight hauler, miner. He was a family man, a man loyal to his brothers and sisters. He was a risk taker, a speculator, a gambler, a horse breeder and finally a sheriff.

He could keep order without gunplay, but never backed away from a fight. Not once was he ever shot or ill in his eighty-one years, a rare statement for those times. He lived by his own rules and his own code of conduct, not the code of the Old West, but his own. Always.

Caro studied the solemn Earp expression in all those portraits. She was positive that the ends of his signature handlebar mustache rarely twitched with silliness. Life was hard for lawmen.

And for law-women.

Fighting crime wasn't an easy life, but it was her choice. She only hoped the cost wouldn't be as high for her as it had been for Wyatt Earp. His family and friends had been easy targets, maimed or murdered because of his life's choice. It could happen to her just as well—a sad thing to contemplate, and another reason Caro stayed alone.

I need someone who can take care of himself—someone I wouldn't have to worry about. Someone like...

She didn't dare complete that thought. She hadn't even

known him for a week! And right now, she had work to do.

She left the section on the Earps and strolled over to the mining exhibit. She'd barely glanced at it when she froze.

There, in a group photograph of miners, was a familiar face.

Despite the graininess of the blowup, that face jumped out at her. Caro pressed her forehead and hands against the glass, slowly reading the lengthy narrative. She didn't have to read far. A name jumped out at her, just as the face had.

Her heart pounded. "Son of a desert jack, but I'm good," she said to herself.

The man in the photo, the man whose face she had reconstructed in clay, was indeed Lem Bodine.

CHAPTER FIFTEEN

CARO STUDIED the photo. No doubt about it. The man in the photograph and her clay face over bone were one and the same. She unlocked the glass case, pulled out Wyatt's camera and carefully inserted it through the opening.

As she took her shots, she marveled again at the photo. There was no question as to the identity of the skeleton, no question at all. Lem Bodine *had* to have been murdered and his remains hidden away. Lies had obviously been spread to protect the killer.

Caro rubbed her temples as she tried to make sense of a century-old crime. "Think this through, Caro," she told herself. "Slow and easy."

The Bodines wouldn't have killed their own father, would they? He was more than just the patriarch. He was the man who'd made the family fortune from cattle ranching when The Silver Dollar Mine had tapped out—the cattle that Wyatt Bodine had, two generations later, cashed into Arabians.

That left the Ellises with a motive. According to that dinner conversation, The Bar E Ranch *hadn't* made a fortune from cattle. Not then, not now, until Kimberly had taken over running the ranch. Suddenly, miraculously, she had it running in the black again.

From stolen gold that came from The Silver Dollar Mine? It was a definite possibility.

But why the skeleton's sudden appearance? Was it a warning from the Bar E? Or a cry for help from Morgan?

"I know why you were killed," Caro said to the photograph. "But I don't know for sure who did it. I suppose there's only one way to find out."

I'll have to go back to the mine.

The long-dead face of Lem Bodine stared back at her. For a moment it blurred, and she almost thought she could see Wyatt's eyes, instead, waiting, watching. Caro blinked, and Wyatt's face changed back to Lem's. She rubbed a hand across her tired eyes, and in a moment her blurry vision cleared. She deliberately turned her back and headed out of the room for the sun—and Wyatt Bodine.

For the first time in her life she was ready to trust a case to someone else. *And ready to trust him with more...*

There were no lights to bother with. The Old Court House had been built for maximum light, and already it was streaming through the windows and from the cupola above. She could see the gallows in the prison exercise yard.

Caro looked for and found the side door that led into the bricked, open-air enclosure.

The gallows didn't look as dangerous as they had earlier. The bottom steps had been removed, the trapdoor nailed firmly shut, and the nooses were much higher than anyone could reach. The barred door, flush against the building, led from the gallows directly to the jail cells.

Strange, Caro thought, how small people were back then. The doors were low, the furniture tiny. Only the gallows itself seemed overwhelmingly huge. Curious, Caro approached the bars of the cell. It was dark and smelled of age.

And something else.

It was the smell of human sweat. Caro tensed, and peered into the gloom. She could see nothing, hear nothing. But she trusted her sense of smell. "Hello? Is someone there?"

A faint groan.

"Are you all right?"

No reply.

Caro snatched Wyatt's key ring from her pocket, her fingers quickly grasping the old brass passkey. It fit the ancient hole in the black barred door, but didn't turn. At her feet Caro noticed heavy chains with padlocks further securing the door, probably to keep visitors off the aged, damaged floor of the cells.

"Damn," Caro swore to herself. Then she raised her voice. "Whoever you are, I'm going around to try to get you," she said. "Just hang on, okay?"

Caro rushed back into the Court House, the keys jangling, her heels pounding on the old wood floors. She grabbed the map out of her jeans pocket, trying to get her bearings. Within minutes she was descending the stairs to the ancient holding cells and their mysterious occupant.

Caro gasped. "Mr. Ellis! Are you okay?"

There was no answer. Hugh was sprawled on the cell floor, his wheelchair overturned, his face hidden in the shadows. Caro didn't bother trying to find a light switch. She fumbled with the passkey and heard the lock click open. A second later she was swinging open the rusty, squealing door of bars and kneeling at Hugh's side.

She felt for a pulse. There was one, but it was weak. "Mr. Ellis? Hugh, can you hear me?"

"My oxygen," he gasped, his eyes still closed. "Behind my chair."

Caro scrambled over to the overturned chair on all fours, her hands feeling in the darkness. When her sensitive fingertips found the plastic tubing, she traced the lines back to the tank. Quickly she dragged the tank closer to Hugh and inserted the tubing in his nostrils.

"Shall I turn up the valve?" she asked.

She heard a yes that sounded more like a groan, then felt for the valve, squinting in the gloom as she carefully adjusted the flow and checked to make sure the lines were uncrimped, the oxygen flowing freely.

"Better?" she asked a moment later, once again checking his pulse. It seemed to be a little stronger, but was still far from strong.

"Mm."

"Are you hurt?"

"Bruised." A gasp and then a wheeze. "Fell out. Floor's rough."

Caro's aching knees could testify to that. She patted Hugh's hand and reached for the wheelchair pillow. "I'll get you some help." Gently she cradled Hugh's neck, slipped the pillow underneath, then lowered his head.

"Who did this to you?" she asked, reaching for the cellular phone at her belt and dialing 911.

"Morgan... Please help Morgan..." he whispered.

"I will! I promise I will. Where is he, Hugh?"

There was no answer, no movement.

"Talk to me! Where's Morgan? Who locked you in here?"

Hugh's eyes fluttered closed. He was unconscious.

Caro lifted the cellular phone to her ear. Nothing but static. She redialed. This time the "no signal" warning light flashed red. She got to her feet. "Hugh," she said, "if you can hear me, I'm going outside. I can't get a phone cell from here in the basement. I'll be right back, okay?"

Caro raced up the brick steps of the jail area, back through the building and into the open air. She barreled into the prison yard, phone in hand. But she never got a chance to use it. From behind the gallows stepped another woman.

It was Kimberly—and she was pointing a gun right at her face—a small, semiautomatic handgun, with a silencer.

"Put your hands up, please."

Caro's answer was inaudible. She took a deep breath,

did as she was told, then said in the calmest voice she could muster, "Kimberly, I just left your grandfather. He's trapped inside a jail cell."

Kimberly smiled. "I know. I put him there."

Caro's jaw dropped. "You?"

"Of course. What better place to hide someone?"

"But he needs an ambulance! He's barely breathing! I was just about to call 911. I found him on the floor, and he wasn't hooked up to his oxygen." Caro glanced pointedly at the phone, her damp palm clasped around it.

"I made sure my grandfather was settled in comfortably before I left. There's food and water for him, even a radio so he can listen to the baseball game. He'll be fine."

"He's not! He's on the floor! Go check if you don't believe me."

"Nice try, but Hugh doesn't need any help. I'm his granddaughter. I'd never hurt him."

"No, you'd just lock him up in a dark, dirty cell so he can't talk to anyone," Caro said contemptuously. "Who was he looking for, Kimberly? Wyatt? Me?"

Kimberly's eyes flashed with fury. "Shut up! Hugh would be home by now if you hadn't insisted on your little tour of the Court House. That's why I was here—to pick him up. Now I have you to deal with."

"Why?"

"Because ever since you showed up, you've created nothing but trouble. Especially between Wyatt and me!"

"I'm not here to ruin the friendship between you and Wyatt. I just wanted to help identify that skeleton." It was the wrong thing to say.

"That's why you're here at the Court House, isn't it? To look at the old photos."

Caro pretended ignorance. "No, I just wanted to tour the place. I'm...interested in Old West history." After all, Kimberly hadn't heard about the skull's re-creation from her. There was a good chance she hadn't heard about it from anyone else, either.

Kimberly's lips twisted in an ugly grimace. "Don't lie to me. You know who the skeleton was, because you kept the skull."

Caro continued to feign ignorance. "What are you talking about? The skull disappeared when the rest of the bones were stolen."

"Nice try. But you're lying. Now ask me how I know."

Caro tried not to stare at Kimberly's gun and asked. "How do you know?"

"Because I stole the body from you and dumped it back where it came from!"

Oh, no. Oh, no.

"This is a small town, city girl. People *will* talk, especially to me. And even small-town dispatchers know all about facial re-creations. Tell me, *Doctor* Hartlan, did you find a match in the mining exhibit? Was his name Lem Bodine?"

Caro couldn't manage a poker face if her life depended on it. But she tried. "Who?" And failed. Her expression gave her away, and she knew it.

"That damn skeleton! I wish it'd never seen the light of day!"

"Then why did you bring it to Boothill?"

"I didn't, you fool!" Kimberly spit out. "Hugh decided to come clean about Lem's death. He asked that Apache girl to find the body and retrieve it."

"Jasentha Cliffwalker?"

"The one and only. Hugh hired Miz One-With-Nature so he could die with a clean conscience. He figured if anyone could find that skeleton and move it, she could. Hugh met her at Boothill in the dead of night and dropped Morgan's keys into the skull to point you all toward the Silver Dollar." She smiled scornfully. "Morgan was careless enough to leave them at my house once when he rode over to see me.''

The mine! The keys were a clue to The Silver Dollar Mine, not The Silver Dollar Ranch! I've made a dreadful mistake!

''When he was done with that, he even gave her an anatomy book and asked her to reassemble the whole cursed thing so you'd spot the broken legs. Like it matters after all these years!'' Kimberly's voice shook, but her gun hand remained dead calm.

Caro tried not to focus on that. ''Hugh couldn't have killed Lem Bodine, Kimberly. He was too young.''

''No, but he knew about it. His father, Jodiah, did the killing—with a branding iron to the head—and Hugh was an accessory. It happened in 1909—Lem had found out about the gold and was stupid enough to tell Jodiah. So Jodiah bashed his head in and made Hugh lie. He was the supposed eyewitness who saw Lem trampled to death in the stampede.''

''*Hugh* was that witness?'' Caro was incredulous.

''At his father's insistence. Everyone was afraid of Great-grandfather Jodiah, Hugh included. I heard he beat his wife, his dogs and his kids alike.''

Caro was disgusted. ''A real gem,'' she muttered.

Kimberly shrugged. ''We Ellises have known about that Bodine gold for four generations, thanks to Jodiah, then Hugh and now me.''

Caro was horrified. ''But Hugh was just a little boy!''

''That's right. Like Jodiah said, who's going to doubt the word of a child? So while Hugh's father was off dumping Lem's body down a pit, eight-year-old Hugh was telling the widow the sad, sad story. It was either that or his father would beat him. Maybe kill him. He had a cruel streak, Jodiah did.''

Caro's heart ached for that young boy of long ago. Hugh

Ellis was just as much a victim of Jodiah Ellis as Lem Bodine was.

"Like you said, this is all in the past," she said desperately. "It has nothing to do with now. Please, Kimberly, let me call an ambulance for your grandfather. He needs help."

"He needs to shut his mouth and keep it shut, or I'll beat him myself. That gold is ours! We waited for the technology to drain it and start mining again."

"The Silver Dollar Mine is on Bodine property."

"But it has an entrance on our property!"

"I don't believe you," Caro scoffed. "You have no mine. Wyatt would've told me."

"We have caves, though. The same system of caves that lies above the Silver Dollar. It slopes down the hills and onto our ranch. Wyatt wasn't the only one who grew up exploring," Kimberly said smugly. "I know those caves as well as anyone—even Jasentha."

"Then you should know exactly where the ore's located. Is there any silver on Ellis land? Or gold, for that matter?" Caro demanded. "Tell me that, Kimberly."

Kimberly's face turned ugly, and Caro knew she had her answer. The gold was on Bodine land.

"The Silver Dollar Mine gave up its silver generations ago, so it doesn't matter," Kimberly snapped. "As for the gold, the Ellis family sweated blood over it. We even *shed* blood over it!"

"And let's not forget grave robbing—twice," came Caro's accusation. "Someone else had to be buried under Lem Bodine's name. In his grave. Who was it?"

"Some nameless drifter who died on Ellis land. He'd been buried in the family cemetery and Jodiah dug him up. His body was thrown under the cattle, then buried in the Bodine family cemetery with Lem's name on the tombstone."

Caro shivered at Kimberly's words. Still, her investigative instincts made her press on. If she was going down, she'd go with all the answers. "Where does Jasentha come into this? Did she know where the true remains were hidden?"

"Only Hugh knew until I stumbled on those bones while I was having the machinery set up."

"That must have been...quite a shock."

"Hardly. More of an annoyance than anything else. But I just couldn't leave the bones there, or bury them in the family plot without arousing suspicion. Hugh knew about the gold. Hugh knew about my pumps. I figured he'd know about the body, too."

Kimberly paused. "What I *didn't* know was that he'd ask Jasentha to transfer them to Boothill. He told her the bones needed a proper burial. I don't know what else he told her—she's an odd bird anyway—but it did the trick. Who would've thought Hugh would develop a conscience so late in life?"

"It's not too late to do the same, Kimberly!"

"Of course it is, even if I wanted to—which I don't. I succeeded where no one else did. Jodiah somehow found out about Lem's gold, and claimed it for the family—"

"You mean killed for it."

Kimberly airily granted Caro that point. "True on both counts, but no Ellis could ever get to it. The mines flooded soon after Jodiah's discovery. There was no way to get down to the flooded veins in those days, but the gold was close enough to the top to make me try."

Kimberley smiled proudly. "I was the one who hired workers who couldn't speak English. I was the one who risked my neck transporting gold to my Mexican bank. I was the only Ellis to succeed! For the first time ever, our ranch is out of the red. That gold belongs to me, and I don't care if it *is* on Bodine land!"

"I won't argue with you, Kimberly. I don't care who gets the gold. I only care that no one gets hurt. Like Hugh." Caro said a quick, silent prayer, then went on, "Kimberly, I'm going to put my hands down and use the phone to call an ambulance. Then we'll both go check on Hugh."

Kimberly's response was instantaneous. She squeezed the trigger. The phone shattered into pieces of sharp-edged plastic as the silenced bullet slammed through it. Stunned, Caro felt a sticky warmth slide down her fingers.

"I'm sorry, but my grandfather stays here. While you—" Kimberly gestured with the gun in an easy motion "—you're coming with me."

CARO SAT BEHIND the wheel of Kimberly's truck, Kimberly right beside her, gun in hand.

"Where are we going?" Caro asked, bumping along on the desert land. She could see a faint path in sight, but nothing looked familiar. Driving was difficult, and her injured hand wasn't helping matters.

"To The Silver Dollar Mine."

"But this isn't the way."

"This is my way. A secret way."

Caro shook her head, confused. "I don't understand."

"I told you I have a system of tunnels on my land that lead straight to the mine. Tombstone is a mining town. This whole area is honeycombed and crisscrossed with tunnels and natural caves. It's like a labyrinth down there. Think subway system, city girl."

Caro threw her captor a withering look. "I'm from Phoenix. They don't have subways in Phoenix."

Kimberly glared at her. "For someone with a gun on her, you're pretty glib."

"Shoot me and you'll crash the truck. Then everyone will know my death wasn't an accident. Just like they'll soon know Lem Bodine's death wasn't an accident. That's what you have planned, right? Shooting me." Caro glanced at her quickly. "You intend to get rid of me in the mines, just like you got rid of Morgan."

Kimberly sighed. She pushed a strand of blowing red hair away from her face with the gun barrel.

"I don't want to kill you. I just wanted to scare you off. But Wyatt had your car checked, and you caught the slashed cinch. I didn't want to kill Morgan, either. But he was as bad as you. Nothing I did would make him leave me alone."

You killed Morgan! What am I going to tell Wyatt? How can I tell him if she kills me?

"But when he found out, I had stop him."

"When did Morgan find out you were stealing gold from the Silver Dollar?"

"The Bodines were always smart stockmen. Give them a bull and a few cows, or a stallion and a few mares, and they made money hand over fist. We never had cash-on-the-hoof luck. But when it came to mining, we were way ahead of the Bodines. They were dead-mule stupid. Still are."

Caro drove through a particularly bumpy wash. The creek beds seemed to be everywhere in this section of pasture, and the flying dust made visibility worse. It took all her concentration to navigate the rough patch before she could talk again. She was glad she had her seat belt tight and snug. Kimberly, like many dirt-road drivers without the highway patrol to fine them, didn't bother with a seat belt. She just grabbed the side of the window with a well-practiced motion.

"Why are the Bodines stupid?" Caro asked. "Because they trusted you? Because they didn't realize you were stealing their gold? Or because they didn't figure out that you murdered one of them for it?"

"All of the above, really. I didn't want to hurt anyone—

I just wanted to keep Hugh from going to Wyatt. I mean, he's been quiet about it all these years. He'll come around, and then everything can go back to the way it was.''

''What about Morgan?''

''I didn't want to hurt him. But what could I do? He was always underfoot, following me, looking at me like a love-sick puppy.'' Kimberly scowled. ''He found out about the gold. One of the local bartenders—who happens to speak Spanish—found out about it from one of my workers. And Morgan favors that same bar. Morgan wanted to go straight to Wyatt. I couldn't let him.''

''What did you do?'' Caro asked. ''Hit *him* in the head with a branding iron before you dumped him down a mining shaft?''

''Hardly,'' Kimberly drawled. ''But Morgan was getting in the way. It all started at the dinner party where you pulled the gold out of Hugh's wheelchair treads. That damn guano and gold must've stuck tight after Jasentha took him over to our caves to retrieve Lem's bones. Then Morgan got suspicious. Wyatt didn't notice the guano in the chair, but Morgan did.''

''And that's why he showed up at the mine when Wyatt and I were there!'' Caro realized with sudden insight. ''*You* cut my cinch—didn't you? And I blamed Morgan...''

''Yes.'' Kimberly actually laughed. ''You know, Morgan's a better detective than either you *or* Wyatt. Too bad he didn't have the same instinct for self-preservation that you do.''

Caro felt sick to her stomach. Morgan couldn't possibly be alive, could he? ''You never answered my question. What did you do to Morgan?''

''Mostly just batted my eyelashes and talked sweet. I told him I wanted to spend the day exploring the caves—with him. I said I'd show him the gold.'' She paused, shaking her head sadly. "Morgan almost ruined everything, you know."

"I don't know," Caro replied. "Tell me."

Kimberly's face grew soft with an almost ethereal beauty. "I love Wyatt. I've always loved Wyatt. I plan to marry him. He'd get a loving wife, and I'd get him."

"Plus, a legal claim to the gold as his spouse."

"Exactly! Only if I decided to tell him—no sense rocking the boat. Until you showed up, it was a win-win situation."

"Don't forget Morgan," Caro said contemptuously. "What did you do, leave him where your family left Lem?"

"Not *exactly* there. But close enough. He's in the mine, all right." She gestured ahead with the gun. Caro could see a man-made opening in the natural rock formation.

"Dead?"

Kimberly smiled, her face still ablaze with that strange, unearthly beauty. "Well, if he wasn't when I shoved him down that pit, he ought to be by now."

"My God!" Caro stared at Kimberly in horror. "How could you do that? He's the brother of the man you love!"

Kimberly merely laughed.

Caro shivered at the sound. *She's crazy.* Despite a hand that was bleeding and raw, she clenched her fingers tight around the steering wheel. She hadn't grown up driving in the desert for nothing. Caro prepared herself to take her foot off the gas pedal, prepared to jam on the brakes, prepared to jerk the steering wheel hard to the right.

I don't have much time. The Bar E's tunnel entrance is dead ahead!

"When it's your turn to die, I'll just think of Wyatt, think of the gold and shove you down, too," Kimberly said matter-of-factly. "Nothing personal."

"I do consider it personal. Very personal."

Kimberly gave her a sad little smile. "It doesn't matter. Because I'll kill you as easily as I killed Morgan."

"Think again, bitch," Caro hissed. *And deliberately rolled the truck,*

CHAPTER SIXTEEN

Sunday, midmorning

"THEY'VE DISAPPEARED, I tell you! Come in, Sheriff! Where in blue blazes are you? Over?"

The police radio on Wyatt's belt squawked with static as Catfish's angry voice boomed out. The noise was so loud his gelding jumped. Wyatt steadied the horse with one hand, turning down the radio with the other.

"Bodine here," he said, reining the gelding in. "What's up, Catfish?"

"I'll tell you what the hell's up! My dander! I'm a retired man. I'm too damn old to be tracking down young fools like you. I'm supposed to be working Boothill, and here I am at your office. Then I get stuck doing dispatch duty when Kimberly doesn't show up—*after* she calls Jamie and tells him to go home! So you get your behind over here and relieve me, because my dispatching days are over. Or find that forensic lady and tell her."

The tirade was followed by several generic curses, a few specific expletives and Catfish's feelings on outsiders who got themselves on the city payroll and didn't even have the courtesy to pitch in when an extra hand was needed. Wyatt interrupted.

"Wait a minute. Caro Hartlan isn't around?" He had a bad feeling about this, a gut instinct that had never failed him.

"Sure as cow patties smell, she ain't here!"

"Then where is she?"

"How in the hell should I know? I dropped her off this morning and ain't seen her since. She's not at the Court House. No one at the motel's seen her. She ain't at your ranch—"

"Did you check with Kimberly?" Wyatt asked abruptly.

"I told you—she hasn't shown up! Don't know where she is. I even tried the Bar E. And Hugh's gone—or he's not answering his phone. Seems like them three have dropped off the face of the earth!"

"I know." Wyatt turned the volume higher, unwilling to miss a word. "Have you called around town?"

"No, I'm a doddering old fool who isn't smart enough to think of that," was the sarcastic answer. "You going deaf, Sheriff?"

"No...but where could they be?"

"Danged if I know." Catfish started swearing again, only this time he swore as only an old miner could swear, and over the air, no less. That worried Wyatt even more. Because when Catfish swore so foully, that wasn't anger. That was fear.

"You're worried," Wyatt said in a flat voice.

"'Course I'm worried! First Morgan, then the doc. Wherever she went, it was important. Or maybe...maybe dangerous. And Kim's supposed to be looking for Morgan, not disappearing herself!" The old voice shook. "What are we going to do, Sheriff?"

"Look for them."

"But where? I've tried every place in town!"

Wyatt racked his brain. Where was his brother? Kimberly? And the woman he loved?

The woman he loved...

That thought astounded him. He'd never truly been in love. He'd felt lust, yes, but those impulses he could, and did, control. But in love? Was this fierce desire to protect and possess, this fierce anger at those who threatened the object of his every waking thought, *love?*

This was a powerful craving greater than the affection he felt for his family and friends. This was a white hot fire that threatened to engulf him with desperation and a deadly, killing fury.

"Sheriff? Wyatt, you there?" Catfish asked.

"Wait. I'm thinking." If anything happened to Caro, there would be hell to pay. If he lost his heart, he'd gladly trade his conscience for revenge.

Wyatt took in a deep breath. He put aside thoughts of love and family and Caro and justice. He put away everything but the cold, deadly side of him, the ability to think like a criminal. And he played back every single aspect of the crime, every minute detail since he'd first seen Caro Hartlan standing over the skeleton at Boothill.

Then he played it back again. And again. Until finally it hit him.

The vultures.

Turkey vultures were like most scavengers, wary and extremely nervous. They didn't circle around the strong and living, only the dying or freshly dead. So why were they circling over a hole with a picked-clean skeleton and a healthy young woman?

Wyatt's brow furrowed as he remembered Caro's words. "Think back, Sheriff. Think about Kimberly's appearance when you pulled her out of the shaft. Think about the way she smelled." And he had. Her blouse was fresh and she smelled of cologne, not guano.

There was more he remembered. Kimberly hadn't stayed at the clinic. She'd gone right home to bed and had sworn to both Hugh and him that she'd be fit for work the next morning. Wyatt felt his blood run cold.

The vultures hadn't been circling over Kimberly! They'd

been circling over the only person missing at that time. *Morgan.*

Wyatt's adrenaline kicked into overdrive, flooding his body with strength. He keyed the microphone button. "Morgan's in the mine."

"In the—?"

"The mine, the mine! It's always been the mine! Call the state police. I want some backup out at the Silver Dollar, and I want it now. Next, call Jamie to relieve you. Then call Luciano, and the two of you meet the police out at the entrance to the mine."

"Got it."

"Have Luciano send some men to check out all the official buildings. Not just the sheriff's office, but the town hall and go through the Old Court House again. Morgan's at the mine, but I doubt Kimberly or Caro are there. Ask the Bar E hands to search their pastures. Are you getting all this?"

"Writin' it down, Sheriff. Keep a-going."

"Make sure you notify the doctor on call at the clinic before you leave my office. I have a feeling we're in for trouble."

A pause, then, "What about me, Sheriff? What do I do after I'm relieved?"

"Go to the motel. Wait for Marta to get back. Maybe she can shed some light on Caro's whereabouts. If I need to reach you, I'll call you there."

"Anything else?"

"Yeah."

"What?"

"Pray."

Morgan drove the gelding hard, cutting corners and taking the shortest route possible to The Silver Dollar Mine. The good-natured animal had long ago stopped being good-natured. His coat was lathered with sweat, and he snorted his annoyance. Wyatt didn't pull up. The gelding's Arabian blood was holding true. Like generations of Arabians before him, the animal had reserves left, despite the distance already traveled, the heat and the instinctive desire to rest when danger wasn't present. But at his rider's relentless urging, he ran even faster.

Wyatt felt the horse tremble, and yet he increased his speed. It didn't matter. If those he loved were dead, dead through his own stupidity and fear, nothing mattered anymore. Not his horse, not his ranch…

Nothing.

His mind raced even faster than the gelding's feet. And then he was there.

The Silver Dollar Mine.

He dismounted, then tethered his horse quickly. He pulled out a flashlight, grabbed his canteen, headed for the entrance. He had to climb to where they'd found Kimberly, where she'd lured them away from Morgan, and he had to do it without help. Because he was alone. He had always been alone, but that didn't matter. He knew that he could be a formidable force, a dangerous force. He knew he'd find his brother, just like he knew he'd find Caro Hartlan, the woman he loved. What he *didn't* know was whether he'd find them dead or alive.

"DAMN YOU!" Kimberly screamed in rage. Then she screamed in terror as the truck jerked and flipped completely over.

Caro felt her teeth go almost through her bottom lip as the vehicle rolled—rolled so hard that the centrifugal force threw Kimberly right out the open window. Caro saw the other woman go flying through the air before she lost all her bearings as the truck flipped over one, two, three more times.

You country girls don't stand a chance against us road-

rally, rush-hour, high-speed city drivers, Kimberly. I'll be walking away from this one, no doubt about it, Caro thought with triumph as the truck jerked hard one last time, then landed on the driver's side, its wheels still spinning, the engine still running.

Caro spit out the sand and blood in her mouth and reached for the clasp of her seat belt. In seconds she was free, upright and out of the truck, her eyes already scanning for Kimberly, her heart praying that the crash had immobilized her enemy.

Her prayers went unanswered. Kimberly was alert and moving. She was on the other side of the truck, already on her hands and knees in a soft patch of sand that must have absorbed much of her body's impact.

Please, Lord, don't let her still have that gun. If she doesn't, I can take her down. Please, please, please.

That prayer went unanswered, too. Caro saw Kimberly push up to her knees and brush the sand out of her face. Then she brushed the sand off the gun lying beside her. Caro's only advantage was that Kimberly was on the far side of the tunnel opening, while Caro was between the truck and the near side.

Caro didn't bother taking any more time to pray or, for that matter, curse. She ran for the tunnel as if her life depended on it.

Which it did.

The Bar E entrance to the system of caves and mines was hidden by natural vegetation and rock formations. But as Caro slipped inside, she saw that the terrain of the interior was graded, flat, easy to walk on. It had obviously been recently worked.

Thank goodness for small miracles, she thought as she ran over the smooth walkway.

And damn them, too! she added as lights came flooding on. The hum of electricity filled the cave. Caro frantically searched for a place to conceal herself, but the best she could do was duck around a curve of the passageway.

"There's no place to hide!" Kimberly called out. "I know this cave like I know my own face. I'll find you sooner or later."

It'll have to be later, Caro silently vowed. She continued running down the passageway, hoping the single tunnel would branch out soon.

"Let's talk!" Kimberly yelled. Caro noted that Kimberly sounded farther away and her voice was ragged. Maybe she hadn't walked away scratch-free from the truck, after all. Caro smiled grimly, even as she went on running as fast as she could. Gun or no gun, she had the upper hand now— as long as the lights stayed on.

But sooner or later Kimberly would figure that out, too. And with the lights off, Caro would be at a disadvantage. She didn't know the mine at all, didn't have a flashlight, didn't have any weapon, except her brain. And her senses.

Finally the tunnel split—into two brightly lit corridors. Caro slowed, wiped her still-bleeding lip, took a valuable second to catch her breath and think. Which way? Right or left?

Suddenly her nose caught a faint whiff. Caro breathed in deeply and held it. She sniffed again and identified the scent of uremic acid. She hugged herself with hope. Where there was bat urine, there were bats. And where there were bats, there were openings to the surface. Without hesitation she headed into the left corridor, blessing the smelly domain of the mammals and vowing to find herself an opening.

She had no choice. Because if Kimberly had her way, only one of them would be leaving the cave alive.

WYATT EMERGED into the fresh air from the bottom of his bat-filled mine and the natural caverns above the Silver Dollar. He was covered in dirt and filth, his feet were sore and his fingernails bled where he'd climbed with more attention to speed than caution.

"Morgan!" he yelled. "It's Wyatt. Where are you?"

He heard only the sound of his own voice. And he saw the turkey vultures, the ones he'd seen yesterday. He hadn't been able to see them from the valley floor, but he certainly could from here. Now, though, there were more than three. There were as many as a dozen—circling, coasting on the desert thermals, waiting for the right moment.

That sight gave Wyatt added strength. If their prey was dead, there wouldn't be a vulture in sight. They'd all be down on the ground, feeding and fighting over choice scraps. Wyatt raced along the route he'd taken to rescue Kimberly—only Kim hadn't really needed rescuing. She'd only provided a diversion from the vultures' real prey.

Part of him was shocked that his dearest childhood friend, a woman he loved as a sister, had deceived him—and worse. But the hidden part of him wasn't shocked a bit. Wyatt Bodine knew there were only three sane motives for murder.

Money, sex and power.

Kimberly was probably stealing gold from his mine. Kimberly most certainly had wanted him in her life—and her bed—for a very long time. And marrying him would ensure her place as the reigning queen of both the Bar E and the Silver Dollar.

Motive for murder times three.

Morgan passed the large cleft in the rock formations where Caro had lowered herself to "rescue" Kim. Was there anyone down there now? He flattened himself on the ground, leaned over the edge and peered down into the crack.

The late-morning sunlight was growing brighter and bolder; visibility at the bottom was much better today. But Wyatt saw no one—and the vultures continued to circle.

He got to his feet and continued along territory he'd never walked before. Around him huge pillars of rock rose in strange formations. Massive bleached boulders threatened to block his way. Except for routine glances forward and behind to check his bearings, Wyatt refused to be stopped. He was as relentless, as persistent, as the vultures overhead.

The rock formations drew tighter and tighter together until it seemed as if even the hot wind couldn't find a single cleft in the wall of rocks. In any other circumstances Wyatt would have turned around, defeated. But the birds' low presence told him he was close. Very close. He could almost feel their excitement.

Boulder by bare boulder, pillar by desolate pillar, Wyatt searched for an alternate route.

Then he found it!

He squeezed between two columns, their massive bulk refusing to yield. He turned sideways, sucked in his breath, ignored his protesting ribs and forced himself through. For a second he was stuck, then he popped out onto a small hollow that dipped and led into a dark, naturally formed cavern. It quickly narrowed into a much smaller passage that dropped sharply. It was almost a pit, but if he moved carefully, he should be able to lower himself down those steep slopes without a rope. He slowly descended. His first few steps yielded two shocking discoveries.

The first was gold—vein after vein of crystalline yellow. It was underfoot, overhead, on his left side, on his right. The clear, untarnished color of the only corrosion-free metal known to man shone clear and true in the largest vein Wyatt had ever seen.

The second discovery was more disturbing. Beneath his feet, as battered and beaten as the gold was pure, was Morgan Bodine.

Wyatt dropped to his knees, his hand searching for his

brother's wrist. He rolled the inert body over, revealing bound hands and feet. Wyatt cursed viciously. He reached for the knife he always carried, slashed the ropes and gently cradled his brother in his lap.

"Oh, Morg, what did she do to you?"

Morgan's right leg bent at a crazy angle. The damage his brother had suffered, still suffered, stabbed at Wyatt's heart, and he moved gingerly, unwilling to cause more pain.

"Morgan? It's Wyatt. Come on, answer me."

He took Morgan's wrist again. He could barely feel a pulse. Wyatt opened his canteen, soaked the bandanna he'd carried in a back pocket and sponged his brother's bruised face. He doubted the touch of the wet cloth would revive Morgan, but perhaps the smell of water would. Desert dwellers learned to treasure everything about water—its smell, its sound, the sight of it. Horses, coyotes, javelina, burrowing owls, even the tiny hummingbirds, knew that moisture meant life. Humans were no exception.

Wyatt continued to sponge his brother's dirty face. He gently ran the edges of the damp bandanna against the blistered lips, stroked the sweat-streaked hair, rocked Morgan in his arms.

"Come back to me, little brother. The ranch needs you. Virgil needs you. Hell, I need you! Now open those damn eyes!"

Nothing. Not even a flicker. If anything, his brother's pulse seemed weaker.

"Please don't die, Morg. Because if you do, I won't be able to stand it." Wyatt's voice broke. "Don't let Kimberly win."

Morgan's lips parted, the air slowly hissing out. Tears ran down Wyatt's face as he braced himself for his brother's death rattle.

"I'll dig that woman's grave myself for what she's done to you, Morg. I swear it by everything I hold dear."

"Take a number, Wyatt," Morgan gasped. "And stand in line."

CHAPTER SEVENTEEN

Sunday—High Noon

THE CAVE ECHOED with the sounds of Caro's frantic flight from Kimberly. Her breath came in ragged puffs as she pushed her body to the limit. She should have spent more time at the gym! Better yet, she should have jogged a couple of miles every morning, she thought, as the stitch in her side grabbed her and forced her to stop.

"Damn it," she swore through gritted teeth. A demented woman with a gun was chasing her, help was miles away, and her own physical fatigue promised her a bullet in the head—or a shove down a rocky pit. Lord knew she'd passed enough of them in this winding maze.

"Things can't get any worse," she muttered.

Then the lights went out. They shut down with a *chunk,* and blackness filled her eyes.

I should've kept my big mouth shut.

Caro tried to take a few more steps, tripped and fell flat on her face. Her lip started bleeding again, and she felt a sticky dampness on one knee beneath her ripped jeans. But that was nothing to the cold fear she felt at Kimberly's words.

"Sorry I forgot to pack an extra flashlight," Kimberly called out. "But if you wait for me, I'll let you share mine." The other woman's laughter echoed bizarrely off the rock walls.

Honey, hire yourself a joke writer. If your bullets don't kill me, your humor will. Caro picked herself up from the stone floor. *Where's the law when you need it?*

An image of Wyatt Bodine came to her, and she felt both longing and regret as she staggered forward in the dark. *If only he was here.* But as usual, she had only herself to rely on. Unfortunately she wasn't at her strongest, especially after that truck roll.

Kimberly changed tactics. "I don't want you to hurt yourself...Caro. Come on out. We'll talk. Maybe there's a way we can resolve this." She sounded closer.

Caro inched forward as quietly, as quickly, as she dared. She glanced over her shoulder, and easily visible in the distance was a shaft of light—the beam from Kimberly's torch. The other woman was headed her way.

"Listen, I'm putting down the gun."

Forget it, Kimberly. I'm not falling for that one. In fact, I don't plan on falling anywhere. I hope.

THE GOLD VEIN grew higher, wider and more developed the deeper Wyatt went. Any other time, he would have been in awe at the bounty of riches all around him in the natural formations above his mine, the caves that sloped down toward Ellis land. This wasn't the time. His blood alternately boiled at the thought of Kimberly and grew chilled as he worried about Morgan.

Morgan had told him in hoarse, stark phrases about the gold beneath the Silver Dollar land.

"The Bar E has...connecting caves to our mine..." Morgan had said after Wyatt slowly, carefully helped him into a concealed, shady area. "I figured it out when Kim...led me up here. The whole place...honeycombed with them."

Wyatt wasn't surprised; he'd already figured that out for himself. What he *was* surprised to hear were Morgan's next words. "Kimberly's here, Wyatt."

"Here?"

"Yes!" Morgan started coughing, then grabbed at Morgan's canteen again. Wyatt only let him take a few careful sips, then urged, "Go on."

"I heard her. Sound travels...in the tunnels. Heard Caro, too."

Wyatt's joy at his brother's still being alive was tempered by fear. "What about Caro?"

"Caro knows. Don't know how—but Caro knows about Lem..."

"I know, Morg. The skeleton is our great-grandfather. Caro re-created the facial features on the skull."

Morgan nodded his understanding. "Hugh's father killed Lem. Hugh helped cover it up. Kimberly's doing the same. She's crazy, Wyatt! She tried to kill me! She'll kill Caro, too! Find them!"

Wyatt looked at his brother's shattered leg, blistered lips and the vultures circling up ahead. He hated to leave Morgan behind, and it clearly showed.

"Go, Wyatt. *Now.*"

Wyatt wasn't surprised by his brother's words. He pulled off his canteen, then his gun and left both with Morgan.

Morgan took the water, but hesitated to accept the gun. "Think that's...wise?"

Wyatt shrugged. "About as wise as you getting yourself in this mess."

"True enough." Morgan took the gun and didn't waste any more time arguing. Neither did Wyatt.

Morgan did add one last request. "Try to save them both, Wyatt. Caro and Kimberly. I...I still love her."

The hard, angry part of him won over his better side— the vicious part that preferred revenge to justice. He stared at the broken, bleeding body of his brother, and wondered if Caro's beautiful body was now broken or bleeding, too. Or even breathing. Wyatt's face was set in hard lines.

"If Caro's dead, I make no promises, Morg. Do you hear me? None..."

CARO CONTINUED her escape in the dark. She was crawling now, keeping low to the ground. The rock gouged her kneecaps, but this way, there was less likelihood of falling down a pit. And it made her a harder target for Kimberly's gun.

Her left knee banged against a rough stalagmite. "Ow!" she cried. She crawled carefully around the jutting piece of rock and ran smack into another. Caro clamped her lips closed, not wanting to give away her position.

Wherever *that* was. She wasn't sure, but she thought—hoped—she was now entering the old man-made tunnels of The Silver Dollar Mine.

Come on, little bats, where are you? Guide me!

She tried hard to focus on something other than her fear. The stench of guano seemed to be getting stronger, closer. But speed was out of the question. Just trying to hurry made her slip in a pile of slick limestone goo caused by the dripping stalactites. She felt the lime burn into her cut hands.

"Come on!" Kimberly was saying. "We can talk this over. There's enough gold for both of us. I'm willing to negotiate."

Caro refused to answer. She wiped her face with a ragged shirtsleeve and went on crawling. She bumped the top of her head on another stalactite. The dizzying, ringing pain made her less than careful as she continued forward.

Suddenly there was nothing but air beneath her hands. Caro frantically tried to pull back, but it was too late. Her balance was severely compromised, and gravity was stronger than her tired body.

She slipped headfirst over the ledge. Then she was falling, falling, falling. The air rushing through her hair mingled with her scream—and with the sound of Kimberly's gun firing twice.

WYATT HEARD the scream and something that had to be gunshots, and shuddered. The scream's high, eerie pitch could only mean three things—fear, pain or death.

But who was hurt? Caro? Kim? Both?

Wyatt moved as fast as he dared. This was new territory to him, and he couldn't traverse it with the easy familiarity he'd felt in the caves of his childhood. One flashlight wasn't much help. The stark fact was, he was no good to either woman if he became lost and needed rescuing himself.

He shut his eyes and listened. The sound was coming from…what direction? He couldn't distinguish north from south, east from west, Ellis from Bodine land in here. But he could tell one thing.

The scream came from below.

CARO'S FALL was a long one. Her scream was totally primitive, something she could neither help nor stop. Even the sound of two gunshots couldn't stop her shrill wail. Her scream was only cut short by her headfirst landing.

But instead of a hard, bone-jarring stop, Caro landed with an icy splash. Water! She'd fallen into a subterranean lake. She gasped at the cold and fought to overcome the cramping of her muscles—and her panic.

Because, no doubt about it, she was panicking. She was below the surface, she was being shot at, and her scream had depleted most of the air in her lungs. Caro kicked and clawed, unable to see surface light or the water's ceiling. Something she'd recently read flashed through her mind— the normal temperature of most caves was a chilly forty-eight degrees Fahrenheit.

That was wrong. Caves and cave lakes were much colder—as cold as death.

She was underwater, totally disoriented, totally lost. Caro realized she had no idea in which direction she was swimming. She couldn't tell up from down, left from right, nor was the sagging weight of her clothes and shoes allowing her to float. Her lungs burned from lack of air as she frantically grabbed for her feet. Thank goodness she was wearing sneakers, instead of boots! The shoes came off without having to be untied. She kicked off her jeans next, working hard for calm as the urge to breathe grew unbearable.

Then—the hardest part of all—she forced herself to relax and let the water take her.

Just when she thought she'd have to gasp for air that wasn't there, her body became buoyant. It gave her the strength to hold on longer as she began to float upward. She hastened the process by kicking like a Sonoran mule for the surface, praying the most fervent prayer of her life.

Please, God, I'm too young to die. And then, *Don't let Kimberly hurt Wyatt. Keep him safe!*

The water, permeated with guano and lime, burned through her tightly closed eyes. Finally, finally, her head broke the surface. Caro sucked in one huge breath after another.

From above she saw a beam of light approaching, then Kimberly's flashlight and gun were hovering at the edge of the sinkhole. Caro chanced one last breath before diving deep into the water, just as Kimberly fired off three more rounds.

The silence of the water enveloped her once again. Caro concentrated desperately on holding her breath. The icy chill seeping into her veins was agony. The thought of never seeing Wyatt again hurt even more. Because of the water, Caro couldn't make out a thing, neither the enemy nor her heart's desire.

But then, neither could Kimberly.

AT THE SOUND of more gunshots, Wyatt clutched the flashlight so tightly that the shape of the On-Off switch was imprinted in his palm.

"Kimberly, no!" he shouted. It had to be Kimberly who'd fired the gun, Kimberly who'd grown up shooting tin cans in the desert with the three Bodine boys.

The gun's report roared through the caves, vibrating in fainter and fainter echoes. Wyatt might not be a caver or a miner, but guns were as familiar to him as a favorite horse. Those reports were as clear as neon arrows advertising cheap beer outside a border cantina.

I'm coming, Caro, he promised. *Hold on, love.* He knew which way he was going now. And nothing, *nothing,* would stop him.

CARO COULD STAND IT no more. She had to surface, had to breathe, had to escape the icy water before her muscles cramped beyond use. She could barely tread water as it was.

She tried to break the water's surface as quietly as possible, but her shirtsleeves were flapping around her arms, and she was shivering so hard her teeth tapped out Morse code.

Caro saw the beam of light swing her way. As it did, she noticed a ledge off to the side. It wasn't very wide, but it would get her out of the water.

Thanks for the help, Kimberly. Remind me to send a thank-you note to whatever jail you're residing in.

And thank God there was another ledge above it. Kimberly would have to hike to the far side of the sinkhole to aim a flashlight—or a bullet—at her. That would buy Caro some time, maybe enough time to figure a way out of this.

She was shivering violently now. In another few minutes she wouldn't be able to control her chilled muscles, let alone save herself—or Wyatt. She was very close to drown-

ing, and she knew it. The flashlight beam was awfully close
to her location again, and she knew that, as well.

Caro's last thought before diving again was the sound of
a man's voice shouting her name.

Wyatt? Is that you?

"WYATT? IS THAT YOU?" Kimberly yelled.

Wyatt immediately slowed his wild descent. He cau-
tiously let the sound of Kimberly's voice draw him toward
her.

"Yes." He quickly formulated a plan—a poker bluff that
might save Caro's life. If she was still among the living.
"I came to check on you!"

"You did?" Kimberly's voice was edgy, suspicious.

"Yes! I think Caro killed Morgan, and she's after you,
too!" The bluff came out so smoothly. "Are you okay?"

"I'm fine, Wyatt! Just fine!" Kimberly called back.
"Where are you?"

"Over here!"

"I can't see you! Wave your torch around!" she urged.

No way in this lifetime, lady. Wyatt deliberately masked
his flashlight with his hand, leaving only the faintest glow
of light for himself and none for her. "Wave yours!"

She did. Wyatt spotted it. "Gotcha, Kim!" He moved
behind the shelter of a stalagmite, keeping out of sight.

"I still can't see you!"

"Be quiet! Don't let Caro hear you!" Now for part one
of his plan. Wyatt decided to take the truth and twist it for
his benefit. It would be easy. All he had to do was substitute
Caro's name for Kimberly's. "She's after the gold in my
mine! She'll do anything to get it."

"What gold?" Kimberly did a good job of sounding surprised, Wyatt noticed. But he wasn't fooled.

"Caro was looking for the original burial site of the skeleton and found a vein of gold above the Silver Dollar.

That's why she's been following me, Kimberly! That's why she killed Morgan!''

Kimberly's staged gasp would do a Hollywood director proud. "She killed Morgan? You found him?"

"I found what was left of him." He continued with his game plan. "I think Caro discovered the gold and wanted to keep it all. Morgan figured it out and tried to stop her. Caro must have lured him up here. The poor fool never knew what happened."

"Oh, no! Your brother's dead?"

You rotting serpent. You left Morgan to suffer, to die slowly. You'll pay dearly for that.

"Really dead, Wyatt?"

Wyatt had to fight for control at the relief in her voice. "Yes! And Caro will kill you, too! She thinks you're her competition for me and my gold."

"We both know that isn't true," Kimberly's voice sounded angry—and much closer. Wyatt gritted his teeth and refused to retreat as she advanced.

"But it is, Kimmie." He deliberately used the old childhood diminutive, calculated to disarm. "I never knew how much I cared until today. Just the thought of Caro chasing you down here... I had to come after you!"

"You don't love her?" Kimberly asked eagerly. "You've never loved her?"

"How could I?" *How could I not?* "She was the one who pushed you down the shaft yesterday, right?"

"Yes! Yes, it was her!"

"Kimmie, why didn't you tell me?"

"I...I didn't think you'd believe me."

Why should I? You lied to me. You lowered yourself down into that pit on a dark, stormy day, and waited in the cool shade for us while my brother lay injured. You probably still had the rope attached somewhere out of sight in case we were late.

"Oh, Wyatt, everything's so messed up!"

Oh, no it's not. Everything is crystal clear. "That's why I'm here, Kimberly. To straighten everything out."

"How can you?" she wailed. "My great-grandfather killed yours. My grandfather helped. We all kept it a secret because of your gold. We never had the Bodine touch for stock."

Her voice was shaky. "How *could* you love me, Wyatt? How could anyone love a family like ours?"

Wyatt didn't trust himself to answer. His rage was building, and he was afraid his voice would transmit it. He drew on years of self-control until he tamed that rage, until his cool, calculating, self was back.

Wyatt carefully tracked her beam of light, positioning himself to his advantage. She was close, very close now. Her gun didn't frighten him. If she took him down, she was going with him. A few more steps, and—

"Wyatt? Wyatt, where *are* you?" Kimberly asked plaintively. "Answer me!"

"I'm over here!" he replied as faintly as he dared. "My flashlight's not working." *Not working because I've turned it off.* "We'll never find Caro at this rate."

Kimberly's sadness immediately shifted into fury. "Is that all you care about? Finding your precious Caro?"

Damn it! Time for damage control. "Only so I know she'll never hurt you again! I intend to lock her up for the rest of her life. She'll pay for what she did to Morgan and for trying to come between us," he bluffed. *Take the bait, you viper. Take the bait.* "She'll pay big time."

"But she already has!"

"She— How?"

"Caro came after me, but I had my gun and I turned the tables on her. I chased her into a sinkhole. If the bullets didn't get her, the fall and the water did."

"She's hurt?"

"She's gone, sweetheart! Dead!"

"Dead?" His voice cracked and drained away, as did whatever good remained in his heart. He couldn't nourish the flame of honor and justice anymore. The rage, the loss, the pain had him in a death grip and fired his desolation into a killing frenzy. He waited as Kimberly came closer, closer...just a few steps away.

"It was self-defense, Wyatt. I swear it was."

Caro...I waited my whole life for you. I'd just started to get to know you. I've loved you and never even knew it until today. And you're gone?

"Dead?" he said again. Somehow that word overwhelmed him.

"Yes. Yes! You should be glad!"

Kimberly was almost within his reach. Close enough for him to grab and tear into pieces. He would kill her, kill her for what she did to Morgan and Caro. Especially Caro.

"Morgan will rest easy," Kimberly continued in a soothing voice. "He's been avenged."

Not yet, you foul piece of carrion. Take a few more steps, you corpse. Just a few more steps. Maybe I'll kill you slowly—like you wanted for Morgan. Or maybe I'll kill you quickly, like—

"Avenged by me. For us, Wyatt. For us."

Either way, you die today. And there is no "us." He tensed behind the wet, dripping pillar of lime and rock. *One more step. Just one more step.*

And then revenge would be his.

CARO PULLED HERSELF up onto the tiny ledge with numbed, clumsy fingers. It was her third try. She lay panting and gasping, trying to remain quiet, trying not to splash or suck in air too loudly. She couldn't tell if she was being noisy or not. The blood pounding in her ears and chest drowned out everything except the chattering of her teeth. Eventually her roaring pulse slowed enough to let her listen. To wait and see if Wyatt or Kimberly had left.

What she heard told her they were both still here. Sound carried easily in the caves and over the water. She listened.

"LET GO! Wyatt, you're hurting me!" It was Kimberly.

"I intend to keep on hurting you. I intend to enjoy hurting you. Until you're as dead as Caro is."

Wyatt's answer chilled Caro even more than the water had. She gasped and tried to sit up but started to slip off the narrow ledge. She lay back down. She knew if she fell off she wouldn't be able to pull herself back.

"But Wyatt…you said—"

"I lied. Just like you lied. How does it feel to be lied to, Kimberly?"

"Please give me back my gun, Wyatt." Kimberly's voice was tinged with just the barest edge of nervousness. "And let go of my arm."

"I'll let you go when you're dead. You almost killed Morgan. You would have if I hadn't found him."

Morgan's alive? Caro thought.

"Morgan's alive?" Kimberly's voice wasn't so calm this time.

"Oh, yes. My brother had a sick, grotesque story to tell, Kimberly. You tried to kill him and you killed Caro. Didn't you?"

"But only in self-defense! Both times, I was fighting for my life!"

Oh, please, lady, give it up! Caro thought. *The man's not stupid. I'm the stupid one for not trusting him. If I had, we'd all be home free.*

And then, in horror, she heard the unmistakable click of a gun's hammer being pulled back. Caro was experienced with firearms; she knew that only in old Westerns on late-night TV did someone pull the hammer back on a gun

Hammers were sensitive, too sensitive to cock. And squeezing the trigger was much quicker than thumbing the hammer.

Pulling the hammer back was done for Hollywood effect. Real-life shooters never cocked the trigger unless they were crazy.

Suddenly she understood. Wyatt *was* crazy! Her supposed death at Kimberly's hands had driven him over the edge. The predator Caro had sensed inside him was out in full play.

He was a good man who was fighting a battle with his worst self—and losing!

"No, Wyatt, don't! I'm alive!" She tried to shout, but her shivering body and stiff vocal cords weren't working. She heard only air, not sound, emerge from her lips.

"You're dead meat, Kimberly. Vulture food." The voice was harsh. Cold. Emotionless. Unrecognizable as Wyatt Bodine's.

Caro shivered again, this time with fear.

"Wyatt!" Kimberly begged. "Please...you can't be serious."

"I'm very serious. Let the punishment fit the crime. The only question is how. Do I push you—or shoot you?"

No, Wyatt! Don't do it!

"Wyatt, please don't do it!" Kimberly cried. "You can't kill me. I did it for you, sweetheart! For us!"

"You did it for yourself. For the gold. For the power. For the easy way out. But it ends here—and now. You're taking the easiest way out of all, *sweetheart*. The big *D*. And I'm here to help you along."

Caro tried to scream Wyatt's name, willing her voice to work. She couldn't. But Kimberly could and did. Her scream ended abruptly—

Cut off when he pressed the cold barrel of the gun against her temple.

CHAPTER EIGHTEEN

WYATT STARED at the gun in his hand. He stared at the woman in front of him. As he prepared to thumb back the hammer one more time, to pull it past the release point, where it would slam down and strike the firing pin, Kimberly smiled.

She actually smiled! It was so unexpected, so bizarre, that he stopped in midmotion.

"You know something, Wyatt? We're more alike that I thought."

"We're nothing alike! Nothing!"

His words echoed off the walls. Kimberly laughed, her laughter echoing with his words.

"Oh, dearest, of course we are. You want the gold all for yourself. You don't feel like sharing. I can understand that. I can even admire you for it. No wonder your Caro won't give you the time of day."

"You killed her!"

"Like you're going to kill me. We're two of a kind, you and I. Two of a kind." She laid her hand on his cheek— the same hand that had killed the woman he loved. "Only, at least I'm honest about it."

Two of a kind? Are we really two of a kind? Is Caro dead because she couldn't trust me? God in heaven, is Kimberly right?

The thought made him even sicker inside, something he'd have sworn was impossible.

"It's not too late to change your mind, Wyatt. All that

gold just waiting for us. No Morgan or Caro to interfere. We could have a lot of fun, you and me. What do you say?''

"I'd rather see you dead." He pressed the gun barrel even harder against her temple, so hard the metal made a circular imprint on her skin.

To Wyatt's amazement, Kimberly didn't resist. She didn't even act surprised. "Oh, well, I tried. It's not much consolation, but it's something." She gave him one last smile. "See you in hell, lover."

She lifted her chin and waited for the end. Wyatt tried to pull the trigger, but Caro Hartlan's face appeared in his mind. *She's the woman I wanted to be worthy of, the woman whose opinion, whose heart and soul, matters more than my own.*

But that woman was gone. Dead. What value could his love hold now if he went against her commitment to life? A commitment he himself shared. Dared he dishonor the purest emotion he'd ever experienced? Was the love he felt for her truer than his rage, his grief, his desire for revenge?

Drawing on strength deep within, a strength he'd never tapped before, he fought the dark side of him with blind fury.

And this time, *this* time, he had it tamed. Wyatt Bodine triumphantly realized he would always be evil's master.

There was no way he would let himself become the kind of man Caro Hartlan would despise. Not even to kill her murderer. He'd saved more than just the pureness of his love for Caro Hartlan. He'd saved himself. *If only I'd been able to save her, as well.*

He lifted the gun from Kimberly's head, pointed it down toward the ground and slowly, delicately, uncocked the hammer and let it rest flush against the metal. Hot tears burned down his face as he took a deep breath and once again became the man he would always be. *A man of the law.*

"Ms. Kimberly Ellis, I'm placing you under arrest for the murder of Dr. Caro Hartlan. I also charge you with two counts of kidnapping—one of Caro Hartlan, the other of Morgan Bodine." The words hurt his throat, but he managed to deliver them in as professional manner as possible. "And the attempted murder of Morgan Bodine."

Kimberly gasped; Wyatt ignored her. "I must warn you—you have the right to remain silent. You have the right to an attorney. If you cannot afford an attorney, one will be appointed for you—"

"And we downtrodden taxpayers will be robbed again."

It was Wyatt's turn to gasp. The faint, tremulous voice belonged to Caro Hartlan. She hung over the edge of the limestone sink, only her shivering wet head and arms visible. She was alive! *Alive!*

"Someone want to give me a hand up, please?" Caro asked weakly. "Or do I have to hang around all day listening to the Miranda statement?"

"Caro! Caro, you're—"

"—going to fall back in the water in about two seconds," she finished for him, gasping. "Now cuff the prisoner and get your slow but adorable sheriff's butt over here. I need rescuing, lawman! Or do I have to crawl to the nearest phone and dial 911?"

Wyatt dropped his flashlight in shock. His grief turned to joy, then to triumph. *He hadn't failed Caro!* But that moment of stunned bliss was all Kimberly needed. She whirled and broke away, leaving him at a dead run.

He couldn't—wouldn't—follow her. Not with Caro nearby and in such need. He raced over to her, yanking her free of the lime sinkhole, clasping her in his arms, pressing her hard against his heart. He felt his body's warmth become hers, her heart's warmth become his. For the first time in his life the words he spoke were wild, crazy, passionate, even incoherent—but the emotion behind them rang true, as did the love he heard between the lines of Caro's glib, irreverent response.

"So, are you glad to see me? Or just happy you don't have to fill out more paperwork?"

"Both, lady. Both." Despite the fleeing Kimberly, despite Caro's obvious physical discomfort, he kissed her. Then he kissed her again. He couldn't help it. Neither could she. Her icy hands were on his cheeks, her dripping hair snagged on his buttons as she nestled against his chest, her cheek over his embroidered sheriff's badge. Below, Wyatt's fallen flashlight illuminated her wet stocking feet below wet bare legs.

"Where are your clothes?" he asked. "You're just wearing…wearing…"

"They're called panties, you idiot, and I think you have a lingerie fetish, after all. What did you expect me to do, swim in my jeans and shoes?"

"No, but…" *Are you cold?* he was going to ask, but Caro interrupted him.

"Skip it, would you? Don't we have to get Morgan to a doctor?" Her question brought everything back into sharp focus.

"You heard us talking?"

"Yes."

Wyatt's heart stopped. "How much did you hear?"

"Every single word."

He closed his eyes. Wyatt Bodine, afraid of nothing, was afraid now. Then he slowly said, "I make no excuses for what I nearly did to Kimberly. I know I was wrong."

Caro sighed. "Well, I was really hoping I'd get to go to Kimberly's funeral, but I suppose you had to let her live."

Wyatt stared. He couldn't believe her words, couldn't

believe she'd heard all the ugliness inside him—and could forgive him. His voice was hoarse. "You don't mind?"

"I can't say I approve of your letting her escape just to steal a kiss from me. Still, I suppose I'll have to get used to all that Bodine testosterone sooner or later."

He could barely see the smile she gave him in the darkness of the cave, but he could feel its warmth and love all the way through to his soul.

"Sorry about that." Wyatt held her gently and touched her dripping shirt. "I'll try to keep my raging hormones under wraps."

"Don't you dare, Wyatt!"

He grinned. "Yes, ma'am."

"I'm so happy Morgan's alive. So happy you found me." Her voice trailed off into another spell of shivering. "So glad I can trust you."

"On everything. Forever," he said. He took off his dry shirt and silently handed it to her. She wrapped it, sarong-style, around her waist. Then Wyatt picked up his flashlight, hooked it to his belt and scooped her up in his arms.

"What do you think you're doing?" Caro asked indignantly.

"Carrying you. You don't have any shoes."

"I still have legs. Put me down."

"But we have to hike uphill to get to Morgan. It's not an easy climb, and you're hurt." Her knees were bleeding, as were her hands.

"I'm banged up a bit. Big deal."

"You'll slip in those socks and cut up your bare legs."

"So I'll take the socks off. Do I look like a lapdog? Or some Barbie doll you have to carry around?"

"I..." Wyatt blinked. His woman had even greater courage and strength than he'd suspected. "No, but—"

"So put me down. I need to move to get warm. I'll freeze

to death if I don't get my blood circulating. And you can get me out into the sun faster if we both walk.''

Only then did he set her down, carefully, tenderly, lovingly.

''Oh, please, you aren't going to go all sappy on me, are you?'' She grabbed his shoulder with one hand to balance herself and pulled off her socks with the other. She shoved them into her pockets. ''Look, if you're afraid of Kimberly, just give me directions and the flashlight. I'll find her myself.''

''What?'' He stared, amazed. He took in the bleeding hands planted defiantly on her hips. It occurred to him that he really had a lot to learn about this woman. One thing for sure—she was as strong as he was. Maybe stronger.

''Fine. Be a wimp,'' she spit out. ''I'll catch that madwoman myself!'' She snatched the flashlight off his belt and set off.

Wyatt grinned again. ''You're going the wrong way!''

Caro hissed out an exasperated breath and stomped back to his side. Wyatt took the flashlight from her. He allowed himself one last wave of pleasure and love and pride before pushing his tenderness out of the way and letting his professional persona come into focus. He grabbed Caro's hand with a businesslike grasp and pointed the flashlight in the right direction.

''Follow me,'' Tombstone's sheriff ordered.

The climb was even harder going uphill, instead of down, but Caro kept pace with him. Once or twice she slipped, but he was always there to steady her.

They kept quiet, their bodies straining at the task, their minds ever alert for sounds of Kimberly. Even without a gun, there were enough weapons Kimberly could use against them in this dangerous area. Wyatt was determined that he and Caro had suffered enough at Kimberly's hands,

as generations of Bodines had suffered at the hands of Ellises. Justice must be done.

Finally they were near the once secret entrance where
Morgan awaited them. Caro merely glanced at the gold
surrounding her, but she cried in sympathy at the sight of
Morgan and rushed to his side.

"How you doing, Morg?" Wyatt asked.

Morgan's response about certain sheriffs and what they
could do with their idiotic questions didn't bear repeating.
Wyatt set down some old planking he'd found on their way
before taking his canteen back from Morgan and passing it
to Caro. She set it down.

"Later. This leg needs tending." She tore the sleeves off
her own ragged shirt and reached for the splinting material.

"I'll do it," Wyatt said. "You need to warm up. Get out
in the sun and dry off."

"Take the water, too," Morgan croaked.

"Forget it! I have more knowledge of anatomy than you,
Wyatt. And, Morgan, I've had enough water for a while."

"Drink!" Morgan insisted.

"Put a lid on it, Bodine. I don't take orders from your
brother, I'm certainly not going to take them from you."
She started tearing her shirtsleeves into strips.

Wyatt watched them argue. They stopped when he
handed Caro his canteen.

"Where are you going?" Morgan asked.

"He's going to find Kimberly," Caro answered for him.
She knows how it is. She lets me do my job.

"She's still alive?" Morgan couldn't hide his shock.

"So far," Caro replied.

"Kimberly gave me the slip, Morg. I have to find her."
His heart ached for Morgan, a man not blessed in love, the
way he himself was. "She needs to stand trial."

"I know. But as long as she's alive, there's hope for

her,'' Morgan said, his voice a hoarse whisper. Wyatt couldn't disagree.

Caro took Morgan's hand in her own, squeezing it for comfort, then went back to tearing her shirt into rags.

"I gotta go, Morg...Caro." What Wyatt really meant was, *This is my life—hard decisions, pain and all.*

"Don't worry about us," she said. "Just be careful."

Wyatt's relief was boundless. There was so much he wanted to say, so much he needed to hear, but now was not the time. "Later, then."

"Later," Caro echoed.

Morgan lifted Wyatt's gun. "You want this?"

"Yeah. I have her gun. Take it and give me mine." The men switched; a man's gun was like his horse—rarely shared. "You be careful, too. She may double back and show up here."

"I'll be watching." Morgan promised. "I'll take good care of your lady, Wyatt."

"Thanks, Morg. But my lady can take care of herself." He allowed himself one last look at the woman he loved, then was gone.

Wyatt painstakingly searched for his childhood companion. He carefully covered familiar and unfamiliar ground— caves where he had played with Kimberly in his youth, caves where Kimberly had almost cost him the love of his life. His search took a long time, longer than it would have if his prey had been a stranger. Still, his steps were sure and silent. He moved with the stealth of the predator he knew he was, yet his chest was tight with sadness.

Wyatt forced that sadness aside and concentrated. His predatory instincts told him Kimberly would be bold, even overconfident where he was concerned. There was a deep-down ruthlessness in Kimberly that he had always recognized; like did indeed call to like. Wyatt knew how dangerous she could be—would be—if she decided to fight him.

The hours ticked by until the sun hung low in the western sky and Wyatt traveled back the way he'd come. He suspected that Kimberly would delay her emergence from the caves until dark. That was what he'd do if the situation was reversed. Perhaps she thought she could escape him in the evening twilight, but Wyatt knew better. He would never let her go until he knew those he loved would be safe. From Kimberly. Forever.

He emerged out into the open. And there, amid the spires of ancient rock, on the other side of a ravine, there she was. She stood outlined against the setting sun at the natural entrance to the caves above The Silver Dollar Mine. Wyatt remembered the last time he was here, remembered the same pillared area where they had "saved" Kim once before.

She was much higher than he was, the old ravine keeping them apart. Her beautiful hair glowed even redder in the sun's fiery light. Wyatt couldn't believe the sun was actually setting. How long had they been in the caves?

He stared at her. *I've never seen her look more beautiful—or more deadly.*

Kimberly spoke first. "I knew you'd come for me."

"I knew you'd be here. You were right, Kimberly. We do think alike."

"We always have. So tell me, Wyatt, what am I thinking now?"

"You've decided to stay in Tombstone and fight."

She nodded. "Go on."

"A tearful performance about my lovesick, sun-addled brother—delirious after his terrible ordeal, of course."

"Of course."

"A little slander accusing Caro of stumbling across my gold and wanting it all for herself."

"Why not?"

"And—let's see—a touch of blackmail regarding my character. After all, the sheriff's an elected position. Your version of my behavior might be frowned on by the voters."

"You did put a gun to my head and threaten to kill me."

"That's the difference between us, Kimberly. I've never acted on my baser impulses."

"You've come awfully close, Wyatt. Why not just cross that line? I have. It's easy. Much easier than resisting."

"No." The sincerity of that simple answer was unmistakable.

Kimberly's eyes flashed a fire as burning as the sun. "You would have, if that plain-faced, straight-shooting forensics woman hadn't come to town."

"I came close," he admitted with shame. Then that changed to rock-hard certainty. "But it won't happen again."

Kimberly sighed, the sound carrying easily. "Be reasonable, Wyatt. You have no idea how wealthy your gold has made me. Anyone with enough cash to hire a fancy lawyer can get away with murder. Besides, I have the perfect defense." She smiled. "I was only trying to save my poor sick grandfather's ranch."

"The same sick man you locked up in a cell! Caro told me all about it on the climb out. Please, Kimberly, if you care anything about your family and friends, if you care anything about *yourself,* give up!"

Kimberly laughed, the melodious, bubbling laugh he'd heard all his life.

"You know me better than that, Wyatt. *You* give up. There's enough gold to buy everyone's silence. Everyone's!"

A deep pain settled in his heart. "Not mine, Kimberly. Never mine."

"You don't think you can spare any gold?" Confused, Kimberly tilted her head. "If you wanted it all for yourself, why didn't you kill me when you had the chance? The new pump's in place—it has the water drained and most of the vein exposed."

"It's not about the gold. It's about right and wrong!"

"Oh, please! Wyatt Earp you're not...*Sheriff* Bodine. You're a black-hearted man wearing a white hat. And you'll never convince me otherwise."

Wyatt glanced down below them into the ravine at what looked like a rising black cloud of smoke. "I can and I will. For starters, you're a dead woman if you don't get away from that ledge."

Kimberly swore, an ugly word that mocked the beauty of her perfect face. "My patience is wearing thin, Wyatt. How stupid do you think I am? You may have a gun, but you'd never use it on me."

"There are more ways to die than from bullets, and I want you alive, Kim. My brother loves you. Your grandfather needs you. It's not too late to start over. I'll help you all I can. We all will!"

"You liar! The only person you want to help is yourself—to the gold I slaved for! You'd never have known it was here if it wasn't for that woman!"

The cloud of black rose higher in the ravine. "Kimberly! You have to get down! The..."

He finished his sentence, but Kimberly didn't hear it. She started swearing, cursing him and all Bodines to suffer whatever torment there was for unfaithful friends and lovers. Wyatt tried again, but her tirade continued and she didn't, couldn't, hear a word; he was so far below, she so high above him.

The expression on his face changed to one of panic, and he gestured frantically, pointing with the forefingers of both hands. "Below you, Kimberly!"

The cloud of black smoke was thousands upon thousands of hungry bats making their way up and out of the caves. The rush of wind created by their wings grew louder, and the squeaks increased as the swarm began to maneuver around the strange object blocking their centuries-old path to freedom.

"Get down, Kim! Get down!"

It was too late. Kimberly jumped in surprise, moving herself into the path of a bat. It managed to avoid the unexpected obstacle with barely a whisper of air between wing and face. Nonetheless Kimberly panicked. Alarmed, she jerked this way and that, looking for a way to escape the cloud of bats, instead of standing still to let it avoid her.

"They won't hurt you—wait it out!" Wyatt yelled.

She ignored him. Then the bulk of the black cloud reached her. Wyatt heard Kimberly's scream, saw her feet move dangerously close to the ledge. Then thousands of bats obscured her from his view.

"Kimmie? Kimmie!"

When the dark swarm finally cleared, all that remained was silence.

Wyatt didn't bother to look deep below into the ravine. He knew what he would see. He closed his eyes for a solemn, tragic moment.

Goodbye…my friend.

Then he turned and walked away.

CHAPTER NINETEEN

Wednesday morning

"ASHES TO ASHES, dust to dust..." The familiar words rang out over Boothill's cemetery. "Remember, man, that you are dust, and to dust you shall return."

Caro listened to the old preacher read over Lem Bodine's newly dug grave. Boothill rarely accepted the recent dead; it had been a full cemetery for many years. But in this case, an exception was made. Wyatt's great-grandfather would rest with the others from his generation. It felt right to everyone.

Four of the five adults present followed the solemn custom of a traditional town and wore black—the preacher, Catfish, Marta and Caro. Only Wyatt was dressed in beige, his jeans and short-sleeved shirt replaced by the complete, formal sheriff's dress uniform. He held his hat in hand, wore his gun at his hip. Also tradition.

The preacher murmured the familiar words of the Twenty-third Psalm. "...though I walk through the valley of..."

At Wyatt's side, Caro almost reached for the sheriff's hand, then stopped herself. He had been cool, official, almost brusque ever since that day high above The Silver Dollar Mine. Of course, he had his reasons.

For starters, Morgan's health was on his mind. Morgan had been admitted to a Tucson hospital for orthopedic surgery to repair his shattered leg. It would take time, but he would eventually heal. Hugh Ellis had also been admitted to the Tucson hospital. His ordeal in the cell, coupled with the news of his granddaughter's death, had hit him hard. But like Morgan, he would survive.

That in itself was a miracle. Hugh had wanted to die, tried his best to die, but Wyatt had been there, comforting, forgiving, telling him that Morgan—the other person who had loved Kimberly—needed him most of all. The Bodines would take care of Hugh's ranch if Hugh would take care of Morgan. Hugh agreed. As far as his ill health would permit, Hugh had rallied.

Both Hugh and Morgan were to be discharged at the end of the week into the care of family and friends at The Silver Dollar Ranch, with follow-up visits planned at the local clinic.

Caro herself had spent a couple of hours in Tombstone's clinic. Her lip didn't need stitches, although her hands had to be cleaned and her raw knees bandaged. Her eyes had bothered her the most and had to be treated for exposure to the dirty cave water. But there was no permanent damage. The doctor assured her she'd be as good as new and told her to have her eyes rechecked the next day if she experienced further problems. She hadn't. Physically she was fine.

The doctors could do nothing for Kimberly. With Jasentha's help, Kimberly's broken body had been recovered. She'd been buried in the old Ellis cemetery on the Bar E at Hugh's request. Save for the invalids, the whole town had turned out for her funeral. The official obituary notice said accidental death; Kimberly had tragically fallen during a foolish sunset hike. That had been Wyatt's doing.

"Let her at least keep her good name," he'd asked those few who knew the truth. "Maybe she didn't deserve it, but let Morgan and Hugh mourn her without censure."

No one saw any reason to argue. And now the last piece of business—the laying to rest of Lem Bodine—was over.

Well, the second-to-last piece, Caro thought. She and Wyatt hadn't spoken privately during the week since Kimberly's accident. There was a lot to be settled between them. Or so she'd thought. Caro was relieved when the preacher finally finished, and all the men clapped on their ever-present hats.

Her gaze moved from the grave site toward Wyatt. He was watching her, too, his face no longer solemn but questioning.

"Now what?" he asked her.

"I guess we both go home. You to your horses and the Silver Dollar—me to my crime sites in the city."

"Is that what you want?"

"No, not at all!" Her voice rose, causing Catfish and Marta to glance at her curiously. She lowered her voice. "But I don't see any other way. You can't be a rancher if you aren't on a ranch, and my services couldn't possibly be required here in Tombstone. I'm not giving up my work. I doubt you'd ever give up your Arabians. Not that I'd ask you…"

"True, horses are in my blood, but…" Wyatt's attention was suddenly diverted by a raucous noise outside the cemetery proper.

"What's that?" Caro had to raise her voice again to be heard, cursing whatever had interrupted such an important conversation. It was impossible to ignore the racket.

Wyatt peered off toward the parking lot, seeing a huge tour bus parked, its doors open, its interior empty. "I'd guess an impatient group of tourists is wanting in."

Caro glanced at her watch. "It *is* way past opening time."

"They can wait. Boothill is a cemetery first and foremost, period. They aren't coming in until..." He gestured off to the side.

Caro noted the grave diggers with the tools of their trade—a miniature bulldozer, two sturdy shovels, a canteen of water and a brand-new cross with "Lem Bodine" carefully lettered, black on white. She knew they were waiting to fill in the grave and set the tombstone as soon as the mourners left. Caro smiled politely and said, "I guess you'd better go to work, Sheriff."

"Yeah... Before that mob storms the entrance." Wyatt was already on his way, his fingers touching his hat brim in both apology and farewell.

Caro read more than a mere "farewell" in that gesture. She read a final "good-bye" as well.

Caro watched Wyatt leave Boothill as she had seen him first arrive.

Without her.

She sighed and caught at her black skirt as the desert wind kicked up dust and blew clothing about. Marta held down her dress as she came over to Caro's side.

"Aren't you going with him?" Marta asked.

"I guess not. You know, he cared deeply for Kimberly. If it wasn't for me, she'd still be alive. Besides, we haven't known each other all that long. I don't know a thing about him, not how he likes his coffee or what his favorite color is or anything."

"You know how he acts during bad times."

"I sure do," Caro said morosely. "Especially since I caused most of them. He hasn't said two words to me since Kimberly's death. I think he's decided to back off—for good."

"Maybe you should stick around and find out."

Caro's smile was sad. "Can't. I have another job waiting. Someone back East is leaving a trail of bodies along Interstate 10. One at every rest stop. I've been called in to help investigate.''

She glanced at her watch. She'd already packed and checked out of the motel, where she'd stayed since that day in the caves. "I'll change into my jeans in the ladies' room, then hit the road. It's a long drive to Phoenix."

"You're actually going home?" Marta asked incredulously.

"Only for the night. I have to drop off my car, pay bills, call the insurance agent, borrow a backup set of forensic tools and catch the airport limo for tomorrow night's red-eye to Florida," she listed, out of breath. "Which reminds me, I owe you some money."

"Forget it," Marta said.

"Sorry. Business is business." Caro reached into the pocket of her skirt and withdrew the check she'd written earlier.

Marta stared at the figure. "Wow. Isn't this a bit high?"

"Nope. It's the standard amount, plus hazard pay. Take it."

Marta nodded and carefully placed the check into her purse. "Well, thanks, Doc. It'll help me pay for a good divorce lawyer."

"Marta, I'm so sorry—"

"Hey, don't be! I think that man over there—" Marta gestured with her chin toward Catfish, who stood patiently waiting "—has possibilities."

That drew a genuine smile from Caro. "I'm happy for you, Marta."

"Well, nothing's settled yet. I'm still legally a married woman. But I've got more news." Marta drew herself up tall. "Guess who Tombstone's new dispatcher is? I'm replacing you-know-who."

"Congratulations! I can't say I'm surprised. I always knew you were one heck of an assistant." Caro held out her hand for Marta to shake. "Thanks for your help. I couldn't have done it without you."

"No, thank *you*." Marta didn't take Caro's hand. She gave her a warm hug, instead. "I needed someone to believe in me, and there you were. Now I believe in myself. Others, too." Marta's tender smile toward Catfish made her seem years younger.

Caro felt years older—not to mention a little jealous. "Best not keep a good man waiting," she said, giving Marta a friendly shove. "Time waits for none of us, you know."

After one last goodbye, Marta headed for the exit through the rows of ancient graves, the stark white crosses broken only by a single piece of granite. Marta stopped abruptly at that gray tombstone, the final resting place of photographer Camillus Sidney Fly. "Oh, I almost forgot! I have something for you!" Marta hurried back, rummaged through her oversize handbag and withdrew a small manila envelope.

Caro stared at the offering. "What is it? More evidence?"

"No, just a reproduction of an old photograph I found in one of Tombstone's antique shops. It's one of his, you know."

Caro followed Marta's gesturing finger. "Fly's?"

"Yep. Thought you might get a kick out of it." Marta gave Caro the envelope, then a quick kiss on the cheek. "Good men are hard to find, Caro, and your sheriff's the pick of the litter. Don't let him get away."

"We'll see," was Caro's nebulous answer, but it was obviously good enough for Marta.

"Great! Well, I've gotta go! I start training for my new job tomorrow, and I've got paperwork to fill out at City Hall. Catfish is giving me a ride in."

"Have a safe trip."

"You, too!"

Another hug, then Marta hurried off, fluttering her hand in farewell. Catfish threw an arm around Marta's shoulder, leaving Caro alone with the silver-and gold-laced mountains.

No doubt about it, Tombstone was a beautiful place. She could see why C. S. Fly would spend more than twenty years photographing it. But there were other places for her, dangerous places where mysteries waited to be solved by someone with her skills.

Tombstone wasn't for her. *Too bad a man from Tombstone was.*

"So much for the girl getting the guy and riding off into the sunset. All I get is some old photo, a paycheck and a few crazy memories." Pensively, she slid the unopened photograph into her blazer pocket.

"Crazy sounds about right," a deep voice answered.

Caro whirled around, embarrassed to be caught talking to herself.

"As for memories," he continued, "I prefer to live in the present. We need to talk."

"You know, you keep saying that."

Wyatt offered her an arm and escorted her away from the past, with its griefs and its deaths. They left behind the old for the new—the front of the gift store and the view of a modern highway, telephone wires, tourists, laughing children.

Wyatt fanned the dust off one of the outside benches with his Stetson. "Please, have a seat," he said.

She did, but Wyatt didn't join her. Instead, he gazed out toward the desert valleys for a long moment. Then he turned slowly and studied her.

"Are you in a hurry?" he finally asked. "This might take a bit."

"I have a few minutes to listen," Caro said evenly, although her heart was racing. "Fire away."

He nodded, his face expressionless. "You know I used to work for the Tucson Drug Enforcement Agency."

She nodded.

"You even implied I'd lost my edge."

"I should never have said that, Wyatt. I'm sorry. I know such intense work can cause burnout. Anyone in law enforcement knows that."

"True, but that wasn't the case with me." Wyatt gave her a tight smile. "I didn't quit because of burnout. I quit because I was enjoying myself too much."

"Enjoying?"

"Relishing. Savoring. Treasuring. I loved thinking better, scheming better than the real drug runners. I loved infiltrating their ranks. I was able to go undercover to trap them because, deep down, I *was* one of them. And they knew it."

Puzzled, Caro said, "What exactly are you saying?"

"There's a twisted part of me that makes me comfortable with these people! There's a part of me that wishes I could join them!"

"I'm glad," Caro said calmly.

"You're *glad?*"

"Of course I am! I'd rather have one of you on our side than a hundred naive, innocent, ineffective lawmen. Only *you* could've helped me and saved Morgan. I don't care how you think. That's your business. I only care how you act. And so far, I approve."

"My God, I nearly killed Kimberly in the caves! Can you condone that?"

"No, but I *can* understand it. If it'd been my sister she'd hogtied and left to die in the desert sun—" Caro shrugged "—who knows what I might've done?"

"But what I did—almost did—to Kimberly was wrong. A mistake."

"Welcome to the human race." Caro stood up and folded her arms across her chest. "Is there a point to this self-recrimination?"

Wyatt met her gaze straight on. "Yes. I'm in love with you. I want to spend the rest of my life with you—as my friend, my partner, my equal." He lowered his voice. "My lover."

Caro's heart leapt with excitement. "Do you now?"

"Only if you understand one thing. I can't change who I am or what I do. I can't change that…that darkness inside me. I can only promise that I'll never use it for anything except the pursuit of justice."

"Well, Wyatt Earp Bodine, I'm kind of into truth and justice myself. Which is why—" her eyes grew dark with sadness "—I can't leave my old life for a new one in Tombstone."

"I don't expect you to, city girl."

"Of course you do! You're an elected official."

"And my term expires in a few months."

"Then what?" Caro ran her fingers through her hair. "I'm in Florida next week, and who knows where after that!"

"So, we'll compromise. I'll travel more—with you, of course—and you'll travel less—staying right here at the Silver Dollar when you're not on a case."

Caro lifted her head.

"Neither of us has to give up our work, Caro. We just have to cut back. In fact, we have it easy."

"Easy?" Caro echoed.

"Yes. We're our own bosses. Do you like solving crimes seven days a week, fifty-two weeks a year?"

"No, I don't." Caro thought of the numerous airline meals she had eaten, the airports that had all started to look the same, the anonymous hotel rooms. "I never took much time between jobs because...well, I never had a good reason to stay home. Never had anyone waiting for me."

"You do now," he said simply, taking her hands in his.

Could it really be that simple? "But what about your horses? Your ranch?"

"Luciano can easily run this place when I'm gone. And I'll be home often enough to supervise the breeding program, take care of business and make love to my lady on my own land. No, change that." He pulled her closer. "Make love to my wife on *our* own land."

"Is that...is that...?" Caro stammered.

"A proposal? Yes, ma'am, it is. I don't intend for us to be separated again, so I've decided to tag along. Wherever you go is where I'll hang my hat—if you'll have me."

Caro gasped. "You'd do that for me?"

"And for me. I'm doing it for purely selfish reasons. Maybe sometimes you'll need a bodyguard. But you do need an assistant. I'm much more experienced than Marta Wenkert."

He reached for her hand and gently pulled her closer.

Caro hesitated. "What about Morgan?"

"I already called my brother Virgil. He'll be here tomorrow to take over running both the Silver Dollar and the Bar E. He'll keep an eye on Morg and Hugh until they're back to their old selves."

"Your brother doesn't mind?"

"No. He might even stand in for me as sheriff until the elections."

"But what about your ranch? What about the gold? Don't you have to mine the gold to get the Silver Dollar out of hock?"

"Oh, I think I've got enough in the bank to finance our honeymoon. And I'll take money on the hoof over money in the ground any day. Mining's too much like work. As for Morgan and the ranch..."

Wyatt's tender expression faded just a bit as he spoke. "Morgan's sold all his diamonds back to the California wholesaler he purchased them from."

"Oh, no! Won't he take a big loss?"

"I'm afraid so. He's put his jewelry store up for sale to cover the difference. He called me from the hospital this morning. As I understand it, some Native American jewelers have gone in together to purchase the place. That sale will put things square again, and cancel out the mortgage on his and Virgil's share of the Silver Dollar."

"But...that shop was Morgan's dream!"

"I know. I told him to take his time about paying back the rest of the money. Virgil said the same thing. But Morgan said he made the mistake, so he'd correct it. And he has."

"But why didn't he just take over Kimberly's mining oper—? Oh." Caro stopped abruptly, remembering again how Kimberly had met her end. The mine would hold bad memories for all the Bodines.

"I'm sorry about your loss," Caro said quietly. "I know you loved her, too."

Wyatt acknowledged her sympathy with a curt nod, then moved on. "Enough about Morgan," Wyatt ordered, dropping her hands to draw her into his arms. The tenderness returned to his manner. "Now...are you going to marry me or not?"

"Are you sure, Wyatt?"

"I'm free to go. If you'll have me."

Caro blinked. She couldn't believe her good fortune—or her hesitation. *Surely it can't be this easy to trust someone with my body, my heart, my soul. Or can it?*

"But you'll have to keep leaving all this—" she gestured widely "—your family's history, your way of life."

"The Silver Dollar Ranch will always be there for us. It's home," he said simply. It always would be home; he would always love the land and the solid old house with its echoes of past Bodines. But he no longer needed a haven. His haven was her.

"Yes, but…" She stalled for more time. "Are we talking long-term commitment here? Forever?"

"Forever. You've seen the worst of me—"

"And the best," she interrupted.

"You once told me that evil doesn't frighten you." Wyatt took her hand. "You also said you'd tell me what *does* frighten you, remember?"

"I remember."

"I'm asking now, Caro. Tell me." His eyes were soft, warm, inviting. Her own eyes filled with unfamiliar tears. This was love—a company of two. Knowing the best and the worst of each other. Accepting both. She could almost see the years of loneliness slip away.

"What frightens me is…" She took a deep breath. *If I'm ever going to trust someone, now's the time, and this is the man.* "What frightens me is spending the rest of my life without you. If you aren't proposing, then I am. Marry me, Sheriff."

She had only a second to feel his heart beat faster, then she was crushed against his chest, her lips against his, her lonely heart finally at peace. When he drew back, she saw that his face was glowing with a radiance she'd never before inspired in another human being.

Did I do that? she wondered in amazement. *Better check and see for sure.* She pressed her mouth against his and placed her trust in his keeping.

They were interrupted by a shout. "Hey, none of that in public, you unmannerly youngsters! We're a God-fearing, law-abiding town here!" It was Catfish. He and Marta were sitting in his truck across the road.

"Go find a minister!" Marta suggested loudly.

"Or rent a room!" Catfish suggested lewdly.

"Ignore them," Wyatt murmured against Caro's lips.

She did for another long kiss, then Wyatt released her.

"They're right, you know. We'll have to find a preacher real quick. Or a justice of the peace."

"I like churches, Wyatt, but when? We can't plan anything." Caro's face fell. "I have a plane to catch tomorrow night."

"So soon?"

"Yes. I have to leave now. When will I see you again?"

Wyatt whistled, then gave Catfish a thumbs-up. Catfish nodded and went around to the back of his pickup truck.

"What's he doing?" Caro asked.

"Getting my bags. I've already packed, said my good-byes, got you an engagement ring. Morgan made it and he's working on the wedding bands." He reached into his pocket and withdrew a jeweler's box. "I hope you like Silver Dollar gold and diamonds."

Caro started to melt at the sight of the box, then pushed him away to plant her hands on her hips. "Pretty sure of yourself, weren't you?"

"That I love you, yes. That you'd love me back...well, I was afraid I'd come up aces and eights."

"Huh?"

"It's a losing hand in poker. And I didn't want to lose you."

"I don't know how to play poker, but don't worry. You won't lose me." She took the box from his hand, slipped on the ring herself and let him gather her in his arms again. She kissed him hard.

"Just for that, Caro, my love, I may teach you to play poker."

"Tonight?"

"If you want. What kind?"

Caro's eyes sparkled devilishly. "How about strip poker?"

Wyatt shook his head. "Not until after the wedding."

"No, before. Now!"

"I'm a traditional man. I want a license in my pocket and two rings on my wife's finger."

Caro looked shocked. "Wow. You really *are* traditional."

"You have a problem with that?" he asked.

Caro smiled a slow, womanly smile. "This," she stated succinctly, "is going to be worth the wait."

"Hell, I hope so. But we'll never find out if we don't get moving."

Caro watched Catfish drop the last of Wyatt's luggage by her car. "Only if you're really sure. I'm good at what I do, Wyatt. I don't want to give it up."

"So who's asking you to? What, you think we country men just want our women barefoot and in the kitchen?"

"Don't forget pregnant," she added.

"I wouldn't mind that sometime down the road, but it's up to you. It's your body."

Caro couldn't believe her ears. "I guess you're not as traditional as I thought."

"Wrong. I can be as possessive as the next guy." Wyatt proved it by picking her up in his arms and carrying her to the car.

"What is this?" Caro shrieked. "Do I look like Scarlet O'Hara? Didn't we have this conversation before? Wyatt, put me down!"

"Fine." Wyatt placed her firmly back on the ground. "I'd better get to wear the pants in this family *some* of the time."

"As long as it's not in the bedroom," Caro replied, her eyes shining with love and anticipation. She dug in her skirt pocket for her car keys, then paused before unlocking the door. "Wyatt..."

"Yes?"

"What did Jasentha say to you when we were looking for Morgan? The time she spoke in Apache so I couldn't understand?"

Wyatt's smile was slow and easy. "I guess I can tell you now. Jaz bet ten bucks that you'd be finding out if cowboys make love with their hats on before the year was out."

"Well?"

"Well, what?"

"Do they?"

He gave her a sharp glance. "You'll have to wait and see."

"Fine." Caro gave him a seductive glance. "Here are the keys. Why don't you unlock my door and put your suitcases in the trunk?"

"Got it. You want me to drive?" He lifted one of her bandaged fingers to his lips and kissed it. "Maybe you should kick back, relax."

"Sounds good, Sheriff."

"You *could* call me something else, you know," he suggested.

"You got it, stud."

"Let's just stick with Wyatt, shall we? I'll go stow your gear."

Caro giggled as she slid into the passenger seat and reached for her seat belt. The crinkling noise from her blazer pocket reminded her that she still had Marta's envelope. Curiously, she pulled it out and tore it open.

A paper-clipped note covered the photo:

Dear Boss—Enclosed please find two pictures of Wyatt Earp. One is a reproduction of a rare photo of him in his youth, long before his handlebar mustache and lawman days. The other is better known. Thought you might want to keep them both. Best, Marta. P.S. I expect an invitation to the wedding!

Marta was wise in the ways of the heart, after all. Caro carefully removed the paper clip and the letter to expose the photos beneath. What she saw made her fingers shake; she dropped the letter on the floor.

Caro studied the photo in her hand. Despite the graininess of the black-and-white reproduction, the likeness of the young Wyatt Earp was clear. Caro jerked her head toward the rear window and stared at an identical face.

It couldn't be. According to all the history books, Wyatt Earp had no living descendants, no children by any of his three wives. And yet...yet...the face in the photograph was a dead ringer for Wyatt Earp Bodine.

Wyatt slammed the trunk shut, came around to the driver's side and slid in. Caro still held both photos in her hand, her mouth agape, the envelope and letter still on the floor.

"More paperwork?" Wyatt asked.

Wordlessly Caro held out the photo of the younger Wyatt Earp. Wyatt Bodine barely flicked a glance at it before starting the car. "Oh, that."

"You've seen this before?" Caro asked incredulously.

Wyatt shrugged. "This is Tombstone. Everyone's seen Fly's photos."

"But you...he..."

Wyatt leaned over and gave her a quick kiss on the cheek, then adjusted the driver's seat and mirrors. "What's the cruising speed on this car?" he asked.

"Around seventy miles an hour," she replied in a shocked whisper.

"You like air-conditioning or fresh air?"

Caro couldn't believe his questions. "Fresh air, but—"

"Then you'd better pick up your paperwork and photos or they'll be flying out the window."

Under his watchful gaze, she recovered the letter and the envelope, then slipped the two photos safely inside. Her eyes were wide, her heart pounded with excitement. "Are you going to tell me about this?"

A tiny smile played on his lips. "Maybe someday—when our first child is born."

I can't wait that long! she started to say. Then she stopped herself. "I can wait," she said.

Now it was Wyatt's turn to be surprised. "You can?"

"Sure." She shifted to the center of the seat and laid her head on his shoulder. "You know why? Because I've got my hands on something better than family legends and old photos."

Wyatt slung his arm around her shoulders. "Now what would that be?"

She pulled off his Stetson, tossed it into the back seat and ran her fingers through his hair.

"Don't you know?" she asked tenderly just before she kissed him hard on the lips. "I caught the sheriff!"

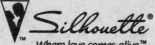

Where love comes alive™

From first love to forever, these love stories are for today's woman with traditional values.

Silhouette® **Desire®**

A highly passionate, emotionally powerful and always provocative read.

Silhouette®

SPECIAL EDITION™

Emotional, compelling stories that capture the intensity of living, loving and creating a family in today's world.

Silhouette®

INTIMATE MOMENTS™

A roller-coaster read that delivers romantic thrills in a world of suspense, adventure and more.